Cowboys Never Cry

"You'll love Cassie Danner, a cowgirl with an environmental bent, as she struggles to overcome an old love and embrace a new one. *Cowboys Never Cry* is as satisfying as the smell of sage in summer rain."
—Sandra Dallas, *New York Times* bestselling author of *Prayers for Sale* and *Whiter Than Snow*

"Tina Welling's newest novel, *Cowboys Never Cry*, is a lively romantic romp that blends the landscape of the heart and the fragile West, where real cowboys and cowgirls really do ride off into the sunset."
—Kris Radish, author of *Hearts on a String*

"Tina Welling has done it again. *Cowboys Never Cry* is a bighearted romp set against the gorgeous landscapes of the American West. Cassie Danner is a tough, generous, grieving protagonist. She also has a sense of humor as grand as the Tetons. This novel is a heady gallop through the tangled thickets of love."
—Alyson Hagy, author of *Ghosts of Wyoming*

"Tina Welling is a wonderfully fresh voice in women's fiction. *Cowboys Never Cry* will keep you up all night reading—and rooting for wounded characters who heal each other through the power of love."
—Joan Johnston, *New York Times* bestselling author of *Shattered*

continued . . .

Written by today's freshest new talents and selected by New American Library, NAL Accent novels touch on subjects close to a woman's heart, from friendship to family to finding our place in the world. The Conversation Guides included in each book are intended to enrich the individual reading experience, as well as encourage us to explore these topics together—because books, and life, are meant for sharing.

Visit us online at www.penguin.com.

"Tina Welling has a sharp eye for the West and an ear to match it. Pick up the book and join her charming characters for a romance-filled ride through Wyoming's spectacular backcountry."
—Jana Richman, author of *The Last Cowgirl*

"Cassie's struggle to overcome the loss of her husband through hard work in a fiercely beautiful and sometimes dangerous landscape makes her a particularly powerful heroine. Her independence is itself an act of defiance against grief. While examining the intricacies of emotional wounds, Tina Welling also miraculously manages to capture the awesome beauty of Wyoming. If you care about the monumental strength of the tenderhearted, you'll love this story."
—Kathleen O'Neal Gear and W. Michael Gear, *New York Times* bestselling authors of *People of the Thunder*

"A charming Western romance sure to please readers."
—Jo-Ann Mapson, author of *The Owl & Moon Cafe* and *Solomon's Oak*

"Welling delivers a winning combination—the cowboy who isn't easy to love and the modern woman who sees through all his pretenses. A novel about a contemporary courtship that is as fresh as today's headlines and as classic as the Old West."
—Kathleen Eagle, *USA Today* bestselling author of *Cool Hand Hank*

"A novel of richness and depth. *Cowboys Never Cry* is a poignant story of love and loss and the healing that can come from the most unexpected people in the most unlikely circumstances. Looming over the story is the beauty and grandeur of Wyoming's Grand Tetons and the almost magical influence that nature exerts on human lives. If you haven't yet read Tina Welling, you don't know what you've been missing. Start here! Start now!"
—Margaret Coel, author of *The Spider's Web*

Fairy Tale Blues

"Those who remember *Crybaby Ranch* will find [Welling's] newest novel equally well-written and satisfying. . . . Either of her books would make excellent book club choices." —*The Herald Journal* (UT)

Crybaby Ranch

"Suzannah's happy ending is a well-earned one that readers of inspirational fiction will appreciate." —*Publishers Weekly*

"Twists and dances like a bouncing bronco, but beneath the humor beats a strong foundation of heart."
—Jacquelyn Mitchard, *New York Times* bestselling author of
No Time to Wave Goodbye

"*Crybaby Ranch* follows the up and down and all-around adventures of a brave woman who's willing to ask questions we've all asked ourselves. The writing is vivid and will hold you through to the end—bringing home fresh answers to old questions about strength and weakness."
—Clyde Edgerton, author of *The Bible Salesman*

"A more winning heroine than Suzannah . . . would be hard to imagine. From page one, we are in love with this wry, insightful, funny survivor of the Sandwich Generation, squeezed between her mother's Alzheimer's and her husband's detachment. In reflections both luminous and humorous, she charts her way to love and independence."
—Sarah Bird, author of *How Perfect Is That*

"Women and men are suddenly revealed in *Crybaby Ranch*, an illuminating arc-of-life writing that unfolds in a rich detail of simple and complex feelings."
—Craig Johnson, author of *Another Man's Moccasins*

"Like a cliff diver, Tina Welling's fiction flies, tucks, and slices into the dark depths of her characters. She writes with insight, humor, and complete control. If they ever make compassion an Olympic sport, Tina will have a roomful of gold."
—Tim Sandlin, author of *Rowdy in Paris*

OTHER NOVELS BY TINA WELLING

Crybaby Ranch

Fairy Tale Blues

COWBOYS NEVER CRY

TINA WELLING

NAL ACCENT
Published by New American Library, a division of
Penguin Group (USA) Inc., 375 Hudson Street,
New York, New York 10014, USA
Penguin Group (Canada), 90 Eglinton Avenue East, Suite 700, Toronto,
Ontario M4P 2Y3, Canada (a division of Pearson Penguin Canada Inc.)
Penguin Books Ltd., 80 Strand, London WC2R 0RL, England
Penguin Ireland, 25 St. Stephen's Green, Dublin 2,
Ireland (a division of Penguin Books Ltd.)
Penguin Group (Australia), 250 Camberwell Road, Camberwell, Victoria 3124,
Australia (a division of Pearson Australia Group Pty. Ltd.)
Penguin Books India Pvt. Ltd., 11 Community Centre, Panchsheel Park,
New Delhi - 110 017, India
Penguin Group (NZ), 67 Apollo Drive, Rosedale, North Shore 0632,
New Zealand (a division of Pearson New Zealand Ltd.)
Penguin Books (South Africa) (Pty.) Ltd., 24 Sturdee Avenue,
Rosebank, Johannesburg 2196, South Africa

Penguin Books Ltd., Registered Offices:
80 Strand, London WC2R 0RL, England

First published by NAL Accent, an imprint of New American Library,
a division of Penguin Group (USA) Inc.

First Printing, October 2010
10   9   8   7   6   5   4   3   2   1

REGISTERED TRADEMARK—MARCA REGISTRADA

Library Of Congress Cataloging-In-Publication Data:
Welling, Tina.
  Cowboys never cry/Tina Welling.
      p.   cm.
  ISBN 978-0-451-23121-5
  1. Widows—Fiction. 2. Cowboys—Fiction. 3. Dude ranches—Fiction. 4. Self-realization in
women—Fiction. 5. Wyoming—Fiction. I. Title.
  PS3623.E4677C69   2010
  813'.6—dc22   2010020128

Set in Garamond
Designed by Spring Hoteling

Printed in the United States of America

This one is for
Tom Welling

ACKNOWLEDGMENTS

Tom Welling, my brother, is a wonderful storyteller. Among his family, friends and associates he's famous for his stories, and every one of them arouses laughter. So, naturally, I steal some of them. Thank you, Tom.

John Buhler, my husband, makes me laugh every day. And he cooks and edits my work, too. Thank you, John.

Ellen Edwards, my editor, fills me with gratitude and admiration for her impeccable sense of taste and fairness. She unfailingly asks the exact questions that lead me toward my own answers. Thank you, Ellen.

Charlotte Sheedy, my agent, believed in my work long before anyone else did, and I love her for that and her generous and tenacious spirit. Meredith Kaffel answers every question with clarity and thoroughness and is good company on top of that. Thank you, Charlotte and Meredith.

Special thanks go to Louise Lasley, Patti Sherlock, Susan Marsh, Jim Moulton, the Wyoming Arts Council and Jackson Hole Writers Conference.

Though the novel is set on a fictional ranch in Jackson Hole, Wyoming, the local ranchers are commended for their conscientious care of the land and the wildlife and are not in any way guilty of the issues that

ACKNOWLEDGMENTS

create contention in the novel. That is not true, however, of ranching throughout the West.

I used the following books for research: *I Always Did Like Horses & Women*, by Earle F. Layser (BookSurge Publishing, 2008); *Welfare Ranching*, edited by George Wuerthner and Molly Matteson (Island Press, 2002); *Cissy: The Extraordinary Life of Eleanor Medill Patterson*, by Ralph G. Martin (Simon & Schuster, 1979); *Cissy*, by Paul F. Healy (Doubleday & Company, 1966). All errors are my own; all people, places and perspectives are of my imagination.

CHAPTER ONE

She scanned the forested slope, her gaze climbing higher and higher until it reached the cathedral spires of the Grand Tetons, glowing silver against the blue sky. She shifted the twenty-pound backpack that rested on her shoulders, cinched the padded waist belt and slid the bear spray around until it was easily within reach of her right hand.

Doing that triggered old fears about hiking alone, much like locking her door before bedtime conjured images of break-ins. But going into these mountains on her own should have felt like camping in her backyard by now; she had lived in Jackson Hole that long and hiked these slopes and canyons that many years. Still, she stepped outside of herself every time and snapped a photo: Cassie Danner, Wyoming Woman. She would mentally send the photo back to her family in Ohio. Those people went nowhere without suitcases and dinner reservations.

If she'd had to describe the way she felt just then, she would have called the sensation jubilant sorrow. A soft sorrow, the kind that opened her, exposing a vulnerable center. The kind that said yes—instead of the harsh, raw sorrow that had once closed her, that said no. And jubilant because there was a lifting, a spreading of this vulnerable center that seemed to allow her to feel more awake than she had felt at any time, before or after Jake's death.

It was probably a law of the universe that grief filled as large a space as the lost love once did. Considering the void Cassie had floundered in for the past three years, only the earth itself could fill her up. So had begun her love affair with the outdoors.

Today, one last overnight into the mountains alone; then she'd start another seasonal job in a long string of seasonal jobs, learning useless skills that would never benefit her life afterward. When Jake was alive and climbing peaks all over the globe, this lifestyle made sense. It allowed her the freedom to travel with him. Now his death demanded she stick with that routine. There were so many bills to pay. She couldn't stop working long enough to give attention to a real career—that is, if she'd had one in mind to begin with. Grief took incredible energy, she had been surprised to realize. Little had been left over to make any future plans for her life.

She checked that she'd locked her truck, tugging on the driver's-side door, then approached the trailhead.

Jake, she thought, and waited for the stab of loss to buckle her forward momentum, as it had done hourly that first year, less so the second. Now that she was well into the third year since the crevasse in the Himalayas had swallowed her husband between its slippery lips, the once sodden mass of grief in her body had lightened and often arose, like now, as a sizzle of joy.

Sometimes she felt that because she hadn't succumbed to numbness in the dull, lonely world left to her, but had stayed awake and aware of the pain of her loss, she had boosted her resonance to the pure throb of liveliness all around her. Sometimes, despite herself, her body celebrated its vitality.

Cassie entered the woods and began the gentle ascent that stretched the muscles in the backs of her legs and tightened them in her pelvis. She was headed for one of the small teal and turquoise lakes that nested in the folds of forest. Sunlight wove into the warp of tree trunks ahead and the rocky trail threaded through them, beckoning like a fairy tale.

Hours later, she paused at the sound of a horse's hooves approaching from an adjacent path. She stepped off where the two paths crossed—in Wyoming, horseback riders had the right-of-way on any trail, even this one deep in the national park. For a moment all she heard was the rhythmic clack of horseshoes against rock; then horse and rider appeared around the curve. The rider reined in when he spotted Cassie.

He rested his hand holding the reins on the pommel of his saddle and gave her a nod. The cowboy nod. Direct eye contact, no smile, one dip of the chin. An age-old mannerism that spoke of a tradition of silence, respect, watchfulness. The spring air was crisp, yet this rider had tied his brown canvas jacket onto the back of his saddle. He was dressed in a faded blue snap-front shirt, sleeves rolled up to expose his tanned wrists. He wore a summer white cowboy hat and a white silk scarf wrapped twice around his neck and knotted in front. His left eye had a murky look to the iris and didn't track with the other eye. She couldn't be sure when she looked at him which eye was actually looking back at her.

Some men Cassie might meet while alone on the trail would make her uneasy, make her finger her bear spray, but not this man. Though tough and masculine, he exuded peacefulness, a composure that suggested a rooted philosophy. Live and let live.

She said, "Good morning."

"Miss." Touched the brim of his hat, nodded once more. He seemed about to ask her something, thought better of it and signaled his horse with an almost imperceptible pressure from his boot in the stirrup and moved past her.

Cassie turned to watch him and his creamy tan horse with the dark mane and tail. They traveled a path that traversed the lower slope and eventually led north to rangelands. She was not immune to the charms of a cowboy; most women weren't. This one was handsome. Still, he hadn't smiled, and that could change things. He might not have all his teeth.

She pulled out her water bottle and wondered what he was doing up there. Not, she guessed, out for a pleasure ride. This cowboy appeared too intent for that, and observant. Likely in those few seconds he had learned everything he needed to know about her: where she had come from—the parking lot at the trailhead; where she was going—five miles farther to Whitebark Lake; how long she was staying out—one night. And because this was a trail deliberately left off tourist guidebooks, he knew she was a longtime local.

She took a sip of water and remembered his eye. He'd apparently been injured. Cowboys were as rough on their bodies as they were on the land. In many ways, he and the others who made their living ranching were the enemy of a woman like her, one who loved the natural world . . . left natural. And the cowboy philosophy of live and let live might apply to people, but it wasn't a typical perspective on anything that got in the way of raising cows—wolves, bears, coyotes, the very creatures that made the wilderness wild and beautiful to her. Interfere with

ranching, and there was no let live about it. What had she gotten herself into, taking a job for the summer among people who
thought like that? Cross Wave Guest Ranch and Cattle Company, here comes your new cook.

But that was tomorrow. Today was hers.

The cowboy's horse swished its dark tail and disappeared
around a bend. Cassie stuck her water bottle back into the side
pocket of her pack and moved on.

The forest of lodgepole pines was dotted with the newly
sprouted lime-colored aspen leaves of early May. The size of
quarters, the leaves spun on their stems and seemed to chime
in the light breeze. Higher up the slope, snow-covered meadows
opened in patches, slanting almost vertically, glittering in the
sunlight like sequined bridal veils. And higher up yet, the granite
peaks of the Tetons. Beside them the moon sat broken, looking
out of place in the day's fresh light.

Cassie took a big breath of moist, pine-scented air and a
honeyed serenity drifted through her muscles and bones. How
could that happen? How could the weight of grief turn into this
lightness? It made her love silence and solitude, because that was
when the gleaming calm descended and swathed her in comfort
and rose all through her body to waft around her in an almost
palpable glow. Her friends had said she looked more beautiful
than ever. Nice to hear when you're in your mid-thirties. But
such experiences explained today's hike. One more outing alone;
one more night sleeping beneath the sky. And that explained her
choice of jobs this summer. She'd do anything that allowed her
to be outdoors.

Several hours later she topped the rise to the lake. Her eyes swept
the scene: partially frozen lake, snowy embankments and, just

as she had anticipated, one small beach area free of snow on the south side where the forest opened; lake water melted there, small waves rustling the icy edges. Her eyes flashed back to the shore.

Somebody was standing there.

Cassie stepped backward into the trees, out of sight, in order to read the situation. She wasn't especially frightened—nobody worked this hard, getting up to a high-altitude lake, in order to commit a crime—though she felt uneasy and she was disappointed. She had counted on camping alone. Who, besides her, would even want to be up there this early in the season? There was still deep snow in the forest, thick ice on much of the lake; temperatures would drop into the low twenties before morning. Yet Jackson Hole was like that, populated with hearty and adventuresome oddballs. Never before had she considered herself one of them, but she was here, wasn't she? Twelve miles down a canyon, nine thousand feet up a mountain slope, intending to camp at the snow line.

Since she hadn't encountered the man's tracks, she assumed he'd come up the north trailhead. His rolled sleeping bag had been tossed on the cleared ground, no other gear or supplies in sight. Cassie stepped into the open and called a greeting.

He turned and Cassie saw a bottle of liquor in his hand. He grinned at her and said, "Well, have I been a good boy or what?"

Under any other circumstances Cassie would not have hesitated; she would have turned on her heel and trotted out of there, unsnapping the safety latch on her bear spray at the same time. But in one hour, darkness would fall with a resounding thud, the blackness abrupt and complete. Moving outside this small patch of snow-free ground in the dark could result in unimaginable dangers.

The man made no move toward her. Instead he sat on a large rock and shrugged, as if in sympathy with her situation . . . or his good luck. He propped his elbows on his knees and dangled the bottle between his legs, watching it swing back and forth. There had been an even, mild tone to his voice that came across without menace, despite his words.

She had better be sure about this.

She recalled the story of two spring hikers the past year who had stepped unknowingly onto a snow moat—a crust of snow covering a deep creek. They plunged through the crust and were washed away beneath the snow in fast-moving water they hadn't realized raged beneath them. Later in the season their bodies were found far downstream. Cassie shuddered at the image.

She glanced at the trail behind her, which was already deeply shadowed. She took a big breath and decided staying was the lesser threat. She walked into the clearing, pulled her arms out of the straps of her backpack and swung it to the ground.

Before losing the light, she needed to set up camp. So she unzipped her pack, pulled out her cooking stove and put it together, then walked to the lake and scooped water into her pan. She lit the stove, set the pan of water on it and, while it heated, she unpacked her food, glancing occasionally at the man.

Close up, she knew who he was; everybody did.

He didn't know her. Although that could be hard to prove, considering the apt insults he began lobbing her way. He lay flat on his back on the stone slab next to the glacier-cut lake, clutching his bottle of Jack Daniel's in his armpit, as if he were trying to keep the whiskey thawed in the frigid mountain air. Mute for a long spell, as Cassie cooked, he occasionally blurted a taunt while staring into the darkening sky. Then dead silence for another fifteen minutes, during which Cassie hoped he'd drifted into unconsciousness. Soon, though, he'd send another zinger through the dusk that so hit the bull's-eye, she wanted to pull out her makeup mirror to see whether her past three years of celibacy were etched upon her features. Why hadn't he fallen asleep by now? If she drank like that, she'd be in a coma. Jacket unzipped, no hat, no gloves, he didn't seem affected by the dropping temperature.

She ate her dinner alone, since he didn't respond to her offers of food.

"What are you keeping it for? Sex isn't like money in the bank, you know. You don't get multiple orgasms by saving up for them."

He didn't seem to expect a response and she didn't give one. He never looked at her, spoke in a flat voice to the sky and sounded as if he were reading lines from one of his movies.

She washed her pot and cup with snow. All around this bare patch of ground beside the lake, where the pines opened to allow the warmth of sunlight during the day, snow cover shone like porcelain and exuded a chilly breath. Cassie had counted on this bare patch, had noticed it during past spring hikes. At the far edge of it she unrolled her sleeping pad and fluffed out her down bag on top of it. Along the edges of the bare patch, the ground lay darkened by a steady seep of snowmelt. Each day this patch would become larger, but tonight, sharing it with a drunk, it didn't feel nearly large enough.

Though he sounded somewhat aggressive, she wasn't afraid of him. Still, after they'd both crawled into their sleeping bags, Cassie waited until his breathing evened and deepened; then she slipped out of her bag, walked softly across the ragged circle of snow-free ground, plucked his boots from beside him and tiptoed over to a lodgepole pine. She hoisted herself up and balanced his boots in the crotch of the tree.

He was Robbin McKeag and she had heard about him all her life—or since the third grade, when she'd begun to pay attention to such things. He was a movie actor who had made it big as a young kid playing in a Western. *Ruby Stallion* was considered a classic now, and McKeag's roles in films were still cowboy types, rugged males in rugged lands. Wooing beautiful women, winning them every time. Exuding confidence, acting masterful.

His fans should see him now. He'd barely made it to his sleeping bag without landing in a face-plant.

She knew he lived here in the valley. Lots of famous people did, and Jackson Hole residents took pride in allowing public personalities their privacy. Nobody, for example, ever gave tourists directions to Harrison Ford's ranch, and when he was spotted in the Valley Bookstore or in the Cadillac Grille with Calista, they were both ignored. Other famous people came for vacations and some bought homes and stayed. Robbin McKeag had been born here.

Cassie recalled some newspaper article about valley homesteaders and how his great-grandfather had been one of them. She didn't care; she was just relieved that he'd finally shut up and gone to sleep.

Beneath the sound of Robbin McKeag's breathing, Cassie heard the trickle of snow melting where the earth still held the warmth of day. The spring thaw was working itself up the mountain. The night air was dry and cold on her cheeks, and it felt good with the rest of her snuggled warmly inside her bag, but if she didn't sit up and braid her hair, it would be an unmanageable tangle in the morning. So she scooted upright and unwound her hair from the twist she pinned daily to the back of her head and let it fall, reaching the ground where she sat. She parted it into sections with her fingers and began a braid, tipping back her head to marvel over the depth of darkness above her, happy to be in the mountains and on her own.

The night sky was a dotted swiss fabric of stars. While she watched, one star separated and flared briefly across the night. She joked to herself that with any luck it wasn't one of the important ones. Say, plucked from the handle of the Big Dipper or one of the three in Orion's Belt.

"Hey."

Cassie jumped.

"I've never slept with anyone with so much long black hair," McKeag drawled from inside his sleeping bag. "Except some bony Oriental once."

Cassie left the job undone and slid deep inside her bag without answering him, then lay motionless and listened to the sound of Robbin McKeag's steady exhale, hoping he'd succumbed to an alcohol-induced sleep once again.

Jake had been famous, too, in his own way. But not hampered by the crazed celebrity this guy lived in. Jake was known globally to other mountain climbers and the people who followed the sport. But he could walk down the street anywhere without being noticed. This guy, across the bare, hard ground, couldn't sit in public and drink a beer without creating chaos among the tourists. She had been at the Cowboy Bar on the town square with friends the past winter and had seen him sitting with a barrier of ranch hands surrounding him, imprisoned by his fame.

Who would have guessed that decades of celebrity would have followed a young kid starring in a horse movie? For her eighth birthday, her parents had taken her and three girlfriends to see *Ruby Stallion*. She remembered the boy who had played Reno, but not as well as the horse that he'd adopted and trained. Cassie and her friends had loved that horse and soon all their bedrooms sported posters of Ruby Stallion. Later, when those friends became teenagers, some had switched to posters of Robbin McKeag, but Cassie had turned to other interests that didn't include either horses or movie stars. Over the years, she had seen more Robbin McKeag movies, even though Westerns didn't particularly interest her—a fact she might consider keeping to herself while working on a ranch this summer.

Cassie lay on her back, hoping to spot another shooting star. This wasn't her first encounter with this guy. That had occurred the day before the January Thaw the past winter, a morning so bitterly cold that the interior of Cassie's nose had frozen stiff with tiny ice crystals. Her thermometer that morning had read twenty-six degrees below zero. She had unplugged her truck's engine-block heater from one of the outside wooden posts housing electrical outlets that lined her apartment drive, as hitching posts once had lined the streets in Jackson Hole. After starting the motor, she reluctantly crawled back out of the truck to scrape her windows. It was so cold, the air itself crystallized and drifted above her in sparkly flakes. She couldn't stand it for more than two seconds. She scraped off one peephole the size of a shoe box and left it at that.

First she failed to see a STOP sign through her peephole and rolled through an intersection. Next she failed to see an old 1950s green Jeep pickup barreling down the ice-packed street from her left. To avoid a collision with her, the Jeep swerved into a five-foot bank of snow lining the side of the road.

Cassie slammed on her brakes, leaped out of her truck and ran over to the other driver's door. She asked the driver if he was hurt; she offered to call a tow truck; she said she was sorry. No response.

She babbled apologies as the man got out of his truck, dug

with his bare hands to free a space around his tires and locked in his front hubs for four-wheel drive. Nothing. He climbed back into his Jeep. Nervously Cassie picked up a handful of snow, packed it and rolled it between her gloved hands as she watched his wheels spin, then take hold on the seven-inch-thick ice pack. The truck slowly began creeping away. Not once had the guy even acknowledged her presence.

Cassie looked down at her hands and saw she had formed a perfect snowball. It seemed only natural to throw it at him.

The snowball hit his back window with a thump. He braked, shifted his eyes to his side mirror.

Like an ass, Cassie waved.

That was when she realized she'd just run the famous Robbin McKeag off the road.

As she watched him drive away, she recalled a silly joke from her childhood. One her father used to tell when he had worked as a laborer before he had begun his own construction company. A bricklayer's joke: A man was building a brick wall in front of an insane asylum and doing a wonderful job of it. A businessman, passing by, stopped to admire the work and ended up offering the bricklayer a job. After giving specific and lengthy information about the project and directions to the site, he suggested the man begin work the next Tuesday. As the businessman walked away, he felt the thud of a brick hitting him between his shoulders. He stopped and turned around, and the bricklayer waved and merrily said, "See you next Tuesday."

Though not a great joke, it stuck with Cassie's family, and forever after an intent nod and "See you next Tuesday" was the traditional response to long and complicated instructions. In those days, craziness was supposed to be funny. Now that nearly everyone was crazy, it was more difficult to find the humor.

Cassie thought if that early-morning encounter had been in a Robbin McKeag cowboy movie, it would have been called a "cute meet."

Like currents of water carrying a collection of sticks downstream, there seemed to be people currents. Cassie found herself often meeting up with the same people at, say, the post office or the grocery store for a few weeks, then not seeing them again for months. As if there were a magnetism that mysteriously held certain people in the same patterns of travel until they were just as mysteriously released and began moving into separate currents. So that wasn't the end of her encounters with Robbin McKeag.

"Cute meet" number two: The next day, the day of the January Thaw, dawned at thirty-three degrees. The sun felt strong. With an upward kick of fifty degrees overnight, icicles—some the size of human beings—ran like faucets from the shop eaves. People walked without coats. Cassie had driven her employer's black SUV into town to do an errand for her. She sat staring at a red light, sunning her arm out the window, dreaming about springtime, which was still five months away.

In the lane next to her idled the same green Jeep pickup. Just as Cassie caught on to that, she saw the driver reach out to the roof of his truck cab, grab a fistful of snow and toss it through his open passenger window. The snowball hit Cassie softly on the shoulder. He nodded at her employer's car and asked, "Eventually *wreck* the other one?"

This was the trouble with living in a small town, she remembered thinking. You do one stupid thing and aren't allowed to forget it until all witnesses have died or moved away.

As they both pulled up to the stoplight on the next block, he called over, "Come to the Cowboy tonight. You can buy me a drink and plead my forgiveness."

Cassie didn't go to the Cowboy Bar that night, so that was the end of it. Until now. "Cute meet" number three.

No movie director would allow a *series* of cute meets. And tonight's scene Hollywood would have edited right out of the film: the big star sprawled drunk on a rock, slack-jawed, hair long and unkempt, as verbose with sexual innuendo now as he had been mute that freezing morning.

Cassie was having trouble falling asleep and she suddenly craved popcorn—all this thinking about movies. She tried to roll over onto her side and it became a big production. She had left her clothes on and they felt bulky inside the slim mummy-style sleeping bag. With her hair unbraided, it twisted around her arms and neck, and she wondered if she would ever nod off. She was a little worried, too, about this new job that started to-morrow, since she had passed herself off as a cook to Mr. Boone, owner of the guest ranch. The salary was good, plus no food costs or rent. She planned to stay in her camper, and though she loved Erin, Becca and Lacy, she was looking forward to living without roommates for a change, while also getting caught up with her bills.

No salaries for mountain climbers; Jake had been supported by endorsements. And for a climber of his stature that meant everything from clothing to cars—or in his case, a Chevy pickup. Cassie had worked to provide groceries and to cover her travel expenses when opportunities arose for meeting up with Jake. She took jobs with the local resorts that made it easy to leave. Winters she taught toddlers at the ski school and worked in a sports gear store; summers she worked sales at a gallery on the town square and booked trips for a rafting company. Every season, something temporary for the tourist business. Waitressing, sales clerking, whatever she could find and quit without regret.

Now a new job. The cooking part worried her, but how hard could it be? She knew *how* to cook. She'd been cooking for two when she was married and for four when she roomed with friends. The recipes would just be tripled or quadrupled or quint-somethinged. She could handle it.

Finally Cassie was getting sleepy. The wind had picked up and the night air on her cheeks that earlier had felt refreshing now felt sharp and icy. She slid deeper into her bag, pulled the hood over her head and set her mental alarm clock for the very first hint of dawn. The plan was to get the heck out of there before McKeag woke up.

The next morning Cassie hiked a couple miles down trail, and stopped beside a fallen tree trunk. Lying in shadow, a patch of small purple flowers bloomed beneath a casing of clear ice. Against all reason, the ice acted as a hothouse.

She decided this was a good place for breakfast and brought out her backpacking stove to boil water for coffee. As planned, she had awakened at first light. She had cached her food, toothpaste and deodorant overnight in a bear vault, a small container that wildlife couldn't open, and lodged it beneath deadfall a hundred feet from camp. She had gathered that and her sleeping bag quietly and moved down the trail, releasing a big breath once she was out of sight. Now a golden glow rimmed the Gros Ventre Mountains across the wide valley to the east. Soon the sun would turn this navy blue sky into a baby blanket blue. She tipped her face up. Devoid of clouds from the Absarokas in the north to the Snake River Range in the south.

She had set an orange, two small wedges of foil-wrapped cheese and a granola bar on the rock for the movie star, so that left her with just an emergency power bar that had been tucked in her backpack all through last summer and the past winter. It was misshapen and tasted stale. Still, she felt happy sitting on the ground, her back against the fallen tree trunk, steam from her freshly brewed coffee rising to warm her cheeks when she sipped.

Below her, near an open marshy meadow, early light struck bare willow stems and they glowed yellow, scarlet and chartreuse. They looked as though they might momentarily burst into flame rather than leaf. The colors kindled so brightly, she bet she could read by them after nightfall.

As she had dropped altitude along the path that morning, it seemed as if she was leaving winter and entering early spring again. There were few birds, except for high overhead, where she watched a flock of snow geese travel a migratory path to the north, a path that Cassie knew was as well-known to birds as Interstate 25 was known to man.

"Do only those things that you love." She'd read that line a few years back in a beat-up book she'd found in a hostel in Kathmandu, where she was waiting to meet Jake after a climb. She loved sitting here, wildness all around her. But she didn't always love doing what she needed to in order to experience these moments. Chiseling away at debt with jobs beneath her abilities, she rented rooms, shared kitchens and purchased her clothes mostly at Browse & Buy, Jackson Hole's secondhand shop. Now she turned to watch sunlight climb down the Tetons as the sun rose higher over the Gros Ventre Mountains. She smiled at the sight.

Poverty with a view, her friends called this.

CHAPTER TWO

"Not Mr. Boone," he corrected Cassie. "Just Boone."

She guessed he was in his mid-sixties. A big man, in good shape. They toured the ranch, and he introduced her to the horses and barn cats in the same respectful manner with which he introduced her to the wranglers. She liked that about him. The two of them headed to his office off the ranch kitchen. Boone turned the padded desk chair around and invited Cassie to sit. He pulled in a wooden chair from the kitchen for himself. He explained he needed a cook this early in May because a small film crew would be basing operations at the ranch while doing a documentary on the wildlife.

Ah, Cassie thought, springtime in the Wyoming Rockies. She could show them the violets encased in ice.

"But that's not for a few days," Boone said, then filled her in on this evening's events. As a favor to a family friend, Cross Wave had accepted four early birds. A cookout was planned at their camp a ways upriver.

"That okay? You can handle cooking in a camp?"

"That's fine," Cassie lied.

Two days earlier, during their interview, Cassie had asked about the duties of the position and Mr. Boone, or rather Boone, had been vague.

"Oh, nothing much," he had answered.

"Nothing much?" she'd asked.

"It varies. You'll do fine," he'd said. "I know you're just the one."

Cassie had accepted the job more on his confidence than her own. Also, she needed an income fast. Her last paycheck from the ski resort had been deposited over a month ago. Many other places wouldn't be hiring until the end of May instead of the beginning, like Cross Wave, and most businesses not until mid-June, when the summer season really took off.

Now in the office, he said, "I'll drive you and your gear out to camp when you're ready; later our foreman, Cody Barlow, will guide the guests out on horseback. Give you some time to get organized. You can pick out the supplies you'll need from the fridge and pantry in the storeroom outside the kitchen. We'll plan to eat early, about five thirty, before it gets too chilly, if that's okay."

None of it was okay. He sounded as if she should already have a menu in mind. She hadn't expected to cook until tomorrow. Not for anyone. What had happened to Orientation Day, like other new jobs?

The back door slammed and from the kitchen someone hollered, "Boone. Hey, I'm home."

Who was that? The voice struck her as oddly familiar, flat, almost atonal. Boone excused himself, leaving the office door ajar. Of course, she thought, a camp cook *would* mean cooking in a camp. No oven, no broiler, no microwave. Earlier, Boone had said that sometimes she'd be cooking here at the house for just the family and he'd flipped open and closed cupboard doors to show her where dishes were stacked and pots and pans stored, as they'd passed through on their way to the office. That's where she'd assumed she would learn the ropes, in an indoor kitchen, and then some other day expand her duties. . . . But why did that voice make her feel even more uneasy?

She listened to the talk in the other room.

"You look like hell," Boone said. "I want you to meet somebody."

"I feel like hell."

Recognition of the voice brought Cassie lurching to her feet. Both hands flew to her chest. She spun toward the desk, leaned over and flipped an envelope on top of a pile of mail to read the name.

Boone McKeag.

She raised her head and listened.

"Some damn woman hid my fucking hiking boots in a *tree*."

"You took a lady friend, Robb?"

"Took me all *morning* to find them."

She'd forgotten to retrieve his boots. Cassie's gaze flew to the window. She considered her chances of escaping.

"You haven't been seeing any ladies."

"*Not* a lady friend. Some mountain harpy, and she took over *my* campsite."

"You said you'd get a haircut before dinner tonight."

"I will. I will. Who's in there?"

Cassie wondered whether they always talked like this, one step behind each other. Maybe this accounted for her failure to get any solid answers to her questions to Boone. She'd been too sequential in her thinking.

Nothing sequential about her thinking now. Random notions of death and disguise tramped through her mind like spooked bison. She knelt to crawl under the desk, pictured how stupid she'd feel being caught there, straightened up and listened for a possible reprieve from the kitchen.

"You'll like her." Boone spoke enthusiastically. "Our new cook."

She heard the sound of boots being kicked off. Something was dropped on the floor, something else was tossed on a chair.

"I said, 'Get one strong, fat and ugly.' How big is she? The bigger they are, the better they cook. A known fact."

"Shhh. Keep it down."

"Pretty big, huh?"

Footsteps.

"Why don't you clean up first, son. Looking pretty rough."

Cassie turned toward the door to watch her fate approach. Boone's steps had overcome his son's; he barred the doorway with an arm.

"Jump in the shower first, Robb. This can wait."

Flooded with relief, Cassie sank back in the chair and turned it toward the desk, dropped her head in her hands and tried to slow her heartbeat.

Abruptly her chair was spun about and she stared at irises so blue with whites so bloodshot the eyes came across as purple.

From behind his son, Boone began, "Cassidy Danner, I'd like you to—"

"*Two hours* I waded in that icy lake water looking for my boots."

"I'm sorry." Her voice rattled in her throat. "I meant to give them back to you."

Boone said, "I'll be doggone. You've met." He chuckled, putting it all together pretty fast. "I get it. Hid his boots so you could run for it if need arose."

Boone grinned at the two of them, then clapped a hand on Robbin's shoulder. "I got us just the cook, Robb, just the very one."

Cassie looked at them, father and son, as they stood close together, looking down at her in the desk chair. Only one of their faces beamed with pleasure.

"Boone," Robbin hollered to his father across the cleared area of the camp within minutes of dismounting his horse. "Look at this. Look what your cook's done."

"Nice-looking haircut, Robb." Boone ambled over to the grill, smiling. "Haven't seen your ears in half a year." He turned Robbin's head from side to side.

"I've got all this shit down my collar."

"Let me see." Boone pulled Robbin's head low and blew down his neck and feathered his fingers beneath his collar. "Better?"

"Thanks. Boone, she's messed up already. Look." Robbin lifted the plastic covering off a blue-speckled enamel bowl. "First, she tells me it's strawberries Romanoff. She stirs it and I hear her mumble. I look in the bowl and there's all this runny stuff. She says she's changed her mind. Made strawberries à la Ritz to serve over biscuits instead. Know what that means? No biscuits with dinner."

Cassie held up a spoonful of soupy whipped cream and berries for Boone to taste.

"Magnificent." Boone saved half the spoonful and fed it to Robbin.

Robbin said, "I never heard of strawberries à la Ritz."

"Good though, isn't it? Over biscuits. I'll look forward to that." Boone stepped to the grill. Cassie watched his smiling face as he took in the two dozen shish kebabs lying across the charcoal fire. Mushrooms, cherry tomatoes, green and yellow peppers, beef tenderloin cubes skewered alternately. He nodded approval at the Dijon mustard and horseradish sauce.

Boone left to build a fire in the circular stone pit, around which chunky logs were arranged as seating for the guests. But before he got far he turned back to Robbin and warned in a mild tone, "No more drinking."

Robbin turned an exaggerated, open-eyed look of betrayal toward Cassie. "Fire her. Right now. We don't need a tattletale hanging around our ranch."

Boone looked perplexed.

Cassie said, "He thinks I told you."

Boone took that in, seemed to imagine her night alone with his drunken son on a mountain. "You should have done more than hide his boots, Miss Cassidy." He shook his head at Robbin in regret. "A fine start this is."

Boone moved off, and Robbin poked around for more evidence against Cassie. He lifted a pan lid. "What's this?"

"Rice pilaf."

"It's all water."

"Maybe rice soup," Cassie said, ready to alter at a moment's notice either her plan or her label. She felt hot and itchy under the collar herself, as if tiny, sharp hairs prickled there. How to fix food for seven people with only a waist-high grill and a small worktable?

"You're not a cook." Robbin gestured toward her skirt. "And you're not a wrangler."

That could be part of the trouble; she hadn't known she was supposed to act like a wrangler, too. She blew on the coals beneath the rice.

"See that dust?" Robbin pointed across a stretch of sage flats to below a cutbank. "The guests are riding in and will be here in eleven minutes. Your rice won't be done for thirty."

Cassie blew harder.

"And blowing ash all the fuck over the shish kebabs isn't going to impress anybody either."

"Well . . ." she said, stumped. An idea occurred to her. "I could take some of the water out." She spoke more to herself than to him. She began to search for a ladle. "No. That won't work." She stopped and stared at the chalky-looking water. "Criminently. Darn."

Robbin watched her with folded arms. "Possibly," he said, "I was wrong about you. You certainly cuss like a wrangler." He relented and bent to a low cupboard built next to the grill, pulled out a long-handled metal spatula and began shoveling coals away from the wildly boiling coffee, pyramiding them high beneath the rice.

Immediately the pot began to rumble and Cassie's shoulders relaxed. She looked up to smile her gratitude, but Robbin had walked away.

"Thanks," she called to him.

He turned back to look at her.

Cassie smiled and lifted her hand in a wave.

Something about that made Robbin halt and squint at her. Cassie was afraid she knew what; she dropped her hand and swiveled back to the worktable. It didn't come to him, but he added before moving off, as if the residual feeling of the half-retrieved memory was jogged, "You cook over open flame as confidently as a blind person drives."

When the foreman, Cody, neared camp with the guests, Cassie recognized the horse first, then the rider. She stopped and stared with a fistful of silverware in her hand. He recognized Cassie, too. He gave her the nod. Eye to eye, sharp dip of the chin. Nothing surprised this guy.

So this was Cody Barlow, manager of the cattle end of the operation. She kept a discreet eye on him as she moved around the long picnic table, distributing mismatched forks and knives. About the same age as Robbin, he had high-cut cheekbones, dark hair and skin, as if there was some Indian blood in his genetic history—some juicy story of a Shoshone maiden and a fur trader, perhaps—and he moved with the grace of a cougar. Built long and lean, the way you'd expect a cowboy to look, accompanied by the expected manners. Unlike the movie star over there. Cassie turned to look. Robbin sat on the ground with his back against a tree, knees bent, reading a paperback. Robbin wasn't particularly tall, maybe five-eleven, maybe not quite; certainly he was not lean. Instead, he was rather well muscled, as if he lifted weights. Light brown, almost blond hair, hairdresser highlights growing out. And a great lack of manners. How the heck had he become the iconic cowboy of film and fantasy? She glanced back at Cody. Hollywood had flubbed.

After giving Cassie the cowboy nod again, Cody walked over to Robbin.

"I couldn't find you up there yesterday."

Robbin didn't lift his head from his book. "That was the idea."

Cody shrugged and walked off. Several yards from the cleared area, he bent his upper body sideways and spit a stream of dark brown fluid into the weeds. Oh, right, Cassie thought. Cowboys and chew. Go together like hikers and trail mix.

Robbin tossed his book aside, pushed himself to his feet with one arm and caught up to Cody. Cassie couldn't hear what he said, but the body language was congenial. Robbin hung a hand on Cody's shoulder and when Cody mounted his horse, he looked down at Robbin and laughed at something he said, then reined to the left and rode out of camp. Teeth all present, Cassie noted.

So far this evening she was acquiring her job description in bits and pieces. She was expected to be not only the cook but also the hostess during dinner. Cook, wrangler, hostess. Sit in the center of the picnic bench and try to balance the conversation, watch for what everyone needed and eat at the same time. So full of questions, Cassie felt bottlenecked with the rush of them and could barely swallow her food past them. Boone kept popping remarks into the conversation like "meals cooked on the raft trips" or "the weekend we host that wedding on horseback." And what were those tent posts doing over there? Did they sleep out here sometimes?

Not tonight, she learned when one of the guests asked. Too early in the season, too cold, Boone answered in English, and Robbin translated in French, for the couple who had traveled from Geneva, Switzerland.

So, Cassie thought, Robbin's no dummy.

The American couple with them, Mr. and Mrs. Carroll, were relatives of Elene Cottrell. And Elene, Cassie gathered from the talk, was Boone's longtime lady friend, who ranched a small spread in Montana, where the two couples were headed next. Mr. Carroll had a large plastic-smooth nose, a thick mustache, and he wore heavy black-rimmed glasses. Like a Groucho Marx mask, Cassie decided. He frequently removed his glasses to gesture, and watching him, she expected every time to see the nose and mustache slip off with the glasses.

Though dinner eventually turned out all right, the struggles with cooking on the grill, the search for every utensil she needed, and especially getting all the dishes cooked and ready to eat at the same time made Cassie wonder where she was going to get the energy for the cleaning-up process. She imagined herself giving in to the urge to wrap up in an extra tablecloth, crawl under the picnic table and take a nap.

Just keep your eyes open and your face out of your pilaf, she warned herself.

"Let me guess: you're not married."

Cassie's head bobbed up. Was Robbin speaking to her? He certainly wasn't using the same animated tone of voice he used to warm up the French couple—"La!" the woman had often exclaimed, while her husband giggled, and Mr. and Mrs. Carroll grinned proudly at providing such an entertaining host.

Cassie looked up and down the table. All eyes were on her. "No," she said.

"How old are you?"

"Now, that's enough, Robb." Boone began to look uneasy. The four guests continued to look toward Cassie, waiting for a response. She could feel each of them making a mental guess.

"Thirty-four."

Genuine surprise from all except Robbin.

"Thirty-four and never married. Sounds suspicious to me."

"I didn't say I was never married."

"Aha. A reject. Come to Wyoming to heal a heart and nab a cowboy. And not too successful at it, obviously."

Boone twitched around in his place across the table and cleared his throat in warning to Robbin.

But Robbin pressed on. "So why'd he drop you?"

"My husband . . . died." Bald, but he'd asked for it. Still, Cassie felt embarrassed for having turned the tide of talk. Then she reprimanded herself for accepting responsibility that rightly belonged to another—a longtime character flaw.

The guests blushed for Robbin . . . or Cassie, but they weren't really unsettled by his rudeness. After all, a millionaire movie star shouldn't have to follow the same rules as everyone else. They appeared more curious about where Robbin would go next with his line of talk than embarrassed by him.

"Hell of a way to escape from you," Robbin said. "Count on it—I'll find an easier method."

By way of balancing the exchange, Boone contributed that Robbin had never been married and he was almost forty. Then, to show his empathy with the experience of losing a mate, he said, "Robbin's mother died when he was three."

Robbin's head cocked sideways, eyebrows lifted, waiting for Cassie to take her turn on commenting how Robbin's own mother knew to connive escape in three short years of association with *him*.

Cassie passed; there was Boone patting her hand across the table.

"Wimpy thing, aren't you?" Robbin noted.

With dessert the Frenchman announced, switching to a halting English, that he'd like to practice his new language skills, if his fellow dinner companions didn't mind. He began by telling them what he hoped to find in the way of souvenirs. He expected to accumulate so many that his small traveling group would be packed into their vehicle like "feeshes in zee can." Meaning sardines, Cassie supposed, and kept her smile within polite bounds.

He said, "I particularly promised my granddaughter a video of *Snow White and the Seven Midgets.*"

It began with a hiccup sound, then a rude bark of a laugh. She bit her lips and lowered her face into a hand, but ended up spilling uncontrollable laughter through her fingers.

She felt hysteria rappel down from the top of her head on a slack rope and swing her dangerously against the wall of sane behavior. Every time she attempted an apology, she soared off again on a wild arc of laughter. Snow White and the Seven *Midgets.* Tears pooled. Worse, Cassie feared she was going to abruptly hit ground with genuine sobs to accompany those tears. She blotted her eyes with her paper napkin.

Boone herded the guests to the campfire and took orders for liqueurs and additional cups of coffee. Once they were out of earshot, Robbin, still sitting at his place down the table from Cassie, said his first pleasant words to her.

"If there was a porno shop in town, I think I might find a video *actually* entitled *Snow White and the Seven Midgets.*"

Robbin delivered the guests back to the ranch in Boone's van, leaving the horses in the corral for a wrangler to deal with later. He returned with the ranch truck to pick up Boone and Cassie and her supplies. She squeezed into the cab between Boone, who now drove, and Robbin, who started right off telling Boone what a mistake he'd made hiring this impersonator to cook for them.

"The deal was I shape up and get a haircut and you hire a *cook.* Strong, fat and ugly. Then we have this nice, calm summer so I can get it together, work on my screenplay and eat well." He bent around Cassie to direct his words to Boone. "You hire some woman who can't even lift her own supply boxes."

Boone murmured, "Now, Robb." Soothing words that did little to stop Robbin's tirade.

"I know her, Boone."

Uh-oh, Cassie thought. Possibly memory had been revived as Robbin jogged over the rough road to and from camp. Or perhaps when he dropped off the guests at their cabins, he'd spotted her truck with the built-in camper, which she'd parked behind some shrubbery. Not hiding it exactly, just keeping it from plain sight for a while.

"She's too lazy to scrape the ice off her windshield on cold mornings. She puts other people in danger and throws snowballs when she's in the wrong. Also, she rebuffs perfectly polite invitations without any good reason. That makes her"—he counted on his fingers— "bone lazy, careless, accident-prone, rude and totally devoid of good taste. She doesn't like me, Boone."

"Already, Miss Cassidy?"

"That's just from our first encounters," Robbin continued. "Here's what else I've learned. She's cold, humorless and probably suffers sexual dysfunction. But most of all, she is not strong, fat and ugly, Boone. And that was the criteria."

"I think this is going to work out great, don't you, Miss Cassidy?" Boone rolled down his window and sucked in a big, hearty breath of the night air, temperature in the low fifties by now.

"It's not going to work out at *all*. I *know* her."

"Did he ask you for a date once, Miss Cassidy?"

"What does that have to do with anything?" Robbin said. "I'm telling you, she threw a snowball at me for no good reason."

"He did, didn't he?" Boone asked her.

Cassie shrugged.

"You turned him down, and he didn't take that very well."

Cassie tipped her head from side to side.

"Got mighty *put out* is my guess."

Cassie sighed.

"So you threw a snowball at him," Boone summed up. "Good for you."

CHAPTER THREE

The next morning Cassie pushed the snooze button on her alarm clock three times. Finally she surfaced, thirty minutes behind schedule. She pulled on Levi's and hiking boots, yanked on a sweater and a down vest. Racing the clock, she left her braids as they were, but managed to wash her face and brush her teeth, then sprinted to the truck that pulled up to take her and the breakfast supplies that she'd gathered the previous night to camp. Once she arrived, she had forty minutes before the guests returned from their early-morning horseback ride.

Robbin started right off. "Look at her. She looks like a fucking Apache. Black hair braided to her ass. Tossing eggshells around like the skulls of the enemy."

Cassie ignored him. Besides, his remarks were directed to Boone. Boone, too, ignored him.

Robbin lounged lengthwise on a picnic table bench, his head cupped in a hand, and watched Cassie pretend to have breakfast under control.

Now that she'd broken all these eggs into a bowl, she was stumped about whether to scramble them or fix French toast.

"Still hungover, Robb?" Boone asked pleasantly, while sweeping the packed dirt around the eating area.

"Throw it up to me. A Spring Binge. I haven't had a drink in four months and won't for another four."

"You're going to do this again in four months?" Boone held his broom still.

"I just meant, with work starting . . ."

"Still, Robbin . . ."

"I'm happy, Boone. Ecstatic. Just thought I'd see if it was still fun. It felt like shit, okay?"

Very seriously: "You looked like shit, Robbin." Boone's head swung around. "Oh, sorry, Miss Cassidy." Then back to his son. "But you shouldn't mess with things like that so soon, Robb."

"I do not have an 'addictive personality.' " He rolled over onto his back. As if mimicking someone, he said to the sky, " 'Robbin is suffering from a spiritual crisis, a failed value system. Robbin needs to be given a serene atmosphere in which to heal himself.' "

"Still, Robb . . ." Boone began to move on with his broom, picking up fallen twigs and pinecones and tossing them toward the campfire as he worked.

"I took the tests. I do not have an undue penchant for very fat women; ergo I am not an alcoholic. God, where do they get that shit?"

Cassie put sausage links on the grill, then began to wonder whether she should have had coffee made by now. Maybe they were waiting for it. Endless minutes passed while the little spigot dribbled enough water to fill the huge stainless steel coffeepot. Just in time and feeling most clever, she thought to smear dish soap all over the outside bottom of the thing. She'd read that somewhere. Made the pots easier to clean. Last night she'd scrubbed for fifteen minutes with an SOS pad to remove the charred soot.

"Remember last summer's cook, Boone?" Robbin asked, staring upward. "Had thighs so huge you'd think she had panniers hidden under her skirt."

"We fired her, Robbin."

"Why'd we go and do a thing like that?" Robbin sounded crestfallen. "Good old Mattie."

"Because," Boone explained, "while you were stoned, good old Mattie was drunk."

"I don't remember that."

"I've got the kind of cook I like right here." Boone swept his way over to the worktable. He patted Cassie on the shoulder.

Cassie grated orange zest into the French toast batter to give it flash. Of course, now she should offer orange syrup, or something compatible, to serve with it. She was going to put herself in a panic again if she wasn't careful. Or was she already there?

"You just hang on with Robbin here," Boone said in what Cassie supposed he thought was a whisper. He twisted his mouth to speak out of the side of it and bent over toward her, tipped his face down secretively, then talked at a perfectly normal volume. "Mattie was sure strong, fat and ugly, but it didn't help her cooking any."

Since Robbin had obviously heard and Cassie wanted to assume the image of a woman so in command of her duties that she could partake of casual repartee, she replied, "Robbin seems to have an undue penchant for fat women to *me*."

"See, Boone." Robbin came alert, bolted upright on the picnic bench and swung a leg down on either side to the ground.

"This is exactly what I don't need. I am not serene. This is not a healing experience."

Hard to say exactly how it happened. The first hint was the smell of a horse burning. No, automobile tires. Hair? Rubber? Both? Cassie swung around and eyed the grill suspiciously—what was it doing to her food now? Then Boone, who was bent over tightening a bolt on a picnic table leg, tipped his nose to the air.

Too late to keep it secret, Cassie caught on that her braid and its elastic holder were smoldering. She waved the braid in the air. She swatted it with a hot pad. The singed hair continued traveling upward, crackling as it went.

"It's still burning, you idiot." Robbin leaped up, ran over and plunged Cassie's braid in the coffeepot.

"Here is your camp cook, Boone," Robbin announced with one hand on the coffeepot handle, the other dunking Cassie's braid up and down in it. "Now you want to tell me why she's still here?"

"Shoot!" Cassie shouted. "The French toast!" She skittered down the griddle, flipping French toast slices and scooping up those that were too darkly grilled to be good for anything but the garbage pail.

Robbin kept pace with her, holding the coffeepot under her braid. "Slow down, will you?"

Boone passed a dish towel to Robbin, who caught the dripping braid in it and squeezed the liquid out.

"I'm late." Cassie sniffed. The smell was awful; it stung her eyes. "My hair's ruined. The French toast is burned."

"Uh . . ." Boone inched away. "Take care of that, Robbin," he said with his head averted.

"My God," Robbin said, siding with Cassie for the moment.

"You may hear rumors about *my* sanity, but"—he nodded toward his father—"it's nothing compared to what crying women do to him." He handed Cassie a paper towel. "Blow."

"I'm *not* crying." Did these two have so little interaction with women that they mistook smoke-stung eyes for the threat of a sob scene? Did they think this job was *that* important to her? She began to dip more bread into her egg mixture.

Robbin pocketed the paper towel and proceeded to explain the deal. He would help her with breakfast, then afterward he'd drive her back to the ranch, and Fee, who had cut Robbin's hair, would cut the gummy stuff out of her braid. After that, she'd tell Boone she was quitting and pack it on out.

Cassie stopped her work. "Are you firing me?"

Robbin said, "I don't have the authority to do that. Look, why don't you just leave? Be a secretary or something."

Over his shoulder, Cassie spotted signs of the approaching riders. She snatched up her spatula.

Robbin detained her with a hand on her shoulder. "Looks like war paint." He rubbed his thumb over a soot smear on her chin, and Cassie practically vibrated with impatience. She held her chin out and from the sides of her eyes watched the dust cloud nearing.

Robbin's ministrations assured Boone that it was safe to come over, and he gathered up silverware and began setting the table. Robbin threw out the old coffee water, rinsed and refilled the pot with fresh. Cassie blended orange juice into brown sugar for her syrup, swiveling from worktable to grill in hopes of surprising any new catastrophe in progress there.

A low droning sound with something of an upbeat contentment to it issued from Boone's mouth. After a couple bars Cassie realized he was singing "Rock of Ages." But it was recognizable only by the duration of his single note repeated and the pauses between the repeats. He smiled benevolently and moved around the table, patting first Robbin, then Cassie as he passed.

When Boone moved out of earshot to fill the dishwater buckets from the stream, Robbin said conversationally, "Boone's theory has always been to pick one note and be faithful to it. That way he's sure to be right *some* of the time."

Cassie handed Robbin a glass of juice.

Silly gestures, every one of them. But, Cassie thought, taking a big breath, what else is a gesture but a silly half act? A white flag not waved, just revealed over the hill. Gestures gave notice of amity, a willingness or a wish to do more. Last fall when her grandmother was dying, it was all she had to give, small and incomplete indications of her benign presence. The offering of them now seemed far less empty to her than she had supposed them to be at the time. Gestures, Cassie thought in her calm aftermath of disorder, might be one of life's greatest gifts.

After Boone returned and set the water buckets beneath the worktable, he put his hands on his hips and looked toward the mountains. "The beginning of a new dude season," he announced. He inhaled the cool morning air and let it out slowly. "You know, Miss Cassidy, many of the folks that will be visiting us don't ever get to stretch their gaze this far without it smacking up against a wall. Never see an animal in the wild. Don't even see stars in the night sky where they call home. This summer they'll be our guests, and we'll have the honor of showing them all this." He stretched his arm out to encompass mountains, sky, sage flats and forest. He added, "It's good work we have ahead of us."

After breakfast Robbin drove Cassie back down the rutted dirt road, over wooden planks serving as a bridge across Elk Tooth

Creek, around Carrion Butte, and pulled up twenty minutes later in front of a small two-story clapboard set behind the guest cabins. To Cassie it felt like twice that long on the bumpy track with the unfamiliar terrain. But by week's end, she figured, she wouldn't ever again experience the assumption that she was in the wilderness while at camp. The dudes, according to Robbin, traveled a more circuitous route by horseback and happily never caught on.

As it turned out, the designated ranch barber, Fee Barlow, was Cody's father. The two of them lived in this house, located down a ranch road a quarter mile from the McKeags'. Fee was a man of wiry build with gray in his beard and a thick head of hair, tall like his son.

Cassie perched on a wooden stool set in the grass and unbraided her hair. Robbin watched the procedure from the porch steps.

"Got us a goddamn coyote den with a half dozen new pups in the hillock over there." Fee cocked his head toward the flats. "Just what we need." He bent his knees and began to wet Cassie's hair with a comb dipped into a jar of water.

Robbin said, "The dudes will be happy. Out there lurking around the sagebrush with their cameras to get shots of the pups playing."

"Hope your dudes can't count. Half the time we got to teach a young one or two out of every batch to stay the hell out of the stock and hope it takes that lesson back to the others."

Cassie said, "You don't kill them, do you?"

"Only when nobody's looking. Don't tell me you're fond of the varmints, missy."

"Fond of all live things," she said, and remembered reading that Edward Abbey claimed coyotes were smarter than ranchers, and more valuable. Not the thing to repeat when a rancher held a sharp instrument near your back.

Behind her, a screen door creaked, cowboy boots walked across wooden porch boards, and the door slammed closed. Cody said, "What's going on?"

Robbin said, "Your dad's broadcasting his joy of shooting coyotes."

Fee stopped his work, and Cassie turned her body around on the stool, keeping her head straight so the hair Fee had fanned across her back was undisturbed.

"Don't mind him," Cody said to her. "Dad loves the old days. If it was up to him, we'd still be stringing up outlaws from the cottonwood trees."

Cassie grinned at him. Cody nodded. And they stared at each other a moment. It felt like a good sign that she had begun to notice men as sexual beings again and was thinking now that Cody was a startlingly handsome man. She couldn't say, though, that she felt more than that for him.

With the jar of water in one hand, comb in the other, Fee stood immobile and glanced first at his son, then at Robbin, finally settling his gaze on Cassie. Everything halted, as if someone had hit the pause button on the scene. Cassie tried to decipher Fee's look, failed to, and turned back around on the stool. After a moment she felt the comb move through her hair again.

"We'll have to lop off five, six inches," Fee warned.

"Cut," Cassie said.

But Robbin leaped up from the porch step when the first chunk hit the ground.

"My God, take it easy, Fee. You can't replace this stuff overnight, you know."

Fee said, "Back off, Robb" in a patient, parental voice that suggested Fee had spent a lifetime correcting younger men.

Robbin shrugged. "Listen, hair's the only thing she's got going for her. She can't cook."

Back in camp, Boone and the guests straggled in from their morning ride in search of wildlife and were amazingly hungry. Time for lunch. Cassie had envisioned everyone wanting to settle down with a book—she did. They reported spotting a mother moose with twins, resting in the willows; a family of otters, floating on their backs in the river; trumpeter swans; and an elk named Earl.

"You could leave your hair loose like that sometimes," Robbin said as Cassie pulled her hair back and twisted her remaining elastic band around it.

"If I'd done that this morning, my whole head would have been ablaze."

Men were drippy over long hair. "Catch them however you can," her friend Erin often counseled. "Weed them out at your leisure." Cassie laid beef patties and chicken breasts on the grill.

Robbin's next conversational gambit sent him directly to Cassie's metaphorical compost pile.

"So . . . how *many* husbands did you kill off?" He leaned against the worktable and was possibly trying to flirt with her. "Just the one?"

Cassie glanced at Robbin over her shoulder as she reached up for dish towels that were drying on a tree limb. He was a good-looking guy. Nice teeth. Eyes blue, with a muscle beneath the left one that tightened when he smiled. She wondered briefly about a two-inch-long scar on the lower-right side of his jaw. Looked fresh. She reminded herself that to be a successful movie actor, a person had to be absurdly self-focused. But this guy had the emotional awareness of an earwig.

Either that or mental problems.

The next day she picked up the notion that perhaps she wasn't too far off the mark.

CHAPTER FOUR

The weekend's guests pulled out before dawn with plans to breakfast at the Lake Hotel in Yellowstone on their way to Montana. At about seven, Cassie let herself into the McKeags' kitchen, moving quietly in case Boone was still sleeping.

"I just don't think she's the sort of woman who's used to that kind of language." Boone's voice came from the adjoining office. "And Mrs. Penny will be coming soon."

"I go on automatic delete with Mrs. Penny." Robbin's voice.

Cassie now decided banging around to be the better courtesy.

"Listen to her out there. Sounds like a fucking bear's loose in the pantry."

"See, Robb, that's what I'm referring to. . . ."

"Fucking shit. This is my home. Let *her* adjust."

Cassie had had time to plan this meal. She aimed at impressing the McKeags now that she was in a real kitchen. A Mexican omelet encircled by sausage links, toast triangling that. Should she trim off the crusts? Would a real cook?

Cassie enjoyed working in the old-fashioned, sunny room as the kitchen filled with the comforting aromas of good food cooking.

The sound of sneakers striding out through the office doorway was followed by the sound of boots. The sneakers, seeming impudent on a ranch, were worn by Robbin, who chose to continue the conversation within earshot of Cassie. "She's prissy, Boone. She'll be carving our radishes into roses and curlicuing our carrots. She doesn't understand our operation here." To Cassie, with a deliberate bend to his body, as if he were onstage and needed to exaggerate his words for those in the back row, he added, "This is a down-home, come-as-you-are, no-frills guest ranch. Not a spa."

So, she'd leave the crusts on the toast.

Cassie handed Boone his breakfast plate. He gave loud sounds of appreciation—to cover up, Cassie was sure, Robbin's suggestion to "Note the arrangement, will you?"

Robbin grabbed his plate. "Just plop the food on there, sweetheart."

"Don't call me sweetheart."

"Don't call Miss Cassidy sweetheart, Robbin." Boone assured Cassie, "Tomorrow he won't do that."

Robbin clunked his plate down on the table. "Shit, Boone, what the fuck is this. . . ."

"Robbin, your language." Boone came up with a novel thought. "Try saying 'phooey.'"

"Let's not teach Robbin new tricks; let's just fire this impostor."

"I like her."

"I don't."

The two of them argued about her aimlessly, while Cassie cut a pork roast into cubes. She decided this might be a routine she'd have to get accustomed to, and though Robbin turned in his chair and directed particular insults toward her rather than toward Boone, it apparently wasn't up to Cassie to defend herself. Boone covered that job well. So, deciding she carried no responsibility, she tuned back in to the dialogue to learn what she could about these two characters she'd be spending the summer with—should she last that long.

"I don't understand this, Robbin. Did your psychiatrist mention regression as part of the healing process?" Boone sounded earnest and truly puzzled.

"I don't need this from you, Boone."

"But, Robbin, you bicker with Cassidy over the silliest—"

"It's Cassidy's fault. She starts it."

"Try, Robbin. Or *I'll* have to be cured from—you know—mental stress."

"Blackmail. Did I ever threaten you with craziness? No, I did not. I just quietly and on my own went crazy, and that's how it should be done." Abruptly Robbin's attention snapped to his food. "What's this hot shit in my eggs?"

"Robb," Boone warned, "she's new—she could make *one* mistake."

"She made that yesterday. Hey, Cassidy." He swung around to address her at the sink. "There's green shit in our eggs and it burns our tongues. Where the hell did you get that name? Sounds as phony as your job title. What'd you do, come west and take on a whole new—"

"It's Mexican."

"Zorro is Mexican."

"The omelet." And she used the occasion to invite them to call her Cassie.

Robbin picked the green chilies out of his omelet and dramatically draped them across an extra paper napkin. To Boone he said, excluding Cassie from the conversation again, as if she were the kitchen slave, "I'll bet her whole damn résumé is a fucking hoax. You really know how to pick them, Boone."

Furtively Boone added his green chilies to the pile on the napkin, while at the same time exuberantly praising Cassie on her inventiveness. "Mexican dishes. I believe Mrs. Penny will like that." To Robbin he said in a whisper, "Clean up . . . the . . . language." Boone's head was tucked down, with his eyes cast covertly at Robbin, the stance of a man who hopes to look like he's doing anything but passing information. Cassie looked, and sure enough, Boone wasn't even moving his lips. He was stretching them across his teeth like an amateur ventriloquist. "Phooey," he reminded his son.

"Phooey with this fucking Zorro food." Robbin scraped back his chair, pulled open the refrigerator and reached for the milk. "I'm fixing a bowl of Cheerios. Want some?"

"Um . . ." One glance at Cassie.

"Yes, he'll have some," she supplied, and removed both their plates.

From now on, Boone told Cassie, she should join them in their meals. Cassie figured his theory was if *she* had to eat burning green shit, she'd be more careful.

That evening Cassie pulled her camper into a permanent spot beneath a big Douglas fir. She leveled the floor by driving a couple feet forward, then backing up a few inches. Forward and to the left a couple inches to get the back left wheel off a root.

On and on, until she had it right—which occurred a good seven minutes past her threshold of patience. She turned on the propane tank that fueled her heater, untangled her extension cord and hooked up to an electrical outlet outside the garage for lights. She ran the garden hose she carried stored behind a door panel to the outdoor water spigot, then connected it to her sink. She swept and shook out her two rag rugs and wished those lilacs in the side yard were in bloom so she could cut some to set on her table. But she'd have to wait. Unlike back home in southern Ohio, where lilacs bloomed in March, Jackson Hole often didn't see lilac blossoms until the Fourth of July.

Cassie gathered a towel and soap, robe and sandals and—congratulating herself on a day without setting her hair on fire—went to bathe.

The bath, originally part of a three-car garage connected to the kitchen, had been renovated some years before with a tiled floor and paneled walls for the dudes as a bath and laundry area. By now, though, each cabin had been upgraded with its own bath, and laundry was hired out. Boone had said the place was all Cassie's. Opposite three toilet stalls were three shower stalls. Cassie undressed in the middle one, wrapped her towel around herself, and was brushing her teeth at one of the three sinks when Robbin came in through a door that opened from the kitchen. He carried a pile of laundry in his arms.

"Out!" Cassie shouted. "This is *my* bathroom."

"This is everybody's bathroom." Robbin opened a washer lid and stuffed his clothes in, added soap, then stretched out on an aluminum chaise with plastic webbing and watched Cassie tug on the bottom of her towel while she rinsed her mouth of toothpaste.

Haughtily, she swished past him toward the shower stall.

Robbin said, "Hey," and reached an arm out sideways to stop her. In a playful manner, but misjudging her speed, he grabbed the bottom edge of her towel in the back with his two fingers.

The towel slipped its tuck across Cassie's breasts. She reached up, whipped out the catch holding her hair in a knot on the back of her head, and her hair fell down like a blackout curtain, following the slipping towel and concealing her bare behind just as she moved into the dress cubicle outside her shower stall.

"Man," Robbin whispered. "Man."

Cassie latched the door.

"Honest to God, that is the most elegant thing I have ever seen." He sounded dazzled. She heard him push out of the chaise. "Cassie? Hey."

She turned on the water and stepped behind the shower curtain.

"Hey," Robbin said again, leaning against the door of her dressing cubicle. "I'm really sorry. I didn't expect it to come *off*." Pause. "Okay?"

Cassie didn't answer. She heard Robbin shift sides and lean the other shoulder against the door.

"Here's your towel," he said, and draped it over the top of the door. Another pause. "Say 'Thank you, Robbin,'" he mimed in a falsetto voice and singingly added, "'You're a dear!'"

Nothing from Cassie.

She lathered herself thickly with soap, as if donning an extra layer of protective clothing. She was thinking about Robbin going quietly crazy.

"Were you flirting with me? Nah." Robbin answered himself and Cassie heard him move away from the door. "Why *don't* you flirt with me?" Footsteps, as he crossed to the other side of the room. Then she heard a new sound, a steady stream of water hitting water. Her mind buckled. "Two days," he said, "and you haven't flirted once." The toilet flushed.

"Boone!" Cassie shrieked. "Boone!"

Robbin ran water at the sink. At least he washes his hands, Cassie thought inanely, realizing she had added and subtracted qualities to and from his character for two days now, trying to decide who he was, always coming out with a minus.

Boone opened the door from the kitchen.

"Boone." Cassie turned off the water and cried, "What's the *matter* with him?"

"We don't really know for sure, Cassidy," Boone answered. He sounded perplexed, but not shaken. "What'd you do, Robb?"

"Pissed. In the toilet." He stopped the washing machine, and Cassie heard liquid pouring into the wash water. "I put down the seat afterward; I washed my hands. You've hired a neurotic."

"He did that in front of me." Cassie held the towel up to herself and talked through the closed door. "*I'm* in here now."

Boone called that they were leaving, the bath was all hers. He also said he and Robbin were fixing sandwiches for the late movie, maybe she'd like one. Ham and melted cheese on a hot roll.

Cassie said no thank you.

Robbin leaned against her door again. "How about just the hot roll?"

"I can't take any more of this," Cassie warned Boone, her voice shrill.

Two payments behind on her truck, she reminded herself while toweling dry. Almost three. If she could hang on long enough to earn one paycheck out of this place, she could send a partial payment. After mailing several good-intention letters in the hope that GMAC wouldn't panic and begin proceedings against her, she knew real money would have to be in the envelope this time.

She had never been careless with money; neither had Jake. The Chevy pickup was sold to Jake with a considerable break in price as an exchange for endorsements and delivered while he was out of the country—no one realizing—on his final climb. Before Jake's accident, an old climbing friend had begun building a wooden camper onto the truck, apparently something Jake had mentioned wanting. His friend hoped to surprise him. There was no giving back the brand-new truck when Jake failed to return from his climb; the friend had removed the rear window and cut through the back of the truck to make the camper accessible from the front, reconfigured the driver and passenger seats and bolted the new construction to the truck bed. Cassie didn't know the particulars of the endorsement, but it was clear the deal was off with Jake's death. And Cassie was left owing for a full-price, brand-new cherry red pickup.

Wages from her last job had been made to look good with the inclusion of a free season ski pass. Even so, Cassie had been coping all right with the usual high rents of a resort town. Then fifty percent of a normal season's entire snowfall was dumped during December, which fooled her and everyone else into high expectations. When the January Thaw continued past its usual four days and temperatures rose to an unheard-of fifty-two degrees for two weeks straight, the snow that didn't dribble downhill avalanched in massive sheets. She had seen trees two feet in diameter lie severed by an avalanche. Towering pines had been uprooted from their deep and icy grip and tossed aside as easily as cocktail straws were plucked from piña coladas. Roaring like the end of the world, one avalanche produced just that for two ski patrolmen who happened across its path. Tourist numbers fell steadily and so did her employer's profits. Next, Cassie's hours were cut back. Slowly, slowly, her funds dwindled to the panic point.

Hair still damp from the shower, Cassie bundled herself into her flannel robe to read in bed. More than her transportation, this camper served as her insurance against homelessness. Otherwise, she would be scrambling for shelter like her roommates. Erin was hoping for a house-sitting situation; Becca and Lacy were in line for a one-room cabin with no electricity back in Pacific Creek, once the snowmelt allowed access. This camper had made Cassie's life in Jackson Hole possible since Jake's death, and living here was her number one priority—her friends were here, as were the mountains she loved.

Everything she needed was built right in, a sink, small refrigerator, a two-burner stove; even a portable toilet was enclosed in one corner. Joe, a carpenter who believed he owed Jake his life from a past climbing incident, had turned the pickup into a fanciful wooden home. Carved trim on the cupboards, a fan window beside the bed, surprise details of grace were added everywhere. Though there were times when Cassie cursed Joe and his gift to her husband, there were just as many times when she was grateful. In the beginning, when she was grasping for any kind of easement from her grief, it had felt as if she were being held in Jake's love, once removed. Someone who loved Jake had created a loving gift for him that now held her.

Grief had stopped keeping her company, and more and more now she longed to share again that deep exchange with one other special person. She couldn't say she was actually looking yet—she wasn't that far along. But not to worry, no candidates had appeared. Lately the possibility had occurred to her that she had played both roles of that deep exchange with Jake—both his and hers. Because when you were married to someone whose life had built-in separations, there were plenty of exchanges that could be delayed . . . indefinitely. Occasionally these days Cassie suspected Jake's love for the mountains had nudged his love for her down a notch. Many things about their relationship made greater sense from that perspective. Her longing to have children, for one; his relentless postponing of that, for another. And why hadn't he told her instead of a buddy about his desire for a truck with a camper?

A knock on Cassie's door interrupted her thoughts. She called out, "Yes?" and sat up straighter.

Boone peeked in. "Brought you a cup of hot cocoa."

She invited him inside, and he sat across from her bed on a built-in cedar chest designed for storing out-of-season clothes.

"My, isn't this nicely done." He looked around, nodded at the elk antler handles on the cupboards, patted the chest he sat on and took a nervous sip of Cassie's cocoa.

His mission, disclosed in his own roundabout way, was to assure Cassie that things would get better—and, Cassie suspected, to assure himself that she wasn't right now battening down in preparation for escape.

"Um," he said, "I want to explain about Robbin." But after several false starts and more sips of the cocoa he'd meant for her to have, Boone said, "Here's what Robbin told me once. It's from that famous speech." Boone cleared his throat and straightened his spine.

"Now, Robbin's the mimic, not me. You have to supply Martin Luther King's voice, but it went kind of like this." Boone took a deep breath, gave a look of reverent dignity to his face by making a crease between his eyebrows, and, as if speaking to an expanse of enthralled followers, boomed, "'I've *been* to the mountain. And I've looked over. I've *seen* the promised land.'" Then Boone relaxed his puffed-up chest and slipped into Robbin's irreverence. "'There ain't nothin' there.'"

After a silence—one of those moments when laughter arm-wrestles empathy—Cassie said, "I think Robbin just got to the top of a Ferris wheel."

She pictured him perched in his high place in the entertainment industry, looking below him—cameras flashing, fans yelling, the whole world glittering and laid out just for him.

"Then he fell off," Boone said. "Because one day, loaded up on everything he could snort, sip and smoke, he checked himself into a mental hospital."

At last, Cassie thought, she was going to hear some of the story.

"Well, that part was easy. Checking himself out was not. When Robbin couldn't get the authorities in charge to release him, he called me to help him escape."

According to Boone, Robbin had run his career wisely and well for all the years of his adult life, keeping himself clean of the pitfalls offered to an entertainer of his standing. Then abruptly he had indulged in every one of them for the next few years.

"I know this," Boone said to the inside of the cocoa mug. "There is only so much you can do for another person. Even for your own son. I wanted to give Robb the chance to heal himself last fall when I brought him home, but for a long time it looked like he was going to pass up the opportunity."

Boone nodded his head, staring into the mug. "The best thing that happened to Robb was his accident."

Cassie watched Boone swirl the chocolate, sugary remains at

the bottom of the mug. She asked softly, "What accident?" She thought of the fresh scar on Robbin's chin.

"Rolled his pickup. My God, why I had to see that . . . I just don't know." Boone tipped the mug, testing himself on how close he could come to the edge with the cocoa dregs and not spill it. "Early January. He was flying down the highway on his way home, ten o'clock in the morning and drunk. He'd taken to joining Fee and the other ranchers for their breakfast shots uptown in the early mornings. We'd had a snow, and the roads were slippery as cow cum. . . ."

Boone blanched. Some of the chocolate spilled onto his pants. "As cow, as cow . . ."

"Manure," Cassie supplied, as if she understood that was what he'd meant.

Boone unbuttoned his wool jacket with one hand as if he'd suddenly heated up. "I was on my way into town and I saw Robbin's green pickup coming from the other direction and watched him trying to maneuver that nasty curve just past the Wolf Fire Ranch. He veered into my lane, overcorrected and skidded off the rise. Rolled twice and smashed into a tree—I saw the whole thing."

Boone looked at Cassie, as if the film was running in his mind. "The spare tire bounced out of the truck bed and flew through the air. It slammed off another tree and . . . and I thought the tire was Robbin's body."

The emotions of that scene traveled across Boone's features, plain enough for Cassie to experience them herself.

"I jumped out of my truck, ran down the embankment, saw the truck windows broken out and the cab empty. . . . I couldn't go any farther. I dropped facedown on the snow and tried to die myself."

Suddenly, to cover the emotion showing on his face, Boone tipped the mug up and swilled the syrupy goo remaining on the bottom. Cassie winced, as did Boone.

"Well, next thing, Robbin's sitting there patting my head. 'Are we dead, Boone?' he asks me. And I say, 'We better be, otherwise I'm going to kill you.' And I roll over and see him looking fine, little cuts here and there, one good one on his chin, but not even shaking, like I myself was. And I say, 'Get your rifle, Robbin.' And he jumps up, feeling real spirited. He says, 'Good idea, Boone; we'll shoot the bugger'—meaning the truck."

Cassie smiled, picturing Robbin still in a party mood after a horrifying tumble in his truck.

"Lucky the damn thing wasn't loaded. I gave Robb a head start, then I chased him, swinging the rifle butt whenever I got close. We acted like a pair of fools out there in the snowy field. Then Robb climbed the embankment and locked himself in my truck. I flagged down the next car and told them to call the police, I had someone drunk and dangerous I wanted them to arrest."

At this point the accident sounded like the best thing that had happened to Boone, if not Robbin, or at least to their relationship.

"Well," he concluded, though Cassie noticed he always said "welp," pressing his lips together in a firm line at the end of the word. "That was the turning point. Robb's a good guy. Might be that he's feeling a lack of control over his life right now. Read that somewhere. Weaning yourself off liquor and getting your license taken away make a fellow feel out of sorts, nasty and a little demanding, though this here business with you is the first evidence of it. Also read we shouldn't take any of it. No coddling."

Boone stood and buttoned his wool jacket back up. "I can

coddle you, though. I'd take it very kindly if you'd stick on here with us." He offered Cassie the next day off and let himself out the door.

Cassie lay back against her pillows. A day off, paid, he'd said.

Boone stuck his head back in. "Say, we'll be using the horses more and more. You know horses?"

From cows. And she knew how she'd be spending her day off. As well as the extra money she'd be paid for it.

CHAPTER FIVE

Years before, Cassie had looked into horseback riding lessons. The first person she'd asked had said, "Back in Ohio, did you take bicycle riding lessons, too?" He was a Wyoming native and entirely serious. Since then she'd been carrying around the name of a ranch that offered a ten-week course, but she'd never found a strong enough interest to follow through on her intention. Now it took her twenty minutes to convince Harley, the rancher, to give her all ten lessons in one day. Even so, in a last attempt to dissuade her, he sent her back to town to purchase proper boots and a box of Epsom salts.

For the first three hours Cassie learned how to saddle and groom. From one o'clock until a couple hours before dark, she rode a horse named Bubba around a corral. All the while, Harley lectured: Horses never hold a grudge. The horse's ears tell its thoughts—standing upright and forward indicates something ahead concerns him, twitching loosely means he's listening for cues from his rider. And horses "boogerhunt"—look for threats, problems, holes in the ground, rocks. A good horse will be on the alert every minute, and so should a good rider.

About six o'clock in the evening, Harley sent Cassie down Game Creek Canyon with Bubba on her own. For ten minutes that worked out well. Then, like an automobile without a driver, Bubba gradually lost speed, coasted off trail and finally stopped altogether.

"Don't let yer horse get away with one dern thing," Harley had said.

To fool Bubba into thinking she meant to stop here, Cassie dismounted. Besides, when in doubt return to the last known place of comfort. Cassie started over. Off with Bubba's saddle, lift each hoof, check the indented sole around the frog. Sling the saddle back on. Fingertips on Bubba's side, measure stirrup to beneath armpit. Grab reins and mount.

At eight o'clock Cassie paid Harley for the ten hours and threw herself on her camper bed, whimpering. Knees ached from pressing them against the sides of the horse. Toes were numb from squeezing them tensely inside her boots. Bridle, cantle, stirrups. Heels down, elbows out, hands off the horn— "It ain't no steering wheel—relax those legs. Spin him to the right, now the left. Lean into it, girl." Cassie moaned out loud at the thought of getting up and sitting in the driver's seat. "*Spring* into that saddle."

Midmorning the next day, Cassie met Boone and Robbin at the barn. Cody led a twelve-year-old buckskin into the corral for Cassie, and Boone, just as he had when she was interviewing for the job, introduced her to the horse.

"Cassie, meet Bruce." He petted the horse's nose. "Bruce, Cassie is your rider this summer; take her easy."

Before anyone could doubt her ability, Cassie walked to meet Cody coming out of the barn, carrying the horse's assigned saddle and blanket. She took those from him and lugged them over to Bruce. Cody and Robbin exchanged looks, so Cassie beefed up her act and chatted with the horse about his withers and fetlock, his forelock and gaskin. As she saddled Bruce, she explained to the horse what she was doing, using all the proper terms she could remember. Bridle and bit, cinch and saddle string.

"Aren't we just horsey as hell this morning," Robbin said.

Boone glanced over while saddling his own horse and Robbin raised his eyebrows at him with skepticism.

After a moment Robbin said, "Bruce is a gelding." He waited to see what Cassie would do with that fact.

Gelding, gelding. What had she heard that word in reference to at the stables yesterday? "Bring out the gelding for this gal," Harley had instructed his hand. "He's a pussy." Cassie hadn't realized at the time. But, of course, she'd heard that happened in the animal kingdom—a homosexual horse. Cassie said to Robbin, "Do you believe in a Bruce Syndrome?"

"You know a lot of eunuchs named Bruce?"

Eunuch. Oh.

Cassie hobbled around to the other side of the horse to gain cover for a possible rejoinder that might surface if she could hide a moment from the watchful blue eyes. Though every muscle whined with pain this morning, the new boots made it impossible to move normally. Band-Aids plastered blisters all over her feet. Still, the boots were beautiful and she expected someone to notice that any minute now. Half a truck payment and not a single word so far. Harley had demanded that she buy good ones; else she'd be better off working horses barefoot, he'd claimed.

"Hey, Boone." Robbin nodded sideways toward Cassie. "Dale Evans has a brand-new pair of boots."

Cassie came around the other side of Bruce, cocked one leg out and tipped her foot from side to side, demonstrating her boot's burnished black leather. "I can practically put my lipstick on in the reflection, they're so shiny." She laughed.

"Welp . . . there's other things to admire about them," Boone said in the tone of a premature apology.

Cody grabbed a bucket, broke through a skim of ice to fill it with water from the horse trough and toted it over. Robbin said, "Let's have them."

Cassie looked to Boone, who said sympathetically, "Better do as he says, honey."

With certain relief, Cassie sat on the middle pole of the buck-and-rail fence, inched her boots off and tugged at her socks, eager now to share the damage with her sympathizers. Warm water sounded more appealing, but in lieu of wearing those boots one more minute she'd soak her feet in anything.

Robbin scooped her boots up and plunged them into the pail. Cassie shrieked and leaped up.

"You could have explained, Robb," Boone reprimanded.

"*Wranglers* already know these things."

"But she didn't. She fancies those boots." Boone reminded Robbin of his first pair and how he'd balked at breaking them in. "Shame on you, Robbin." Then Boone began inching himself away from the likely fray to follow.

Cody said, "Sorry, but we're going to have to soak these all day."

Robbin explained. "And tomorrow you wear them wet. All day. Until they dry on your feet."

"You're making that up."

She looked toward Boone, but he'd swiftly mounted his horse and was leaning over from the saddle to unlatch the gate of the corral. When she glanced at Cody, he nodded, then leaned to the side and spit a brown stream of chew.

Robbin said, "Tomorrow's forecasted for a temperature plunge with high winds."

"But I'll be cold."

"Cowboy up, Cassie."

It amazed Cassie that she had lived in this valley for all these years, yet knew so little about the ranching lifestyle. Among her friends, mountain sports overwhelmed all else; the cowboy culture was merely the background against which skiing, hiking, climbing, rafting and fly-fishing played out. According to Cassie's experience, it just happened to be the flavor of this particular area that some of the stop signs said WHOA. That the downtown had boardwalks, the stores were built with false fronts and even the snowmen wore cowboy hats. She bought into the western style herself. Her rear bumper sported a sticker with a gleaming red ski boot strapped by a silver spur and her favorite earrings were turquoise stones.

Cassie sat back down on the fence to get off her sore feet and watched her beautiful boots soak in water. "Cowboy boots ain't just for dancin'," Harley had informed her. To ride a horse with anything other than a proper boot was foolhardy. The pointed toe was needed to quickly slip into the stirrup, the raised heel to keep it there. The high leather tops were protection from snakes and other "varmints." Even so, Cassie had figured they'd look great worn with a skirt.

As Robbin stooped over the bucket, cupping water in his hands to fill the inside of her boots, his blue cotton sweater rode up, and Cassie saw that he wore the requisite cowboy belt—wide embossed leather. Yesterday at the stables, she'd encountered five men who had each worn a similar brown leather belt, distinguished only by their choice of buckles and their first names in raised letters across the back: Harley, Dave, Smoke, Gerry and Chuck. Across the back of Robbin's belt was stamped BELT. Catching the joke, Cassie smiled to herself.

Boone decided to postpone the ride till Cassie's boots were broken in and Robbin drove her across the yard to her camper since she was barefoot. Two plastic water bottles and an empty root beer can rolled around the floor of Robbin's truck.

Cassie said, "I'll take these." She gathered them up along with her socks. These people didn't do one thing about recycling. No wonder that among her friends ranchers carried a reputation for using and abusing the land without giving back.

"Just leave those," Robbin said. "I'll toss them out later."

"I'll stick them in the recycling bins."

"We don't have any."

"Soon you will."

Later that night, Robbin brought Cassie's boots to her camper, knocking on her door and announcing himself. She called for him to come in, from the edge of her bed where she sat tending her feet. She was using Bag Balm, a veterinary salve normally used for cows' teats, and hoped Robbin noticed that— it might give her some credibility. All her women friends in Jackson Hole used it for first aid or dry hands; Erin claimed it was perfect for vaginal infections.

Robbin admired the workmanship of her camper and said he'd been curious about the inside, so Cassie pointed out all the tiny drawers and cupboards concealed in odd available spaces. When Robbin discovered her Porta-Potty behind a door, Cassie wondered what she'd do if he unzipped now and began to use it.

"This idea you have about recycling. Give it up. Nobody here is going to go for that." He stood above her as she sat on the edge of her bed, the tips of his fingers stuck in the front pockets of his Levi's.

"How about you? Will you go for it?"

"I don't have anything against it. But you're new here. Not a good idea to start off changing things. Just thought I'd mention that." He set his hand on the doorknob.

"But if there was a place to separate out bottles and cans and other recyclables, you'd go along with it?"

"What's the point? So we bury our shit—who does it bother?"

"I'll do it all myself. Set up bins, sort it, cart it to the town's recycling center."

"You're looking for trouble." He opened the door and stepped down from the camper.

Cassie followed him to the door, held it open and said, "It takes a thousand years before a plastic water bottle even *begins* to decompose when it's buried."

Robbin paused, shifted his eyes to Cassie's and held them a moment, then continued on into the dark toward his cabin.

Her first day at the ranch she'd spotted the ceiling-high column of cases filled with bottled water. During a single summer this ranch must go through truckloads of it. Recycling wasn't the only routine here she planned on initiating. The water in this valley was icy cold and delicious right out of the faucet; why not pass out refillable water bottles?

Boone's goal for the next couple of weeks was to get the ranch shaped up for the summer. The horses needed to become accustomed to riders again after their long winter on the open range. Tents and river rafts needed patching and sealer applied. Boone requested that everyone chip in to cover all necessary jobs until the full staff arrived in mid-June. Fee, Cody and their wranglers joined the effort.

Cassie took over much of the book work, all the guest correspondence, and provided lunches in camp for those working there. She deep-cleaned the main house kitchen, moved on to the dining room and just kept going into the living room, piling a winter's worth of old newspapers and magazines into her new recycling system set up in the storeroom adjoining the kitchen. She dusted and vacuumed and shoveled out ashes from the fireplace. The hearth and chimney were made of moss stone and looked faded, so she found a spray bottle and dampened the lichen. Suddenly the fireplace stone was enlivened with shades of orange and lime green. She stood back and admired her work.

The two sofas and several overstuffed chairs looked comfortable, but were as worn as the lamp shades and draperies. With Boone's permission, she rearranged the main house living room. The furniture, which was pushed unimaginatively against the four walls of the large rectangular room, she set into comfortable groupings for reading and watching television.

Robbin was the first to comment on the change.

"For one god-awful moment I thought I'd gotten married," he said that evening.

Cassie laughed self-consciously. She loved rearranging furniture. Her first year of marriage, Jake kept saying with awe, "I *heard* new wives did this, but jeez, Cassie." He claimed they'd be the only two people who'd wear out their furniture from the bottom up. "I'd swear the legs on this sofa were two inches higher last month."

Tomorrow the movie crew would arrive. No need to plan

events to entertain them. Cassie would provide a large urn of coffee and muffins in the mornings and pack lunches for the five of them to carry into the field. The group looked forward to going into town for dinners to sample the many fine restaurants offering everything from sushi to bison burgers.

That night after the three of them finished eating, Boone explained the family tradition of playing Hollywood gin for fun after dinner; the loser had to clean up the kitchen. He laid the ground rules needed for the three-handed game.

Robbin brought over the coffeepot. "Rule number one: we are not playing for kitchen duty. We hired the Apache for that."

Cassie said, "Let's play for money."

They agreed on half a cent a point.

"By God," Boone said when Cassie won the first game and he tallied up, "she skunked us. Fifty each for that. Twenty-five for under the hump. She got three boxes on each of us, and the bonus for winning. . . ." He shifted figures up and down the margin of the score sheet. "You know what she's got," Boone said.

In unison he and Robbin announced, "Horseshit luck."

Cassie wasn't new at this. She'd been raised on card games at home. Hearts, canasta, pinochle. Her parents thought it was good brain exercise for her and her brother, Dole, as they were growing up.

The next two hands brought Cassie's score down and Robbin's up, and Boone became riled. Sitting up straight on his chair, he watched every move with tense alertness. After Cassie's turn, Boone discarded a seven of clubs, presuming it to be a safe card, after having seen Robbin discard a red seven during his previous turn. Robbin promptly snatched it up.

"Baiter, baiter," Boone sang accusingly in a monotone, like

an old, well-used litany. "Baiter, baiter, masturbator." And then he froze.

It was quiet enough to hear a mouse's toenails click tile, until Robbin fell back in his chair and howled. Cassie joined him, unsure which was funnier, Boone's slipup or his embarrassment over it.

"Stop the silliness, both of you," Boone said gruffly, and ordered Cassie to take her turn.

For Cassie the gin game felt like an initiation into Boone and Robbin's inner circle. The three of them played for themselves, while teaming up during the game with one of the others to better their chances. As in their table talk, affiliation continually shifted.

But the game was rife with sexual terms—hump, box, going down—and Robbin misused the camaraderie of laughing together at Boone to make Cassie as uncomfortable as he legitimately could in front of his father.

When the game was over Boone lectured Robbin with the gusto of the night's big loser. "You could have done better for yourself if you'd saved your little cards and gone down. Could have caught us with our pants at our knees," Boone added, managing to display his ability to pick up subliminally on the undercurrents without his own awareness. "But nooo," he drawled, "you have to ram it in for the big play."

"That's my style," Robbin said, eyes on Cassie, having fun at her expense again.

If only he knew how dated that style was. Yet how could that be true of a movie star, whose image depended on being current? The guy must have had all the women he ever wanted, beginning in his early teens. For sure, any of Cassie's girlhood friends, whose rooms had been plastered with McKeag posters, would have happily made themselves available. Maybe that was it: women made themselves available and Robbin didn't have to do a thing.

Clearly he was experienced in intimate relationships; the love between him and his father was palpable. And in the corral the day of her boot dunking, Cassie had marveled at how attuned Robbin and Cody were. One thought "bucket of water" and the other dipped it into the horse trough. Perhaps it was only with women that Robbin seemed out of his depth.

If Robbin McKeag thought she was titillated by his crassness, he had no *idea* who he was dealing with, Cassie thought later, lying in her camper bed. The guy would have no reference point for comprehending her romance with Jake. Cassie had married the best of them; Jake was dead now, but she still had the gauge with which to measure others. She had dated Jake while they were both in their senior year of college in Bowling Green, Ohio. When she felt sure he was the one, she let him take her to his parents' cottage, three hours away on Lake Erie. She remembered the time was mid-March, cold, gray and damp. They stopped in Port Clinton that night for groceries; then Cassie waited in the car while Jake bought condoms at the drugstore.

They lit the oil heater and crawled into a bed in their clothes to wait until the cottage warmed up. After a time, Jake jumped out to get the condoms, searching by flashlight since the electricity was disconnected for the winter. When they finished making love and he pulled out of her, the condom wasn't there—where it belonged.

In united horror, they realized the *only* other place the condom could be.

"Let me get it," Jake said.

"No," Cassie said, "I should." After pondering the etiquette of the situation, she added, "I'll go into the bathroom."

"You shouldn't move. Maybe it's still okay, if we hurry." He rose to his knees beside her, one hand resting on her abdomen, the other about to press her thigh aside and go fishing for the wayward condom. Cassie flung an arm over her face from embarrassment. To enter exotic territory under the dizzy passion of romance was one thing, but it was quite another to go there with scientific deliberation to search and seize alien matter. An investigative foray. Perhaps he'd have to use his flashlight.

Her hands shot out to halt Jake. "I don't know you well enough for this."

The absurdity of her words struck them, and they began laughing.

"Now we've done it," Jake said, feeling her stomach clench in the laughter. "The condom's sure to be empty now."

Worry, laughter, the intimacy of the condom retrieval, with each of them feeling they'd been stupid, moved gracefully into a sort of wonder. What if, right now, a child was being formed, blink-of-an-eye mating of egg and sperm, his and hers? Imagine. Jake rested his hand there as though to feel the vibration of it. Perhaps this child would be conceived from the act of laughing as well as loving.

"We should get married," Jake said. "Right now, before we know, so the baby will always understand we chose each other."

The following day they found a justice of the peace. But there hadn't been a child, not for all the nine years of their life together, and they never tried again to prevent one. Cassie had assumed the blame was hers, though medical exams had never backed that up. Then a recent encounter had thrown that assumption and others involving her marriage into new light, or rather into new darkness. Another reason she needed to live alone this summer: to sort out her history with Jake, recasting memories and beliefs.

Cassie sat up and rearranged her covers. Outside her camper window the ranch lay quiet. One lamp glowed in Robbin's cabin across the yard.

Being around Robbin McKeag, she decided, was like skiing through the Beaver Creek Burn the first winter after the forest fire had blazed across those acres. No matter how careful she'd been, her clothes had become streaked with soot from the charred trees.

She cracked her bedside window to prevent condensation from forming overnight inside the camper, and she remembered that she'd also experienced a cleanliness within the burn. Vertical, blackened poles, stripped of limbs, rose up against the pristine snow like a Quaker meetinghouse. Simple strokes and sunlight, all else cleared away. And another thing: the burn opened the view to the peaks of the mountain ranges beyond it and she could see forever in that place where, once, she couldn't see the forest for the trees.

She thought now that as tragic as that wide sweep of angry orange flame had seemed, consuming a mountain slope, it was not a misfortune but a renewing process, a healing.

Perhaps this would be true of Robbin after his conflagration.

Because she knew now that the only way a lodgepole forest could be naturally reseeded was through fire. The pinecones holding the seeds were glued together by resin. At 125 degrees the resin melted, the cone exploded and the seeds were released. Those seeds with their featherlike tails, held aloft by flaming air currents, were the cure for tired forests.

She had to figure that if that much purpose and pattern sparked a forest fire, who should say it wasn't within nature's plan for people to go crazy once in a while?

That was what they'd said about her when she'd left Ohio again after Jake's death and returned to Wyoming, jobless and homeless—crazy with grief, they'd said. Sometimes she had wondered herself if it was true. Tonight, though, she saw that returning to this valley, even without Jake, whose climbing career had originally drawn them here, was her way of taking the healing into her own hands.

Maybe Robbin had gone crazy with grief. Gotten to the top of his Ferris wheel, looked over the carnival below and decided to burn it all to hell. Start fresh.

Still, he was charred, and she'd have to be careful not to come away from him with swipes of soot on her clothes.

CHAPTER SIX

A s a survival tactic, Cassie began to gather clues about Robbin. She felt reluctant to ask her friends for information, as
they assumed *she* was the authority now. But when she met
Erin, Becca and Lacy for a drink one evening, a story came
up about Robbin encountering a wooden dummy, an Indian,
propped on a bench outside a souvenir shop. Robbin invited
the dummy to the Cowboy Bar for a beer. The two got into
an argument and later fought it out in the alley. Somehow, the
dummy won.

Her friends were too polite to ask intrusive questions about
Robbin, but by retelling old stories they had hoped to prompt
Cassie into disclosing some of her own. All she could offer was
that Robbin didn't like her much and the feeling was mutual.

What she needed to do was replace some of the mystery
about the guy with facts. She needed to get him to talk. Mystery
came with an imbalanced leverage of power, as she had discovered the past winter when for the first time since Jake's death

she'd found herself interested in a man. He wore a blue ski-racing suit and they exchanged hot-eyed stares while passing each other around the ski village—on the slopes, picking up lattes—until Cassie's blood felt like soda pop as it fizzed through her veins. Finally, one night while having a beer in the Mangy Moose she got the skier to talk. He spoke in T-shirt slogans: "Live to ski, ski to die." "Faster, faster, till the fear of death overcomes the fear of speed." Up close she noticed that a dagger earring dangled from one ear and that his upper arms, now bared, were covered in mean-looking tattoos. Could she have picked anyone more unpromising? The bubble burst, and Cassie plummeted back into herself, thankful for the ownership but lethargic for the rest of the winter.

Recalling this, she realized that episode marked her first experience of feeling like a single woman again, not just like Jake's widow.

"I wonder," Cassie said haltingly to Robbin that afternoon, "if we could—you know—talk."

Robbin's blue eyes became slinky, and Cassie glanced at his earlobes, then dropped to his upper arms—were tattoos lurking beneath his sweater?

Robbin grinned.

In case he thought she was admiring his biceps, she decided it was best to clarify her intentions. "I think," she began. "It's not . . . what you think," she tumbled out.

Robbin pushed his hands deep into the pockets of his khakis, leaned one shoulder against a cottonwood tree and said in humorous despair, "Fuck."

"No," Cassie said hurriedly, "it's not that."

Feeling stupid, she spun on her boot heel and rushed away, certain that her embarrassment was thick enough to leave a red stain in the air behind her. She could hear Robbin until she shut the door on her camper, and she wished he'd *die* laughing.

That evening during dinner, as if to make it up to her, Robbin charmed both Cassie and Boone, telling stories on himself.

One night in the Neon Spur during his heavy-drinking days last summer, Robbin told them, he'd gone into the restroom right after seeing Cody head in that direction. Just one stall was occupied. Robbin took the stall next to it and in an assumed voice began making noises as if he were falling into the toilet—gurgle, gurgle, flushing it, calling for help in a fading voice. Nothing from the next stall. Total silence.

Robbin stepped up the pace. "Hey, cutie!" He knocked on the divider, made suggestions in a falsetto voice. Still no response from Cody in the next stall. But they knew each other so well, Robbin assumed that Cody was holding back as a form of jocular competition, so Robbin upped the ante. He reached under the divider, pulled up the man's pant leg and plucked a leg hair above his boot top. The voice of a total stranger said, "Hey! What's the matter with you, buddy?"

Robbin was a good mimic, and Boone and Cassie laughed hard. More than anything else the humor came from Robbin's body language, as if something was built into his muscle structure that made his movements, like a dancer's, graced with natural rhythm.

After dinner, Robbin invited Cassie for a walk down to the creek. The trumpeter swans had stayed over the winter, since a warm spring kept ice from forming in a wide bend of the creek. The sounds of the swans bullying the smaller waterfowl, whomping their massive wings on the surface of the water, drifted through the trees as Cassie walked with Robbin down the path. As they approached the water, the swans, having chased off the geese, settled beside perfect reflections of themselves and continued their sedate, long-throated float. The gracious sight conflicted with the fact that Cassie knew one swat of those wings could knock a coyote crazy.

Robbin stretched out on the grassy bank and lay on his back, his hands beneath his head. Cassie sat with her back against a boulder and watched the sun smear cranberry stains across the blue cloth of the sky.

Robbin said, "Ask me something."

Cassie was startled, then realized Robbin was probably more accustomed to being interviewed than having conversations with certain people. Apparently he'd defined her need to talk— perhaps correctly—as an interview. She thought back to cooking her first breakfast in camp and Robbin complaining to Boone that he needed serenity to write.

"You mentioned you were writing. What are you working on?"

"Researching a screenplay."

A couple more questions; a couple more brief responses, then Cassie hit the jackpot and Robbin rolled over on his side to face her. His head propped on his hand, he began to tell her what his research had uncovered.

"I'd always heard about Cissy Patterson, the countess and newspaper heiress, and Cal Carrington, a hunting guide with an outlaw reputation. They met here in Jackson Hole at a dude ranch back in the 1920s. So I began to investigate and found it's a damn great story."

"Did they fall in love?"

"That's what the research suggests—if anyone still believes in that these days."

"You don't?"

Robbin grinned. "I'll bet you mean for longer than one night. Nah, but those two were sure into something big. They spent most of their lives together."

"How are you going to write about something you don't believe exists?"

"The same way I play roles in film. It's not hard to act as if I'm in love for the camera." Robbin grinned at her and said, "I suppose you were in love with that guy you married."

Cassie nodded. She noted the past tense and considered correcting that to present tense, but maybe she was nearing the time to let that go.

"What was his name?"

"Jake."

"Jake." Robbin sat up. "Jake Danner? The mountain climber? My God, why didn't you say so?"

Cassie shrugged. Once, she had rarely failed to jump at any opportunity to say Jake's name. The first few months after his death she didn't wait for an opportunity, just injected his name into every conversation, as if saying "Jake" over and over would resuscitate him.

"He was bigger than life," Robbin said. "I followed his career. We even met a few times." He looked at Cassie for a moment. "He was a damn nice guy."

Robbin plucked a stem of grass from between his bent knees and tied it into a knot. "I always used to remind myself that what I was doing was no big deal—not risking my life, climbing mountains like Jake Danner, I used to think. People have such an obsession with fame; it could give a guy the big head. Jake never seemed to fall for that."

"It's true; he didn't."

"So . . ." Robbin stopped himself. He laughed. "I was

just going to ask you what people always ask my friends and family."

"What?"

"What was he really like?"

Cassie smiled and said, "Jake had a very smooth stability about him. Not much rattled him. And you're right—his fame never affected his personality. People thought he was different from them. But the only difference, he claimed, was that spotlight shining on him, which meant to Jake that since people watched him, he carried a greater obligation to express important qualities, like kindness and generosity."

"I'd heard that he made a point of contributing to the villages where he based his climbs—helped build hospitals and stocked the communities with medical supplies." Cassie said that was true. Robbin said, "Jake was right about fame. Some people have this need to isolate others as being special for some reason and they heap all this glory and expectation on them, then get damn mad if the person doesn't measure up. I'm sick to death of it."

That remark reminded Cassie that she still didn't understand about Robbin's mental issues, and that had been her reason for talking to him. So she prompted, "And now you're healing from that."

"I guess. I've done everything else—drank myself into stupors, gave in to the huge amounts of cocaine pressed on me, jetted all over the planet, hobnobbed with the rich and royal, went crazy. I'm out of options."

Was he going to stop there? Cassie prompted again. "Going crazy was an option?"

"The idea felt kind of good, after the rest of it failed to get me anywhere. Supposedly I'd risen to the place where hordes of people dreamed of being, but it wasn't doing a thing for me. I mean, you can climb high enough in the ranks of our culture until there's no more climbing to do. If you're like me and have done nothing else since you were a kid, eventually hopelessness sets in. So I . . ." Robbin shrugged.

"So you . . . ?"

"Tried what else the world had to offer."

"Drugs, drinking . . ." Cassie prompted.

". . . And craziness. I went all out for thrills. I scared myself—deliberately. Drove too fast, partied with dangerous people . . . Adrenaline pumping into my stomach was my religion. But eventually I recognized that it was just another drug. In a moment of realization, I checked myself in at an institution in New England, far from Hollywood, thinking I was on an enforced retreat. You know? I'd be cornered into a kind of equanimity. No drugs, alcohol, fans, agents, producers—the whole damn world held at bay."

Robbin was on a roll; he talked like he hadn't unfurled his scroll for eons. Cassie found herself taken in. She smiled and laughed when he did, sobered to reflect his shift in mood. He was coming alive and taking on dimension right before her eyes. And she liked him.

"That hospital was hell," he said.

"Tell me about it."

"It was like a special little kingdom. You stepped into it and you were who they saw you as being, until you fought your way out. The belief was that you were crazy, or why else were you there? You had to *get yourself out* before they'd believe otherwise."

Cassie tried to imagine. She looked toward the river. The Canada geese had returned and now dipped their heads in search of river bottom vegetation, flashing their white undersides to reflect the setting sun, like mirrored signals in a mysterious code.

She wondered if Robbin's experiences were similar to the way every friend and family member had offered a solution to her grief when Jake died. As if being troubled gave everyone license to dabble in your inner life.

"Sometimes," Robbin said, "it seemed to me they were determined to break me, show me my broken self, make me own up to it, then promise to put me back together *their* way. Shit. I had a drug problem and a loss of philosophy. Debilitating, both of them. But what they offered was their own brand of drugs—a greater variety and amount than *I'd* ever experienced—and a bland choice of philosophies."

"What did it? What got you out?"

"I asked myself why I expected a meaningful life to come to me effortlessly. I didn't just idly *dream* about a successful acting career, though imagination is an important part of it—it's the fire. But dreaming has to be mated with action. I needed to get out of that hospital and begin my real life." He looked off to the forest, his gaze settling behind Cassie for a moment, then shifting back to her. She sat quietly, not wanting to interrupt his flow of thought.

"That idea began to work on me. The desire burned, was fanned by my imagination—just like the early years when I was on my way up in the film business, once I had discovered I really wanted to be good at that work—and finally it flared brightly enough to show me how to take action. In a way it was easy." Robbin grinned at the simplicity of his solution.

"One day last fall I saw that the mental walls keeping all of us inside the sanatorium were invisible to me, and I walked away. I phoned Boone to come help me get out of town. He'd been told by the doctors that as a parent he was a likely source of my trouble and it was not beneficial that he contact me. Can you imagine what that did to Boone? The bastards."

"Then what happened?"

"I hid in the woods without money, food or a coat for two and half days, waiting for Boone to drive across the country. This was last fall. I had told him to come to a park on the edge of a big forested area. I said buy an ice cream cone at the snack hut. Vanilla if it's safe for me to come out, chocolate if I should wait."

Robbin laughed.

"Boone bought strawberry. Hell, I thought, what the fuck does that mean? Then I made myself settle down and think about it. Boone, I decided, was a worse wreck than me, and probably incapable of deciding what was safe or not. He'd been kept in the dark about my condition. Besides, decisions are not Boone's strong suit."

"Then what?" Cassie wanted more and more words to bridge the gap between them.

"I watched him pace with his strawberry ice cream cone. Then he threw it away, purchased a double-dip vanilla and held it up high. Oh, God, we hugged and cried for fifteen minutes, and then we drove the hell out of that state."

Cassie laughed. "A strawberry ice cream cone."

"It's a family catchphrase now," Robbin said. "We can't decide something, we say 'Hell, let's get strawberry.'"

"You weren't crazy?" She wouldn't mind hearing an official diagnosis.

"Just flirting with the notion—not exactly a sane thing to do in itself. But for so long I had a one-track dynamic in life: be a successful actor. It kept me steady and on course until I reached my altitude, then . . . nothing. No inner radar system to keep me directed. I flew in circles until I was bored to lifelessness."

"What will keep you on course now?"

"I'm learning what I care about. So far I've distilled it down to a creative life and my love for this land. And, of course, my family and my friends here. Those are my guiding lights for now and they're a hell of a lot more worthy than the opinion of *People* magazine—which, along with the rest of them, has canceled me out since the institution."

"You've been spared," Cassie said.

"Hollywood can handle drug overdoses, alcoholism, broken families. But do not talk about mental institutions . . . or you will disappear without fanfare. It doesn't end with the press; Cody doesn't get it either. Probably thinks I should 'cowboy up'—you know, stop whining, get back on the horse. The western tradition."

Cassie was familiar with people thinking similar things about her grieving over Jake. She said, "No one can really know what you've experienced. Besides, not many people want to deal with their inner life at all." She was happy to learn that Robbin wasn't one of them. With some surprise and obvious pleasure, Cassie said, "You're nice to talk to."

"Yeah?" Robbin was lying back on the grass again, his head propped in his hand. "Want to make it?"

The smile collapsed on Cassie's face. "We're having a nice talk. Don't demean it." She leaned away from the boulder and stood up.

"So." Robbin pushed himself one-handed to his feet, immediately triggered for defense. "Baring souls is okay. Baring asses is demeaning. Who's off base here? Asses should come before souls in my book."

"You're insensitive, improper. . . ." Then the exact word came to mind. "You're crazy." She immediately regretted the outburst, was horrified at herself for saying that. Robbin had used the word so freely, it just leaped to mind. She didn't know how to correct herself, was more motivated to get away from him, and began to leave.

Robbin shot an arm out to the boulder behind her, barricading her route of escape. "You're the one calling a crazy person crazy. Not even the numbed-out nurses at Pleasant Meadows were that insensitive. Improper? You think it's more intimate to take your pants down than your ego barriers? You're the crazy person here. You have something we can name: anhedonia. A resistance to fun. One of the fundamental human needs and pleasures—sex—arouses you to hysteria."

He glared at her. Then he dipped his head down and smiled to himself. He ran a thumbnail across his upper lip as he looked at Cassie through the tops of his eyes. He dropped his jaw in a shy, bad-boy grin and said to her, pressed against the boulder, "You're between a rock and a hard place, Cassie."

Completely without her consent, she felt her eyes flash downward to the front of his pants.

Later, alone in her camper, Cassie realized there was going to have to be a first time. It had been well over three years now since she'd made love with Jake. She was thirty-four years old; it was unrealistic to hold out for love again.

It wasn't that she wouldn't consider sleeping with someone out of sheer lust, but that she was afraid lust would abruptly leave at an inopportune moment—say, once she was sprawled naked in another person's bed. Because just as lust made surprise appearances—like on a snowy slope with a slinky-eyed skier—it made just as sudden disappearances. Love was a chancy thing, but lust chancier.

Erin had said she needed to loosen up. "Think of it like

dancing. You're not committed for a lifetime, just one song." But Cassie recalled dancing with some men for one song that felt like a lifetime. Some men danced without taking into consideration that they had a partner, just jived wildly to the music without bringing her along. Others started off joining their rhythm to hers, then faded away like a windup toy, barely tapping a toe, while she was left jiggling her butt all alone. The trouble was, you didn't know this when the music started. It wasn't like meeting Jake in school and becoming acquainted before committing to a date and then dating for a while before committing to sex. At her age, two evenings out and the expectation was . . . She just wasn't ready yet.

The next afternoon while she was taking a walk around the ranch, she ran into Cody and his two blue heeler dingoes. He was looking as well put together as usual, even repairing a barbed wire fence, wire stretchers in one hand, wire cutters at his feet. He wore a herringbone tweed vest. His jeans were dark blue, not faded and worn on the thighs, as were most of the workers' jeans. His blue shirt looked fresh and a red silk scarf was tucked inside the collar. Handsome as Cody was, Cassie felt no particular resonance with him, other than finding him likable. Once, she would have attributed her lack of interest to the grieving process. Now she knew there was more to it; she just didn't know what.

She deliberately walked across the pasture and started a conversation with him—her new method for confronting mysteries, since it had worked with Robbin . . . somewhat. She stooped down and reached the back of her hand out to the dingoes first. They sniffed and let her pet them, then curled into the shade of her body.

"What are their names?"

"The older female is Kelty; her daughter's name is Cairn."

"Karen?"

"Cairn. Like the rock pile."

"Oh, nice."

Silence. Cody leaned on the fence post and looked down at her, still kneeling on one knee so as not to disturb the shape of the shady spot for the dogs. She watched him toss aside his tool and decided that his lack of complexity made him comfortable to be around but not intriguing. The opposite of Robbin, whom Cassie found uncomfortable to be around but quite intriguing. It made sense that the two of them were close; they balanced each other.

Cody looked up to the sky and seemed about to comment on the weather as a last conversational resort. So Cassie said, "You must be glad to have Robbin around this year. Sounds from stories I've heard like you two have been friends all your lives." She had picked up only the merest outline of the two families' history—Cody and Robbin's—so didn't have much to go on with this remark, other than that the families had ranched side by side for four generations.

Cody said, "Yep. But he's a handful." He laughed. There was affection in his smile.

"How's that?" Cassie hoped her voice didn't display the interest this statement aroused. She petted the nearest dog—Cairn, she thought it was—to suggest a lack of eagerness for his answer.

"He likes to go into town most evenings and he's used to me going with him. Well, I really need to."

"You need to?" Cassie switched her eye contact from Cody's left eye to his right, then back again. One of these days she hoped to hear the story of his injury.

"He gets pounded with guys wanting to fight him and girls wanting to f—uh, be fans."

"So you protect him from that?"

"The hands and I do. Our numbers dissuade whatever drunk decides to get himself a name around town—you know, 'I beat up the star of *Sun Mountain*.' And I ask girls out for him."

"You what?" Cassie stood up. "He doesn't have a right to ask you to be his pimp." She shouldn't have said that and wished she hadn't. Cody shrugged and Cassie quickly changed the subject. "You have anyone special yourself?"

"Diana." Cody smiled at the ground.

"Pretty name." Cassie was relieved to have moved to a safe topic that especially interested Cody. "How long have you known her?"

"Since high school. She married another guy. They had a couple kids, but divorced a while back. I started seeing her, then Robbin came home last fall, so I eased off. But, you know . . . she's real special."

"Tell that to Robbin. Diana sounds too good to lose."

Almost to himself, Cody added, "Again." He nodded to Cassie, as if in thanks.

Before she created any more trouble, Cassie began to move away. "Have an easy day," she said, nodded at his work and added, "if that's possible." She bent to pet the dogs once more and ambled off.

To round off her investigation of Robbin, Cassie fanned through sloppy piles of old clippings, photos and magazines stuffed on a shelf in the McKeags' living room. Boone's record of his son's career. Eight years ago the March issue of *Playboy* had published an interview with Robbin.

How odd to look at the three pictures along the bottom of the page—Robbin's face caught in its various moods. Thoughtful—eyes off to the upper left, right thumbnail over top lip. Humorous—muscle beneath his eye tucked, waiting for a slower wit to catch his drift. Laughing right out loud—thumb and forefinger over an eyebrow, fingers stretched out, the hand ready to shoot upward to describe the wild thought.

He looked . . . she didn't know . . . so famous. The opposite from the intent of the shots, she supposed—Robbin McKeag au naturel. But suddenly he was to her what everyone had been saying he was—a celebrity.

The caption beneath the center photo was typical Robbin in her experience: "I was getting off at the Denver airport—oh, I forgot who I was talking to. Getting off *the plane* at the Denver airport."

She skipped through the article until she got to this question.

Interviewer: How do you think of yourself in the romance department?

McKeag: This is *Playboy*—what do you want to know? I screwed my first girl at the late age of twenty.

Interviewer: Was it romantic?

McKeag: Romance is an idea based on no actual fact. I act romance; I don't live it.

Interviewer: What we're trying to get at—is Robbin McKeag, star of some of the most romantic scenes in film, a romantic kind of guy?

McKeag: I play along. A woman sets up a fantasy. If I like it, I engage in it with her . . . for a while.

Interviewer: Sounds cynical. (Robbin shrugs.) First sexual encounter at twenty. That *is* late.

McKeag: I was one-tracked about my career.

Interviewer: Tell us about your first time.

McKeag: (Robbin laughs.) God, you guys are strange. Okay. It's a good story. My promotional tour hit Atlanta, Georgia, that spring and a big party gathered after the premier—local journalists, girls everywhere. Usually I tipped a beer or two, then went to my room, but that night there was this pretty girl . . . blond, sweet-faced, shy as I was, it seemed. I guess you'd say I was feeling romantic toward her. She was . . . God, all the princesses, goddesses, dreams rolled into one at that moment. I worked myself up and approached her. Some guy from a local TV channel pulled me aside and gave me this helpful hint: "Gianna there"—he nodded toward my new love—"likes to take on two at a time, if you need a partner." (Robbin laughs.) I'd just wanted to kiss her before the week was out. But I'm a fast learner. I didn't choose that guy to join us, though—he wasn't my type.

CHAPTER SEVEN

"De-ja-vu, Cassie," Robbin drawled as Cassie broke the yolk while frying an egg. His greeting this morning as he came in for breakfast was intended to remind her she hadn't succeeded in making him an egg over easy yet in the couple weeks she'd been cooking.

Once all of them were seated at the breakfast table, Cassie watched Boone slide his English muffin out from under the ham slice, then pull the egg with melted cheese off that. He arranged each in a separate area on his plate. Then he propped up the front-page section of the newspaper.

Several bites later Robbin said, "Cody is getting serious about some woman."

That brought Boone's newspaper down. "Is that right?"

"She's got two little girls, manages the spa at Snake River Lodge. Cody says he's beginning to feel like my pimp. Somebody referred to him as that, I guess. It's been bothering him."

Cassie radiated nonchalance and chugged her orange juice to stall for time, in case the "somebody" had been identified.

Robbin continued. "He introduced me to three girls last night."

"A stockpile." Boone chuckled.

"Cody gets *all* your dates?" Somehow she hadn't pictured it that way. Just the occasional bar pickup.

"I choose them," Robbin said. "Cody asks them."

"But why?" Cassie cried in amazement.

"He knows how!" Robbin shot back.

Boone said, "While boys were asking girls to sock hops in middle school, Robbin had tutors on movie sets." He added in his son's defense, "He missed out on that stuff."

So, Cassie added to herself, he needed go-betweens and set-ups. Complete with instructions, she thought, remembering the *Playboy* interview.

Outside, rain drizzled monotonously, calling to a halt the work scheduled for the morning. All three of them dawdled over coffee and passed the newspaper around.

"Couple easterners drowned fishing the Snake," Boone reported, passing the section to Cassie. "Their waders filled with river water and pulled them under." Cassie read the story. Mountain snowmelt this time of year made the river run fast and rowdy with treacherous currents and submerged debris. A difficult place for experienced fishermen, but lethal for people unfamiliar with the area. After grieving over so many unnecessary tragedies from tourists getting into trouble, Cassie noticed, she was beginning to understand why longtime locals often hardened their grief into humor. She passed the story to Robbin.

Cassie turned on the radio and sat back down at the table

to watch the rain turn into icy balls, just as the weatherman predicted hail. She stretched her feet onto a second chair and knocked the toes of her boots together. She was all caught up on her office work and had hoped to get her camp kitchen in better shape, but the rain crossed that out; the place would be a muddy morass this morning. Out loud she complained about not having anything to do.

From behind the *Jackson Hole News & Guide*, Robbin offered a suggestion. "You could go wading in the Snake."

The prevalent pastime for rainy days with her younger brother, Dole, surfaced and Cassie mused, "I just can't conceive of a forty-year-old man who's incapable of making his own dates with women." She had been a "master baiter" in those days, teasing her younger brother into a froth with little effort. Lucky for her, Dole hadn't known the McKeags' little jingle—"Baiter, baiter, masturbator."

"Thirty-nine," Robbin corrected. He folded his newspaper section. "*I* can't conceive of a woman who'd resort to working on a Wyoming ranch just to get a man."

Cassie scoffed at the idea.

"Why else would an Ohio-raised woman live where the nearest shopping mall is ninety miles away? Because," he answered himself, "there are purported to be from four to eight men for every woman."

"That's enough," Boone warned, shaking out the classified section to read, driven there by tedium.

"We all know the statistical chances of a thirty-four-year-old woman getting married," Robbin continued.

"I've *been* married. The statistics on forty-year-old men who *never have* are more telling."

"Boone, did you hear that?"

Just like her brother, Dole; things got interesting and Robbin called a parent into the fracas.

Robbin continued in his defense. "I've had relationships with *several* women—all at the same time." He was on the edge of his chair now and leaning across the table at her. "With thousands of *screaming* women."

"Girls," Cassie corrected. "Men with shaky egos prefer girls over women. And groups over individuals." During the years of growing up with Dole, she had perfected her calm and irritating manner. Her brother would always lose it, just like Robbin was doing now, getting loud and aggressive. Then her parents would step into the room, see Dole red with anger, about to slug his sister, and send him for time-out. The best part was when her parents returned to their business and Cassie could strut past Dole's closed bedroom door and whisper something to get him started yelling again. Another half hour would be tagged onto his punishment.

Robbin said, "And you prefer situations as the only female on the premises this side of menopause."

Aha. Just like her brother, he had gone too far.

Boone abruptly stood, scraping his chair back. "Now that's definitely enough!" He gathered all the newspaper sections. "I don't think we should be talking about these things." With a leery glance around, as if he knew it was unwise to leave, he disappeared behind the office door.

Ignoring Boone, Robbin accused Cassie of reverse snobbery. "Refusing to be impressed by my fame places you along with everybody else who only responds to me as a movie actor."

"Because that is the way you present yourself. You react to other people's reactions to you." As if he saw the world from a spotlighted stage and, blinded by the light, was aware only of himself up there, receiving waves of response from a face-less crowd. Cassie discovered real anger beneath her baiting. She shoved her chair back and began gathering the used coffee cups. "You do it with me. You don't know me as a person; you only know how I react to you. And I don't like it." She carried the cups to the sink.

Robbin followed her. "I'll bet you get your mileage out of it. Reflected glory and all. Your friends badger you with questions, right?"

Cassie wiped her hands on a dish towel and turned to face him. "I tell them the same thing I'll tell you: Robbin McKeag is witty and handsome, but I don't like the way he treats me. To him I'm just this year's cook and a handy female face."

"You lie like that, and tell them you're a cook?"

Reluctantly Cassie half smiled.

In the background the radio news segued into music, the oldie by the Casinos, "Then You Can Tell Me Goodbye." Taking advantage of the crack in her anger, Robbin jacked up the song loudly and swooped Cassie into an exaggerated dance around the kitchen, making her laugh. When the song ended, he dipped her almost to the floor.

"Such a *pretty* handy face." He brought Cassie up from the dip. "Mention to your friends that he's a good dancer, too." Flash of white teeth, then he sprinted through the downpour to his cabin. Cassie watched him from the screen door, her heart-beat as loud and fast as the raindrops on the tin roof above her. He might not know how to ask women for dates, but she'd bet he excelled at everything that came afterward.

The gray drizzle washed on. Stopped by the weather, the film crew, who'd arrived earlier in the week, wandered into the main house kitchen. Cassie made another pot of coffee. A girlfriend of one of the filmmakers freelanced as a still-shot photographer for women's magazines. Marley Otter offered Cassie twelve thousand dollars to drop her hair—this was the seller—and pose against a backdrop of mountains and buck-and-rail fences to depict the lifestyle of the New West. She had been able to sell the idea with a proposal and shots she'd taken of Cassie around the ranch a couple days ago, which she had e-mailed off to her agent.

Cassie calculated in her head. Twelve thousand dollars would bring her a lot closer to paying off the truck. At least the amount of the loan would no longer be higher than the price for which she could sell it. She practically smelled the freedom that would offer. No more taking jobs just for the money; she could concentrate on work she loved. As the grip of grief from losing Jake had eased, energy had risen for beginning her life anew, but she felt that debt holding her down.

Right now her chest felt the way a fully leafed aspen tree looked when breezes moved through it. Every leaf twirled and flashed sunlight, and the tree with its slender white trunk turned into a spirit dance of celebration. Who would she be without debt and grief weighing on her? Though perhaps she should give those double weights a bow of gratitude, because they had kept her grounded in this valley and within her private sense of self. She was stronger because of them: she had a home within herself and without. But the photography shoot would open a gate and, like a bucking bronco, she'd be off, kicking up her heels.

Marley scheduled test shots for tomorrow when the weather cleared. The actual shooting would take place among the wildflowers of mid-July, when Marley would return, bringing a crew of her own. Cassie was not to change a thing, not her weight, not her hairstyle, not even her early-summer tan.

With the rest of her unexpected free time that afternoon, Cassie drove into town. She had learned a couple of important things while talking to Robbin the other night. One was that Boone was known for his indecisiveness—despite his being pretty decisive about hiring her—and two, Robbin cared about the land, which made him the one to win over to her recycling plan. Today she would pop in on Becca, who worked at an ad agency, and see what kind of price she could quote Cassie for reusable water bottles with the Cross Wave Guest Ranch and Cattle Company logo on them. Cassie's figures suggested that with the amount of bottled water each guest consumed during a visit, she could offer Boone a deal that would cut down on the use of plastic while also offering guests a take-home souvenir.

As the staff filled out, visions of sign-in sheets and duty rosters beckoned. But the phrase "job description" was unheard of at Cross Wave and—Cassie caught on just in time—unwelcome.

The guest ranch housed, fed and entertained up to a dozen and a half dudes at a time with riding, rafting, hiking and fishing expeditions. The cattle operation involved fence mending, irrigation, haying and emergency veterinary care for four hundred head of cattle. Despite the fifteen- to twenty-member staff supporting these two enterprises, Cross Wave operated under a continual state of emergency.

Ultimately, Cassie suspected, this worked in Boone's favor, because his refusal to acknowledge responsibility prompted his staff to carry the burden. Untouched by the raging chaos about him, he abruptly postponed a cattle drive, even though Cross Wave was two weeks later than other valley ranches in trailing its herd to the high country for the summer. Instead Boone announced a staff float trip.

Boone's deliberate, though clumsy, maneuver to assign

Cassie to Robbin's raft was made on the pretense that she was new and Robbin was the most experienced boatman. Guiding river trips had been Robbin's summer job, when he wasn't filming, since he'd been a kid. But last night Cassie had overheard Boone making long-distance phone plans to visit Elene Cottrell, his lady friend in Montana. Apparently he anticipated trouble between his new cook and his son during his absence and had worried out loud to Elene about returning to discover his delicately assembled staff in shambles just as Mrs. Penny—their special yearly guest—arrived. The raft trip was supposed to resolve all tensions and lay a foundation of fun.

Mrs. Penny, annually the first official guest of the season, the only one to stay the entire summer and the last to leave, was a widow now, but she had been coming to Cross Wave for decades, before and after Mr. Penny was no longer a soul among the chatty. Cassie understood that Mrs. Penny, her likes and dislikes, established the standards that Boone maintained on his guest ranch.

For the sake of Boone's love life Cassie assumed a camaraderie toward Robbin and, to demonstrate that, during dinner that night she asked him how his screenplay was coming along.

Boone said, "Oh, so you know about Robb's work."

"A little." She pretended not to notice Boone's satisfied smile.

"Tell her the title, Robb. It's a good one."

"'The Countess and the Cowboy.' What do you think?" Perhaps Robbin, too, was making a special effort to reassure Boone.

"I like it. Right away I want to know more."

"The story opens with Eleanor Patterson, known as Cissy. She was a red-haired beauty with a reputation for strong-headed wildness all her life. Her best girlhood friend was Alice Roosevelt, so that tells you something. Later she married a Polish count and they had a daughter, Felicia. Cissy ran the gamut of experiences, from rich debutante to international socialite to newspaper publisher, feuding with everyone around the globe. I want to open with her marriage to Count Gizycki, who had a reputation for being a womanizer, a heavy drinker, and a gambler with serious debts."

Cassie asked, "Did she know that about him before the marriage or find out the hard way?"

"His reputation was widely known, but she didn't realize the extent of it. Her first day as a new bride, her carriage arrived at the castle gates, and a young boy and girl, bedecked in flowers, presented themselves to the count and made a plea for the right to marry. The count granted their marriage, and Cissy learned that by law the count had the right to be the first to sleep with that new bride and, in fact, all new brides in his village on their wedding night."

"He didn't do that, though, did he?" Boone asked, looking upset at such cruelty.

"He absolutely did. And that piece of information explained to Cissy why she had noticed so many of the children in the village looking like her husband. He also turned out to be a wife beater. Eventually she divorced him. But while that was happening he abducted their daughter and hid her in a Polish nunnery."

"Gosh," Cassie said.

"Her story just never stops. I want to show it against the background of her coming here to Jackson Hole and meeting Cal Carrington, a reputed outlaw, and how she carried on a loving relationship with him for the rest of her life."

"You've got quite a job ahead of you, son."

While everyone was invested in being especially friendly this evening, Cassie took the opportunity to mention something she'd been worrying about.

"I ran into Fee out irrigating this afternoon. It was a bad encounter. I meant to be conversational and couldn't think up anything to talk about that would interest Fee, except the land. So I said it looked like his irrigation ditches were seeping . . . and had been for years. He became quite angry."

"Fee's got a temper." Boone nodded.

"What do you mean about seeping?" Robbin asked.

"There's so much groundwater from seepage that willows are growing near the ditch in that field. Along with all the evaporation, it makes for big water losses." Cassie looked first at Boone and then at Robbin. "We're in the eighth year of a drought."

Boone said, "Welp, Fee knows his business. Better let him do it his way."

"I don't get it. Why would you know a thing like that?" Robbin asked.

"Everybody knows about the drought."

"No, I mean about ground seepage, willows."

"I hike a lot. Hikers need to know how to find water."
Robbin nodded.

"Anyway, I was going for a walk. I saw this line of willows, and since they typically grow alongside creeks, I figured it would be a pretty place to check out. When I got over there, I saw it wasn't a creek . . . and it wasn't a pretty place. Lots of land damage in that pasture from past overgrazing. Then Fee rode up." She didn't mention she had hoped to find where the ranch dumped its trash, because she was sure there was a place hidden where the dudes wouldn't see it.

Robbin said, "Can't be helped. Ditch water seeps into the ground."

"That's what Fee said, but it isn't true. It can be helped—though that's as far as I got with him. He began railing at me like I was some tree-hugger hippie that was going to chain myself to his barn door and start a protest." His yelling had come as a shock and the memory of it felt just as sore now as it had that afternoon. Without warning, Fee had become loudly defensive. Cassie said now, "I thought you should know, because he made a threat."

"What did he say?" Robbin asked.

Boone was following the conversation, but Cassie suspected that his mind was more on the brownies she had baked for dessert. Before dinner he'd been breaking off small pieces once they came out of the oven, and now his gaze shifted over to them on the countertop and settled there. She got up and returned to the table with the pan of brownies and three plates.

"Fee said, 'Don't you stir up things with Robbin, missy, or I'll make trouble for both of you.'" Cassie sat back down. "And then, before riding off, he hollered over his shoulder, 'Rabble-rousing women don't belong here. And you aren't the first woman I told that to.'"

Boone said, "He means Laraine." He saw Cassie's next question before she asked it and added, "That's his wife. She moved away years back."

Robbin said, "I guess some ranchers line their ditches with plastic. Is that what you meant to say he should do?"

"I had no intention of saying he should do anything. I was just reaching for small talk." And speaking before thinking, she added to herself. She cut the brownies into squares and passed out the plates.

Boone said, "Just let that go by. Fee doesn't mean harm."

"Fee means harm every chance he gets and you know it, Boone," Robbin said. "That bastard is negative and defensive as hell. But he's our neighbor and friend and practically family, so we put up with him. Talk about a rabble-rouser; he's the biggest one in Wyoming. Trouble is, the other ranchers listen to him. I swear, that guy's probably the single reason I stopped doing morning shots in town. I couldn't stand to hear Fee ranting and reviling all through breakfast."

"I'd say the single reason was that your truck was too wrecked to get you there," Boone said. And he reached for another brownie.

"What's the deal about morning shots in town?" Cassie asked.

"It's a thing with some of the older ranchers. They get together and talk politics." Robbin took a bite of his brownie. "They rile themselves up and figure out how they can get the younger guys to carry out the plans they concoct. Damn." He looked back down at his plate. "These are great."

People were so used to brownies made from a box that ones baked from scratch wowed them. It was the first time Robbin had complimented anything she'd cooked.

Unless the entire Wyoming legislature indulged in morning shots, Cassie was mystified as to why so many laws favored ranching over the land and wildlife. Ranchers could shoot wolves if found near their cattle, despite wolves' being on the endangered list. They could shoot and poison coyotes anywhere outside of town limits. Presently ranchers were lobbying for the vaccination of elk and bison against brucellosis, a disease that created a high incidence of aborted pregnancies. They feared it would be transmitted from the wildlife to their livestock, despite no proof of such a problem. Cattle numbered three thousand in the state of Wyoming, whereas elk and bison numbered in the many thousands, but cattle got the most legal protection.

"Why would other ranchers listen to Fee?" she asked. He appeared impressive—sixtysomething, as handsome as his son, and as graceful in his movements, with a dazzling big smile and rich laugh. However, she had just experienced how that friendliness flipped easily into anger and sharp words. He must know how far-reaching the water loss was and that all it took to make a big difference was pipe, instead of open ditches, lined or not. That might be an extra expense, but every business required concessions to the well-being of the planet, which these days could no longer be postponed.

"They listen to Fee because he's on the Wyoming legislature and has been for years. He's got quite a bit of power around here," Robbin said. "Down in the capital, too."

She should have known. Who else can take two months off in the winter and travel to Cheyenne to sit in the legislature other than ranchers? It wasn't right. "Do you know what percentage of income cattle produce in Wyoming?" she asked Robbin.

"I'd guess oil drilling brings in the most, then tourism and ranching."

"Cattle produce *one* percent of the income in the whole state of Wyoming."

"You're kidding," Boone said.

"How do you know that?" Robbin asked.

"I care about the land. I pay attention to the regulations that are made regarding it." She added, "Tourism is the number one producing income, and that thrives on protecting the wildlife." She let that sink in. Because here at Cross Wave the two opposing value systems of the cattle company and the guest ranch were trying to work it out for the benefit of both. Cassie hoped they succeeded, because one value contributed by ranching that couldn't be measured by income percentage was the preservation of the open land, left undeveloped by housing or industry. The Grand Teton Mountains needed the foreground of vast open spaces.

CHAPTER EIGHT

After leaving one truck, a trailer and Boone's Suburban down-stream for the takeout, Cody, Fee, Boone, Robbin and the wranglers loaded three rafts with food and drinks. Cassie complied with Boone's plan for her to ride in Robbin's raft. She also made it easy for one of the new wranglers to join them. Lannie was a would-be actor who hoped to weasel his way into Robbin's movie entourage—apparently many of the wranglers worked on film sets during the winter. From there, he had confessed to Cassie, he hoped to land acting roles.

They pushed off at ten. About twelve, they banked for a picnic lunch. About two, the first raft—guided by the most experienced boatman—got into trouble.

Cassie had just filled her plastic wineglass and settled with her legs pulled up and crossed on the raft's forward seat, when suddenly the raft swept sideways in the fast current of the spring runoff and was pulled beneath limbs from a recently fallen, half-submerged tree. Wine was in Cassie's hair before she could grab a chicken rope.

Robbin shouted, "Down!"

All three of them hit the bottom of the raft face-first to avoid getting knocked witless by the overhang. But the imbalance of bodies lunging to one side and the unexpected white water created by the downed tree tipped the boat over.

Cassie's last sight was of Robbin scrambling to correct their inevitable dipping and another submerged branch knocking one of his oars overboard. Lannie was out of sight, out of mind. A dark interlude of terror contracted Cassie's thoughts to survival. She was so dazed at first, she didn't know whether she was under or above the water. Immobilizing fear spun inside her chest like the agitated waters of the Snake River around her, which—she just remembered—was called by the Indians who once canoed its treacherous currents the *Mad* River. The power of a turbulent eddy tugged Cassie deeper and deeper underwater, then trapped her there, braced against a mass of debris in a nightmare entanglement with branches and her own hair, now loosened and twisted around her neck.

Moments passed as she tried to fight her way clear and then suddenly Robbin's face appeared; he grabbed her shirtfront and yanked her upward. She emerged gasping for breath, then wailing, like a newborn from the birth waters.

He boosted her onto the horizontal tree trunk, wrapped her arms around a strong limb, then climbed higher on the fallen tree for a better view.

"Fee just picked up Lannie," he called down to her.

Cassie clung to the tree limb, soothing herself into calmness, keeping her eyes on Robbin, as if her safety depended on it.

"Boone's retrieving our raft."

She watched Robbin signal with big, sweeping arm movements that the two of them were safe.

Minutes later, after a wade to shore, Cassie lay on the grassy riverbank, Robbin beside her. Her breathing became regular; then the sounds of life returned—water lapping, birds singing, tall weeds swishing.

Robbin said, "Feel that?"

"Oh, yes." She felt it. A quiet euphoria seeped out from the base of her spine, surged upward toward her skull and into the forefront of her mind, traveled down through her chest, stomach and into her legs. Then cycled through again. She felt fully aware, fully at peace. Everything beat and flowed and circled as it should. More than bliss, more than intoxication, she felt a frenzy of ecstatic vibration.

Robbin said, "If I had sex right now, I'd probably die."

Cassie listened to her bloodstream chanting in unison with the cosmos.

Then Robbin said, "Hey, that wouldn't make it more appealing to you, would it?"

They laughed hard. So hard that breathing seemed set aside in favor of the hilarity that built on itself and rippled through their bodies.

It was adrenaline, Cassie knew, that surged through her system. But she wanted to remember this total awareness. It seemed the very essence of being alive, and she'd like to learn to call on it again.

Boone seemed to think he'd pulled a slick one, as if he'd engineered the spill and the rescue himself. Turned sideways in the front seat of the car, he beamed fondly at Cassie and Robbin in the backseat during the ride home, as they told their story and fell against each other laughing. Cassie felt the two of them bonding in an unspoken collusion to assure Boone of his weekend getaway without worry. Fee, who was driving, glanced often in the rearview mirror and never cracked a smile. He seemed to be reading something entirely different in this collusion of friendliness. It didn't make any sense, but it felt as if teams were lining up and Fee was suspicious of who was choosing which side.

Most of Cross Wave followed Boone's example and took the three-day Memorial Day weekend off. Last chance before the season really got under way. Fee and Cody drove down to Denver to look at stock; the wranglers streamed to town, where they'd have first stab at romances with this year's resort workers. Robbin planned to use the time to write. And Cassie hiked during the day and spent the evenings with Erin, Becca and Lacy, enjoying someone else's cooking for a change.

Saturday the ranch looked deserted when Cassie drove in after midnight. Unable to sleep, restless in the twisted sheets and confines of her camper, she got out of bed and pulled on her jeans beneath her summer pajama top, pushed into her boots and stepped outside. All day a soft wind had blown through the valley, melting the last of the snow mounds tucked in the darkest shadows beneath rock ledges and stands of pine, where previously only deep wells had melted around each trunk. The air now was still and as inviting as bathwater. The moon, high and nearly full, sent down a creamy path of light. Cassie stooped and gathered dew from the grass and smoothed it across her cheeks like a potion.

She sat on the buck-and-rail fence that enclosed two dozen horses standing motionless in dark clumps here and there. Even the aspen leaves hung silently, not a rustle in the sage, or a batting of wings from the river. She considered getting her watercolors, the small backpacking set she took on hikes, to try to capture the light, but instead leaned against the trunk of the Engelmann spruce growing beside the fence. She sat there motionlessly for so long that she felt she had become the tree, a curvy burl, smooth against its trunk. She expected to feel a chill on her bare arms or a cool stray current of breeze beneath her loose-hanging pajama top, but instead the muted sound of a motor intruded upon her passive state of mind.

The soft rumble drew nearer and materialized into two sets of low-light beams that flicked off as she watched. The shapes turned left onto a dirt road less than a quarter of a mile on the other side of the horse pasture, and the haze of red brake lights revealed the silhouettes of two small stock trucks. The trucks crept slowly down the road toward the spring cattle pastures behind Carrion Butte. Cassie felt she could have dreamed it, so still was the night after the trucks' passage and so still her thoughts.

Spooked into avoiding loud noises, Cassie knocked softly on Robbin's door twice. When he didn't answer, she stepped into his one-room cabin and knelt on the floor next to his pillow and woke him.

"Hey," he said quietly. "Hi." And he reached out and held the side of her face with a sleep-warmed hand.

"Robbin," she whispered, breathless from her jog across the yard and her gathering alarm.

He whispered back, "Cassie." His look shifted downward to take in her lacy white pajama top.

She said, "I'm scared—"

"Don't be." He moved his thumb to the corner of her mouth and caressed it.

Cassie got lost in the sensation for a moment, then recalled herself. "Were you going to sell some cattle?"

"Sure," Robbin whispered comfortingly. "We'll talk a little

first." He propped his head up with his other hand. "No," he answered seriously, "we're not selling any cattle. It's not done until the fall." All the while he traced her mouth with his thumb and once touched the edges of her bottom teeth.

"Then they must be stealing them."

"Hmm?" Robbin put pressure on the back of Cassie's neck with his fingers to draw her face nearer and he leaned toward her with his lips parted.

"Stealing the cattle."

Robbin stilled. His look shifted up from her mouth to her eyes. "You know, Cassie, I don't like you one damn bit."

Cassie waited outside while Robbin threw on some clothes and they both hopped in his pickup, kept their own headlights off and took a Jeep track past the corrals and off across open range. As he drove, Robbin directed Cassie to get a box of cartridges from the glove compartment and lift the two rifles out of the rack across the rear window. Most Wyoming pickups had a rack like this, though Cassie had noticed that some carried only fishing rods or, in the winter, long-handled windshield scrapers. She hoped Robbin regretted his decision about waiting to call the police until later, when he saw how clumsy she was handling the rifles. To prove her incompetence, she spilled the whole box of ammunition on the truck floor. Twenty cartridges rolled and bounced under her seat.

"This is just a prank, I think," Robbin said.

"Then why the guns?"

"Rifles. Just to scare them off. We're not going to shoot anybody." They bounced over an especially rutted section. "Probably some of the same guys in the bar that kept challenging me at the pool table earlier tonight." Robbin added, "I'd bet on it."

Wondering out loud whether he'd bet her life on it, Cassie banged her head on the underside of the dashboard, trying to collect the dropped shells into the gathered pouch of her pajama top.

"We should have called the police," she said, sitting upright and rubbing the back of her head.

"We'll call them. But first I'm going to save myself the trouble of rounding up our cattle from the town square or some damn place." They both flew off their seat when the tires hit a pothole. "All we have to do is discourage them."

He made it sound like fun, and maybe it was for him, but Cassie's heart beat as loudly as the truck's shock absorbers clanged. Soon Robbin slowed, stuck his head out the window to listen, then parked behind a clump of willows and turned the engine off. He slid out of his truck door, barely opening it so the interior lights didn't go on, and stood on the running board to scan the scene. He came to Cassie's side of the truck, eased her out, and whispered his plan to stampede the small herd of twenty to thirty head of cattle that the so-called rustlers were rounding up with the intention of moving them toward their trucks. He loaded the rifles, showed her how to do it, and stuffed extra shells into Cassie's pockets. He stationed her with a rifle behind a hillock. Hunched down low, Robbin ran to another spot several hundred feet away. All Cassie had to do was lie on her stomach and wait for Robbin's first shot, then fire off a series of her own shots with the rifle pointing to the sky.

Four dark figures. Three out among the cattle hissed the steers into a tight circle, slapping their butts to get them gathered near the trucks; the fourth figure was approaching the barbed wire fence with wire cutters.

Robbin shot twice in the air.

The sudden activity of scared animals and startled men disrupted Cassie's internal dialogue with herself to stay calm, to follow directions, to uphold her end and pay attention. A half minute passed by in which she did nothing but lie on the ground and watch dozens of beasts stampede her way, pounding the earth beneath her stomach with such force that her spine vibrated.

Finally she pulled the trigger.

Rifle fire exploded into the air. The cattle instantly veered away from her and the men darted for the cover of their trucks. From then on Cassie rode a power surge. She shot the sky until her magazine was empty. Like Calamity Jane herself, Cassie rolled over onto her back, stretched out her right leg in order to allow her fist to grab another handful of cartridges from her Levi's pocket, and reloaded the way Robbin had shown her.

Robbin placed his shots on the dirt road just in front of the trucks as their lights were turned on in preparation for escape. Little explosions of dust hit the road and glittered in the headlights. And Cassie, uncertain that she could aim her empty threats that precisely, continued to shoot out the stars until the trucks disappeared into the distance. Too rattled with her own racket to think, she failed to get the license plate numbers on the first truck before it was too far away, but forgave herself when she saw the second truck had deliberately smeared mud across its plates.

"Hey, hey, we did it." Robbin trotted over the small rise to Cassie and fell to the ground beside her. "You didn't shoot off your braids or anything, did you?"

She laughed nervously, still shaky from the flurry of rifle fire that had made the last few minutes seem more dangerous than they actually were at any point. Her rifle grip was slick from the sweat of her palms, and her fingers wouldn't uncrook from around the trigger until the second message to do so arrived from her slow-working brain. Then she pushed the rifle to arm's length away and wanted nothing more to do with it.

Robbin sprawled on his back. "What a sky. Look at that, Cassie."

Cassie sat up and arched her neck back to let the moon bathe her face like sunshine. Not black, not even navy blue, the sky was nearer a deep royal; the moon was so large, so bright.

"Let's have sex," Robbin said, sounding happy to have thought of a way to unwind. He reached up to touch Cassie beneath the chin. "Let's," he said softly. He cupped the side of her face. "Lapis lazuli."

"What?"

"Your eyes. Like tonight's sky. Deep blue, little specks of sparkle. You're beautiful, Cassie."

Robbin moved his hand down her neck, across her bare shoulder, and the strap of her pajama top shifted with his touch, and now dropped to her upper arm. "I always think so," he said. "Really beautiful."

One coyote not too far away began to bay at the bright moon. Another joined and another. Cassie felt something in her chest resonate to these lonesome howls. She wanted to answer them, howl herself. Grow an extra set of legs and bound off across the glossy land. Or something. Something wild and unlike herself.

Robbin said, "Let me take your top off. See the moonlight on your breasts."

Cassie tried to decide what to do.

"The air smells like sage, the grass feels silky, the moon's shining. We shouldn't let that slip away, Cassie." His hand worked back along the top of her lace neckline with his fingers draped inside, smoothing her skin as it rounded onto the top of her right breast.

Cassie rose to her knees. "We don't like each other very well," she reminded him, hoping he'd argue the point. She felt breathless.

"We don't have to." Robbin began to talk faster, like a salesman with the door easing shut and his foot not firmly planted on the sill. "Feel this night air, Cassie. We should enjoy this. We'll have sex together and never be sorry for wasting this time."

Robbin's other hand moved upward beneath the hem of her top, and Cassie clutched it, uncertain whether she was obstructing his progress or congratulating him for it.

"It's time, Cassie, that we do this."

Purchase this set of encyclopedias; I'll throw in the bookcase. Easy monthly payments. It'll look good in your home. And your friends will be impressed.

Cassie stood.

She walked downhill to the truck.

In frustrated anger Robbin slapped the ground next to him.

On the way home her breasts felt sensitive to the jolts from the bumpy track, and Cassie pulled tightly on the bottom of her pajama top to brace them. Perhaps she should have made love with Robbin. But then, he hadn't said that; he'd said "have sex."

Still, she worried that she had missed something perhaps especially lovely that the world had to offer her. Full moons, soft night breezes, enchanting words, desire meeting desire. Perhaps it was even *wrong* to pass up such offerings—perhaps she was ungrateful in the face of rare opportunity. But then, afterward, she would have no defense against this difficult man, his abrasiveness or his requests for other nights.

In her camper again, Cassie pulled off her boots and her jeans and got back into bed. Soon Robbin's headlights swung around the drive from the main house, where he'd gone to call in the police report, and next shone into her window and bounced off the mirror above her sink and lit up her whole camper. The truck braked to a halt a few feet from her window. She heard the door slam and rose up on her knees in bed in time to see Robbin yank open her camper door.

"Just tell me this. And tell me the truth. You *wanted* to, didn't you?"

"Yes."

"Then *why didn't you?*"

"You don't care about me."

"You've got *that* right." He slammed back out through her doorway, wrenched the gears into reverse and spun off.

CHAPTER NINE

Cassie cooked an early lunch in camp the next day for the crew, who had been clearing the nearby trails of the last of the fallen trees. Somehow, as she gathered up the dirty dishes afterward, a hot dog stuck to the bottom of a plate and wound up lying in wait for her beneath the soapsuds in the dishpan. She blindly felt about for the last of the silverware, grabbed the long, slippery thing, screamed and threw it up in the air.

In light of the previous night's episode with Robbin, that reaction felt like a direct comment on the state of her libido.

Boone returned from his Montana trip later that afternoon, and an hour after that the ranch van delivered Mrs. Penny from the airport. Eighty-five years old, Mrs. Penny was a large woman of commanding presence. She stood with her back straight and her awareness all-encompassing. Anyone could tell that she considered herself to be in charge of the space she inhabited and of everyone who happened to share it with her.

Five first-time travelers to this side of the Mississippi accompanied Mrs. Penny in the van—one of whom wanted to know what all that white stuff was high on the mountains.

Cassie laughed politely, assuming this to be the humorous gambit of a nervous newcomer. She'd heard before, but never believed, that this was the number one most-asked question by summer tourists in Jackson Hole. The second question being, When do the moose turn into elk?—something about the shedding of the antlers confusing the matter.

Robbin, more accustomed to the naïveté of flatlanders and looking for an outlet for his ill temper today, said it was cotton batting for the cattle to sleep on. "Keeps their meat tender."

"Robbin!" Mrs. Penny clicked her tongue, and Cassie thought for a moment that the woman was going to pat Robbin's behind in reprimand. "It's snow, dears. Isn't that exciting?" Mrs. Penny pursed her lips at Robbin and looked him over. "Your arms are bigger."

"Weights."

"Well, that's silly; your arms were perfectly useful before. What else have you done this year to improve yourself?" With heavy dark eyebrows raised, she waited for Robbin's report.

"Mrs. Penny, look, my fingernails are clean." He spread them out for display. "I've been brushing my teeth before bedtime for thirty-five years. Aren't you ever going to decide I'm a good boy?"

"I sent you five dollars on your birthday."

Even Cassie could tell Mrs. Penny was laying a trap.

Seemed Robbin suspected it, too, and he was ready. "I put it in my savings account."

"You didn't send me a thank-you note."

Mrs. Penny proclaimed to the other guests that as she was Robbin's godmother, her Christian vow was to set standards for his moral upbringing. "I stood next to your mother, Laura, and promised this before the altar of God." Over the winter she had seen pictures of Robbin in a magazine. Mrs. Penny raised her tarnished silver hairline a good inch. "A position of global prominence in this incarnation, and you squander it posing with female undergarments dangling from your fingertips."

Later Mrs. Penny took charge of the conversation at dinner. She began by delving into the guests' lineage. "Hunt . . . Hunt. Now is this the Hunt from the Harvard endowment? You know, my grandfather and Mr. Andover Hunt were dearest of friends. Impeccable family, the Hunts." After running through her historical knowledge of Danners, none of which Cassie recognized, Mrs. Penny next inquired about ranch news, and conversation turned to last night's cattle raid.

Two Teton County sheriff's deputies had stopped by the ranch that morning to fill out their report. Before the deputies ducked their cream-colored cowboy hats back into their white Bronco, Cassie learned that cattle rustling remained a problem in Wyoming for the same reason it historically had: vast stretches of unpopulated land. These days, some bolder thieves parked on Interstate 80, which cut across the high plains south, snipped barbed wire and trotted a couple dozen head of cattle into two-story tractor trailers.

In Jackson Hole, such attempts were unwise.

"Nope, with escape limited to three mountain passes and one river canyon, strike-and-run crime is hard to pull off in this valley," one of the deputies announced, as if he'd thought up the crime-fighting device on his own.

Neither Cassie nor Robbin had mentioned that it was almost pulled off last night, though the sheriff's office had stationed lookouts at all four exits from the valley as soon as they got Robbin's call. Robbin was still convinced it was a personal prank and had mentioned to Cassie last night on their way to the scene that he was relieved Fee was out of town. "He'd be madder than hell and kick up a big stink all over the valley. He probably still will when he finds out."

Now Mrs. Penny said, "Those tick-brains could have cost you a lot of money, Boone." She wanted to know how such a thing had happened.

Cassie thought Mrs. Penny said *dick*-brains and was one step behind in the table talk. So she missed Boone's excuses, and next Mrs. Penny asked how Boone proposed to safeguard his cattle. By the time Cassie tuned in, Boone had cleared his throat a few times, then made the leap.

"Welp, starting tonight, ah, we're scheduling . . . a watch," he said. And looked around to see who was buying it.

Not Cassie. The word "schedule" tipped her off. Boone was making this up on the spot.

"Um, we're going to have a . . . a relay of wranglers cruising the back pasture. Yep, dark to dawn."

Mrs. Penny said, "Your cattle have no business being down here this late, Boone. If you're going to *schedule* anything, *schedule* your cattle drive up Sky Rider Mountain, where they'll be safe and your pastures won't get overgrazed."

Cassie was feeling fonder and fonder of Mrs. Penny.

Later that evening Fee returned from his weekend in Denver, arriving at camp in time to drive Mrs. Penny and the guests back to the ranch after dinner. He was told about the cattle rustling event, but brushed it off. Instead of being surprised about that, Boone and Robbin acted relieved. To get on Fee's good side, Cassie looked for an opening in which to tell her part in discovering the trucks' approach, and it appeared while the two of them carried supplies to the back of the van.

Fee said, "Nice that you and Robbin were up so late together and able to spot the intruders."

Eager to correct the image of her and Robbin deliberately together at three in the morning, Cassie sounded like Boone, stumbling around for a way to start. Finally she said, "No, we weren't." And meant to elaborate.

Fee said, "Yes. You were, missy." And he slammed himself inside the ranch van and rifled through the glove compartment with his head averted. Cassie gave up and walked away.

In what she was learning was typical Cross Wave fashion, the watches turned into guerrilla night games. Some nights the wranglers, Robbin and Cody included, played hide-and-seek with clues given over walkie-talkies—cell phones didn't get a signal anywhere on the ranch. Some nights they played tag in their trucks with their headlights off and their brake lights disconnected. They ambushed one another in the dark, using dried cow patties for ammunition. Of course, if the watches hadn't been so much fun, the cattle would have been trailed to the high country immediately. But Cassie kept that to herself and relied on Mrs. Penny to bring it up.

Cassie would have liked to ask Robbin why he thought Fee was taking the cattle rustling event so casually, but he was angry with her. As it was, now it seemed she had made two enemies—Robbin and Fee—when all her life she had never before made one. The time alone allowed her to think, and what she thought about mostly was the kind of work she'd like to do once the truck was paid off. How could the love of wilderness, watercolor painting and the desire to make enough money to buy a house in Jackson Hole come together into a new career? Ideally, one in which she didn't have to work for anyone else for once. She was dreaming, which Robbin had said was an important ingredient for success.

In hopes of understanding Fee and his antagonism toward her and "rabble-rousing" women, Cassie took her cup of coffee over to sit with Mrs. Penny in her patch of sunlight the next morning, after the others had ridden off from camp. She wanted to know more about Fee's wife, Laraine.

"Well, now, that's an interesting time," Mrs. Penny began and pulled her shawl, woven in purples and greens, up higher on her shoulders. "They met back in the sixties, while Laraine was in the valley protesting the killing of rattlesnakes—there were yearly Rattlesnake Round-ups in Wyoming back then, and her group came out from California and spread across the state to march and hold up signs in the communities. Little did any of them know that Jackson Hole never had rattlesnakes—altitude too high. The valley is truly a paradise that way."

Cassie settled in the lawn chair she'd pulled up, took a sip of her coffee and wondered if she really had time for all that she'd have to listen to in response to her question. Mrs. Penny was the walking history book of the Cross Wave Guest Ranch and Cattle Company.

"Anyway," Mrs. Penny continued, "that's when Laraine met up with Fee, and those two—I'll never forget—bang! Smoke and fire. When the sparks settled, there was the newborn Cody, there was Laraine out of her element *entirely*, and there was Fee tangling with all of his wife's no meat-eating, no killing, let-everything-live-and-love-it-all ways." She fingered the fringe on her shawl and smiled to herself.

"I, of course, admire how those two handled it in the end.

They did not let that love for each other turn nasty, though it was heading that way, spooking the folks around them and threatening to trample every good thing in its path."

She sipped her coffee. "Well, I put my foot down, and the two of them came up with a plan to keep their love intact and their marriage strong enough to hold Cody."

Cassie said, "And now she lives in California and Fee and Cody live here?"

Mrs. Penny continued as if Cassie hadn't asked her question. "It turned out eventually, the only way to do that was to live separate lives—she there, he here. Because Fee is a born rancher. Grasslands and cow manure are in his blood and bones. His heart only knows how to beat beneath a huge expanse of cloudless sky. And Laraine, of course, was a California gal and intent on the spiritual life. The three of them get together in my home out there several times a year, often for weeks at a time. They are devoted to one another and quite the family. Fee will always take good care of Laraine. He loves that woman."

Her words were spoken with such fervor that Cassie was startled to realize Mrs. Penny still missed her husband so many years after his death—it had been twenty-six years now. She felt embarrassed momentarily as she caught herself believing that only someone as young as she herself was would feel the passion of missing her mate. Cassie imagined herself at Mrs. Penny's age still longing for Jake.

Kindly, Cassie asked, "Would you like more coffee?"

"Certainly not." Mrs. Penny could make any response sound like a reprimand, and Cassie felt a pinprick of guilt, then annoyance at the woman. She stood to leave.

Mrs. Penny wasn't finished. "Fee, now, won't let anything threaten his way of life and the fact is nothing ever did until

Laraine showed up and he fell head over behind and fathered Cody. He's been on the lookout since for the same thing happening to his son. However, that boy is quite stable—if a bit brainwashed about his father's wishes to carry on the ranching tradition."

Cassie thanked Mrs. Penny for the nice chat and moved on to the worktable to finish up the breakfast dishes and begin lunch. She was glad for the background on Fee. "Head over behind" was a bit difficult to picture with the mighty Fee and his quick, sharp temper. If she worked on it, though, it could make him more accessible.

She should also keep in mind that Fee was a man whose lifestyle was dependent on capricious weather, wild predators, a fluctuating market and, from what she picked up from casual talk, the financial support of Robbin's film career, in itself dependent on the mercurial whims of the public. Ranching in general was an endangered enterprise. Ranchers knew that and acted aggressively to protect their rights. For example, the right to be charged minimally for grazing privately owned cattle on publicly owned lands. The Bureau of Land Management, known as the BLM, charged ranchers mere cents per acre to graze their cattle, and in most of the West it took five acres per cow-calf unit. Lately, ranchers were pressuring the government to kill or remove wild horse herds from the public lands throughout the West, because they were in competition with their cattle for grazing. Ranchers were once again, as they were in the 1930s, the force behind the legislation to eliminate the recently reintroduced wolf population, because the wolves were occasionally predatory with calves. Ranchers had once succeeded in wiping out every last wolf across the West.

Yet Cassie knew most ranchers in Jackson Hole loved the

land as much as she did. They removed fencing so the elk, moose and antelope could migrate through their property, protected the wetlands, never overgrazed or wasted water. This love and respect came from the joys and struggles they shared with the wildlife, while living off the same land together generation after generation.

Fee had to know how much water he was wasting with his unlined irrigation canals and his method of periodically flooding his fields to keep them green. He had to know, also, that the extermination of wolves had resulted in a greater population of coyotes and that his killing coyotes was creating an overabundance of prairie dogs. How could he miss recognizing this chain of events?

Cassie hung her dish towels on a tree bough to dry and wondered about Cody. Where did he stand on wildlife conservation? Probably he and Robbin, like most people Cassie knew who were raised in Jackson Hole, had shot prairie dogs—chizzlers, they were called around here—as kids for summertime fun. With Robbin it was clear: he stood firmly on the side of glamorizing the Old West and its traditions in his films. He accomplished the same thing the Saturday rodeo and the nightly shoot-out on the town square did. He kept alive a history that had once served a meaningful purpose but now was largely energized by image. These were the events that sold thousands of embossed leather cowboy boots and felt Stetsons to the tourists.

Cassie had lived in Jackson Hole long enough to love its history of ranching but to also see beyond the glamour of it. What she would like to have happen now was for the power of that glamorous image from the past—open land, adventurous people, the partnership between humans and animals that made up the settling of the West—to gather into a momentum for celebrating and protecting the beauty and the spiritedness of the present. She imagined ranches that maintained the open spaces, protected native plant life, conserved water and honored both domestic and wild animals. Who could resist being a part of that?

A couple days after the cattle rustling event, Cassie took an early-morning stroll around the compound before going to the kitchen to start breakfast. She came from behind the row of guest cabins to the parking lot and saw Robbin shirtless and barefoot, standing with a woman next to a strange blue sedan.

Cassie stopped, one hand flattened against her chest, and stood at attention as though surprised by a flag-raising ceremony. Close your mouth, she commanded herself. Loosen those eyes. A puppeteer in control of the strings, she ordered herself to turn around and walk herself offstage. But before she could perform the movement, Robbin caught her eyes over the woman's shoulder and held her look defiantly. Held it long enough for the woman to turn around to see what Robbin was staring at with such grim challenge.

Cassie made that hand over her heart twist about and wave woodenly. Now move those feet.

"Cassidy."

She stopped. Robbin now stood side by side with the woman, his arm flung around her neck. "Can you fix an extra breakfast?"

She made herself bob her chin.

"Good."

Fifteen minutes later, Robbin, showered and dressed, ushered his pert young guest into the kitchen. "This is nice of you," she said to Cassie. "Are you related to Robb?"

"Um . . ." Cassie began, trying to decide which way to go with this. "I'm his cousin," she said unconvincingly.

Robbin said, "You don't have to lie, Cassie."

"Okay. I'm his wife."

The dewy cheeks with overly applied moisturizer drew inward and the perfectly made-up eyes widened.

"That's not true," Robbin was quick to say to the woman. "She's not my wife." Then, turning his back to her, he faced Cassie up close and hissed a warning. "Shape. Up."

Cassie ducked around Robbin's face and smiled at the woman. "We'll be with you in a minute," she sang. To Robbin, she shrugged gamely and spoke loud enough for the woman to hear, "Well, Robbie, introduce me however you like."

"She's the cook. Cassie the cook."

"Yes." Cassie practiced her line out loud to their guest. "I am the cook."

Boone entered the kitchen, smoothing his cheeks with the last hint of aftershave gracing his palms. "Oh," he said, stopping in his tracks, surprised to see a stranger preparing to sit at his breakfast table. "Hello." And he looked to Cassie for an introduction, apparently assuming it was a friend of hers.

For Robbin's benefit, Cassie swept her hand magnanimously to indicate an early sixties we-must-try-everything attitude and said gaily, "Robbin has brought another woman into our home."

Boone asked for introductions.

"This is Randy," Robbin offered.

"Well, tell us her last name, Robb," Boone prompted.

"You pronounce it, Randy," Robbin suggested.

"Cunningham." Randy said it slowly as though it were a name from Uzbekistan with clusters of consonants and a scarcity of vowels. Cun-ning-ham.

"Randy has to be in town for work by eight," Robbin said to Cassie. "Could you hurry up with some of that?"

"Certainly. We'll try to get her out of here soon as possible," Cassie said cheerily.

Robbin was apparently having second thoughts, a certain regret about having his bed partner at the family breakfast table. He sat sullenly, watching Randy take dainty sips of her coffee. When her eggs were served, he pushed the salt and pepper her way, said, "No time for sausage, right, Randy?" And a second later, "This clock's always slow."

Boone attempted cordiality. He asked questions. Where did she work? The bank. Did she like it? She did. What did she do there?

"Counts money," Robbin interjected. "She doesn't have time for talk, Boone. You want the rest of that, Randy?" He pushed his chair back and stood up. She guessed not, and Robbin walked her outside to her car.

When he returned and the three of them were seated and starting breakfast, Boone asked, "Was she someone special, Robbin?"

"No," he answered.

"Then don't bring her to breakfast again. If you'd like to invite a guest to join us sometime, make it dinner. And make your intention clear ahead of time." He boosted his position by adding, "Cassie doesn't need the unexpected work."

"Cassie should wear an apron. And a name tag. Shit, Randy thought she was my *wife*. She couldn't even think straight, she was so upset. She's actually a very bright girl."

"She can count money," Cassie reminded him.

"And if I need another reason," Boone supplied, "I don't *like* it."

Robbin pushed his coffee cup over to Cassie for a refill. "And how does the Apache feel?"

"Randy is darling. I'm going to ask her to spend the night with *me* sometime." That would gel Cassie's flower-child role in Randy's mind.

"Goddamn." Robbin set his coffee cup down hard. "Why do I have to put up with this?"

He addressed his outburst to Boone, who rattled his newspaper and turned a disgusted eye in response before retreating deeply into page two. Seemed a good idea, so Cassie reached for a newspaper section and pretended an enthusiasm for sports scores.

That left only advertising flyers for Robbin. In the long silence that followed, Robbin pushed his food around. Cassie assumed a studious stare at the inside crease of the *Casper Star-Tribune*. And only Boone appeared to thoroughly enjoy his breakfast and his reading.

After a while Robbin asked, "So what does Dear Abby say this morning?"

"She says"—Cassie turned back a page—"in reply to a letter asking why some men have casual, indiscriminate sex, that it is an attitude showing a dearth of self-respect, self-confidence and a deep-seated need to escape themselves. Oh, this is interesting. Abby goes on to imply that playboys display an inability to relate to women on the deeper levels of intimacy. It seems"—Cassie continued to pretend to read—"that womanizers actually *do not like* women."

"That's funny," Boone said. "Dear Abby is in this section, too." Catching on to Cassie's ruse a beat too late, he cast a guilty eye her way, followed by an apologetic one-shoulder shrug.

Robbin yanked down Cassie's newspaper, exposing two pages of stock market listings.

"Goddamn you."

Boone scraped his chair back from the table and said, "I believe I'd rather work than sit here another goldern minute." He headed for the office.

Cassie decided to exit as well. She pushed her chair back and stood.

Robbin said, "Is that what you really think?"

"Are you attempting to relate on the deeper levels of intimacy with me?" Cassie went to the sink and ran water into it for no good reason other than to turn her back on Robbin.

Robbin bolted out of his chair. He reached Cassie at the sink in three long strides and spun her around. "Jealous," he accused. "Jealous of Randy."

"Why would I be jealous of Randy? I can count money, too."

"I'm tired of your smart mouth, Cassie, and I'm tired of your supercilious attitude. Am I relating deeply enough for you?" He braced his arms on each side of her, pinning her against the sink. "We could analyze *your* inability to relate to men on *any* level. Let's relate *deeply*, Cassie, and see if we can come up with a reason for your total *lack* of a sex life."

"Sex life," Cassie repeated scornfully. "That's a media term; nobody has a sex *life*."

"You sure as hell don't."

"Do you have a *food* life, too?"

"Not since you've been in charge of it. But that's about to end." He shot across the room and pounded on the office door. "Boone!" he shouted. "Boone!"

"Goldernit." Boone swung the door open. "You scared me out of my shorts."

"Fire her. Fire her *right* now."

Wearily Boone rubbed a hand down his face. "Not enough excitement for you, Robb? A strange woman at breakfast, a shoot-out over the weekend . . . You have to stir up more trouble?"

Cassie was uneasy with the escalation of events. She didn't know what to do—wash dishes, apologize for stirring up a crazy man or just stand here with the faucet running.

Boone sat heavily onto a kitchen chair. "Maybe it's been *too* exciting. Maybe you need a rest."

"You do that every time. You know how that frustrated me when I was a kid? Every time I made a complaint you'd say I needed a nap." Robbin paced the kitchen, gesturing dramatically. "The least show of discontent, you'd say 'Robbin's tired.' 'Better put Robbin down for a nap.' Hell. All my life I've solved problems with an escape into unconsciousness—*sleep* of one kind or another."

Robbin's speaking voice fascinated Cassie; it was not the voice of an actor, or maybe it was—sure, it must be. Though his rhythm was dramatic and accentuated, his voice was keyed at one place in the back of his throat and rarely varied, kind of like Boone's singing, she decided. She found herself listening sometimes to its even timbre and failing to react to the impact of his words.

Cassie turned off the running water. This time the impact of his words was way too strong.

"It's your fault I got into drugs—I started with sleeping pills, you know. 'Robbin is grumpy, Robbin should sleep'—so I did. One way or another I slept several goddamn years away."

At those words Boone dropped his head into his hands.

Robbin stopped his pacing, and the three of them were as motionless as plastic figures in a diorama.

"Oh, God," Robbin breathed. "I didn't mean that."

Without raising his head, Boone said, "I knew all along that I carried blame for that. I just never before understood how."

Swiftly, Robbin moved behind Boone's seat. He laid a hand on the back of his father's head. "It's not true, Boone." With his other hand he held Boone's shoulder. "You *saved* my life. Honest to God, Boone, you did."

Robbin described his friends, others who still struggled with their lack of love and acceptance and approval, despite their fame, because they never got it from their parents. "They're a mess, Boone. I mean, they need so much. . . . They'll never be whole."

Robbin squeezed Boone's shoulders. "You know I'm whole. Just got snagged there for a while. But I'm on the mend. I'm going to be okay," he said. "And that's because you have always made certain I knew that you loved me."

Boone kept his head down, didn't respond.

Robbin looked to Cassie. "Tell him, Cassie. Tell him how come I'm a son of a bitch."

Startled to be asked to testify, Cassie lifted her eyes from the floor. She looked at Robbin.

He nodded urgently.

Why *was* Robbin such a son of a bitch? She couldn't choose one reason over another. Robbin waited expectantly, a plea and encouragement in his eyes. "Because . . ." Cassie said, stalling for time, then grabbing the strongest thought. "Because he misuses the gifts he has been given." Robbin nodded her on. "But, he's right—it's just temporary. He's testing them . . . and the source of these gifts, suspecting they come from someplace bigger than himself, but . . . resisting the work it takes to find out."

"That's good," Robbin said appreciatively and slapped Boone on the shoulder. "Right on the nose—hey, Boone? I'm a lazy damn bastard." He was so energetic in his self-condemnation, so pleased with Cassie's diagnosis, that she giggled, and a low vibration of mirth erupted from Boone.

"It sounds perfectly right," Robbin said contemplatively, forgetting in his self-involvement the purpose of the discussion. "Which brings us to why we can't have her around anymore."

Boone let it go in loud, full chuckles and dropped his arms to rest on the table. Cassie regretted not taking the floor for a full thirty-minute rundown of *all* Robbin's flaws.

Robbin let his remark stand as a joke and set his chin on top of Boone's head. And those two faces, one above the other, watching her from across the table, the one warm, the other wary, caught Cassie strangely. Like a picture of home when you're miles away, or months before you've acquired one.

Boone reached above him to pat his son's head. While smiling at Cassie, he said to Robbin, "You do something nice for each of us before the sun sets today, and we'll consider this over."

"I can't remember what it is that keeps this from happening." Robbin held up his hands. He had Rice Krispies and melted marshmallows stuck up to his elbows. Rice Krispies were on the floor, marshmallow smears on the cupboard knobs and the refrigerator handle.

"Butter."

"Butter," Robbin said, and hit his forehead. Smashed Rice Krispies crumbled down past his eyes and marshmallow stuff stuck to the front of his hair.

"I'm leaving." Cassie crunched her way back toward the kitchen door, forgetting what she had come in for and deciding that whatever it was wasn't worth it. "You're sure Boone is going to like this?"

"He *loves* Rice Krispies squares. When I was fourteen, I made him mad and had to do something nice before sundown and I made these. He'll remember that."

Cassie asked, "Because the kitchen looked like this when you were finished?"

"Damn near," Robbin said, looking around. He lifted one foot, which came away from the sticky floor sounding as if the sole had torn off.

Cassie rode Bruce the Eunuch out to camp to prepare her cook area for tomorrow's lunch ride. The sun was lowering in the west, and she wondered about her "something nice" from Robbin. She hoped her "something nice" was his cleaning up his mess from Boone's "something nice."

Just as the sun dropped onto a sharp peak of the Tetons, and just before the peak pierced it like a party balloon to explode its fragments of color all over the sky, Robbin drove into camp. He hopped out of his truck carrying a CD player. Without speaking, he put the earphones in her ears and pushed the PLAY button.

Robbin's voice. She listened while he watched her. "This is for Cassie." Then he began reading his screenplay, "The Countess and the Cowboy."

Cassie's hand went directly to her heart.

Robbin pressed the STOP button. "I recorded what I already told you and the next section, where Cissy Patterson first comes to Wyoming." He added, "You seemed to like the story."

"Oh, I do. I like it a lot. This is a wonderful present."

Robbin said the CD player was for her to keep and that he'd add following installments of the screenplay as he wrote them, if she liked. He handed it to her.

She put the earphones back in and turned on the CD player

again. Robbin watched her as she began listening to his story. The muscle beneath his eye contracted as he smiled in response to her pleasure. Her smile got bigger and bigger and so did Robbin's. This was Robbin full out, all prisms flashing—talented, generous, soft, absolutely present with her—and Cassie had never liked him better.

Trained to spot this, Robbin moved in. Came down slowly, dropped his eyes and covered her mouth with his.

Then he walked to his truck and didn't meet her gaze again until he was inside. There he looked at her suspiciously from behind the windshield as he leaned one shoulder forward and turned the ignition.

Cassie watched him leave and thought she could have erotic dreams for years based on that kiss, with Robbin intimately storytelling in her ears like that. Did he know all he had to do was direct his full attention to her and the rest would be easy?

Of course he did. This was his life, she reminded herself. She was the only novice here.

She started the CD from the beginning again.

Cissy Patterson, her eleven-year-old daughter, Felicia, and their French maid traveled by train to Victor, Idaho, on the other side of Teton Pass from Jackson Hole. It was 1916, springtime. They spent the night in the only hotel in Victor, with working cowboys spitting tobacco in the lobby. Cissy complained about the grubby bed linens and foul food.

The next morning a wagon came to fetch them over the pass and take them to the Bar BC Guest Ranch, where Cissy planned to spend the summer as an escape from society life in the East, which, she had claimed to her daughter, was a bore. At dawn Cissy's seven trunks were loaded on the wagon and the little group faced a ten-hour trip up a pass so steep the three of them had to get out and walk in order for the horses to make the climb. Arriving at the peak, they saw Jackson Hole spread below them in all its splendor.

Cassie could imagine Cissy's thrill at this sight; she had seen it herself often and each time she was freshly astonished at the view of mountain ranges circled around the valley floor, the green, rounded buttes of early summer rising, and the silvery thread of the Snake River unraveling from one end of the valley to the other. Cassie had hiked the Old Pass Road, now replaced by a newer route for cars, with her watercolors, stopping to paint the wildflowers, the dark pines, the shimmering pale aspens and clear streams. Each visit struck her with the same raw power of her first.

The downside of the pass still faced the easterners, and it was a harrowing trip in the wagon, as it pitched into the valley. Once again the countess, her daughter and the French maid walked. Cissy was dressed in her Parisian travel tweeds with laced-up walking boots. The journey was hot and dusty, later turning wet and muddy as spring rains poured and lasted for hours. By the time the small group arrived at the ranch it was dark, the rains were torrential and Cissy was convinced she'd made a great error in traveling all this distance from her home in Washington, DC.

The Bar BC Ranch was holding its yearly costume party when Cissy arrived. The wife of the married couple who owned the ranch greeted Cissy dressed as a cavewoman. Cissy demanded a hot bath, dinner on a tray and a hired motorcar for the next morning to take her back to the Victor train station. But, of course, there was no such thing to hire and neither was there going to be a hot bath or dinner on a tray. In fact, there was no plumbing, no electricity, and Cissy wasn't finished walking through the rain. She was directed to hike up the hill on a muddy path to find her cabin.

At that point the Countess Cissy Gizycka raged that she, her daughter and the French maid would return home the following morning no matter what they had to do to accomplish that.

Then she met the cowboy Cal Carrington.

End of the recording. Cassie turned off the CD player and thought of Robbin's kiss—soft, slow, romantic. Was it possible that writing a romantic story created a romantic screenwriter?

CHAPTER TEN

Cassie stayed with Erin on her day off. After her morning shower, she said to Erin at breakfast, "I think I've gained a few pounds."

Erin said, "No, you haven't. I set the scale on five instead of zero."

"But you really know it's five pounds over the actual weight?"

Erin said, "Of course I do. I'm not stupid, just gullible."

It kept her on her toes, she claimed. Erin was in no need of fooling herself; she was one of those women who made you wonder how they could be thin everywhere it's desirable yet voluptuous in all the right places, too.

She was a real estate agent and had succeeded in finding a house-sitting arrangement for the coming year while waiting for the big sale that would establish her reputation in the field. The family that owned the house spent only a month there, during the Christmas holidays. Aside from the spectacular beauty of the valley, the lack of Wyoming income tax accounted for the influx of part-time home owners, Erin had long ago explained. And recent jet service made it easy for people to establish vacation homes here.

After Erin headed off to her office, Cassie spent the day working with her watercolors on Erin's beautiful deck overlooking a stretch of wetlands, a small pond, and beyond that, the pine-covered slopes of mountains.

One thing Cassie loved about working at Cross Wave was that almost every day she was able to spend some time outdoors hiking, and she always carried her Winsor & Newton pocket-sized watercolor set. It held twelve small cubes of color, which could be exchanged for others or replaced when used. The tiny brush that came with the set was, in her opinion, useless, so she carried a one-inch Kolinsky made of sable hair instead. Lately, she had become fond of working on 140-pound cold-press postcards. They were designed for addressing and writing a small note on one side and painting on the other side and easily fit in a pocket beside her watercolor set. By now she had quite a collection of postcards, even though she mailed many back east to family and friends.

Watercolor was all about light. The love of light. Fred Kingwell had taught her that when she took her first class with him during those early years of living in the valley. Jake had taken off to climb Aconcagua in Argentina, the highest peak in the Western Hemisphere, and as Cassie recalled that time, it seemed to mark the beginning of a split between them. After Jake's success on Aconcagua and Cassie's passion for watercolors flowered, the two of them led separate lives together. In Cassie's philosophy of marriage that was just the way it should work: the two of them supporting each other in their individual passions. But at some point down the line the two paths needed to converge. And infinity, as the geometric question posed, wasn't soon enough for Cassie. Though perhaps it was for Jake.

"The rocks are real," Jake had said. "The rocks stay, we don't. We come, we go; the rocks stay. I don't know, Cassie," he'd said early in his career, "how to explain it, but that knowledge changes a person."

He loved her, Cassie knew that. Though when she had told him what she wanted for her life, he'd said to her, "Gardens, babies—they're not solid, you know?" So maybe she wasn't solid to him either. Not solid enough that he would tell her the one fact of his life that would have cast her hopes in a wholly different light. He knew it, and he didn't tell her. She had found out just months ago, by accident, three years after his death and the funeral back home in Ohio.

She watched a western tanager land near a quartered orange she had set in the crotch of an aspen tree in the hope of luring the pair she had spotted during breakfast. The sun glistened off the bird's yellow, red and black feathers, the green heart-shaped aspen leaves, the juicy insides of the orange. She dipped her brush in water, preparing to lay down color. But then she let the brush dangle between her fingers and just watched.

Late this past winter she had encountered the sports physician Jake regularly saw for checkups and inoculations before his climbing trips. It could so easily never have happened. Didn't in fact happen when it was most likely—three years earlier, at the memorial service Jake's friends had held for him in Jackson Hole. Instead she had run into the doctor at a trailhead, as they were both loading their backpacks for a cross-country ski. The doctor ambled across the snowy parking lot to say hello.

"I think of Jake often," he'd said.

Cassie had smiled and said, "Me, too." But in an easy, warm way, not laying any of her remaining grief on this kind man. And then he'd said, "I suppose your regret over his sterility leaves you doubly bereft. Having a child can help soothe the loss of a mate."

"His sterility," she repeated.

"He said a few years before his death that you very much wanted children. He took that news harder than his cancer diagnosis just before the accident."

"Cancer."

Cassie's knees gave out and she leaned heavily on her ski poles. And then she began to shake. Neither she nor the doctor went skiing that day. This man who apparently knew her husband more intimately than she did helped her remove her skis, leaned them against her truck and took her inside her camper, where he turned on her propane heater to warm them and the stove to make tea.

For days afterward she had felt as if she'd fallen into an icy crevasse herself. Jake, the familiar husband of her heart, had died all over again, as memories of their life together shifted and rolled into new slots. Once more, watercolors had painted the path through that darkness into new light. She understood now that Jake had coped with all the large issues in his life the best way he could—by taking them to the mountains.

For a long while Cassie couldn't paint the Grand Teton Mountains; all she saw when looking at them were places where a husband could fall and die. She painted instead what many people failed to experience but recognized having seen once they viewed Cassie's paintings: the beauty at their feet. The microcosmic communities of the natural world. And in this way she discovered her own unique territory in a place where the obvious splendor of the dramatic peaks was generally irresistible to painters.

Today she set aside her plans to paint the tanagers and worked instead to enhance a watercolor she had begun in the field, a small setting discovered near the old Lucas/Fabian cabins on Cottonwood Creek in Grand Teton National Park. A decaying chunk of log, twelve inches long, weathered gray with two knotholes. An orange lichen–covered rock beside it, graced on one side by red-leafed Oregon grape, the leaves leathery as dancing shoes, and on the other side by an ebony-bodied ant, glistening in the sunlight like a pair of jet beads. Unseen in the painting, yet felt while viewing it, was the murmur of the creek, the blueness of sky, the high-country snowfields crisping the air. If she did the painting just right, Cassie would be able to look at it and feel all the sounds and smells that were left out of the painting itself. Fred had taught her that. His definition of color was something you felt. With oils or acrylic paints, light came to the surface and bounced back, he said. With watercolors, light went through the paint to the paper and came back to the viewer.

Cassie picked up a piece of sandpaper to rub on the layers of paint, to give her rock texture. Then she dipped an old toothbrush in raw umber and flicked her thumb over it to speckle the rock with yet another layer of color.

Mrs. Penny had spotted Cassie painting one of her postcards outside during a free afternoon break last week, and had asked to see her other work. She told Cassie that with her permission, she would take a dozen of the postcard paintings with her to display in the ranch gift shop and sell for whatever price Cassie put on them. Cassie pictured them tucked around the window frames of the old log cabin and figured they'd might as well be there as stacked in her cupboard. She said, "Five dollars each?" She could use the mocha latte money.

She had shown her work around the valley before. Some of the local restaurants hung paintings and sold them for the artists. Snake River Brewery, Pearl Street Bagels, Shades, Betty Rock. Cassie had exhibited in them all and had sold several larger paintings while Jake was still alive. The trouble came when she had to purchase frames for the work—a requirement for hanging publicly—and that became expensive. So she hadn't shown her work during the past three years. Watercolor postcards for five dollars didn't require frames.

During Jake's long absences and later after his death, Cassie used her images as medicine and sent them through her body to awaken the painful parts that took refuge in numbness. Being married to a mountain climber had demanded a strong sense of equilibrium, a solid foundation of enjoying the moment in the moment. She never knew when she kissed Jake good-bye how long that kiss might need to comfort her. And finally she realized it couldn't comfort her at all past the actual kiss, unless she chose to live in memory, and then, reason followed, that entailed giving up the actual moment of the kiss. Because you don't get to do both. If she filled her mind with memory, Cassie learned, she shielded herself from immediate experience—the good and the bad.

She paused with her paintbrush now and looked up and over the wetlands to see the wind shake free yellow pollen from the pine trees on the mountain. Like golden smoke it swept across the slope.

When Cassie returned to the ranch, good news awaited her. Several postcard paintings had sold already. Boone handed her $370.

"This is a mistake," Cassie said.

"No, Mrs. Penny and her two visiting friends bought five of your paintings."

"They're just five dollars each."

When all this got untangled, Cassie learned that Mrs. Penny had taken it upon herself to get the postcard paintings double-matted and framed at Master's Studio, then hung them in the shop with price tags of $185 to $250 each. Mrs. Penny explained that it was her gamble. The paintings were worth it, and Cassie had already paid her back for the frame work with the first three paintings she'd sold. The money in Cassie's hand represented the two other paintings, sold free and clear.

Right now Cassie would trot that $370 back into town and straight to the bank, so she could mail off another check to GMAC. Next month she'd have her modeling fee to send as well, because the other piece of good news was a phone call from Marley Otter, who had gotten her crew together for the photographic layout; the piece was slotted for a late-winter issue. Cassie was feeling in good spirits. She would feel even better if her truck would at least make a noise when she turned the key. Lately there had been a problem with the battery keeping its charge. As she lifted the hood, she wondered whether this was the trouble she'd been warned by the mechanics to watch for.

"I think it's my altimeter," she told Boone at lunch.

"Altimeter?" Robbin said.

"They said I might need a new one soon."

"Airplanes have altimeters, honey," Boone informed her. "Cars don't."

"Then something else that begins with an *A*," she said.

"Alternator?"

"That's it."

Robbin offered to deal with the mechanics. They'd see Cassie walk in with her $370 and sell her a pair of propellers. And yes, Boone said, it would take at least that much. She didn't know how she was going to afford this or manage without her truck for the next couple days.

Part of her problem was solved later that afternoon. Robbin was called away and gave Cassie the use of his truck while he was gone, and Boone offered a spare room upstairs for her to stay in.

Seemed a friend who had once covered for Robbin during his years of trouble was in intensive care, recuperating from a near fatal overdose. With only hours' notice, Robbin was returning the favor, filling in at a two-day fund-raising marathon, plus a few TV appearances promoting it.

He seemed uneasy, to say the least, about coming out of his temporary retirement prematurely. While waiting for Cody to pick him up, Robbin buried his discomfort by taunting Cassie about her belief that Jake was a one-woman man. "If by some quirk of nature that was true, you think he'd want you broadcasting his bad luck? You loved him; he was a good guy. You don't have to exaggerate his perfection."

When she snapped back at him that his range of experience in the area of love and faithfulness compared to that of a snowshoe rabbit, her chin puckered momentarily and he caught that and apologized—sort of. "I'm sorry. But you don't have to be so sensitive."

"That's not a crime; that's a goal."

Only Cassie felt uncomplicated enthusiasm over Robbin's departure. Boone was so worried he worked himself into anger over Robbin's insults to Cassie. And in order to avoid waiting for Robbin to leave, he kicked Robbin and his suitcase out to wait on the porch for his ride to the airport. Even so, he needed to pull Cassie into position as his backup.

"And Cassie and I don't want you coming back here with some disease either. You've tested clean once, buster. Don't press your luck with strange women."

"Shit, Boone. Tell her about my circumcision, too, why don't you?"

Then Cody was tapping on the horn, and Cassie figured chances were good that softhearted Boone had seen Cody's truck approaching before booting Robbin out the door.

"I'll be all right, Boone," Robbin called, as he lobbed his suitcase into the bed of Cody's truck and added, "Honest."

Later, still stung by Robbin's dismissal of Jake's fidelity, Cassie called home. "Mom, you think Dad has ever . . . you know . . . had an affair while you were married?"

Without pause her mother answered, "I don't go in for this progressive mother-daughter stuff, Cassie. You want a recipe, I'll send it."

"Please, Mom. I need to know."

"No one but me."

"How can you be sure?" Cassie asked.

"No need to doubt Jake, if that's what this is about. A wife knows those things about the man she loves. Women who are surprised with strange phone numbers in their husband's pockets don't want to know how their marriage is faring; they want evidence of having been wronged. Those women are just looking for the needle to break the camel's back," her mother concluded.

"Straw, Mom. The needle was in the haystack."

"Straw, hay—don't be smart with your mother."

Conversations had been smoother when they were more regular. Once-a-month phone calls over the past three years failed to keep Cassie tolerant of her mother's idiomatic carnage.

Robbin could shape clouds. Boone had offered this fact to Cassie as a point of passing interest while the two of them had ridden horseback into camp that afternoon. Small billowy puffs cast spotted shadows on the open fields before them. "A cloud like that"—Boone pointed above them— "turned into a steer's head in just a few minutes." It was an exercise of concentration Robbin used. Boone remembered Robbin had stumbled upon the trick when he was a kid. He'd lie alone in the grass and look for figures in the cloud shapes, then notice the clouds began slowly to take on the shapes he wished for them. Boone had seen him do it a number of times.

Cassie took into consideration Boone's need to upholster his son's character in his absence, concerned as he was over Robbin's ability to hold his own in the midst of drink, drugs and dire sexual viruses. But now, Cassie sat away from the evening camp, near the river, and tried it herself. She picked out one small, rounded cloud and stared at it, trying to turn it into a rabbit. She found the exercise exceedingly dull, but just before giving it up she thought she detected the beginning of ear sprouts. Make it a cat, she thought, and gave it up to watch instead a pair of trumpeter swans whomp their lethal wings against the surface of the river on takeoff and skim low, mirroring their moonlike images on the water, before landing pillow-soft fifty yards closer to her. Their two signets, still gray, followed behind and looked dingy enough to have been victims of an oil spill.

Cassie wondered what differences were created in a person raised where the first sounds heard as an infant were the trumpeting of swans and elk versus the sirens of a city. Yesterday, she had lifted her eyes to the mountains outside the kitchen window and traced their peaks and dips with her gaze and realized that Robbin had lived all his childhood with that immovable splendor in sight. It had to mark a mind. Mark it more indelibly than even years in the spotlight did.

She agitated Robbin as much as he did her; she knew that. She believed he was more willing to accept the possibility of a love like hers and Jake's than he let on, that his disputing her claim of Jake's faithfulness was, in fact, Robbin challenging his own past notions of how love worked or didn't work. Just as he was challenging his talents and the source of those talents—the remarks she used for convincing Boone why Robbin was a son of a bitch, but only temporarily. She enjoyed Robbin, arguing with him, baiting him, talking to him. He had set himself the task of finding out who he was beneath his successful image and taking action on the discovery. She admired that. And the ranch felt rather lackluster without him.

The half-moon sat in the sky just as the sun sank behind the Tetons. Cassie felt the tension build while color and light suddenly drained from the sky. The pause gathered attention to itself, then—beat one, two, three—the whole western sky lit up with infant hues. Baby blue and pink, lavender and peach, traces of pale green where sky blues met sun yellows, and in the midst of the shifting colors swam that moon, and below that the swans, and below that the images of both in the river.

Cassie thought then: people should live in the place they think is the most beautiful. To her at that moment and on so many occasions before, living here was worth all she had to give up in trade.

She was learning things other than the cloud shaping about Robbin during his absence. She learned he was a speed reader and that he had an IQ of 153—this from Boone. That he wasted his eyes on spy novels and his intelligence on the Sunday *New York Times* crossword puzzles—this from Mrs. Penny. From Boone again, that Robbin finished those books in half a day and the puzzles in half an hour.

Cody added his fond remembrance: Robbin plucked boiling eggs out of their cooking water bare-handed. Now that everyone had convinced themselves Robbin was a living saint and there was every chance that he'd hold up against all temptations, Cassie wondered how long they would carry that vision once Robbin returned home—which he was scheduled to do tomorrow—and once again became, in Cody's words, "a handful."

"Where is she?"

"Who?"

"Cassie."

"Cassie?"

"Boone, did she leave?"

"What's all this interest?"

"Shit, she isn't here."

In Boone's office with the door ajar, Cassie was online sending in the order to Becca for refillable water bottles with the ranch logo. Her proposal had been accepted—no more disposable water bottles at Cross Wave. She followed the sounds from the kitchen: Boone getting a clean glass from the dishwasher, the faucet running, Robbin taking quick steps around the table.

"Slow down," Boone said between long drinks.

"You could have told me. That whole long drive from the airport and you don't say a thing." He had apparently noticed her camper missing, which was still in the garage, longer than expected, awaiting today's paycheck to cover the payment for her new alternator. In an hour, Lannie would be taking her into town to pick it up.

Boone's glass clunked down on the counter. "She's in the office."

Robbin whispered, "Behind that door?"

Cassie smiled to herself.

"Sure, go on in."

"Never mind." He added in a moderately loud tone, "Just wondered if there was anything to eat."

Cassie heard footsteps opening cupboard doors nearer and nearer to the office, so she slipped on the earphones from her CD player. *Why do we save men from their own stupidities?* she asked herself. *To maintain superiority,* she answered. Paradoxically, if women resisted showing men how dumb they were at times, men would forgo the effort to improve, thereby giving women the eternal edge. She pushed the PLAY button on the machine, expecting to hear music. But she heard instead the beginning of the final cut on a Dave Chappelle CD that she'd borrowed from Robbin before he'd left. With the comedian's first line, she laughed right out loud.

"What's so goddamn funny?" Robbin demanded, barging through the door. "Oh," he said, calmer, seeing her CD player.

Cassie turned off the player and removed her earphones. "You're home."

Robbin turned her desk chair around, braced a hand on each arm of her chair and grinned. "Did you miss me?"

"*Pined* for you." She smiled back. "The whole two days you were gone."

"I was gone five days."

"Oh."

"Shit." Robbin straightened up, frowned at her, then tipped his head toward the kitchen. "Come share a beer with Boone and me."

In the kitchen Cassie asked, "Are you hungry?" She opened the refrigerator door.

"Nah." Then Robbin glanced toward Boone. He added, "Maybe some cheese and crackers." Robbin's drinking rules for the summer allowed him to have an occasional beer or two, but only at home with the family, never at his usual haunts; there he nursed root beer. He got out three tall glass mugs and mentioned the possibility had crossed his mind that Cassie had moved on.

"I think Robbin missed you, Cassidy," Boone said.

"I just missed conversation. Nobody knew how to treat me. They looked at me like 'Poor Robbin, he used to be so merry on drugs. We'll have to be careful around him.' It was like hanging out with a bunch of damn nurses."

"Cassie looks pretty in this dress, don't you think?" Boone was testing the atmosphere.

"Very." Eyes as blue as a match flame, Robbin let her enjoy his long approval. "What's the occasion?"

Cassie lifted her beer mug. "I was planning on going out."

"A date?" Robbin halted his pouring of the beer into the three glasses.

"You didn't mention another date, Cassie." Boone sat forward.

"No, you didn't." Robbin jumped on board. He turned to Boone in surprise. "*Another?*"

Cassie hid her smile behind a sip of beer. She hoped Robbin's behavior indicated that Boone was right—he'd missed her—because she had missed him.

"That's two in a row, Cassie. You going to be out real late again tonight, too?"

The two of them were hunched over the table together waiting for her answer, as if she was supposed to justify such excesses during her time off. Cassie set her beer mug down. She said, "Well, gee."

"You don't have to get huffy," Robbin said. "We just asked you a simple question."

The situation called for an alliance shift and Boone obligingly danced over toward Cassie in the *pas de trois*. He said, "Right. That's her personal life." He picked up a mail-order catalog from the chair beside him and spread it open before him as a shield and vowed, "Not another word about Cassie's private doings."

"How late was she last night?" Robbin asked.

"That's Cassie's business."

Cassie dipped her head smugly toward Robbin. The fact was that she had come in darn late. She'd been helping Erin stage a new house that was going on the market today, and the two of them had scooted furniture around and hung art until the wee hours.

Robbin got a second bottle of beer and once again poured a third of it into everyone's mug. "So . . . Boone, did you catch last night's late movie?"

Cassie knew Robbin was going to work every bit of information he wanted out of Boone. She sat back with her arms folded and waited.

"Yep. Fine old Gary Cooper movie. Enjoyed it."

"Then hit the sack?" Robbin sounded so casual as to be almost disinterested.

"Sat through another one. A terrible bore, and I'd seen it twice before. *Wreck of the Mary Deare* or some such."

With her eyebrows raised, Cassie watched Robbin getting warmer. He said, "But you stayed up and saw it through?"

"*And* part of a third one—which was even worse—before she pulled in."

"Hah." Robbin celebrated his success. He stood beside the table and tallied up two full movies and part of a third. "Four hours and . . . say, forty-five minutes past ten thirty."

Boone's eyes shifted guiltily over the top of the catalog toward Cassie's iron gaze.

"Three fifteen," Robbin pronounced and pulled Boone's catalog down. "Right?"

"Welp," Boone said accusingly to Cassie, "you said it'd be an early night. Gary Cooper's ridden off into the sunset, the *Mary Deare* is home to an octopus, James Dean mumbles me half to sleep, and you're still out. Three thirty is not an early night, Cassidy."

"So?" Cassie spread her arms wide.

"That's right, that's right," Boone said apologetically. "Now, damn it, Robbin."

"Who was she with?" Robbin pounced, bending toward Boone with both palms on the table.

"I don't know, but she had on another pretty dress."

"Jeez. You two are really something." Cassie pushed away from the table. If she'd had something more interesting going on than spending time with her women friends, she might have announced it to the two of them. As it was, she decided to keep them wondering.

"You said 'early night,'" Boone mumbled and lifted the catalog up to his face again.

"That's right," Robbin chimed in. "From now on when you say 'early night' you get home before Gary Cooper does."

CHAPTER ELEVEN

Fee held up a one-liter water bottle with Cassie's design of the ranch's entrance—two massive upright logs, another log lodged horizontally across the top, and hanging from that the Cross Wave Guest Ranch and Cattle Company logo painted on a rough wood sign. In the background she had sketched three peaks of the Tetons. "Where the hell did these come from and what're they doing in my barn?"

"These are for you and the ranch hands," Cassie said. "Choose whichever color you'd like." The bottles were done in a variety of colors so people could identify their own more easily. She was pleased with how well the design had turned out and she had to bite her tongue to keep from listing all the colors to Fee, from turquoise to ruby red. She'd carried a box of the bottles to the stables to encourage the wranglers to use them instead of popping off the cap of a fresh plastic bottle of water to guzzle several times a day. She scooted the box nearer the open stable doors so everyone coming in would see them.

"Goddamn," Fee mumbled. "This your idea?"

Cassie felt irked at Fee's manner. With a slyness untypical of her, she said, "The ranch dump was going to fill up soon with all those plastic bottles the dudes go through."

"That's not your problem, missy." He tossed the bottle into the box, where it bounced and clanked against the other bottles. He said, "Too pretty for Cross Wave wranglers. Don't expect them to go for this gimmick."

"If they do, there's a box of them," Cassie said and decided to let someone else deal with Fee's scorn. As he was fond of telling her, it wasn't her problem. She hadn't found a ranch dump, but Fee had just practically told her there was one.

She had sold Boone on the idea of refillable water bottles with mathematics alone. It was just plain cheaper in the long run, even in the short run. Robbin had shrugged at the news, but when the Cross Wave bottles had arrived that afternoon, he'd picked out a purple one and notched the cap with his pocketknife, so he'd know it was his. Cassie carried a box to the guests' main lodge, passing Robbin's cabin next door. She spotted him through the window working on his laptop, with his new water bottle at hand. He often spent full days toting his computer from place to place, working on his screenplay.

Inside the lodge Cassie set the box on a table and wrote out a sign stating the water bottles were a gift from Cross Wave. Mrs. Penny is going to love this idea, Cassie thought, then reprimanded herself for falling into the same mind-set as the McKeags, trying to please that woman.

Cassie looked around the lodge, checking on the maids' housework—a supervisory job added to her responsibilities after Mrs. Penny complained about spiderwebs between the antlers of the elk, moose and pronghorn heads that hung high on the log walls. The maids had cleaned well. The logs shone with the golden light that streamed through the sparkling windows and the whole lodge smelled like Murphy Oil Soap.

Cassie never tired of looking at the framed family photographs hanging in the lodge. Robbin and Cody as young boys, toting guns and the small game they had hunted. Robbin, towheaded at five, napping on the back of a heifer, sprawled out shirtless with a stripe of sunlight across his bare back. Groups of dudes on horseback against the mountains and blue sky; Mrs. Penny sitting in her special lawn chair at camp; Mrs. Penny flyfishing with Mr. Penny a couple decades back; a preteen Cody posing beside the antlers of a seven-point bull elk, Robbin standing by in admiration. Along the wall behind the drinks table hung something that was even familiar to Cassie: a poster of Robbin's first movie, *Ruby Stallion*. Ruby in the foreground, Robbin in the background. Cassie looked closer. Robbin had dark hair in this photo and it didn't quite look like him, but she knew it must be. Actually, it looked more like Cody.

The spiffy-looking lodge was quite a contrast to the McKeags' living quarters. It was Cassie's guess that when the furniture got worn out here, it was moved to the ranch house. The lodge was used as a common room for the guests and a place where they ate when the weather prohibited picnics. Elk antler chandeliers hung over tables covered in blue-and-white-checkered cloths, with red paisley bandannas knotted for napkins. The other side of the room held sofas, big leather easy chairs, walls of bookshelves, bent wicker end tables holding wrought-iron lamps. And one god-awful chair made of horseshoes welded together. Boone had said it was Mrs. Penny's favorite, designed with a spacious seat, swooping arms and a tall back. Mr. Penny had made it for her with the help of Fee one summer at the ranch. No one else was allowed to sit in it, but Cassie figured no one else would want to.

Cassie picked out a sky blue bottle for herself and another light jade one and walked outside to the long porch, where rockers were lined up in the dappled shade of the pines. She was going to find Cody, test the water bottle response. What Cody liked, the wranglers liked. Or at least she was betting on that.

She found him coming out of the tent shed, a small building where the tents were stored and repaired. Soon, he said, they'd be putting them up at camp.

"Should have done it a few weeks ago. We seem to have been off schedule all spring."

"You mean the cattle and all."

"I mean the works. I hadn't even caught up on my sleep until Robb went to California for his friend. Otherwise it was late nights in the bar."

"You take good care of him, don't you?"

"Just until you get the hang of it."

"What? Me?" She started shaking her head and couldn't seem to stop. "I don't take care of grown men." She thought for a second. "Why would you say that?"

"Guess I got that from Dad. Says you two are tight."

"No, that's not true."

"He doesn't ask me to get him dates anymore, so . . . I just thought—"

"No." There were messages in this exchange, but Cassie couldn't sort them all out. She stood staring at the mountains against the horizon, bouncing the green water bottle against her leg. "Oh," she said. "I brought this for you."

"Nice." Cody dragged out the word "niii-ice," while nodding his head and admiring Cassie's design. He looked up. "Thanks."

"Do you think you'll use it? I mean instead of opening a fresh bottle of water? That's what I was hoping everybody would do. We got them for the dudes." Before he could answer, she added, "And I put a box of them in the stable for your wranglers." She was talking too much; she sounded suspiciously like she was trying to sell him something, and if she said one more word, Cody would know for sure she was. "Do you really like it?" Darn. Shut up.

"It's okay," Cody said. Backing off, Cassie thought, picking up that there was a message in the bottle.

He said, "So you and Robb aren't—"

She didn't let him finish. "No."

"Hmm." He set the bottle on the ground and reached into the shed to drag out a heavy rolled-up canvas. He began to spread it on the grass and as soon as he did, his dingos, Kelty and Cairn, trotted over from the shady patch where they'd been napping, walked onto the cloth, circled three times and lay down.

Cassie set her own bottle aside and helped Cody with the canvas. "You know, Robbin seems to have done all right on his trip, so maybe you don't have to worry." She added, "He seems pretty steady. Though, of course, I don't know him like you do. You've been practically brothers, raised together. . . ." Was she talking too much again? Or did it just seem that way compared to this cowboy of few words? She wouldn't mind hearing a little more about the two of them growing up or why Cody thought she and Robbin were . . . whatever he thought. And she wouldn't mind knowing which eye to look into when she talked to him.

Cody stood looking at the tarp. "Robb and I been taking care of each other most our life. Usually it's him taking care of me."

That was a surprise. Cassie held rules similar to those of a TV courtroom drama: if a subject was raised by one party, law allowed questions on the subject from the other party. So she said, "How's that?"

"This place, for one. All my operations, for another." He indicated his eye.

"Gosh. A lot of operations?"

"One, sometimes two, every year from the time of the accident, when Robb and I were eleven until we were nineteen."

"Accident?" Now she was in a position to be of few words herself.

Cody said the two of them were out playing with their BB guns. Unlike most kids that age, these two had been around guns since they were kindergartners and knew how to handle them safely. Still, accidents happened.

That summer the eleven-year-old Cody and Robbin stood in the woods, near each other, and both aimed at a pinecone on a limb. Robbin took first shot. The BB hit the tree's trunk, ricocheted off and hit Cody in the eye. He screamed with pain and fell to his knees. Robbin threw himself down beside him and when he realized what had happened, he wrapped his bandanna around both Cody's eyes to keep the injured one closed and guided Cody, blind, back to the ranch. Both boys were scared and crying.

"So that was the end of my film career."

"What?" Cassie was certain her jaw dropped. "Film career?"

Cody said, "Come over here; there's a water spigot. We can fill up our new bottles."

She followed him to the other side of the shed and watched him bend over, turn on the faucet and hold his bottle under it.

He shook it and threw the water out, then did the same with hers. Filled them both. Cassie said, "You're going to drink out of it?"

"Sure. What was your plan?"

She laughed. "I thought you might not think it was western enough. You know, cowboys should drink out of creeks or something."

"That would be 'cricks' to you."

She laughed again, Cody turned the water off, and Cassie followed him back around the front of the tent shed. "You were in films when you were a kid?"

"Almost." Cody stooped to check the strength of a few seams, then began to roll the tarp back up, nudging the dingos off as he neared center. "Earlier that same summer we had some movie people here. A producer from Los Angeles was dragging his family around the West—Colorado, Montana and finally Wyoming—looking for a young kid to play the lead in his movie about a boy and a horse." Cody carted the rolled canvas back into the shed and brought out another one.

Cassie helped him lay this piece out flat. The dogs once again found their spot and Cassie crawled around with Cody, checking seams and worn spots. When they found one, Cody marked it and set the tarp aside for repairs.

"Robbin and I used to round up the horses at dawn every morning and drive them into camp so the dudes could ride before breakfast. And sometimes we'd guide the rides out to spot wildlife ourselves; we always knew where to find the critters." Cody paused.

"Hand me that marker. I found a split." He circled it and moved on around the tarp.

"So, anyway, the first morning the guy—his name was Dave Dorrey—told Boone he'd found his star. And he pointed to me."

"Everybody must have been thrilled."

"Overwhelmed, more like. Dad was consulted and eventually agreed to us going to California," Cody continued. "Things moved along. Film tests, posters made, tutors lined up for the school year. . . . I don't know all, but I was suddenly doing much of what I always did here, but not allowed to get my clothes dirty while doing it, and cameras followed me."

"Here's something to check," Cassie said and Cody crawled over to look. "Go on," she said.

"All that was just preliminary work. The film project itself was scheduled for the fall. That's why I'd need tutors; I was going to be pulled out of school most of the year. Lots of money involved. Dad had big plans for that. Came back to the ranch for a few weeks the end of summer, before the film schedule kicked in, and he started negotiations to purchase some land."

They dragged another tent out.

"So that *is* you in the poster in the lodge?"

"Yep."

Cassie was starting to worry about the time. She needed to get dinner preparations going. The shed held more rolled canvases than she could imagine them needing and a lot more than she would have time to help with. Yet she didn't want to miss any of this story. They crawled around another canvas.

Abruptly Cody concluded, "Then the accident."

Cassie sat back on her heels.

"They dropped you?"

"They took Robbin instead."

"Oh." Her hand went to her chest. "Gosh, Cody." Images

flew through her mind, each one sparking an emotion the young Cody must have experienced—resentment, anger, envy. How could the two young boys' friendship have survived?

"Robb didn't tell you any of this?"

"I told you, we're not particularly friends."

"I don't know. Something's going on with him."

"How could that happen?"

"He doesn't tell me everything."

"I mean, how could that Dorrey guy do that to you? And your friendship with Robbin? And how did your fathers deal with it?" No stew tonight for dinner. Maybe a pasta dish. Pasta, a big salad, quickly stir up some dessert.

"You know, it worked out. I never had bad feelings about it. I don't know about Dad; he doesn't talk about things that bother him. At the time it was more like our families together had caused a problem for Dorrey, his financial backers and a bunch of other people in California. Putting Robbin in the film was the easiest answer. Boone made it work out financially for Fee and me, plus Robbin's earnings took care of all my medical bills. Of course, everybody thought we were talking about one single movie, which I wasn't all that interested in anyway. Just did it so Fee could buy his land. We didn't know we were talking about a lifetime career."

Cassie was thinking that they didn't know they were talking about covering the expenses for eight years of surgery either. "So now that it's turned out to be a lifetime career, how do you feel?"

"Goddamn relieved." Cody laughed.

"Really?"

"Does Robb look like a lucky guy to you?"

"Not particularly, but most people would think so."

"Most people don't think. Period. If they did, they'd feel sorry for some of those pathetic folks on the cover of *People* magazine."

Cassie said, "I think you're remarkable."

Cody laughed. "Could you send a letter of recommendation to Diana? Because she's not convinced; she's stalling on me."

"I'd be happy to. But I doubt you need it."

"Like I mentioned to you a while back, I let Diana go once before. It was right after we graduated high school. Dad was pressuring me about learning the ranching business, and she went off and married somebody else. Can't let that happen again."

"All you need to do is offer her your full attention—it's all any of us wants from someone we love." Jake had traveled so much, but when he was home, his attention was focused fully on her and it made up for a lot.

Cody stopped his work and looked at Cassie. "You're right."

They continued their work, quiet for several minutes. Then Cody said, "That's why Robb and I are such good friends, brothers really, like you said. He gives me his full attention and I've always done the same."

They were quiet again.

Cody said, "The problem for me is—how do you do that with more than one person?" He stopped his work and so did Cassie.

She was about to say she didn't know, but his need for an answer to this question felt palpable. She glanced at Cody and saw that his expression held a shade of desperation. She realized now that Cody had hoped there was something romantic going on between her and Robbin, because that would let him off the hook of dividing his attention between his friend and his lover.

She said, "If you love Diana and hope to partner for life with her, she is the one you give your full attention to. Diana, her daughters, then keep following your heart."

"But I love Robb, too. I don't want to mess with that."

"Sure, you want to keep true to that. Though I don't think you were hanging out at the Cowboy Bar because you loved being there or even loved Robbin being there." Those two, Cassie thought, both needed to tune in to themselves. It felt as if their tragedy of fame and almost-fame had linked them in some relationship that made them each think that the best way to live was to check out on himself and lock in to the other. It reminded her of some marriages in which neither the man nor the woman had a sense of being an individual but only a pair, a unit of two bodies, one mind.

Nobody had ever told Cassie that because she had lost someone she loved, other people would think that made her wise. Yet over and over again during the past three years she had been approached and asked for advice. At the very least, people spilled their intimate stories to her, their sadness and concerns. As if they recognized she was cut wide-open by her loss, yet living on, strong enough to hear their suffering, acknowledge it and set them on the path toward healing. She wondered at times if her heart, bereft of its beloved, worked like a vacuum and just naturally filled itself with the longings and confusion of others. Whatever it was, Cassie had been surprised that she could send them off feeling better, when often she couldn't do that for herself.

She checked her watch. "I need to start dinner." She stood and brushed her hands on her jeans.

Cody stood, too, and wiped his hands on a bandanna he'd pulled from his rear jeans pocket. "Dad always used to say to

Robb and me that someday a woman would come between us. I've worked hard to watch out for that."

"It doesn't have to happen that way." Even cowboys need to grow up, Cassie thought, get married, move on.

"I was worried about the woman being Diana, but Dad said it was you. You were the woman that was going to come between us."

"Cody, no. No. That couldn't happen." She felt stung to realize someone would think such a malicious thing about her. Not someone. Fee. She stood shaking her head, speechless.

"That's what I told him." He looked up to the sky. "You can count on Dad to see the dark side. Ranching can do that to you."

Cassie hurried back to the ranch house to begin dinner, detouring through the storeroom to pick up ingredients for her pasta dish and standing for a moment before the stack of shiny colored water bottles. Perhaps this was going to work out and never again would the big Pepsi truck rumble down the dirt road to deliver cases and cases of water, far less fresh and far less nutritious than what streamed right out of the ranch well.

It felt good to care about something, feel a passion for accomplishing a task. It had been a long time. She felt like herself, yet a deeper, more expansive self than before her loss.

Then the thought of Fee's accusation struck her anew. It didn't make sense. Why would he say such a thing? She was not a woman who would threaten Cody and Robbin's friendship.

CHAPTER TWELVE

Once Cassie learned that Lannie, the cook for pack trips and overnight rafting trips, had been called home for a family emergency, she skulked around the ranch like a bandit coyote. By Sunday evening no one else had been found to cook and assist Robbin on the five-day, eighty-five-mile float trip. Right now a wrangler with a fresh sprig of sage in his hatband was greeting the paid-in-advance floaters at the airport.

Cassie's fists clenched every time Boone addressed her. Finally, before dinnertime, she blurted it out. "No, Boone, I can't do it. I can't take Lannie's place."

"Well, that's the most indisputable remark I've heard all day."

Robbin came out of the office where he'd been calling other valley ranches, trying to borrow someone for the trip. Boone said to him, "Cassie, here, is afraid *she'll* have to take Lannie's place."

Was there a note of testing, or was Cassie just paranoid?

"I won't do it," she reaffirmed.

"Welp, now, Cassie, you probably won't have to." Boone patted Cassie's hand, to distract her—she was sure—from his interjection of the word "probably."

Separately that evening, both father and son made late-night visits to Cassie's camper to convince her she shouldn't miss the opportunity of a five-day rafting trip. The float had become an *opportunity* sometime between dinner and eleven o'clock Sunday night. Robbin laid the groundwork. Boone just popped by later to tell her she'd made a good choice. At what exact time it became a *choice* was harder to pinpoint.

Cassie had thought to keep this proposal at bay by turning off her light and going to bed early. But there was Robbin, pushing her legs over to make room for himself to sit on her bed as he described the wonders of a five-day float: quiet and serene, sometimes exciting and wet; they'd see sandhill cranes, blue herons, white pelicans; moose and elk, deer and antelope. "When an eagle screams overhead, you'll hope we never have to come back."

He'd be loonier than he was if he didn't have river trips every summer, he told her. On the river nobody gave one damn about his fame. All that mattered was that he was a good boatman.

"I'll make it work," Robbin said. "Honest."

Ten minutes later, another knock on her door and "Cassie, hon?" Boone stuck his head in. "I appreciate this. You've got yourself two days off when you come back. I've scheduled it in already." Boone put a foot on her step. "One other thing. There's a code word in our family. It's the word 'honest,'" he said. "One of us says that, it's the truth and no going back on it. I just want you to know Robbin used that word with me. He promised he'd make this a nice trip for you. Robbin is fierce about his promises." Boone nodded his head. "Otherwise I wouldn't put you in for this. That help at all?"

There were moments for Cassie when the float trip seemed an analogy for living: that if she just interacted with the passing scenery and weather in an open-ended willingness to deal with change, all would forever be well. As obvious as that was, the power of change had never fully occurred to her as a major element of life. Maybe she had changed from new bride to grieving widow—and maybe she should have caught on then—but she had operated under the misconception that change was an aberration of the law of life, not a hard-and-fast rule.

Three days out, it struck her: a person either grows—changes—or dies. Every friend, family member and acquaintance shifted in her mind into two categories: those who chose life with the willingness to grow and change and those who refused to change and thereby chose death in its many assumed disguises—self-imposed limitations, ignorance, fearfulness, addiction.

Jake's life and death took on a different perspective. Whenever she had spoken of the future and her longing to begin their family, Jake would assume a funny half smile and make jokes about the unlikelihood of a mountain climber growing old enough to walk a daughter down the aisle. He was afraid of moving beyond the strong, courageous athlete he knew himself to be. Suddenly she saw that had he not died when he did, she would eventually have had to leave him. Jake was never going to be a full-time husband, never a father, never a grandfather.

The cancer diagnosis and his decision to keep it to himself suggested that perhaps he may have decided against future change of any kind. People often let such decisions be carried out for them by accident.

Cassie looked behind her to Robbin guiding the raft; he smiled and motioned toward the fishing efforts of an osprey circling above them. Robbin, too, had made his decision. Cassie might have failed at times to admire his progress, but he had chosen life. He had demonstrated his willingness to change by grabbing hold of himself and pulling out of the race to fame. He had wanted more. He had made the decision to change his life and grow. And, Cassie thought, she would need to carefully examine her own life through this lens.

The fourth day out turned rainy, cold and miserable. No dry wood for their lunch break meant cold food to eat and damp clothes to wear the rest of the afternoon, despite their rain suits. Cassie's sole comfort was that she hadn't paid a couple thousand dollars for these wretched conditions. One of the guests, Harry Harrison, took comfort by pulling out another one of his many bottles and making dull jokes about preferring his scotch without water. By Cassie's new classification Harry was not choosing life and change, while on the face of it his pretty wife, whose idea it was to come on this rafting trip, was. But by now Cassie had realized Anita was going to go wherever Harry chose for them. She was allowed only to select the entertainments along the way.

Robbin exhibited enough exuberance and humor to carry the rest of the guests through a Pawnee attack without any ammunition of their own or rations to bargain with. One more hour of this, he forecasted, and the sun would be out. Until then they'd keep warm by paddling. Was he going to fabricate all those clouds into donuts, so the sun could shine through their holes? Or did he just know Wyoming's weather was usually predicted by stating the exact opposite of present conditions?

He was the last to crawl into his tent at night, the first out of it every morning. And he kept up his promise with Cassie. He made it comfortable for her to work as his assistant, paddling and cooking, putting up tents, chopping wood, washing dishes, carrying water, singing campfire songs. Robbin had brought along a harmonica and a pear-wood recorder and tried to think up songs Cassie and the guests could accompany him on. Songs like "Five Hundred Miles" in which the lyrics were repetitious enough for everyone to catch on to after the first run-through.

The clouds thinned to mists a few miles downstream and in another half hour the sun burned through. They beached the raft and hung bedding and clothing over bushes and low-hanging pine boughs until camp looked like the aftermath of a massacre.

Harry continued to sit in his wet gear, tipping a bottle to his face. Stress-heightened situations served Harry better, Cassie decided. He came across calmer than the rest, rather than just plain drunk, as he did now. Anita urged food on Harry at dinnertime, and afterward he shared all but one of his remaining bottles with the group to celebrate their final night out.

Robbin held to apple juice and Anita joined him, but Cassie got just a bit giggly with the others around the campfire. She wasn't used to strong liquor, only the occasional glass of wine or beer, so it hit her harder than expected. She recalled another song whose lyrics consisted mostly of repeating the title. Robbin remembered it with a groan. Captain and Tennille's "Do It to Me One More Time." They sat facing each other straddling a log, singing "Do it to me one more time," Cassie aware that she was acting a bit flirty, but it felt so good she didn't want to stop. Robbin played the flute runs with his recorder. "Do it to me one more time." When they finished, Cassie said, "Again."

Robbin laughed and shook his head. "I don't think so, Cass." He stuck the recorder in his back pocket.

One by one, everybody moved off to their tents, to the river to brush their teeth, to the woods behind camp. This was the worst time for Cassie. She was so afraid of being surprised while crouched indignantly in a bush, she puttered around the cook area till all the others had settled into their bags.

Tonight she failed to count heads properly. She went into the trees wearing a long T-shirt over her panties and unlaced sneakers—it was hard enough to keep her feet from getting wet, let alone a pair of long pants bunched around her ankles. Then she went to the river, washed, and brushed her teeth. He leaped out at her from behind her tent as she was returning. And Harry Harrison, whose breath alone could have done the job, overpowered her, clutching her in a crunching squeeze. "Do it to me just *one* time," he said and smashed his face against hers, wet mouth opening and closing somewhere near her nose, his hands all over the backs of her bare legs, trying to find the edge of her shirt.

Cassie opened her mouth to yell—first in surprise, next in disgust—then foolishly thought of his wife seeing this and clenched her teeth. But Harry wasn't dissuaded by her struggles and as loath as she was to touch him further, she clamped her teeth on a piece of his loose neck skin and Harry himself yelled.

Robbin grabbed a wildly searching hand from Cassie's butt and twisted it behind Harry's back, and the scuffle was over. Without speaking a word, Robbin walked Harry around the back of Cassie's tent. She waited to hear the smash of fist against jawbone but heard only "Good night, Harry" and a grunt as Harry's arm was released, followed by a cushioned thud on his sleeping bag. Then Robbin was back and Cassie got the shakes.

"The son-of-a-bitching bastard," Robbin said and folded her into his arms. "Are you all right, Cass?"

He held her until her breathing settled, then ushered her into her tent and said, "See you in the morning."

She couldn't sleep. She lay in her tiny backpacking tent for almost two hours. In the past she had used two standard remedies for insomnia. One fail-safe method was to get up, get a glass of milk and wander around sipping it for twenty minutes. The other was to *visualize* getting up and drinking the milk. Occasionally, before she had finished half the glass of imagined milk, she was out.

Not tonight, of course. Cassie reached for her pants and scooted into them half-lying down, then grabbed her sneakers. She remembered that only powdered milk was packed in the supply boxes, so she'd have to use her imagination anyway just to swallow the lumpy stuff. With a sneaker in each hand, she crawled out through the low flap of the nylon tent and took two steps toward a pine tree that she could lean against to put her shoes on. She stumbled against a body. One steely grip on her ankle, a yank, and she was prone across somebody's sleeping bag.

Both of them perfectly mute, they wrestled in the dark for a few seconds. The muffled thump of a soft rubber sole slapped the top of a head, and Robbin whispered, "Shit." Cassie began laughing into his shoulder. "I thought you were Harry. What are you doing here?" she whispered into his ear.

"Protecting you from another episode with him," he whispered back.

"That's so nice." She didn't move from her sprawl across his sleeping bag. He ran his hand over her back.

"Cass, once we get home . . . let's give it a go. Okay?"

She nodded into his shoulder. "Okay."

She woke early the next morning. Her first thought was about Robbin and how the two of them would "give it a go." Her next thought was about Jake. Little beads of memory surfaced and strung themselves together into a necklace that thumped and rattled against her breastbone throughout the first hour of their float; then she flung it off and gave her attention to the moment.

Meanwhile, she got the feeling that Robbin was uncertain how to proceed in their new relationship. He moved through their day together as cautiously as a hiker might make his way through an unmapped bog. Territory was in sight in which he was adept. But first the bog of snowmelt, one tentative step at a time. His long gazes and clumsiness with chores he'd done all his life created a sweet stress between them.

Harry and Anita were especially lovey with each other all day, which Cassie thought was creepy. She received a heartfelt apology that morning and a hefty tip discreetly presented in a blue envelope—both from Anita.

At four o'clock they paddled into the pickup point, and everyone jumped into the river to pull the raft onto the sandy bank, then got sidetracked by hilarity and had a water fight instead. Cassie spotted Boone, waiting beside his van and raft trailer, keeping a certain distance until he could read the results of putting his son and his cook together with paying customers for five days. Before they had left on the float trip she'd overheard Boone on the office phone talking to his lady friend, Elene: "Good God, those poor people trapped on a raft with the two of them for five days. I'll have to make it up to them somehow."

When Boone realized the mood was positive, he said incongruently, "Oh, I guess we don't need these" and glanced down to the two dew-beaded bottles he held. Then he cheered and said, "By golly, let's have champagne to *celebrate*, then."

Cassie was ordered to consider her work done once the floaters returned. She luxuriated in a long, hot shower and now mingled with the guests that had gathered around Fee's outdoor grill, enjoying his stories about life in the West while he painted barbecue sauce on slabs of beef. On the days when she woke up early enough to go for a walk before starting her cook day, she sometimes spotted Fee in his bathrobe, knobby knees above a pair of cowboy boots, his black Stetson stuck on top of uncombed hair, sternly smoking the only cigarette he allowed himself each day. But knowing he was cranky at the best of times, Cassie always made a wide arc around him first thing in the morning.

This evening, though, Fee generously flashed his bright smile, framed by two long creases that no one within swatting distance would dare refer to as dimples.

"How long does summer last around here?" one of the guests asked.

"Summer began yesterday and we're halfway through it," Fee said to laughter. Cassie hadn't seen this side of the man before. He was funny, charming and knew how to cook—he'd taken her place cooking for the guests while she was gone on the float trip.

"You know how guest ranches got started, don't you?" He held a bottle of beer in one hand, barbecue fork in the other. "Life around here got to be nine months of wearing overboots and three of relatives that we hardly knew visiting us, so we decided to start charging."

All of this week's guests were new to the ranch, though often the cabins were occupied with people who had been coming for many years; some who were now close friends with other guests scheduled visits for the same weeks each summer. Aside from Mrs. Penny, most stayed a week or two, though a few reserved their same cabin and horse year after year for a month's stay.

Mrs. Penny whispered to Cassie, "Fee and his old stories. He always brings them out for the newcomers."

Cassie took her place in line as it passed the long table holding fruit, beans and salads and ended in Fee's slicing station.

"What will you have, missy? Well-done, medium or rare?"

"I'll pass tonight, thanks."

Fee lowered his knife and said, "You hear that, folks? We've got a subversive among us. This gal here isn't eating meat." He spoke jovially and captured the diners' attention. They stood with their plates in their hands, expecting another funny story from him. A few laughed in anticipation.

But Fee's manner shifted to dead seriousness. "You're a vegetarian. Isn't that right, missy?"

The guests stood, looking from Fee to Cassie, waiting for an answer. Boone and Robbin, too, watched for her response. Cassie could practically see the photos flipping through their minds of the many meals the three of them had shared. They were no doubt asking themselves: Did she eat meat or did she just cook and serve meat?

And the answer was she just cooked and served meat. She didn't eat it, couldn't eat it. Had stopped eating beef once she had learned how destructive cattle ranching could be to the land. But this wasn't the time or place to mention that.

"I'm not a strict vegetarian," she said, "though I rarely eat meat." Meaning she ate fish and chicken occasionally.

"I hate to be the one to point out that a cattle ranch is an odd place for someone who doesn't eat beef." Fee allowed a pause, then dropped his next words into that silence. "Those your friends who came late one night and tried to steal our cattle shortly after you were hired?"

Cody stepped up, with Robbin right beside him. Cody said, "Dad—"

"Fee, for God's sake," Robbin said at the same time. "I told you it was just some drunk pranksters from the bar." He looked at Cassie. "She had nothing to do with that."

Fee raised his head over the guests toward Boone. "What do you say, Boone?"

"I say we move this line along and begin to eat some of this fine food you fixed us."

"You heard the boss. Try some of our fine food, Miss Vegetarian." And Fee dropped a slice of the rarest beef onto Cassie's plate. She watched the blood from the meat seep into her potato salad, mix with the juice from her slice of melon.

She couldn't address this action, couldn't lift her head and make eye contact with Fee. But she did set her plate down right there before him and return to the other end of the table to make up another.

During dinner, at a table with Fee, Cody, Mrs. Penny and the McKeags, the talk moved to Fee's wife and her long involvement with a religious group in California. Fee said, perhaps to make amends or to make himself look kinder, "My wife Laraine's a vegetarian, too, missy. I don't understand it, but I love the woman."

He added, "Laraine's been living at the retreat center in Santa Barbara for thirty years or so now. Which seniority affords her status as a Cosmic Rainbow Flame."

"Hmm," Cassie said, impressed, trying to meet Fee's friend-liness and forgetting for the moment the silliness of such a title.

"Yeah," Robbin said, "there's only five of them."

Then Fee muttered, "Cosmic Rainbow Flame," and they all laughed. Though Fee didn't share his wife's religion, it was clear he wished her well. Cassie had known about this before, but even so, an unconventional marriage arrangement was not something she would have expected of Fee.

He said, "Laraine reports some unrest there at the center."

"Well, one day," Mrs. Penny said, "Laraine will have her own land for a retreat cen—"

Fee's fork stilled midway to his mouth and he caught Mrs. Penny's eye with a stern and wordless reprimand. She dropped her sentence and suddenly flushed. An awkward lull spread along the table.

Cassie attributed the scene to the rule that the speaker may say any harsh thing about his own family member, but no one else had better. Still, to see Mrs. Penny admonished was an event.

"What are you talking about, Mrs. P?" Robbin asked, unin-timidated by Fee's grim silence.

"Imagine, Robbin, dear, that it doesn't involve *you*, for once."

Cassie wasn't convinced; everything around Cross Wave in-volved Robbin.

Up till now, Cassie's private life had been the exception to this rule, but as soon as dinner was over, she slipped away, know-ing that Robbin would follow.

He caught up with her on the path to her camper, where she grabbed a sweater. Then they walked to the river and sat on the grass atop a small hill. Behind and below them the river slowed its flow with a deep bend, then seeped into a scoop of wetlands, thick with willows. The elk often ventured out there with their young, early mornings and late evenings. It was a favored haunt of Earl, an imperial bull elk with a seven-point rack branching from his head, furred still with the velvet that he would soon rub off on tree trunks. Earl had been a neighbor of the McKeags' for seventeen years now.

"He has a harem," Robbin said. "Twelve, thirteen females."

"A polygamist," Cassie noted and unlocked her clasp from around her drawn-up knees, then leaned back to brace against an arm. Seven of Earl's females nosed around the willows below and silently kept watch over their young.

"You think Earl's immoral?" Robbin asked.

"No, but I like the trumpeter swan's vow of fidelity. One partner for life." She remembered out loud a story she'd heard in Florida from Petersen, an elderly gentleman who'd befriended her during reality escapes the past three years, when she had to drive fast and hard to someplace far away and grieve till she thought she could return again to home and friends. Sandhill cranes, which also mated for life, frequented her friend's golf club, and a pair were standing together on the green. An impatient golfer took his shot anyway. From 140 yards away, the golf ball struck the male smack in the breast. The female watched her mate keel to his death on the seventh hole, par three. The golfer shouted, "Birdie!" and made jokes about adjusting his score card to reflect his success.

Cassie said, "I always felt sad thinking of the female having to go on alone." She supposed the story had stayed with her because of her own loss of a life partner.

Robbin said, "Sounds like a good argument for the harem method of mating."

Cassie gave him the benefit of the doubt here; likely he hadn't intended the conversation to go in this direction. She decided not to help him out, though; his awkwardness gave her confidence. She'd deliberately forgotten her sweater earlier, using that to excuse herself from the barbecue in order to give Robbin an opening. And she liked being in control.

"So you think we are a different species," Robbin said.

"What do you suppose the sandhill crane did after her mate was killed by the golfer?"

"I think she joined Earl's harem," Robbin said. He lifted Cassie's free hand and held it. Looked down toward the willow flats and extended his theory into a fairy tale. "She decided to see the world. Came to Wyoming, and met up with Earl down there by the willows. She stretched her slender neck up to Earl's muzzle and dazzled him with her feathered self." Robbin turned toward Cassie and ran his fingers along her wrist to the inside of her elbow. "She rubbed her long beak against Earl's antlers and freed them of spring velvet and polished them to a glow with her soft breast."

Cassie said, "Then what?"

"Earl forgot his harem entirely. Left his females to summer on their own, and attempted to fly."

"Until the first frost," Cassie continued, "when one late night the sandhill crane lifted her red-crowned face to the strange and eerie sound of her stag elk bugling its might and glory to herald the advent of mating season. Then she knew she'd be alone again, as sure as when the golfer birdied hole seven."

Robbin pressed closer to Cassie and moved his hand to her neck. He said, "Maybe Earl would do his instinctive duty for animalkind, but maybe he'd forgo his harem for a reed nest on the edge of a prairie pond—we have sandhills here, too, you know." He smoothed the hair off Cassie's face and continued his fable.

"Perhaps the two of them would create a third species brand new to the world. Feathers and fur blended with the ability to soar above the trees and bugle throughout the forest." Robbin pressed on Cassie's inner elbow, collapsing her braced arm, and drawing her down to the grass. "Maybe they'd do that."

"Break all known barriers of the species . . ." she said skeptically.

"Yes. Maybe." Robbin held her face and kissed her. Not too tentatively, not tentatively enough. Cassie drew away.

"I don't believe that could happen," she said.

"Cassie," Robbin warned, pulling her face toward him again, "I'm telling you, I'll grow some goddamn feathers and fly."

Maybe he had been right when he'd accused her of seeing him as famous. Maybe she should release the image of Robbin McKeag with crowds of women seeking autographs . . . or whatever else he'd like to give them. It was getting in the way.

The darkness deepened and so did the kisses.

Robbin said, "Let's go to my cabin."

Cassie slid out from beneath Robbin and stood up. "I'm not ready for that." She slipped her feet back into her sandals and bent down for her sweater.

"But, Cass"—Robbin sat up—"you're leaving for two days."

That was true. She'd announced before the float trip that she was using the days off that Boone had offered for a solo overnight hike, thinking she would appreciate the time alone after living so closely with strangers for almost a week.

"Cass?" Robbin called after her. She paused a few feet away and turned to him. "Have you had many lovers since Jake?"

"No."

"Any?"

"No."

"Holy Christ."

Darkness swooped like a raven wing over the forest as Cassie walked back to her camper. A turquoise rim that traced the shadowed mountains to the west offered just enough light through the pines to follow the path that wound behind the Barlow house. The stillness, the last of the birdsong made this a favorite time of day for her.

"I heard you talking to that gal tonight."

"Cassie?"

When she heard her name, Cassie paused reflexively and turned in the direction of the voices. Still in the trees, she stepped around to view the front of the house. Fee and Cody stood in the yard, near the dying coals of the cookfire, Fee scraping the grill with a long-handled spatula, Cody bagging unused napkins and paper plates from the folding table behind Fee.

"What did she say about that garbage you were carting off after the cookout?" Fee asked.

"She wanted to separate the paper from the plastic for her recycling bins."

"Recycling bins. That girl should understand that we've been taking care of the land for four generations now and we know how. Four generations, by damn; that demands some respect. We don't need a newcomer coming in here to show us how tree huggers do it. She's probably been talking to Robbin and next she'll have him nailing up pooper scooper stations on every other tree for your dingoes."

"They don't talk much, Dad. They're not real friendly."

"Apparently you missed your buddy slipping off on the heels

of that gal right after dinner. And you don't see neither of them right now, do you?" Fee scraped with extra effort at a spot, bending into the job. "I'm taking bets I can find them for you. Just two places to look—his bed or hers."

Cassie advised herself to just move on down the path and pretend she hadn't heard these remarks. She and Fee had tangled enough for one night.

But she didn't take her own advice.

She stepped into Fee's front yard.

"Hi. Sorry I didn't get here sooner," she said as if she had intended all along to return to help with the cleanup and was just now getting around to it. She began to knot the top of the plastic garbage bag in which she'd earlier packed the paper trash and dragged it toward the path she'd come from, leading to the main house. Then she returned, gathered up the remaining plastic spoons and forks, spilled out the dregs of wine, beer and lemonade from the cups as she moved around the tables. Silence and stares from Fee and Cody. She stuffed the load in the bag holding the used plastic. She kept her head down while she worked. Let Fee wonder how much she had heard.

"Just leave those here, missy. We'll burn them later," he said.

"Burning this stuff pollutes the air. Besides, if we don't support the town's recycling center, it will fold. I don't mind taking care of it."

She picked up the two bags and threw one over each shoulder. "It was nice to be a guest instead of the cook tonight, Mr. Barlow. Thank you." Neither Fee nor Cody responded, just watched her as she turned to walk back into the dark trees where she had come from.

She had accomplished nothing with her little stunt, she

reprimanded herself, only indulged her ego in a game of one-upmanship with Fee. The two trash bags bounced against her back as she followed the path toward the main house in the diminishing light. Even so, it was satisfying to replay the scene in her mind. She had walked right into the firelight and shown herself, before Fee could have taken a breath from his remarks about her. He must have been quite surprised, but her moment of superiority was already fading. If anything, she had done a disservice to her goal of making the ranch residents aware of some bad environmental habits they held by turning their lack of awareness against them.

Cross Wave was in a position to set an example for the many guests who might carry good ecological routines back home with them. Was there any more perfect place to represent the value of taking care of the earth than this valley with its abundance of beauty and wildlife? Rather than greeting hundreds of thousands of travelers entering Jackson Hole with a sign that said WELCOME TO THE HOME OF THE OLD WEST, there could be a sign that alerted visitors to a model of the New West, where taking care of the planet was more important than maintaining the anachronistic traditions of cattle ranching.

She sighed. Fee knew what she was up to, and she had better put her ego and her desire to prove him wrong behind her if she wanted to accomplish anything.

CHAPTER THIRTEEN

To appease Boone, Cassie wrote down her destination and gave him permission to send out the troops if she didn't show for work Monday morning. Of course, the troops would consist of Cody all by himself. He was known as an excellent tracker. Robbin had told her that when they were kids he never had to tell Cody where he was going or what time he left. Cody read the scuffed leaves and pine duff and knew it all—unless Robbin chose not to make it so easy. It became their language and sometimes their game, as he worked to cover his tracks or leave false clues. Robbin said he tracked intuitively—he could find Cody just because he knew him so well; Cody was physical in his pursuit—he used all five senses, trained through his boyhood to acuity. Often now Cody was called by Teton County Search and Rescue to help find a lost hunter or hiker. He had read the tracks after the cattle rustling, yet so much activity had taken place before he and Fee returned from Denver that he found very little to work with. Still, he continued to check tire treads whenever he was in town.

Despite Cassie's assuring Boone that she had often gone on solo overnights in the mountains, he was worried. He kept offering advice and weapons. Finally she had accepted the use of an old ranch truck to save her shock absorbers. Her trailhead was many miles down a rutted dirt road, and the garage had warned her earlier that the shocks on her camper were next in line for replacement.

After five days of going without some of her favorite treats on the float trip, what mattered to Cassie for this trip was packing really good food, which also meant extra weight. Real eggs, not powdered. Fruit, vegetables and cheese, instead of envelopes of dust that magically perked into protein after adding water. She left at first light, drove into town and picked up a mocha latte and pastry at the Bunnery. A power breakfast.

Two trails led to the destination Cassie had in mind. She'd told Boone she would use the footpath, rather than the horse trail, so she pulled into the first unmarked road to her left instead of driving another half mile north. Her pack weighed enough to push out a grunt just pulling it off the truck bed. She looked around self-consciously. It often felt like this at the beginning of a solo hike, as if a thousand eyes were watching from behind sage clumps and distant pines. She felt very aware of the need to impress herself with outdoor finesse, as if her indoor upbringing in Ohio challenged her abilities in the wilderness.

Hot air was pulsing off the sage flats now, but above the tree line snow could fall by sundown, so she needed to carry cold-weather gear. Still, she wasn't going to die if she removed her extra pair of pants, one of her two books and the can of Pepsi. Keep the hazelnut chocolate bar at all costs. After doing that, she slung the pack over her back and strapped herself into it with cheers from the invisible onlookers.

By now, early in the second week of July, the wildflowers had neared their peak. Purple harebell, pink geranium, the aspen sunflower, Indian paintbrush, blue columbine. The meadows held a crayon box of vivid color. Cassie crossed elk tracks, deer droppings and coyote scat and smelled bobcat scent left on a nearby boulder. She knew that, unseen, the bighorns had lambed, buffalo were nursing calves, the velvety antlers of the moose were fully developed and young raptors were learning to fly from their nests—and she was alone with this splendor of secret activity. To Cassie the world seemed swollen with surprise, opulent with possibility.

And so when she ascended the last of the switchbacks late that afternoon and discovered an enchanted camp, it seemed momentarily possible that it had been set up and was waiting just for her. She paused and lifted the bottom end of her pack away from her wet shirt and let the cool air thrill the hot skin beneath it.

Someone knew how to do things right. Two horses grazed, tethered to shrubs, their munching sounding like juice briskly shaken in a Mason jar. With the help of packhorses, campers could bring candelabra and fine crystal to dine in romantic glory at nine thousand feet. This particular couple was roughing it, but a sleeping tarp had been erected and dinner simmered in a black iron pot over hot coals. A tablecloth covered one flat boulder and was kept from blowing away by a pyramid of oranges and apples, and a Maxwell House coffee tin, rusted and fire-scorched, sat beside the fruit, crammed with wildflowers. She was Goldilocks peering in the window of Papa Bear's house.

These two had made a honeymoon hideaway and were now probably swimming naked in the lake just down the trail. But she didn't hear a thing and amended that to making love on the beach.

Approaching footsteps still hidden by a curve of trees spurred her to move on. She released the weight of her pack to let it hang again on her sweat-soaked shoulders. She loosened the waist cinch as she walked, so the heft of her pack rode lower on her hips, and head down, she watched her footing and hoped an empty site waited for her farther on, but not too much farther.

"Hey," a familiar voice hollered.

Cassie couldn't decide whether to hide in a bush or curl herself into a tight ball and roll downhill to her parking spot, but her first thought was escape. She had realized last night while being with Robbin that she needed this lone outing to prepare for the transition from being Jake's widow to Robbin's lover. It wasn't a simple process, no matter how much she wanted it to succeed.

Behind her an armful of wood clattered to the ground, hands were brushed on pants, fast steps came toward her. Cassie dropped down on a pathside boulder, one with pointy protuberances that dimpled her butt, and waited for her future to approach from behind her.

"Scared isn't a good enough reason."

"I wasn't scared."

"Sure you were. One man—then *none* for three years."

Insects buzzed and a hummingbird hovered over a red monkey flower. Slopes and valleys stretched out below her, rock faces in the near distance, the tiny sparkle of a lake miles and miles away on the valley floor. Cassie tried to place herself in the pattern, tried to think what lake that was.

"I made a nice camp," he said.

Somewhere along the way she had lost control of things. But

where? When was it that accident, coincidence, problems and shortages had taken control like a parent who swooped down upon a happy child, removed her toys and sang out, "Playtime over"? If someone else had described such a life, she would have thought that person was young, that person refused to know something and that person was demanding that fate take charge. *Discipline yourself or life does it for you*, she'd say. Yet if it were a person whom she respected who reported this, someone who lived life consciously and carefully, she would say, *You're all right— this isn't a discipline; this is an opening, an invitation. Follow the flow.*

"I made vegetable stew and I bought some chocolate cheesecake muffins from the Bunnery. You said you liked those."

He must have been practically on her heels this morning. Must have passed beneath the Bunnery's GET YOUR BUNS IN HERE sign only moments after she had. And then he'd taken the horse trail up, arrived probably three hours before her, with time enough to set up a portable love nest. A cloud skimmed across the sun, reminding her of the darkness that would come. The momentary coolness on her face reminded her, too, of how hot she was. She looked at Robbin.

He took that as acquiescence, uncinched her waist belt and lifted her pack off her shoulders.

Cassie waited for a sign of its impressive weight, a grunt, a raised eyebrow. He slung one strap over his shoulder, grinned and escorted her to their room for the night.

She watched his exuberance mounting. He loped down the path to the lake and fetched up a dripping can of Pepsi, sprayed it open and handed it to her. While she sat on a log and sipped it gratefully, he unstrapped her sleeping bag and opened it out as a blanket and spread it on top of his bag, already opened out flat on the ground cloth. He folded the edges of her top bag around and under the sleeping bag mattress and secured the bottom edge, corner to corner, with water-worn rocks. Then he came over to her, stooped down and smoothed her cheek.

"We're going to make love together," he said, "and you'll remember how wonderful it is." He kissed her lightly. "You've just forgotten."

"Has it occurred to you that I *choose* not to sleep with you for other reasons?"

Robbin stood up, looked down at Cassie and laughed.

"Robb, we haven't talked enough."

"No problem. We'll talk." Robbin bounded over to stir the stew, then stacked the extra wood beside the fire.

Cassie followed him. "It's not just sex, you know? It's an intimacy, something of a promise that we'll follow this thing between us as far as it takes us." She wanted to make him understand what such a bonding had to mean to her, but he was rustling through the panniers. She stopped talking. "Darn. Criminently."

"Watch your mouth, babe."

"You're not listening," she said from behind him.

"Sure, I'm listening. I know I remembered to bring salt. Bonding," he said. "Go on. Here's the pepper; where's the goddamn salt?"

Cassie sighed. "I'm going to the lake to bathe." She grabbed her dinky backpacking towel, clean clothes and headed down. When she returned, Robbin took a quick dip. Then they sat on logs around the fire and ate dinner.

After cleaning up and securing the food from bears, Robbin said, "Let's take our coffee up that knoll and watch the sun go down." He added, "I brought Grand Marnier to put in it."

"Did you bring more alcohol?"

"No, just this little sample bottle." He pulled it out of the food storage, then swung his head around. "Shit, would that have helped?"

He was trying, and she appreciated it. She followed him up the knoll, carrying her mug. It was just that she had already accepted the sexual magnetism between them, knew it was strong and wonderful, and had left on this solo outing to sort out what else there was going on. Such things couldn't be easily defined, so maybe even if she'd had the two days to herself she wouldn't have come up with anything more than what she already knew: she liked being around him, wanted to know what he thought, and cared about how he felt. He made her laugh, he interested her, she loved the way he looked and how his body moved, and his skin and breath smelled like home. She kept her head down, watching her footing, careful not to spill her coffee. Likely she had settled with herself as much as she was ever going to over this last leave-taking of Jake. When you loved a man for many years and were sexually true to him and he to you, sex represented so much more than physical lovemaking. Still, it was time to move on from being a widow.

And Robbin, how was it for him? She looked up at the back of his head as he led the way uphill. She remembered a photo of Robbin with the beautiful Juliana DeLuca in an old *Esquire* magazine stacked in Boone's pile of memorabilia. And there were many, many more photos of him posing with stars and models who were dressed in spangly dresses to skimpy bikinis, kissing, dining, dancing in Hollywood, Prague, Geneva and Paris.

But there could be variations on this theme she hadn't yet considered. The romance here could be that Robbin McKeag, once jaded, crazy, famous and rich, recognized something in her that he needed to make life valuable to himself again. That out of all the women he had been around she stood out in some way. Sure, and there were flying coyotes that dropped silver dollars over the campsites of good little girls. But it was just as unrealistic to believe he would drag her down to his promiscuous level, that if she slept with him tonight she'd become the tart of Teton County.

From the top of the knoll she turned and looked back over the lovely camp Robbin had created. Perfect fire circle of stones. Wood stacked to one side. Open-ended canvas tarp, three sides and a roof, facing the fire and the morning sun. She thought of Robbin selecting their menu, packing the panniers, maybe thinking tonight could be the beginning of—as the song goes—something big.

Look at him. He was sitting beside her on the grass, offering her the time she needed. Give him credit, she counseled herself. He wasn't lewdly chasing her around the campfire. He was letting her ready herself in whatever way she needed.

And she guessed she was ready. She turned toward him.

He checked her eyes. "Aw, Cass," he whispered. He took her coffee mug and set it on the ground beside his own. He took her face in both his hands. "Welcome back, Cassie."

She smiled. "Back to what?"

"To this." He laid small, gentle kisses all around her face. "And this." He kissed her on the mouth deeply. "And this." He laid her down, lifted her shirt and kissed her bare stomach.

Before it got too dark to find their footing, they headed back downhill to camp, forgetting their mugs.

Cassie and Robbin untied their hiking boots and stepped out of them before walking across the bedding, then began undressing. She did well with the removal of her socks and sweater and Levi's, but lost momentum when it came to her long underwear, top and bottoms, which she'd donned after the cold swim. She felt a sob gather in her throat. So much emotion crowded her, she couldn't label it. Was it the farewell to Jake as her last lover or the welcoming of Robbin as her first in three years? Was it the sensual overload of the moment or the long years of celibacy from the past?

Not long ago, Cassie had bemoaned the fact of her naïveté to Erin. She'd said, "Naïveté at thirty-four is not *cute*." Erin had replied, "Oh, cheer up. Somebody will think so."

Cassie swallowed back the lump of emotion and sniffed.

Robbin pulled her away from his bare chest. He scanned her face and then incriminated himself with a long series of hind-sighted errors. "Practically a goddamn virgin and I expect you to bounce into bed with me." He wiped a tear from the corner of her eye. "And when I barge in unexpectedly on your lone campout, too." On and on he went in his low, atonal voice, evenly inflected as always.

Cassie soaked it up like sage flats do an August rainfall. And in no time at all she was just as devoid of puddles.

Then, pretending he'd discovered himself committing a new transgression in the very act of asking forgiveness for past ones, Robbin said, "Good God" and covered her face with his hands. "I'm naked."

She was charmed by him and laughed. He shifted their bodies to lie beneath the covers, her head on his arm, and he adjusted the top sleeping bag to cover them both. "Now, how slow do we have to go?" He seemed to be asking himself. "We'll just neck," he answered. "No petting below the waist. Isn't that how it starts?"

Apart from lying on her side with her knees bent to keep alive the custom of bundling, Cassie put up no resistance to

Robbin from that moment on, and he put up no resistance to the knees. He attended Cassie with fingers and tongue, using only the tips and grazing only her surfaces, the very edges of her mouth, the very edges of her nostrils and, imperceptibly drawing away from her bent knees and bending his own knees between them, he volunteered to provide the barrier between their bodies himself.

And once in control of the drawbridge, Robbin suckered her into diving headfirst into deep water. By the time Cassie came up for air, she was leaning over a grinning Robbin.

"That's what I wanted," he said. He pulled the end of Cassie's single braid around and unwound the elastic holder and combed her hair out with his fingers; her hair fell around them like a blackout shade. Then he set to work.

Robbin moved his hand beneath Cassie's thermal top so slowly toward her breast that Cassie felt herself scoot downward to meet his approaching touch. He whispered wonderful words about her beauty. Mostly about her hair. Her hair excited him, Cassie could tell. Rolling her over onto her back, he took a long time pulling her top over her head, through her long, long hair, stretching his arm way out until he had to rise to his knees to pull it through to the end, and then he sat back on his heels to view the effect.

For the first time in three years Cassie looked at a naked man and his penis interested her. She laid her hand on him. Here was a strong-muscled man, she thought, a man whose face grew stubble this time of night, who had nothing about his body that made her think soft, until touching the skin on his penis, skin perhaps softer than her own vaginal walls.

Robbin gripped the waistband of Cassie's thermal bottoms. "Say yes, Cassie."

She did. More than once.

Robbin kissed her bare stomach, and his kisses followed the removal of her thermal pants. He knelt between her legs. "Good God, you are so beautiful with your hair fanned out like that."

"It's just hair," she said and wished he would lower himself down near her, to become one with their lovemaking, rather than viewing it. He took hold of his penis and placed it between her opened legs and caressed her with it there. When he was fully inside her, he stopped, and she felt him pulsing and felt, too, a rhythm of her own begin to direct her movements.

"You don't know how long I've wanted this," Robbin said, still kneeling, up and away from her. "To be here between your legs, your hair all loose . . ." He set the two of them into a slow pace. "I just wanted to fuck you with your hair strewn about."

And he lost her.

Cassie went cold.

He thrust strongly into her, holding his body away from hers, sitting back on his heels with her hips in his tight grip, off and unaware that she was no longer with him.

Cassie flung her arm across her eyes and a panel of hair came with it. And this set Robbin into a ferocious series of plunges, her lying there, faceless, with long, dark hair fanned around her.

She thought he would go on forever, banging against her, his testicles bobbing at her underside, his hands gripping her buttocks, and then she felt him release and rinse through her.

He flung himself down to the sleeping bag, breathing hard. He reached his hand over to rest between her breasts and said, "Don't go to sleep yet," then went limp with sleep himself.

Cassie lay in total stillness, while his fluids slowly seeped out of her and his breathing deepened and evened. When she was very certain he was soundly unconscious, she eased away and quietly got dressed. She put truck keys and credit cards in her jacket pocket and sat on the stump beside the campfire, her toes near the baking coals, to wait for dawn.

From the draws and coulees of her mind, flashbacks prowled. She recalled going to the Cowboy Bar one night with Robbin and the wranglers. They had sat on the saddles that served as barstools, backs to the counter in order to watch a high-stakes pool game, when out of the crowd emerged this lewd grin and hearty greeting.

"Cock Robbin. Hey, how you doing, buddy? This tonight's little birdie?" Incontinent eyes stained Cassie head to toe, then shifted to nod leering approval to Robbin.

"Camber . . ." Robbin warned.

Camber spoke to the group, with a special intention of entertaining Robbin with a reworked adage. "Cock Robbin ought to know that if you make a bird come in your hand, she'll let you come twice in her bush."

It wasn't that she had forgotten this episode till now, but rather had retained more faithfully what had occurred after.

Robbin had followed Cassie's escape into the women's restroom. "I don't know him. I don't like him. He's just one of those assholes that tries to chum up to certain people."

Cassie remembered a woman beside the sanitary products machine watching the two of them in the mirror, while she slowly peeled the paper on a Tampax like a candy bar she was about to eat.

Robbin had said, "I know some *nice* people. Honest, I do." And he'd taken her elbow and directed her out of the restroom, out of the bar and onto the boardwalk, where the night breezes were tethered to the rodeo grounds six blocks to the south and scents of horse manure and hay saddled the air. Tourists window-shopped around the town square. A cowboy cradled his infant inside his upturned Stetson and another strolled by with his border collie leading the way, the dog carrying a small white bag from the deli in its mouth.

Robbin took Cassie into the Cadillac Grille next door. Immediately a friend called, "Hey, Mac." Cassie could tell Robbin had counted on knowing someone in there. "Come celebrate with my wife and me. Our kid just graduated from junior high tonight."

After introductions, the two of them took seats. Robbin's friend continued, "God, Mac, he's my baby. The other day I was cutting his fingernails, and Roger says, 'Come on, Dad, I'm twelve years old—I can do this myself.' I said to him, 'Shut up. Let me see your toes.'"

Cassie remembered Robbin looking over as she laughed, as if to say, See, I told you. Nice people.

And that was the memory Cassie had pushed to the front pastures of her mind like a blue ribbon breeder. But now starved night creatures slunk out of hiding, and in the way of predators working the edges of the herd, yipped at the heels of her huddled misery until it stampeded into anger.

First light drew the moisture up from the ground and sharpened the chill. Cassie stood and, before leaving, let the cramps ease out of her legs.

Robbin stirred, reached to pull the covers around himself tighter, then rose up on an elbow with the discovery of Cassie's absence. He looked toward the fire, now ash-covered embers, and sat up.

"Cass?"

He said it as sort of a warning to himself. Then testing the equipment, a kind of one-two, one-two, are we on? into the microphone, he monotonally said, "Come back to bed, Cassie; it's too early to get up."

Cassie's rage ballooned and split.

"Nobody *fucks* my hair." She kicked at the dying coals, and sparks and ash lifted to lend power to her wrath. "Nobody," she yelled, bending at the waist with the effort. "Do you get that, *Cock Robbin*?"

Robbin had sat up during her tirade and now his head collapsed into his hands.

Cassie spun around and headed down the path, disappearing into the mist that rose up the mountain as the valley's warm night air met with the cool air of the higher altitudes.

CHAPTER FOURTEEN

Cassie's hairstylist wore a rose quartz crystal on a chain around her neck, which had once become entwined with Cassie's hair during a trim. For long minutes it had looked as if the only solution was to cut off twenty inches of her hair. Today that wouldn't be any problem at all.

After leaving Robbin on the mountain that morning, Cassie drove her borrowed pickup to Snow King Resort, reserved a room, showered and presented herself to Kara. While Kara stared at her in the mirror and plotted, Cassie looked around the familiar shop as it was reflected in the mirror.

Geodes lined the shelves along with natural-ingredient hair and skin potions. A small sign next to the products read: PLEASE DON'T STEAL THINGS, IT'S BAD FOR YOUR KARMA. An old song of Meat Loaf's trickled from the small speakers in the ceiling corners. "I want you. I need you. There ain't no way I'm ever going to love you." "Two Out of Three Ain't Bad."

Kara guessed it: some men you can wash out of your hair;

others you have to cut out. Cassie agreed to her suggestion of donating her hair to be made into wigs for cancer patients. That involved cutting it all in one great hank.

"You have to be sure, though."

"I'm sure."

Kara gathered her gear and Cassie picked up a book lying nearby. *The I Ching.* She flipped through the pages, not really absorbing anything.

Kara came over to stand behind Cassie and began her work. She talked about how she'd house-trained her white German shepherd, Farkas, who wore a crystal as well, and lay in the doorway of Kara's shop, probably scaring off as many clients as he charmed. The training had to do with Farkas wearing Pampers. Cassie didn't think she was paying enough attention to fool Kara. She couldn't keep her mind on the story. She sat in Kara's chair, her head feeling lighter and lighter as Kara snipped around her skull, loosening the gathered and bound swag of hair.

But maybe it wasn't the loss of hair that made her head feel lighter. The lightness seemed to come from inside, as if inner congestion was now descending to her chest area, like a bad cold first impacts the sinuses, then drops to weigh heavily as a bronchial infection. Cassie felt as if some animal were clinging with all four clawed feet to the inside of her breastbone, the way an opossum clings to a tree trunk. And like that homely marsupial, Cassie worried that the sad weight might be largely nocturnal. She hoped not; all she wanted was to be rid of that hair and then succumb to hours of sleep.

Monday mornings were breakfast rides; Cassie needed to be in the horse barn by six to get camp set up and breakfast ready by nine. With a half hour to spare, she drove the pickup into the

ranch, parked it and walked first to her camper. She opened the
door to find Robbin asleep on top of her bed.

He woke instantly and swung his feet to the floor. "Thank
God. Cassie, you scared the shit out of me. I haven't slept all
night." He rubbed the heel of each hand into his eyes as he sat
on the edge of her bed. "Listen, Cass . . ." He stood.

"My God. What have you done?" He spun her around to
view the back of her head, where the great length of her tresses
now wisped at the nape of her neck. Cut so short, each hair
seemed to spike outward in chagrin over its radical fate.

Robbin pressed his forehead against the back of Cassie's
head and held her tightly from behind for a long, silent moment. Then without meeting her eyes again, he let himself out
her door.

Cassie dressed carefully in full ranch regalia: jeans, cowboy
boots, cotton knit undertop, long-sleeved flannel shirt, down
vest, bandanna rolled and tied at the tips to hang around her
neck. The royal blue felt hat, which she usually crammed down
on her head, she folded and stuck in her back pocket. In this
outfit she could peel off layers as it warmed during the day, then
layer them back on as it cooled. Most every summer day began
in the forties, warmed to the eighties, cooled off again after sunset. She stuck her leather gloves in her other back pocket to flap
halfway out and set off for the barn.

She thought on her way that Robbin was like bad money.
Counterfeit didn't hurt anyone as long as it was passed lightly
along to the next unsuspecting customer. When someone
stopped to examine its actual worth was when the damage occurred. Her job was to let Robbin pass lightly through her life.
Her plan was twofold: get through the day, then tell Boone it
was her last.

Cassie entered the barn, and the movement and soft morning talk that had been in progress halted.

She said, "Good morning." Walked directly to fetch Bruce's saddle from its resting place, flung across the partition of the last stall—and found it gone. She had rehearsed each of these steps in her mind and now, as if she were in a grade school play and one of the props was missing, she wanted to bolt offstage.

She ad-libbed. "My saddle . . ."

Nobody answered her.

She turned and caught Boone and three wranglers staring at her. All eyes shifted to Robbin, who sat on a bale of hay with elbows on his knees, hands dangling between them. His own gaze was fastened to the floor. He did offer her an exit line. "Bruce is ready to go," he said without looking up.

She walked through the barn toward the corral, where her horse was tied near the gate. She wondered what it said about the atmosphere that not one person had referred to her as "*Butch Cassidy*."

Lannie had provided the stew, Cassie had learned when she'd complimented Robbin on it two nights ago, and Lannie, according to Robbin, was the only person he'd let in on his plan to camp with Cassie. Lannie, who wanted more than anything to be an actor like Robbin, had been sworn to secrecy.

Now Boone stalled Cassie's progress. He stepped forward and touched her arm. "Did you forget?"

"What?"

"Your photography shoot is this weekend."

Act like you don't care that you just impetuously lopped off twelve thousand dollars, she recommended to herself. Act like you realized that all along. Say, What's money when a woman wants a new hairdo? Say something quick. They're all looking at you.

Robbin dropped his head into one hand at Boone's words and was now leaving the premises. The wranglers watched his back, and Cassie felt them trying to put the pieces together. He wasn't known to pass up prime taunting material.

"Cassie," Boone pressed, "you forgot, didn't you?"

She nodded, speechless at what she had done to herself.

"Think they'll still want you?"

"They wanted the hair." Cassie watched Robbin's retreat. "They all want the hair." She mustered some gaiety for her on-lookers. "Guess I'll tell them where to find it." Then she left for the welcome sunshine of the corral.

Boone followed her out. "You'll be worrying next," he said, "about your camper payments." Cassie turned to smooth Bruce's neck to keep the extent of this blow from being a full-frontal exposure of fear to Boone's kind face. "Welp," he said, "this is a good time to tell you what I did."

He explained that GMAC had sent someone to repossess her vehicle. Only a full payment of the loan would suffice to halt that action. Boone had opened his office safe and paid cash for the full amount; her title was waiting in the office for her. "Now you can pay it off at your leisure and not worry anymore. And you look real pretty with your hair like that."

He watched himself shuffle his feet a moment. "Say," he ventured hesitantly, "you don't have to have a head operation or anything, do you?"

Cassie leaned her forehead into Bruce's mane and laughed like she had not imagined being up to doing that day. Boone went on that she seemed darned tame this morning, so did Robbin, and maybe they knew something. He said, "That's very *short* hair."

Cassie could use that on the phone later to describe her new hairdo to Marley the photographer. Think of surgical prep, she could say.

Robbin stayed out of sight the rest of the day, didn't show up for dinner, so it was just Cassie and Boone eating alone in the kitchen. Afterward, Boone read the papers he'd missed because of the breakfast ride, while Cassie cleaned up the kitchen and cooked for tomorrow. In the weekend's mail she had received a recipe from her mother for making ten piecrusts at one time. Each unbaked piecrust was rolled into a ball and frozen till needed. That was her mother's way of reestablishing a more conventional relationship, Cassie assumed, after their discussion about unfaithful husbands. But it was a big help. Apparently everyone but her knew cowboys and pie go together like hillbillies and grits.

Her mother would probably approve of Cassie's haircut. She'd alluded before to women over thirty wearing long hair as being considered unseemly in her day. But her mother said many strange things. When Cassie had mentioned that she parked her camper beneath a Douglas fir, her mother had said, "Do you name all the trees out there?"

Once, as she mixed her piecrust recipe, she paused to pop into the bathroom to check her image in the mirror. At first glance she looked fresh-faced with her new haircut; with further study she looked like a pileated woodpecker.

Cassie decided to bake two pies, one peach, one apple. She felt compelled to get serious about providing the expected, since she was indebted up to her *pileum* to Cross Wave, but she preferred to think of it as a wise career move.

The telephone rang and Boone got up to answer it. Cassie could tell it was Marley. Boone exchanged pleasantries with Marley before handing the phone to Cassie, then pulled the phone back again and said encouragingly to Marley, "You'll really like her hair like this."

So much for working up to the bad news. Marley's first words were, "Say you didn't cut it."

Back to her crust making. The phone rang again and again Boone handed it to her. She heard bar noises in the background. She said, "Hello."

"Could this just be a lovers' spat? Because if it is, I'm sorry for what I said and I forgive you for cutting your hair all off."

Without responding, Cassie hung up.

Boone raised his eyebrows to her. She said, "Obscene phone call."

Boone lifted his chin in response, then shook his head regretfully before returning to his reading. His head snapped back up. "But that was Robbin."

Cassie suspected this was the joy of victimhood: this center of peace where she felt very innocent, very good, stainless. Her disposition was even; mildness was her middle name. She had done no wrong and she owed no one—unless you counted the thousands of dollars she would repay Boone by handing over two-thirds of her paycheck for the remaining weeks of the season.

As for Robbin, he left a gift-wrapped box inside Cassie's camper door the morning after his obscene phone call. A lapis lazuli pendant, beautifully designed by the goldsmith on the square. On the back was engraved: CASSIE LOVE ROBBIN. No punctuation. It read like a command.

Maybe she'd wear it someday, she thought while examining it, because someday Robbin wouldn't have anything to do with her life. He'd continue to be a famous somebody and she'd be whoever she was, and life would go on.

In fact, she realized even now that Robbin was a decent person, spiritually lazy, emotionally backward, but good. As the ancient *I Ching* philosophy might say, Robbin had a deep well, rich with good, clear water, but his bucket had a hole in it. Or was that sentiment put forth by Ricky Nelson?

She put the lapis lazuli away in a drawer and took out Jake's field watch, with the extra hole she'd once punched in higher up the strap. She wore the huge watch to bed that night and kept it on, except for showers, as she'd first done after Jake's death.

The new water bottles were taking off well. Mrs. Penny especially loved the idea and she promoted the use of them in her aristocratically bullying way. Next Cassie had planned to introduce some vegetarian meals, then stir up a little awareness of how the cattle were destroying the streambeds, but she had no energy, as if she were on the verge of coming down with the flu. No energy, no interest, just moved along from chore to chore.

Robbin began to tease Cassie in front of the guests during dinner again. Offered a sweeter, more playful version of his earlier barbs. Tonight he set her up like a pro with flirty lines for her comebacks, but Cassie, nestled in her cozy apathy, failed to produce her share of the entertainment. Briefly Robbin ventured into hostility, but he quickly drew back from that in the face of her palpable vulnerability.

"Ennui dulls one's intellect," Mrs. Penny informed Robbin, coming to Cassie's defense. She folded her dinner napkin over her finished plate to discourage flies. "A grown man needs more purpose to his life than writing little stories and bedeviling busy people." And if actual work was not to Robbin's liking, perhaps he should consider rounding out his scholarship, because if she recalled correctly, Robbin had not studied many of the classics.

"Not having read *Walden Pond*, for instance, is a disgraceful lack in anyone's education," Mrs. Penny said.

Discovering a sturdy opponent in Mrs. Penny, Robbin attacked. "Thoreau was a wimp."

"Why . . ." Mrs. Penny's cheeks reddened.

"Thoreau made a big whoop out of 'roughing it' two miles from his mama's kitchen. He strolled home for *lunch* half the time he was claiming a life of solitude in the wilderness. Thoreau," Robbin said, "was a mama's boy."

"A great mind," Mrs. Penny pronounced, "and a great man."

"A pansy. A boob. Can you imagine when his book came out what the townspeople thought? Hell, they walked their toddlers to Walden Pond after naps every day to sail toy boats, and here's old Henry writing about it like he was camping in the tundra."

"Shame on you, Robbin McKeag. Just shame on you for your lazy mind. The easy way out is to criticize and belittle."

Robbin reminded Mrs. Penny that she was at the moment criticizing and belittling him.

"I'll have my Drambuie now, Boone," she said. "Cassidy, I shall sit by the fire and you may bring my coffee at your leisure." Mrs. Penny thumped her director's chair away from the end of the picnic table, where she always sat, too dignified and too arthritic to manage the benches.

Cassie joined Mrs. Penny at the campfire after clearing the table, feeling that any antagonist of Robbin's was a friend of hers.

"That lad has to be made to want something more than he is capable of getting with his toothy smile and sulky film scenes," Mrs. Penny confided. She sipped her Drambuie and, with a fingertip, tucked a silver hairpin deeper into her chignon. "If it takes some rough language and a few hard knocks to his ego, so be it. I'll contribute what I can." Mrs. Penny threw back the rest of her Drambuie, then poured a swallow of her coffee into the glass and swished it around. She confessed to Cassie, "I have long yearned to take a studded belt to the boy's backside." She tossed back her concoction.

Sometimes Cassie liked Mrs. Penny quite a bit. Sometimes she felt they had a lot in common.

Afterward Cassie wandered off down a wooded path along the wide stream. A moose stood knee-deep in a beaver pond and dunked for river-bottom vegetation near the opposite bank. The moose lifted her head to stare Cassie down, then resumed her murky grazing.

From behind her Robbin said, "Guess what was found in the cellar of Thoreau's cabin at Walden Pond?"

Cassie swung her head over her shoulder. Robbin stood there with his hands in the pockets of his khakis, his crew neck cotton sweater sleeves pushed up past the elbows. Wondering how he could come up so silently behind her that not even the cow moose noticed his presence, she glanced down to his sneakers, then turned away from him again to discourage his company.

"Bent nails," he answered for her. Cassie didn't react. "Hundreds of bent nails. The pantywaist couldn't hit a goddamn nail on the head."

Cassie thought she'd use the second hand on Jake's watch to time how long the moose could browse underwater; she had read that their nostrils closed.

Again without a sound, Robbin enfolded Cassie in his arms from behind. "Cassie, can't you get over this?" He set his face cheek to cheek with hers. "You don't insult me anymore, you don't talk to anybody. You're so lonesome, Cass, and I don't know what to do about it."

Robbin's arms were parallel bars across Cassie's front, and one hand gripped the inside of her elbow, where his thumb brushed a small patch on her skin over and over till the skin there began to feel raw to her. Twenty-three seconds. The moose was still submerged.

Not hiding the action from Robbin, Cassie glanced at Jake's watch, twisting her wrist around so she could see it.

Robbin said, "Jake was a good guy. He'd beat the hell out of me, if he knew." He set his nose against Cassie's cheek. "Two lovers and one of them is a shit," he said sympathetically. "I would want Jake to approve of me."

Leave it to Robbin to be concerned about a popularity poll among the dead, Cassie thought. She stood as apart from Robbin as she psychically could, pulling her energy away from those places he pressed against, her arms and back and face, holding her real self in a tightly contracted knob in her chest.

"I'd want him to think you were passing from one good guy to another," Robbin was saying, and something about Jake having lived in a way that made her expect honorable treatment from men. He drew back to look at the side of Cassie's face.

Her eyes were cast patiently across the stream. Surely by now the moose needed air. She fought an urge to rush into the water and jerk the moose's head up. Cassie felt suffocated herself.

"You want me to leave, don't you?"

She nodded.

Robbin laid his forehead on the top of her hair, then dropped his hold on her. A few paces away, he said, "Here's the big one: tin cans. Piles and piles of them in Thoreau's basement. But don't tell Mrs. Penny. It would demoralize her."

CHAPTER FIFTEEN

From her window midmorning the following day, Cassie watched Robbin's truck pull in behind her camper as she was putting fresh sheets on her bed. He was driving illegally again, just as he had a number of times that summer. His license had been suspended as a result of his accident last winter. In five more days it would be restored to him. He challenged fate like an adolescent, Cassie thought, and just like an adolescent, he would be chagrined over his bad luck should he get caught.

Robbin jumped out of the driver's seat and hollered, "Hey, Cass."

She went to her door. "Don't you think it's rather stupid to drive and risk having your license revoked again?" She stood a foot above him in her doorway. "Why gamble another six months of having to inconvenience your friends and coworkers by relying on them to get you everywhere you want to go?" She sounded like an irked fishwife, but she didn't care; his carelessness annoyed her.

Robbin had an open, expectant look on his face and impatiently cast a warm glance back toward his truck. He said, brushing away the most trivial of her criticisms, "They don't mind."

"That's not the point—" she began.

"Cass," he interrupted, a tinge of restrained excitement to his voice. He glanced back once again toward his truck. "Come see what I've got." He came over and took her hand. He walked her over to peer into his open truck window, stepping aside with a soft, anticipatory smile to watch her.

"Aw," she cooed. A golden ring of fur lay circled in sleep on the front passenger seat.

He opened the door and lifted the small body into Cassie's arms. "It's for you." And in the surprised silence that followed, he prompted, "It's a puppy." Then he hastily followed with a series of facts about its breeding and personality. Golden retriever, registered, with papers, a male and eight weeks old. He'd driven to Dubois early that morning to see the litter.

"You drove all that way?" There and back was more than a hundred-mile round-trip.

"All the pups were great, but this little guy was the best."

"He's so beautiful."

As if recognizing an important moment, the puppy woke, raised his heavily lashed eyes and bobbed his tail. Both faces bent to greet his awakening and like a shy toddler, the puppy buried his head beneath Cassie's chin.

"Aw," she cooed again.

"Will you keep him?"

"I would love to."

Oddly, it was Robbin who said, "Thank you." As if she were doing him a favor by accepting his gift. "He'll keep you company," he said. "He'll help."

Before Robbin got back in his truck he stuck his face down

to rub noses with the puppy in Cassie's arms, then with Cassie. He said again, "Thanks."

She saw that smitten, milky look in his eyes as he watched her from the driver's seat. She smiled, and he shifted into reverse and backed out. She had read once that there were two kinds of sexual energy expended. One was inspiriting, exalting; the other was dispiriting, deflating. The first was an act of exhilaration and delight in union, and the second was a release of tension. Robbin, Cassie decided, thinking of his softened gaze just now and how it pulled her in and excited her heart, caught his prey with a promise of the first in order to exercise the second.

The puppy squirmed in her arms and she carried him to the shady spot beside her camper and sat down in the grass to play with him. She laughed as he pounced on pinecones. When he crawled back into her lap to nap again, she checked Jake's watch and decided to make a run into town. She moved her jar of wildflowers from the counter to the sink, put the puppy on her bed and pulled out from beneath the shade of the Douglas fir. She would need things for this new puppy: food, dishes, a bandanna for his neck. Also, they could stop at the bank, where all the tellers at the drive-up windows passed out Milk Bones.

When she came out of Kmart with her bag of purchases, the puppy sat whimpering for her beside a glistening puddle on the floor. She'd forgotten that part. She cleaned the floor. To keep the puppy from missing her, Cassie pulled a purple sock with red and yellow stripes out of her laundry bag and gave it to him for company, then trotted back across the parking lot for a big box of newborn-sized Pampers.

"I don't think we can have that, babe," Robbin said gently when he first spotted the puppy wearing a disposable diaper. "I mean, Cass, that's not the way it's done. . . ." But he was interrupted by Boone entering the kitchen for lunch, which was a bit late today.

"So, so, so," Boone sang out. "I hear Robbin gave you a present." Big one-armed shoulder squeeze to Cassie. "A present from Robbin," he said again to ensure that she got the fact. "Where is the little fellow?"

Before Cassie could answer, she saw Robbin cock his head toward the puppy on the floor, with a warning to Boone in his eyes.

"Hmm," Boone said, spotting the pup lying flat on his stomach, back legs stretched out, with his Pampers bunched up. "Is he hurt?" Boone asked, with a careful eye out for any hints from Robbin as to how he should conduct himself.

Cassie explained her hairstylist's fail-safe method of potty training. It would be completely accomplished in only five days. Leave the diaper on in the house and around the camp eating area, take it off everywhere else. The idea was that dogs refused to potty on themselves.

"You know," Boone cheered, "I think Mrs. Penny is going to like this idea."

"Mrs. P would like to see *all* animals wear diapers," Robbin said.

"What's the little fellow going to be called?" Boone asked.

And Cassie relayed another theory, pleased to discover she had two already as a new pet owner. "The puppy will *earn* his name. I'll live with him for a while and watch him draw the perfect name to himself."

Rested, the puppy was now ready for play and bounded out from beneath the kitchen table with Cassie's sock hanging from his mouth, emitting little puffs of baby powder fragrance from the Pamper. He sat before Robbin, and Robbin stooped down to play with him.

"I don't think you should do that," Cassie said, when Robbin began tugging playfully on the puppy's sock. "It gives him the idea that disobedience is fun."

And so began their own tug-of-war about how the puppy should be raised. It was important according to Robbin that the puppy experience a masculine influence in his life. Robbin took it upon himself to provide that. Which, as far as Cassie could tell, meant that Robbin roughhoused with him, tried to get him to carry a stick around in his mouth instead of a purple striped sock—"He's a retriever, for God's sake"—and removed his diaper at every opportunity.

"Fan-fucking-tastic, Cassidy."

"What?"

"Your puppy 'pottied'—as you call it—in my shoe."

"He did not."

"Oh, great." Robbin shot his eyes skyward. "You're supposed to be his *mother*, Cassie, not his *lawyer*. He shit in my shoe."

"Then," she concluded, "it's your fault."

"You're raising a little pansy hoodlum, Cassie." One broad finger stretched outward. "He ate my Chips Ahoy." Two fingers out. "He dragged my clean laundry all the fuck over the place." Three fingers. "And he shit in my shoe." She was emasculating the little bugger, and he wasn't going along with it; in his cabin the puppy was not wearing a *diaper*. "I took him out to a tree and showed him the *right* way."

Cassie got that mental picture—Robbin standing before a tree, teaching by example how real men urinate—and burst into laughter.

"Laugh, Cassie. He squats like a girl. He does not lift his leg."

She reminded him that all puppies potty like that until they mature, but Robbin refused to back down. "You've made him peculiar."

Among the new batch of guests this Sunday were recruits of Mrs. Penny, a first-chair cellist from the New York Philharmonic, scheduled to make a guest appearance at the Grand Teton Music Festival, and his twenty-six-year-old daughter, Betsy, also a musician. Boone, Robbin, Cassie and as many of the Cross Wave guests and staffers as Mrs. Penny could bully were gathered on the lawn as the welcoming party when Cody drove the van into the driveway. Cody had been handpicked by Mrs. Penny to meet the Slaters' flight due to his penchant for fancy western wear. This morning he looked like the movie cowboy he was once fated to become, with his embossed Lucchese boots, leather vest, and a turquoise silk bandanna wrapped twice around his neck. His best summer Stetson shaded his handsome features.

During the introductions Betsy Slater warbled over Robbin's remarkable talent. "Robbin! I adore your movies." She quoted praises published in various reviews. She herself was dressed in expensive cowgirl attire, what was termed in Jackson Hole "Hollywood Western": cowboy boots with purple and red butterflies and a western-cut shirt in lavender velvet. Nobody could work in such clothes, not even ride a horse. Her pants were so tight, Cassie winced with the discomfort she imagined they inflicted on the woman. Betsy wore heavy silver bracelets on each arm and turquoise earrings that swung against her shoulder-length blond hair.

When the puppy loped up, without his Pampers but dragging his sock, Betsy mewed, "What a sweet, darling dog. Robbin! May I pet him?"

Would she throughout her weekend stay, Cassie wondered, pronounce Robbin's name with surprise, as if she'd just discovered his astonishing presence within her field of vision?

Robbin said, "That's *not* my dog." Wishing to get this straight before the diapers appeared, Cassie guessed.

Boone said, "Not mine either."

They both looked to Cassie. She owned up. And added, "I wouldn't pet him—he bites." She regretted the lie instantly, fearing it served as a neon indicator of her feelings for Betsy Slater, who was leggy as a model, very smooth, mannered, poised and musically talented. Her only physical blemish, as far as Cassie could detect, was an ugly yellow-green bruise on the side of her neck, from her lifetime of violin playing. But even that was a badge of expertise and dedication.

Cassie was still struggling with her own lack of expertise and dedication, feeling stuck by the debt Jake's death had created and her own poor choice had extended—she still couldn't think of the thousands of dollars cutting her hair had cost her without slapping her forehead. But after the truck was paid off and she had no more excuses for delaying her life, what then? She had no particular talents, though she wasn't a bad watercolorist; no driving passions, except for the love of this mountain valley. Neither would buy her groceries or keep her puppy in dog food. Whereas Betsy Slater, not yet out of her twenties, was a professional violinist.

At the moment Cassie felt midwestern and dull. The new haircut didn't help, even though Erin, Becca and Lacy had raved over it, using words like "dramatic" and "stunning."

Now, despite Cassie's warning, Betsy swooped down toward

the puppy, and fulfilling Cassie's fantasy, Betsy did not pet the dog but tugged on the purple sock. The puppy growled in a croaky young voice and bared tiny sharp baby teeth. Betsy shot upright and looked around, as if searching for a chair and a whip.

As Cassie had experienced in certain social circles back east, introductory conversation during dinner at camp involved an exchange of school names. As soon as the Slaters learned that Cassie had attended an obscure state university in Ohio, she felt dismissed. Next, dinner talk moved into favorite French cafés, exquisite out-of-the-way murals in Italian chapels and walled German villages that Cassie knew nothing about. References made to other people were prefaced with brief listings of their advanced degrees and their families' historical lineage.

Cassie could discuss the personal and the intimate with universal perspective, but she could not discuss the global and the cosmopolitan with intimacy. Her favorite subjects, psychological motivations and their spiritual outworkings, for instance, seldom set off the trail of happy-talk that common memories of quaint European gardens so easily did.

If she had thought to find sympathetic company in the cowboy McKeags, she was wrong. Robbin had traveled all over Europe, filming and partying, often inviting Boone along. And they could both drop names with the best of them. If the rich and famous hadn't visited their ranch, they had visited the rich and famous. Until now Cassie had been a star among her peers as a woman who boldly traveled alone to unheard-of villages in Nepal, Pakistan, Peru and Patagonia in order to meet up with Jake. But tonight she was pitied for never having visited the museums in Europe.

"Robbin. I'd love to see the river."

"Um . . . sorry, I have to help Cassie with the dishes." Robbin received a beaming smile from Boone with those words, an astonished nod of approval from Mrs. Penny, and simple astonishment from Cassie.

"Let's give her the night off!" Betsy exclaimed. "You wash. I'll dry."

It didn't quite happen that way. Robbin broke the first glass and cut his palm.

Cassie had caught on earlier in the summer that she was expected to follow the tradition of the chuck-wagon cook on roundups and be prepared for every event this side of orthopedic surgery. She had read up on first aid and had stocked an emergency kit. Not that this shallow slice called for anything more than a paper towel blotted twice on the wound.

Robbin followed Cassie to her tent and while she was smearing antiseptic on his hand, he whispered, "Betsy-Wetsy has her goddamn sleeping bag in my tent already."

"Why are you telling *me*?" she hissed back at him and slapped a bandage over the cut.

"Well . . . I don't know. . . ."

Cassie ended up washing the dishes. Betsy couldn't, due to an allergy to detergent. She offered instead to help Robbin dry.

"Robbin! I have *all* your DVDs. Every one of them."

"Every one. Hmm. Cassie doesn't have any."

"Cassie. Shame." Betsy shook a long pink fingernail at Cassie's nose.

"I have many of your father's CDs," she said to even the score.

"Isn't that cute? I don't have a single one." Betsy giggled and posed against the grill. "Of course I *grew up* hearing his music. Mother says I learned classical prenatally. Mother is a pianist, as you know. When I was a teeny thing I hummed Beethoven before I spoke. You see, I learned it *in utero*. I knew all the pieces Mother performed the winter she was pregnant with me. Knew them by heart. Oh, look what I've done."

A long black band of burned grease graced the white jeans on Betsy's backside from leaning against the grill.

"Robbin! Very carefully dab a soapy cloth on my tush and get this awful stuff off me."

Suddenly Cassie felt ancient, bored and unnecessary.

"Betsy," she said dully, "go change your clothes. Robbin, go with her." Cassie tossed her dishcloth in the soapy water and walked away from camp. How could people do that? Just get naked and squirm around with each other hours after meeting? Share emissions and involuntary muscle contractions without any foundation of intimacy?

The puppy romped beside her, excited that they were going somewhere new. Cassie walked through the trees, then out across the flats. She followed a faint game trail that wove through the sage toward a single giant boulder mysteriously sitting in the open. Glacial erratics. During the massive upheaval that had created the Tetons, this lone boulder, as big as a barn, had rolled and rolled till it landed there. She climbed up an easy slant on the side, the puppy under her arm, and sat on the flat top of the big rock. The puppy explored, then perched on a high point and seemed to take in the view.

The more Cassie examined the mentality that must lie beneath the ability to freely partake of sexual delight with anyone who was physically desirable, the more she found the idea startlingly appealing. To live that frivolously could bring its own rewards. She bet Robbin didn't lie awake nights pondering whether he'd met the day's encounters with his best self. Not Betsy either.

Yet, twenty minutes later when Robbin climbed the boulder to sit beside Cassie, she soon heard herself arguing defensively against just that.

"What do you *want*?" Robbin began. "Why the hell can't I get anywhere with you?" He quickly added, "I'm not committing to anything, but you can at least let me know."

So Cassie tried.

"You're not . . . sensitive to me—other than in the broadest way physically."

"Shit, Cassie. I want to sleep with you. Plain and simple. So how is that going to take place—and just tell me that plain and simple."

Cassie leaned back on her hands and laughed—he sounded so frustrated and riled. "Over my dead body."

"That's how I remember it last time," Robbin muttered. "Me over your dead body." He looked out over the sage flats toward the rocky tracings of peaks on which the setting sun balanced. "I was *sensitive* about your lonesomeness and got you a puppy," he said in his own defense. "Nobody *told* me."

"That was perfect." She loved the little guy and reached over to pet him. She smiled at Robbin. A dozen times a day she marveled that he knew to do that for her. "That was wonderfully insightful." She watched the sun being absorbed in jagged, toothy bites by the rocky tips of the mountains. It sank out of sight, and the hush that always followed descended on the birds. The land darkened briefly, and if Cassie hadn't known better, she would've thought it was time to gather her belongings and head hurriedly for home, but minutes later the sun angled just right and a rose-gold glow spread across the sky. The birds twittered happily, like children given an extra half hour to play.

"You're too goddamn much trouble, Cassie. I feel you *pull-*

ing at me for something. Something not there. It's not *anywhere*, Cassie."

Robbin got to his feet to leave. He stood above her. "You know what *I* want? A woman—with brains and beauty. I want her in bed with me . . . until the fantasy wears off. Then I want another one." Before turning to leave, he added, "You hear moans and groans in the night—it's not the wind in the trees."

Betsy-Wetsy.

"You're kind of a jerk, Robbin."

He stepped over her, straddled her legs and stooped down before her. "You're kind of a cock—"

She pressed her hand over his mouth to stop him. He held her wrist. It was a staredown for a moment. Then she removed her hand.

"We could have had such a great summer, Cassie."

"I know."

"You made me bite my lip," he said, testing the soreness with the tip of his tongue.

Cassie leaned forward and lightly kissed his lower lip. She tasted blood and like a good sheepdog turned bad, Cassie moved in closer and went for more, acting like the teaser he'd accused her of being. After the kiss ended, she wished she was Robbin's kind of woman, because it really could have been such a great summer.

She leaned back on her hands again, and Robbin swung himself over to sit beside her. Across the brush, the community of chizzlers popped in and out of holes in the ground, scurrying behind sage for one last hunt before dark. The puppy was thrilled at the sight of them, circling the top of the rock to keep them all in view.

"You dislike me," Robbin stated.

"No," Cassie said, surprised he'd think that. "I don't dislike you."

"What, then? What is it?"

She had to drop more deeply into herself to find the true answer to that.

And there existed only one unfortunate but obvious answer for a woman like her. Women like her, if any remained, invariably fell in love with men to whom they'd given their bodies. By the time they had come that far, women like her were already deeply attuned to the man in question and wanted to share more. Cassie shook her head and shrugged her shoulders. Robbin dropped his head and seemed to have given up hope of understanding, then lifted his face to her and appealed one last time. "Tell me."

It seemed only fair, so Cassie said, "I love you. But it's nothing to worry about."

Robbin's upper body straightened in a stunned silence; he seemed to vibrate with alertness. Cassie rose and gathered the puppy in her arms and climbed down the boulder. As she scuffed through the sparse woods back to camp, a mental argument ensued. The voices took on British accents and the debate sounded to her a lot like a Monty Python skit on BBC.

This woman is a deviant. An aberration. Her actions are a defection from the norm.

Naw, this woman is just principled. Untainted, unsullied. She's an innocent.

She's not an innocent! This woman is an oddity—a thumbless glove, a finless fish. This woman is eccentric. Diagnostic.

She's distinctive. Piquant.

Pee-kant! She's silly. An absurd specimen of womankind. This woman is an anomaly. She belongs in a zoo!

This woman is of the worthy species of virtuous females we need to see more of. She's moralistic. Notably matchless.

She's a freak!

Well-ll . . . a bit.

Few people still sat around the campfire beyond Cassie's tent. Most had retired for the night. She saw by the flickering of firelight that Robbin had finished the dishes before he'd joined her on the boulder. She spotted distinct signs of his workmanship—the soggy dishcloth clumped at the bottom of the empty dishpan along with the towels, and her bathwater set on the cook grill to warm over the embers. After depositing the puppy in his horse blanket nest under the worktable, she wrung out the dishcloth and hung it and the towels over a branch, then carried the bucket of warmed water to her tent.

Aside from exhibiting atypical tendencies of the sexual and emotional sort, loving Robbin, Cassie decided, would involve no discomfort. She wasn't heartbroken. She wasn't mooning. It felt more like a virus that would eventually pass. If an antidote was available, it was that jewel of wisdom: hair of the dog. Which was built into her natural environment for the summer. Robbin himself would cure her.

But really, she thought, moving the washcloth languidly over her body, face to feet, she had the morals of medieval mystics with Bibles gripped close to their chests. One thing she could count on: Robbin would take this confession of hers as an admission ticket to her sleeping mat.

What would a freak do if she didn't want to join the circus?

Right. Hair of the dog in one potent dose. She'd get ready for him.

Twenty minutes later she lifted her tent flap to set her bucket of bathwater outside. Robbin was sitting on a picnic table facing her, his feet on the bench.

He said, "Like a sister."

She said, "No."

And she stepped back inside her tent. She blew out her kerosene lantern and stood in her long T-shirt, kicking her foot free of her underpants, which in a last-ditch change of mind she'd felt compelled to put on after bathing. Her eyes adjusted to the dark and she watched fingers curl around her tent flap.

"Robbin. There you are." Betsy called in her distinctly schooled pronunciation.

"Night, Betsy," Robbin called back, and ducked inside Cassie's tent.

Cassie bent quickly to grab her panties from around one ankle. Her white underwear, now dangling from her fingers, seemed to fairly glow in the dark. She stood facing Robbin and listened to Betsy's steps fade.

Finally, Robbin stepped nearer. He took Cassie's panties from her—as if they were a belated gift he hadn't decided to accept until now. He placed his arms around her in a gentle greeting, then laid her on her sleeping mat.

For a crazy moment, Cassie thought he was just going to tuck her in, there was such restraint to his movements.

He stood above her, cupped a hand behind the heel of each

of his shoes, and scooped them off. He pulled his sweater over his head and knelt beside her.

All, blessedly, without speaking a word. Perhaps at last he had caught on to the factor that had been primary in his defeat up till now.

Robbin lifted Cassie's right hand and flattened his tongue on her palm and drew it along the length of her middle finger, then sucked the tip of it until Cassie's breath caught and she reached for him.

CHAPTER SIXTEEN

An hour before first light, Cassie felt Robbin easing himself out of her bed, limb by limb, pulling his warmth with him. She slept another half hour.

Up alone now, starting breakfast preparations in the stillness of dawn, she listened as only a few birds tested single notes at the new day. Once it had been a painful hour, when she craved more warm sleep, but now Cassie had begun to favor it above others. The time never lasted long enough. No matter how early a start she got, how often she envisioned getting everything to the point of readiness with time to spare for a quiet cup of coffee alone, thirty minutes after she lit the fire, happy campers began to call greetings to one another and meander to the Porta-Potties set in the trees. Then the rush was on. Lucy Ricardo working in the candy factory. One thing never finished before a second and third needed tending, complicated further now with the puppy chasing her pant cuffs.

"Hi," Robbin said, the first one to arrive in the camp kitchen. His eyes were sweet as they caught hers.

Pancakes to flip, eggs to fry, sausages to brown. Cassie moved up and down the grill, breaking off to slice strawberries at the worktable, pour juice at the picnic table, set out syrup, butter, cream and sugar. Robbin didn't appear to notice; he leaned against the cutting board built between the grill and her worktable.

"Isn't this a great, beautiful day? Honest to God, Cassie, I could wrestle a goddamn bear. Come on, demand the eyetooth of a grizzly—I'll bring it before your coffee cools."

In her attempt to keep up with the frenzied pace that now generated its own momentum, Cassie raced from worktable to grill, detouring around Robbin.

"I feel full of clichés. 'I never knew it could be like that.' 'Bells are ringing.' 'The earth moved.' 'I'm all shook up—da dum.'" He laughed at himself.

Bent down for a mixing bowl, Cassie held the door of the lower cabinet and nudged Robbin's leg with it as a hint to move.

"One of us," Robbin announced, looking down at her, "is gushy this morning."

She rose. "Sorry." She looked him in the eyes. In case it wasn't obvious, she said, "It's a rushed time for me." She grabbed a fistful of silverware and napkins and held them toward him on her way to rescue a pancake. "Help me?"

"Cassie, really, I never knew . . . Cassie? Hey." He pulled her shoulder back. The pancake, in mid-flip, missed the griddle and landed runny side down on the bars of the grill. She looked at Robbin—he'd get the message now, wouldn't he? "We got it on last night, Cass—what is this?" Robbin's lower lids squinted upward a bit. Robert Redford did that in his movies. He would look at a woman studiously, and those lower lids would squinch up, and the audience would know that the man had an insight. Robbin was having an insight. "I get it. You're busy."

Cassie moved around him to finish slicing strawberries into the fruit bowl. Then reached for the bananas.

"Just tell me this." Robbin turned to follow her. "I made it with you, and you didn't scream at me for fucking your hair or some damn thing. I did it right. Right?"

His self-involvement at the moment reflected his lovemaking of the night before. She wanted to say to him, a year off the movie set and you're still successful at arousing women; you've lost none of your skill. That had seemed to be his goal last night and the assurance he needed this morning.

She paused slicing a banana. "You were good, Robbin. So good it's a shame there are only two of us to applaud you this morning."

The lower lids came up for an encore.

Cassie moved back down to the grill.

Robbin laid the silverware and napkins down. "You're not doing this to me again," he said and circled around the work-table to face her across the grill. "You were *there* with me. The whole route."

Cassie scooped up sausage links and set them in the warming oven.

"You're not going to rattle me, Cassie." He bent over the grill with his hands flattened to lean closer, then leaped back as his palms were nearly branded by the hot bars. "I *know* what happened last night," he said, rubbing the singed hairs on his wrist where a flame had licked. He looked around to see who else might have spotted him nearly frying his palms crisp. "You were *there*. I made sure of it."

Cassie headed for the picnic table to set the silverware out herself. Robbin came around the grill and grabbed her wrist. "I made *love* to you last night."

Cassie gave him her full attention. "You *played* to me last night."

"I made you crazy. I made you cry."

"Congratulations. We'll tell them at breakfast."

"Stop that," he hissed, then flashed his eyes over her shoulder as others approached the area. "Give me another chance." He nodded to someone coming up behind Cassie, released her arm and assumed a casual facial expression for the company. He half sat on the corner of the picnic table with his hands in his pockets. "Everybody gets at least three chances," he said conversationally, as if talking about a base-ball player up to bat.

"Oh, give the boy another chance," Mrs. Penny said, passing to her seat at the other end of the picnic table. "He's right. Everybody deserves three." Playfully, she shook Robbin's shoulder. "But no more." Then added that he should not be sitting on the table where decent people were planning to eat. "Shoo."

Others seated themselves, and breakfast was on. Afterward, with the horses saddled and waiting outside the corral, Mrs. Penny, the Slaters, Boone and seven other guests mounted for a midmorning trail ride into the mountains.

"Come along, Robb, we're ready to ride," Boone called.

"I'm not coming."

"Welp, don't hang around and pester Cassie." Boone hoisted himself into the saddle. "What're you going to do?"

"Pester Cassie."

"That's fine, son." Boone turned his horse toward the trail. "See you later."

Robbin watched the single-file line of horses and riders move into the trees, then grabbed Cassie around her waist. "What's going on?"

"It's true you made me crazy last night; you're a wonderful lover. And you made me cry; I was completely there with you. But, Robbin"—she paused to get the right words— "afterward . . . I felt like a teen screamer in the theater audience. What I got last night was a performance. Robbin in the role of Sensitive Lover. Robbin needing only one take to show a little tenderness here, a little wowing there, long build to the crescendo, the sweet fade-out."

She thought he looked a bit pleased at her description. He also seemed to recognize that she was going to carry this discussion in a direction he wasn't prepared to follow. He tried to reroute it; he traced a finger around the scalloped hairline at the edge of her cheek. She became still and intent, the way a restless animal did when petted and not used to the feeling.

"You love me."

"I know." Cassie shrugged one shoulder; everybody had their crosses to bear. She turned to her dishwashing. Then she tried once more. "What did you give me last night?" she asked.

"A good time, Teacher?"

Robbin was losing interest in this talk; he was ready for more activity, but Cassie pressed on. "What did you *exchange* with me?"

Robbin smoothed his hand heavily down his own face, forehead to chin. He glanced at the sky, then swung himself up on the picnic table and rested his feet on the bench. He propped his forearms on his knees and, looking defeated, he sighed. "Body fluids is not the right answer."

Cassie was sure Robbin never failed to give his all during any performance, and he had given his all last night. And maybe that was the extent of what he had to give. It would be simple if that was enough for her. There was the sensuousness of Robbin's mouth, his blue eyes, that muscle beneath his eye that tucked when he smiled. There was the vitality of his everyday body language, his open rapport with the world, his easy flow of energy, wide affections. Most of all, she was attracted to his hunger for something beyond the bright star he'd made of himself. It was Robbin's potential that she had fallen for.

But potential, Cassie knew, didn't always sprout. Seeds sometimes remained seeds, hardening their hulls for a long dormancy—nuts, for example.

Maybe she was an anomaly, an absurd specimen of womankind, but way at the other side of the zoo was Robbin, and he was on the same side of the bars she was.

He sat now, sulking—as Cassie interpreted it—and watched her while she shook out tablecloths, packed food back into the truck bed, and stored the clean dishes in plastic bags to keep them dust-free in the cupboard beneath the worktable.

After his long silence Robbin said, "Betsy-Wetsy asked me to take her to the concert tonight."

Whole other worlds of morality existed that Cassie was a stranger to. She thought of last night when the three of them had washed dishes. Betsy had rattled on about her mother—still married to Betsy's father, Alexander—who disliked traveling; her father's mistress, Joanna, who enjoyed traveling but disliked parties; and a new girlfriend of her father's who adored parties, giving them and attending them, but disliked leaving New York City. Since Joanna, the mistress, was recovering from a hysterectomy and couldn't accompany Alex west, Betsy was filling in. Cassie supposed it made perfect sense to Betsy that Robbin may have chosen Cassie's bed over hers last night without that precluding a possible vacancy in his love life.

Robbin said now, "They were wondering if you'd like to be

Alex's special guest tonight. A reception is being held afterward in his honor at the conductor's home."

"They?"

"Betsy and Alex. Betsy says her father has taken a fancy to you."

Cassie said, "I don't think so. I don't want to be the cause of Alexander Slater's infidelity to his wife, mistress and girlfriend."

"It's okay—he often dates other women."

Cassie had felt lonesome before in the company of others. This lonely sensation slithering its webbed fingers over her heart was not new. But she had not felt it before with a man she'd lain with all night. One she let lick her straying teardrops, among other things. She sat down at another picnic table across from the one on which Robbin perched, set her chin on her folded arms and stared at the mountains.

Robbin approached and laid a hand on the back of her head. "I did that on purpose. I wanted you to know there are worse men than me. You're not very experienced, Cassie; there *are* worse men, or plenty just as bad. Doesn't that cheer you up?"

His rationale briefly sent Cassie into laughter, and Robbin straddled the bench beside her. "Also, I'd hoped to make you jealous. I didn't tell Betsy I would take her tonight."

Easy to forget with Robbin's sexual expertise that he was still so inexperienced socially that he would attempt such a crude maneuver. No one past the stage of rented prom tuxes would consider that a slick move. Cassie could laugh again. Though Robbin hadn't said he'd told Betsy he *wouldn't* take her either, so perhaps he was a man after Mr. Slater's own heart.

Cassie lifted her head. "Robb, you may as well go with her. There won't be any more nights for us. I just need more than you're interested in us having together."

"Goddamn you, Cassie." Robbin stood and turned partly away from her with his hands on his hips. Then he turned back and kicked the bench leg with the side of his sneaker. "Just stay off your high horse, Cassie. Even I don't pretend to *love* who I fuck." He strode off to his truck, cranked the ignition too hard and squealed off.

Cassie thought she might stay there all day with her head in her arms. She could mope all day and then, later, when everybody waved good-bye in their evening clothes for the concert and party, she could be Cinderella cleaning up the kitchen.

Before she'd become aware that she was stranded without a way to get back to the ranch, Robbin spun back down the road in reverse. Looking straight ahead, he said emphatically, "Get the fuck in."

After they bounced down the dirt road a mile, she said, "We have to manage this." She was thinking about the long stretch of working together all summer.

He glanced briefly out his side window, a gesture before answering. Though it took him another moment to respond. "We will . . . I guess."

During her late-afternoon break, that lazy time of the day after lunch was cleaned up and before dinner preparations began, Cassie returned to her camper and saw that Robbin had left a CD on her countertop, the next installment of "The Countess and the Cowboy." That was a good sign. Perhaps he had settled something within himself and felt friendlier toward her. She had a couple hours, so she grabbed her CD player, called the puppy and took off for a spot beside the river.

Cal Carrington was six feet tall and then some, blue-eyed, big-chested, small-waisted and handsome. He carried a reputation as a supreme horseman and hunter, knowledgeable about the wilderness and almost savage in his fearlessness. He dressed in traditional western wear with the added drama of silver-studded leather cuffs, a colorful scarf knotted and flared behind him, a tall hat, leather chaps, and high-heeled boots with fancy stitching. He was forty-one years old, and Cissy had never met anyone like him.

Cal had never met anyone like Cissy either. At age thirty-five, she was beautiful, elegant, aristocratic, a proficient rider and small-game hunter herself. She was a powerful figure in society, wealthy, with a reputation for getting what she wanted or going into a rage until she did. And what she wanted when she arrived in Jackson Hole and decided to stay was Cal Carrington as her guide. Cissy sent the French maid and six of her trunks back east that first morning. She and her daughter, Felicia, would stay. Cal had promised he'd guide another party on a pack trip, but Cissy handed him a fistful of money, more than he had ever seen, and said she wanted him to take her instead. Off they rode with a string of packhorses loaded with supplies. They stayed out for twenty-two days, camping and hunting, leaving Felicia with a cowhand to watch over her.

Cal called Cissy his "fancy dude" and from that time on they spent the summer in each other's company, riding during the days, dancing in town at night, disappearing for weeks in the Teton Wilderness, hunting big game. Cissy wanted trophies for her home back east in Dupont Circle. The two of them were the talk of the valley. Cal took Cissy to his Flat Creek Ranch, six miles of rough trail up Sheep Canyon, and she fell in love with the remoteness and beauty of the setting.

That evening after dinner Cassie drove into town and she thought about the story of the countess and the cowboy. That could have been the kind of summer she and Robbin spent: a romance against the backdrop of the Teton Mountains by day; dancing at the Cowboy Bar at night. She was probably too serious for her own good.

Cassie knew Sheep Canyon and Flat Creek Ranch. She recalled driving that two-track to the headwaters of Flat Creek, where the ranch was located, no faster than fifteen miles per hour, the road was so rough and embedded with boulders. She had hiked around the lake and had seen what Cissy had seen and understood how the woman had fallen in love with the land there. Anyone could tell, as well, why Cal had chosen it. If the rumors were true that he had been a horse thief at one time, this canyon would be the place to hide the horses. Only one way in and easily guarded.

Cassie understood this love for a piece of land. She was falling in love with Cross Wave. The ranch was in a varied and beautiful area. It held both mountain views and flowing water, forests and wide-open flats. By now she had covered every inch of it during her hikes and knew the old adage was true that people loved what they knew well.

Tonight she was meeting Erin for dinner at the Cadillac Grille. Erin's lover was from Bozeman, Montana, a political figure with a marriage not quite cleared in the courts yet; often he wasn't free during conventional date nights—a situation that worked well for Cassie, since she was invariably free.

Afterward, she and Erin walked next door to the Cowboy Bar for a drink. Harrison Ford was between movies and back in the valley, and his houseguest was rumored to be Jimmy Buffett. Erin always knew the scuttlebutt. Since she worked in real estate, she considered it her job. If Buffett was visiting, and if Erin could leave her card with him, and if he was interested in purchasing

property, and if she sold it to him, Erin would be in sheared beaver and sapphires before you could say "Margaritaville." Erin's
broker had handled the deal many years ago on Ford's ranch,
then bought a spread of his own with the commission.

Erin claimed a small table for them where she could keep
her eye on the action.

"Robbin has his band of merry men providing a buffer guard
for the stars," Erin said, looking toward the back corner.

"Robbin's here?" Cassie was surprised. She sat up straighter.
"Is he with a kittenish bottle-blond thing?"

"No women, just nine, ten guys."

Erin named the faces she recognized besides the locals—
the writer Jim Harrison, the painter Russell Chatham, Jimmy
Buffett.

So Robbin hadn't gone to the concert after all. The realization had barely sunk in when Cassie spotted Cody stopping the
waitress on her way to their table. He gave her some money, then
came over.

"Are you Rin? Robb said nobody's looking for property right
now, but he'll pass your cards around."

"What a sweetheart." Erin leaned over to dig into her big
leather bag, placed on the empty chair beside her, pulled out her
business cards and handed several to Cody. He said Robbin was
sending drinks over for them.

"Robbin's really okay," Erin said, after Cody returned to the
group of tables pushed together in the back corner.

That was exactly what Robbin had said to Cassie a while
back about Erin—except he'd referred to her as Rin, short for
Erin-tin-tin, alluding to the unfriendly watchdog qualities Erin
had exhibited over Cassie during their first meeting, right here
in the Cowboy earlier in the summer.

"You don't like him," Cassie reminded Erin. "You think he's a flasher." Erin had once said Robbin threw open his soul just to hear girls scream.

"I think you ought to give him a whirl, Cassie. You live too safely."

So it worked, Cassie thought, remembering another night here when Robbin had glanced off Lacy's shy flirtations and Becca's warm politeness to melt down Erin's glacial-lily presence. "Get the guard dog charmed and you're halfway into the vault," Robbin had said later.

Eventually Becca and her date joined their table, then a couple of ski patrolmen who had worked in the ski village with Cassie this past winter, and soon Lacy brought in two men from Cleveland, Ohio, in town for a petroleum conference. She had met them at the Four Seasons concierge desk where she worked.

The tourists, Lacy whispered, had been afraid to come to the Cowboy Bar. They'd heard stories. Bar fights. Cowboys beating up anyone wearing a necktie. Horses galloping through with drunk riders, shooting up the ceiling.

Cassie and her friends played on the tourists' fears and related the terrors of living in the Wild West, along with the delights. Cassie told about skiing every day last winter during her lunch break. Becca described once living in a yurt and having to snowshoe a mile to her car. And Lacy narrated her famous story of being charged by a bull moose while making a call on a pay phone—not one block from the town square.

One of the Cleveland men, dazzled by the locals' lifestyle amid such glorious everyday beauty, said, "I'd move here in a minute, except I couldn't find work that would even cover my medical insurance."

"Insurance?" Cassie said, as if it were a foreign word, and her friends laughed.

"You don't have any?"

Erin said, "I had the money once for insurance, but then I couldn't have afforded my season ski pass."

"You *ski* without *insurance?*"

"That's stupid," the other Cleveland man pointed out.

It always ended like this. Tourists were fun for only a little while.

Busy promoting her philosophy of mastering the ability to take risks as a form of security, Cassie didn't notice at first that Robbin had approached. He stood beside her chair with a cocktail straw clamped in his teeth.

Pleased that he was feeling friendly toward her, she greeted him. "No luck in picking up anyone tonight?"

Robbin looked down at her, his head straight and eyelids lowered. He said, "How about you, chick? Wanna go home with me?"

"I was holding out for an offer from someone wearing a prize rodeo belt buckle."

"I need a ride," Robbin said. "Will you settle for just a belt buckle?"

"You have one?"

He tapped the brass square at his waist. "L.L.Bean."

"Let's go, stud."

Before the two of them got away, Lacy, in her enthusiasm to impress upon the tourists that she and her friends were more than stupid people who skied without insurance, introduced Robbin McKeag, movie star. It gave points to the locals—they weren't all losers—but it wasn't fair play and broke the unspoken code of the valley: locals never gave away the identities of resident or visiting notables.

Robbin took it well. Greeted each of the men by name and shook their hands. On the drive home Cassie thanked Robbin for the new installment of his screenplay and praised his work. Though she wasn't any authority on screenplays, she was a big reader and knew a good story when she encountered one. It was a relief that she and Robbin had moved past their sore place. She would have missed him if he'd decided not to be friendly.

When she dropped him off at the main house, he shut the passenger door, then stuck his head back through the open window. "You love me," he reminded her.

"Will you *drop* that?" Cassie said. "I'm never going to tell you another thing."

CHAPTER SEVENTEEN

A week later Cassie strolled along the riverbank and watched her puppy sniff small piles of mud and sticks that muskrats had left as scent mounds. The puppy, still without a name and still untrained, had outgrown newborn Pampers and moved into the toddler size. She laughed as his furry head hunkered down between his shoulders and he stalked something that only he had heard in the weeds. Abruptly he leaped, coyote-like, his golden body arcing in the air, and landed deep in the tall grass.

Summer was at its peak now, and this morning everything seemed to buzz and blossom. Cassie watched a calliope hummingbird, the tiniest bird in America, return to a nest that sat like a flattened pinecone on the limb of a conifer. The nest was an inch and a half wide and barely distinguishable among the pine needles with its covering of pale green lichen. She knew the nest had been built with shredded bark and moss, held together with spider silk, because she'd found one on a fallen limb, had taken it home and investigated it. In her backpack she carried small

Ziploc bags in which to collect findings to examine more closely. She remembered the time Fee spotted her sorting through dried grizzly bear scat with a twig. He came upon her just as she unearthed the skull of a rodent. She held up her prize with a big grin, and Fee said, "Something for your soup pot, missy." For the first time they had laughed together and she hoped that Fee felt, as she had, that maybe the other person was okay after all. A sighting like the hummingbird nest took a trained eye or someone whose curiosity about the natural world stirred a passionate awareness. If she could make a wish, it would be to share the magic of that world with others. She imagined someday walking with her children into the forest, whispering to them about the discoveries they were making. She often thought she would enjoy taking out a group of ranch guests, but she was busy enough cooking for them.

By now her days and evenings had fallen into a comfortable pattern. The ranch and the surrounding meadows, forests and riverbanks felt like home. The cattle had been trailed to the high country in the national forest and would stay there until late fall. The ranch pastures seemed to be restoring themselves in the strong sun, though they needed summer's typical late-afternoon showers and those had been lacking.

She had found the ranch dump and it wasn't pretty. An old computer, a refrigerator and cans and bottles were mounded in a dip in the land that kept the mess from view. Worse, near the barns and repair sheds she had spotted places where used motor oil from trucks and tractors had been poured right into the ground. The good news was that Robbin had begun to ask her questions about her interest in land and wildlife preservation. She had gathered along the way that Robbin's income supported both the cattle and guest operations on the ranch, yet his career had put him at a distance concerning the actual control over how his money was spent. He trusted Boone, Cody and Fee with that. Lately his interest in how that control was exercised was tipping the balance in ways new to all four of them, perhaps most particularly Fee.

She glanced at her watch. Time to return to the main house. Robbin was lending himself and his truck to carry the recycling bags into town. A big step right there.

Without calling the puppy, Cassie stepped off the path and ducked behind a cotoneaster bush. She was teaching him that it was his job to stay alerted to her, not her job to call him to attention. This was Robbin's idea, and she thought it was a good one. Soon the pup perked his ears and turned in all directions, looking for her, then darted up the path a few yards, down the path, then back toward the river again. He settled himself a moment and used his nose. Cassie laughed when he found her. He wriggled his hindquarters so hard that tail met snout.

Robbin's truck was parked by the storeroom and he was just slamming the tailgate closed. He had already loaded up all the trash bags.

"Robb, you should have let me help."

"Didn't take long."

Five minutes later, after gathering her things, Cassie opened the passenger door and lifted the puppy to deposit him in the front seat.

"Huh-uh," Robbin said from behind the steering wheel. "We are not taking Baby Huey."

Dismally, Cassie looked from Robbin to the puppy in her arms. The big lug had paws the size of cow patties. Baby powder fragrance puffed up from his Pampers, the purple sock hung from his mouth. But Baby Huey? She remembered the cartoon character from her childhood. He was a sweet, dumpy, bonnet-wearing duck whose diaper was pinned in front of his big tummy.

"Just like you said he would, Cass. He *earned* his name."

He added, "I'm not going into town with a dog wearing a diaper."

"I thought you were a big star," Cassie challenged, turning her dismay into an attack on him. "What good does it do you if you can't do stuff like this?"

"You think I worked my ass off so I could drive around my hometown with a diapered dog? I did it so I could refuse stupid things like that."

Later, after the truck was unloaded at the recycling center south of town and everything had been sorted into the proper bins, Robbin drove back into Jackson and accompanied Cassie to the Valley Bookstore to pick up a book she'd ordered. She had a running list of books she wanted, always did. Someday she'd have a home with books everywhere, on bookshelves, tables, chairs, stacked on the floor, lined along the steps of a staircase. She wanted to open books, read bits and pieces, set them aside, read bits and pieces of others. Have them with markers hanging out, have them read twice, and have some not read yet at all.

Robbin collected his usual paperback conspiracies, then lingered near Cassie in the philosophy section. He picked up M. Scott Peck's *The Road Less Traveled* from the shelf in front of him and leafed through it.

"Hey, Cass. This guy says sex is a path to spiritual growth. Listen to this—"

"He says more than that," she interrupted. "I've read that book."

"He says orgasm breaks our ego boundaries, expands us. And when our ego boundaries are cracked we can become one with the universe." Robbin looked up. "I think we should crack our egos together some more, Cassie. Get more enlightened," he said, squinting his eyes to assume a frown of seriousness.

Cassie had five books piled in her arms. She was getting great tips along with thank-you notes from guests—a thing she hadn't expected—plus she had sold more paintings from the ranch gift shop. She was keeping ahead of her planned payments to Boone on her truck, but even so, she would need to cull out three of her choices and buy them another time. Robbin gathered his stack together and followed her to the register.

Back home Robbin whipped through Peck's book in no time, using a lime green highlighter to indicate the passages Cassie should reread. She used a hot pink one to respond. He made another trip into town for more books from the philosophy section. He highlighted a quote that said it was a far more enlightening experience to love a sinner than a saint. And another that said sex was a meeting of the carnal and the spiritual—that it grounded the sacred and raised the earthly to the heavenly. "You're a fast reader," Cassie joked, "but a slow learner."

"You're not getting it, Cass. Sex is everywhere. Sex is *it*." He described the interaction of river water evaporating upward to meet warm air in order to become rainfall in sensuous detail, and he pointed to the peaks of the Tetons thrusting through cloud matter. To believe Robbin, the whole world was working in continual orgasm. And it was entirely spiritual.

She had begun to love their talks.

One evening they went walking, Baby Huey romping ahead of them, and Robbin said, "What is it you want to do most of all?"

That was easy. "Get out of debt."

"After that. What about your painting? What do you want to do with that?"

"Just be able to keep on doing it. Sell enough paintings to buy more paints, cold-press paper and frames."

"You're quite good. Someday you could support yourself with your painting."

"That would be wonderful." The image stirred her.

"Then aim for that. Get that desire clear in your mind. Construct your daily life toward that goal." He added, "I know that's hard around here." They walked farther. "We could talk to Boone about clearing a room someplace where you can work and not have to pack up your stuff all the time, like I see you do in the kitchen."

Some sweet sensation rose in Cassie's chest as she imagined such a room. And the sweetness filled her further as she imagined herself living her life as a painter. Yes, that was what she wanted. Paint. Be outdoors. Those two things. Support herself with what she loved. Then, as the old jump rope jingle of her girlhood went: "Next comes love, then comes marriage, then comes Cassie with a baby carriage."

Robbin said, "It might take years, but if you want painting to play a big role in your life, you have to start living that way now." They walked a while and then he said, "Every time you take action on a dream like that, it's as if you're constructing that experience you want, piece by piece. It's no different than anything else we create—like one of your paintings in which you layer color over color. Or one of my films that involves take after take. Or how those cabins over there were built with log on top of log. You know?"

"I think so. That's how relationships work as well."

Robbin was silent for a few steps; then he said, "Sure, makes sense."

At the end of the evening, Robbin said good night, bent down to rumple Baby Huey's ears, then straightened and kissed Cassie on the cheek and left for his cabin. Kissed her like it was a regular thing, she thought, watching him cross the lawn between her camper and the cabins. A part of the routine. A nightly tradition.

Someone had clued the press in on the fact that Robbin was out of the loony bin—as one headline phrased it—and was in Jackson Hole writing a screenplay. Since not many people knew about his writing, in fact only the two families and a few of the wranglers, suspicion began to drift toward the only person who might see himself as benefiting from this leak. Lannie, young and handsome in Robbin's blond, muscular sort of way, carried considerable ambition toward the spotlight. Asked about it, Lannie denied any involvement. But who else would invite the kind of attention now pummeling the ranch? Constant phone calls, photographers parked along the road, a few brazen enough to tromp across pastures, even approach the main house. Reporters milled around town asking the locals questions. Robbin's agent had gotten wind and was pressuring Robbin to walk through this door that was opening for him. But Robbin was adamant. No interviews, no photographs. And Lannie was advised that his job on the ranch was threatened.

"Didn't do it, wouldn't do it, boss." Lannie had stopped drinking, now ordered root beer—Robbin's favorite brand—at the Cowboy Bar, wore khakis instead of jeans, sneakers instead of boots. Cassie hoped Lannie shaped up, because it was unlikely anyone could find a backup cook this late in the season. And she knew exactly who would be burdened with the extra work if he was let go.

Meanwhile, Robbin announced to Boone during dinner in the main house that Cassie was an artist.

"Why, I know that. She makes nice pictures."

"No, I mean she's a real artist, Boone. She needs a place to work."

Cassie let them talk about her and followed the discussion between son and father. She loved to watch them together.

Before dinner, while Cassie was washing lettuce she'd gotten in town from the farmer's market, she and Robbin had talked more about success, because Cassie felt conflicted about what that idea meant and how it would affect her life. She wasn't after the same things Robbin had experienced.

He had said, "Success isn't being a hit with others. It's doing what you care about and letting go of the outcome."

That had been his challenge throughout his career. The movie industry was based wholly on the outcome. A film was seen as a product and success was rated by the revenue that product generated. Eventually Robbin had had to learn to separate himself from that viewpoint and work with his own gauge of what success meant. He had to learn to let go of the outcome.

Cassie asked him, "What do you mean by that?"

"You do your work—you do it carefully, with all your attention and love. Then you let it go. What happens after that is not your business." He repeated, "It is just not your business." That had been hard for him to learn; the culture tried to make it an artist's business. Robbin had learned over the years that such a goal sucked creative energy dry. He wanted her to learn from his mistake.

"Welp," Boone said now, thinking for a moment, "what about your old room upstairs?"

Robbin nodded and turned to Cassie. She felt that delicious warmth fill her chest again. This was really going to happen. "It's got good light," Robbin said.

She moved her paints and papers in after dinner. From the storage compartment beneath her camper bed she unpacked all her brushes. Found an old enamel coffeepot in the kitchen to hold them and set it on the table Boone and Robbin had carried up for her and moved before a window. A scarred maple twin bed was pushed against the wall and the top of the matching chest of drawers cleared for her books on technique. The shades on the two windows were pulled up to expose a view of the front yard and the side yard over the kitchen, her camper under the fir. That night Cassie stayed up late, painting and painting. In between she walked around the square corner room, hugging herself and dreaming about possibilities.

She tried not to stare at Robbin's fake mustache, its rakish droop, the way its angle echoed the line of his eyebrows and the slant of his haircut. She pretended to read his cap: KING ROPES, SHERIDAN, WYOMING, with a lasso encircling the logo. The royal blue of this cap was Robbin's color. Those eyes, even narrowed with his habit of dropping his lids to look down at her, dazzled blue like the thermal hot pots at Yellowstone on a bright day. Entering the Cowboy Bar during peak tourist season without the buffer of wranglers and with the recent attention of the press demanded subterfuge, and Robbin explained about the disguise he kept under his truck seat. To Cassie he looked transformed—unschooled, rough. But once in the bar, Robbin was just another one of the men in Levi's and dirty caps with surplus hair on the face.

"Ever been kissed by a man with a mustache?" Robbin asked, catching her stare. He steered her toward the bar. "Want to be?" he asked when Cassie admitted she hadn't.

"If I find a man who interests me in here, I'll send him over to borrow it," she said.

"You're kind of a prude." Robbin checked her with wonder, like she was an armless trapeze artist. "I've never known a prude," he said and studied the phenomenon of being caught out on a night in town with one, as they sat at the bar. Robbin turned and surveyed the noisy room behind them—Cassie figured in order to see if any of the wranglers had beat them in. But he returned his eyes to her and said, "You're by far the prettiest woman here, though." So maybe he'd been considering dumping her for someone more promising.

"Real or root?" the bartender asked Robbin, referring to beer. And Robbin ordered one of each, real for Cassie, root for himself.

"Can I look in here?"

The way Robbin anticipated opening her bag when she agreed reminded Cassie of the delight she once took in being allowed to rummage through her mother's purse as a child. The possibility of finding a stray Life Saver, lost in the lint on the bottom, or a stiff piece of forgotten Beemans gum was heightened by the secrets she might discover about her mother's personal life. That hadn't been so thrilling for Erin, who'd reported pulling out an extra pair of panties from her mother's purse and getting slapped for the discovery.

"God." Robbin held up Cassie's eyelash curler. "What *is* this?"

In his hands it looked like a medieval torture device, and Cassie's lashes had stuck to it often enough for her to view it as one. She described its purpose to Robbin.

"No kidding." He looked at her. He rummaged around in the bag some more, then got to the part he'd obviously been saving, her leather folder containing credit cards and identification. He read the statistics on her driver's license.

"Uh-oh." He pulled out a snapshot. "Jake." He examined the photo, bobbing his head up once to thank Ted the bartender for delivering their drinks, then resumed his perusal. "Does he look angry to you, even a little accusatory?"

Cassie had taken this photograph of Jake at his parents' lakeside cottage, two years before his death. He had been fishing, and Cassie had had a sudden urge to capture his contentment, and her own.

"He looks accusatory," Robbin determined. "He is looking right in my eyes and thinking I am not good enough to buy you a fucking beer."

Sure, Robbin *would* think a dead man was peering from a photograph taken five years before Robbin even knew Cassie, and take it personally. Robbin took everything personally. Boone had put it differently: "Someone hollers 'Horseshit,' Robbin, and you come sliding in."

"No, Robb," Cassie said. "He is thinking: 'When I am dead, five years from now, I hope my beloved wife, who I am presently smiling at on the boat dock, has her sad widowhood enhanced by the wooing of a movie star.'"

"I am not wooing you. I don't woo."

"That was a gentle term for our past encounters." Cassie looked away.

Also the word came to mind because Robbin had not only

taken to giving her cheek a good-night kiss, but had added a kiss to his breakfast greeting as well. He'd sneaked it in at first, distracting her with lifting pot lids on the stove, his hand on her back; then he'd swooped down and tagged her cheek. "Morning, babe." By now, Cassie was tipping her face for it each day.

"You think I'm wooing," Robbin accused, lowering the photo. "I'm not wooing. If I were wooing, I'd have requested to peer into your goddamn pants, not your purse."

"You get nasty quick."

He returned all the stuff to her bag, lobbing it in like a ball through a hoop. He plopped her bag back on the bar top between them and threw down a slug of his root beer, then stared straight ahead at the shelved liquor bottles lined against the mirrored wall behind the bar. "Woo."

Cassie sighed.

Robbin muttered, "Shit." The toes of his sneakers bounced in agitation. Glancing at his reflection between the bottles, Cassie saw his eyes make tiny darting movements like he was arguing nonverbally with someone. "You wear his watch all the time. You're still in love with him. Woo—it sounds like a Chinese soup. A Chinese sap. So? Are you?" He didn't look at her; he continued to stare straight ahead, but his body settled, waiting for her answer.

"I would say no," Cassie responded thoughtfully, interested herself in the answer, "since I'm not engaged in the loss of him any longer."

"Just love him, like you do a dead person."

"Right. Like you do your mother." Around the newel post at the bottom of the staircase leading to Cassie's painting room hung an old stiff leather saddlebag with the initials LRM stamped on it. Laura Robbin McKeag.

Robbin nodded, then stood up. "Let's play pool." He slipped the straps of her bag onto her shoulder. "Woo." Hand on her neck to guide her toward the pool tables, he said, "Woo a prude."

It sounded like a bumper sticker, Cassie thought. Like a reason put forth by florists to purchase flowers.

Later that night, driving home, Robbin said, "Was he perfect?"

Cassie looked over toward Robbin behind the steering wheel, mustache and ball cap stashed under his seat again, his face lit by the dashboard lights. He wasn't looking at her. "No," she said. "Nobody is perfect and Jake wasn't either."

"Is it too soon after his death for you to tell me something that wasn't perfect about him?"

One thing came immediately to mind. The one thing she had the most trouble with even beyond Jake not telling her at the end, before leaving on his final climb, that he'd just been diagnosed with cancer. Cassie took a moment. The night passing her car window was blacker than many people ever experienced. She'd read once that most Americans had never seen the Milky Way, that great sparkling path that crossed the sky and was seen all over in Wyoming, no matter where you were, even in Casper, the largest city. She hadn't told anyone this, not even Erin. "He was unable to have children, knew it for some years, and didn't tell me." She noticed this didn't hurt as much as it once had. She'd made progress in forgiving him. "Low sperm count." She continued, "I wanted to have a baby so much, was heartbroken every month when it didn't happen." She took a big breath. "I could have managed, if he'd told me." She swallowed past the lump swelling in her throat.

"He didn't want to hurt you." They drove a couple miles in

the dark, once in a while spotting the red eyes of an elk in the headlights along the roadside. "He should have told you." Another mile passed. "Nice guys have trouble saying hard things. Boone's like that."

Cassie was grateful for Robbin's generosity toward Jake. "Thanks, that helps," she replied.

The drive was forty miles long and as always in this part of Wyoming, large animals could be on the road. It wasn't wise to go too fast, so the trip took an hour at night. Later Robbin said, "So you're a vegetarian and probably don't think much of ranchers."

"There are ranchers who love the land and work very hard to take good care of it."

"How's Cross Wave fit in to that?"

"Really? You want to know?"

"Yeah, I do."

"Cross Wave could take some measures to work better with the wildlife, like fences that let the animals through. I've found bones at the fences, particularly below Carrion Butte near the migration trail. And earlier in the summer . . ." This had been difficult to see and was difficult to describe now. She turned her head to look out the side window for a moment.

"What?"

"A trumpeter swan got caught in the barbed wire fencing. It was long dead when I found it, probably happened during the early spring. It was near the river where the swans take off and land."

"Oh, God. That shouldn't happen."

"They can't see the wire. A mule deer tried to jump the fence some time back. Its hide is still draped over the wire." She explained that if wood replaced the top wire of the fence, that would have saved the creatures in both cases. Once buck-and-rail fencing—where two crossed bucks were connected with three thinner rails—was used all over the valley. The design was chosen due to the rocky ground and the difficulty of digging postholes through the glacial debris left from several thousand years ago. Cross Wave retained the buck-and-rail fencing in the dude area of the ranch, but strung wire to fence in the cattle and keep out the wildlife elsewhere.

"Show me sometime, okay? What else?"

"Some things I don't know about, like whether the wranglers are under orders to shoot coyotes or wolves they see around the stock, either on the ranch or on the summer grazing land in the mountains. I know, by law, ranchers can do that."

Robbin said, "The idea we go by is that coyotes and wolves are good for the dude operation, even if not so good for the cattle company. But God help you if you get Fee started on that. Cody, too. They see them as predators, as stealing money right out of their pockets."

Cassie could see that Robbin was risking something big by caring about the land he'd financially supported and others had run all his life. With any changes, he would be slammed right up against tradition and his own beloved family, the Barlows most particularly.

He said, "Losses with the cattle aren't the whole story. In the fall, like a lot of ranchers, Cody is a hunting guide. Every elk a wolf takes down is one his clients can't shoot. For Cody, that's a couple thousand bucks gone."

CHAPTER EIGHTEEN

The next morning a five-day campout with a group of camera buffs would begin. The week would work much as it did during the fall hunting season, Boone explained. He told Cassie the main object was to shoot wildlife—in this case using cameras. Elk, eagles, moose, antelope, coyotes, wolves, swans and bears. The gear was as profuse as with the hunters and the hours similar—up before dawn, portable breakfast and out on foot or horseback, in camp hungry at staggered times throughout the day, an early dinner, one sunset ride for last-chance photos and bed for the night.

Robbin also packed out for the five days in order to escape the incessant demands of his career, recently stirred up afresh by the anonymous tip to the press. As that had occurred on the heels of the public appearances he made for his hospitalized friend, he was badgered with offers, each demanding a decision—even if the decision consisted of being true to his original plan to maintain a private life for a full year. Camp remained the one place where he was left undisturbed. Mostly he sat on the ground, leaning against a narrowleaf cottonwood near the creek, working on his laptop. Brief and polite responses at mealtimes pressed the limits of his gregariousness. He didn't strike Cassie as moody during these two days, but rather thoughtful. Even so, during his withdrawal she realized that Robbin filled space with the essence of himself the way stored alfalfa sweetened a barn. In the past, the inner lining of her chest had seemed to swell with irritation from his consuming nearness. The abrasion of his presence would build unconsciously in her until, suddenly, she would snap out a series of insults, like sneezes, from the tiny particles of him that had lodged in her chest cavity. Now, like a homeopathic cure, those same tiny particles comforted her.

She and Baby Huey went for long outings, seven-mile hikes, often twice a day. The pup expanded Cassie's experience in the outdoors. It was Baby Huey who thought to lick the water cupped in a leaf, who tunneled into thick willows off trail, stuck his paws into ground holes and his nose into scent markings. His fur was fragrant with sagebrush. He was her five senses reaching farther, her muscles bounding across the land in new ways; she had never loved the natural world more. And finally she was realizing her goal of potty-training him. Tonight she would remove the Pampers around camp for good.

Cody's dingoes roamed freely, so Cassie had worried out loud to him a couple weeks back about Baby Huey going off exploring on his own while she cooked. Cody had said, "He can't get lost. Wherever he goes, he's home." After that she had learned from others that her pup visited the barn, was spotted near the river and explored the woods. Baby Huey always returned within a couple hours, so eventually Cassie relaxed and let him go, knowing he was happy with his freedom.

Once again this afternoon, at the time of day when a light rain typically fell, only a few gathered clouds dimmed the sunshine; then, one puff at a time, the clouds slipped between the walls of the canyon like white shirt buttons, opening again to the blue breast of sky. The wildflowers were fading quickly and the sage drooped with layers of dust. Three weeks without a single drop of moisture played hard on the land at Cross Wave, and eyes were cast often toward those white disks in hope of detecting a reprieve.

After dinner, Cassie realized that Baby Huey's food still sat ready for him, uneaten. He had been gone longer than usual. Three dozen horses sifted dirt in the corral into a fine powder that swirled ankle-high, as Boone cut out mounts for the guests who were riding to the old sawmill ponds. Fresh horses were provided twice a day for each guest while in camp. Tonight the guests would sit behind willows with their expensive cameras and await the evening appearance of the moose. The dudes milled about, grabbing sweatshirts and jackets, stuffing extra film canisters into their pockets and finishing their coffee.

Robbin had retreated to his tree and out of the range of Mrs. Penny's persuasive shaming of everyone to "get off your bums and finish the day with a show of western spirit." With Mrs. Penny's zeal toward activity after her day of indolence, she reminded Cassie of a carousing TV evangelist preaching marital fidelity. On her chaise lounge by the river's edge, set there each morning by a wrangler, Mrs. Penny sat with her lap desk and imparted her opinions to addresses around the world, her mailing list so vast that Cassie figured any catalog company would pay lavishly to acquire it. In return, her mailbox at the lodge overflowed with responses from her friends.

Cassie sipped coffee at a picnic table still littered with dishes and wondered again why her pup hadn't appeared yet for his favorite event of the day—mealtime. She rose, started gathering dishes, and noticed Fee riding up. He reined in at the edge of camp and beckoned Boone over to talk privately to him. Cassie set the dishes down and watched, though she didn't know why this interested her especially. Then she saw Fee look toward her, speak further to Boone, and Boone turned to look at her.

She read it on Boone's face.

She heard an abrupt, horrified cry, and realized it was her own.

"Robbin," Cassie cried. "Robbin, Robbin." And though he was there instantly with his arms wrapped around her, she continued to cry his name. "Robbin, Robbin, Robbin."

Boone came and spoke in his son's ear and Robbin, knowing she heard, buried Cassie's face in his arms and began to sway with her, gently from side to side.

"Shot, Cassie. It was an accident. He's dead."

Boone left to confer with Mrs. Penny, who then raised her voice to hector the guests into their saddles. She poked horses with her cane from her fragile perch atop her own horse, then bossed the guests into attending to their spooked mounts, creating a more immediate disturbance to distract them. Since Mrs. Penny bossed everyone at all times and somehow managed to make most feel flattered by the attention, the dudes bumbled along, many unaware of the puppy's death.

Boone approached again and patted both Cassie and Robbin on the back, one hand to each, as they swayed together, Cassie dry-eyed, her face on Robbin's chest and staring vacantly at his shoes. "She going to cry?" Boone asked Robbin.

"Soon," Robbin answered, moving with Cassie so indiscernibly it felt like a heartbeat.

"See if she'd like some ice cream. That always worked with you. When your mother died, we gave you ice cream."

"I should have cried."

"Oh, now . . . you were just a tyke, Robb."

"Doesn't matter. Should have told me she died." He talked into Cassie's hair. He lifted her face now. "Your puppy got shot; he was chasing a colt and Fee mistook him for a coyote. Now he's dead. You hear?"

Boone shifted his feet. "Robbin . . ." he warned uneasily.

Cassie blinked dry-eyed.

"Dead, Cassie."

"That's enough, Robbin." Boone bent his knees and dipped down to level his face with Cassie's. "You want some ice cream, hon? How about a little dish?"

"We don't have ice cream in camp, Boone," Robbin informed him.

"Don't tell her that."

Cassie believed she had vacated the premises, though she leaned against Robbin with her hands and face on his chest, enveloped in his arms, feeling his solid warmth. If asked, she didn't need anything just now. She was without expectations, hope or dread. It was the perfect time to enter a long, empty sleep, but she didn't want that either.

"Boone," Robbin said without an elaborate show of impatience, "you better catch up with the others. I'll take care of things." Then he sat Cassie on the picnic bench and escorted his father over to his horse, talking to him. After the riders left, Robbin returned, pulled Cassie up to him. "Tell me you know Baby Huey is dead."

"He's dead."

"Good. Now, you want to go to your tent, or what?"

"Go to your tent."

"What?"

Cassie said, "I don't know."

"Hmm." Robbin brushed her hair off her forehead. Then smoothed hair behind her ears. Her face was clear of hair now and he hadn't decided for sure what to do.

"Goddamn," he said. "I just caught myself about to be a jerk." He took hold of her shoulders and pressed her away from himself. "Wait here."

Robbin returned with an old quilt, which he spread out on a good patch of grass. He walked Cassie over to it, sat her in the center of it, then got her a cup of coffee. He left again to begin the dishes, but first she saw him get a paper towel and blow his nose and throw water on his face. He had shed tears. She wondered why she couldn't. She sat watching the twenty horses remaining in the corral. Bruce the Eunuch was there. Baby Huey liked to bend his small body down, twist his head around to dip the spot behind his right ear in horse manure with the pleasure of a young boy testing aftershave lotion. Sometimes if she didn't call to him, he'd roll his whole body in it. Many nights she had to bathe him in the creek before she let him in her tent. But Baby Huey was gone. Everything goes eventually, she thought. Life is just a matter of waiting.

Robbin called from the dishwashing basin. "How are you doing?"

She couldn't gather the energy required to respond, so she didn't. He came over, drying his hands with a dish towel. He said, "It's a terrible thing, losing our pup." When she didn't respond, he said, "Isn't it?"

"What?"

"Baby Huey."

He stooped down. "What are you feeling?"

"Nothing."

He sat on the edge of the quilt, an old raggedy thing, its batting showing through in some places. He dangled the dish towel between his bent knees. "You like that? Feeling nothing?"

"I'd like to feel something."

Robbin took the coffee cup from Cassie's hand. She hadn't drunk any of it, so he threw the coffee in an arc across the grass and set the cup on the edge of the quilt. Cassie watched indirectly from her disengaged state. Then Robbin startled her out of her apathy; he swatted her with the dish towel. He did it again, same place, across her lower legs, swathed in Levi's.

Mildly, she said, "Hey."

Robbin said, "Let's wrestle."

The notion intrigued her—it was that silly. It got through.

He lurched at her and got her head in an armlock. She wasn't too responsive, so he rubbed the balled-up dish towel in her face. She giggled a bit, but didn't resist. He stuck her head under his knee, then lifted her lower half up in the air until she laughed his name and began to put up a fight.

He tumbled her all over the quilt. She tried to get leverage over him, but he used her own momentum to topple her. She laughed harder and breathed faster. It felt good, like a gentle chiropractic workout. She made a decent effort to get Robbin in an inferior position, but he easily turned all her tricks into opportunities for himself.

He had her head in an armlock of her own two arms and imprisoned both her feet in his free hand, which he bent up behind her back. He rocked her, back-bended like that, pushing her face into the quilt until her laughter turned into sobs.

"There we go," he said and lifted her onto his lap, and sat

cross-legged with her on the quilt. She cried, and he rocked her like a baby.

"I have to see him," she said. "Will you come with me?"

"We can't do that." Boone had said Fee and Cody had buried the pup as soon as they'd realized their mistake. Gotten the backhoe, dug a hole, rolled rocks on top.

"I never get to say good-bye."

"It was like that with Jake, wasn't it?"

She nodded. "My grandmother, too." She had died last winter, after Cassie left Ohio, thinking she was going to be okay.

They were quiet.

Robbin said, "This might be over for you now, these deaths."

"Why do you say that?"

"I don't know. Something feels finished."

Birds sang, trilling over and over, building crescendos, as if celebrating the fact that they could create such beautiful sounds. Cassie could almost feel the pleasure they took in the notes rolling through the stretch of their throats, the tight grip of their perch on the tree limb, could imagine the view they sang to way across the sage flats, the glacial erratics, the sunlight beading the river, the snowfields on the mountains.

She said, "Are you going to make love to me now?"

"Nope." Robbin sounded proud of himself. As if he'd considered it and chosen the high road.

Cassie sat upright in the circle of his legs. "Why not?"

Robbin smiled with superiority. Then he sobered. "Goddamn. You'd like that, wouldn't you?" he said. "You want to keep me in my place."

Cassie leaned back against his chest. "I don't know what you're talking about." Already twice now she'd begun to think she should look for her puppy and had to remind herself that Baby Huey was gone. When did things begin falling away from her? Maybe she didn't know how to hold what she loved to herself anymore or maybe she didn't know how to properly let go, so had to keep practicing until she got it right.

Robbin said, "You're cunning, Cassie. What you do *not* want is for me to come through for you." He pulled farther back to look at her. "You *want* me to be the big shit you got me tagged for." Then he seemed to remember what his job was at the moment and he held her against himself again and rocked her some more.

"I probably wouldn't have gotten anything out of it anyway."

She expected him to leap into a defense of his manhood, his ability as a lover. She expected him to forget her feelings and express, with exaggerated gestures, his indignation.

He didn't rise to the bait.

He said quietly into her hair, "Hmm, short memory." He kissed the top of her head and added softly, "Your Richter scale registered eight point five." With his chin on her head, he said, "That topples tall buildings."

She felt his breath in her hair, the warmth of his body against hers. She heard the birdsong. And she knew the loss of Baby Huey was another vacancy in her life that would need healing. Robbin laid his cheek against her forehead. He spoke soothingly. "Small mammals ran for cover."

CHAPTER NINETEEN

The first night without Baby Huey was hard. Cassie missed him rustling underfoot in his Pampers, lapping her bathwater, chasing her washcloth as it traveled over her legs and feet. She settled into her sleeping bag, missing her puppy's soft snores. The loss would have been more painful without Robbin. It comforted her knowing that he was determined to give her this wide cushion of companionship, even when she had offered to narrow it in order to distract herself from grief. Prior to the campout, she had felt him moving in closer each day. An arm around her waist as he looked into the cooking pots, a hand on her back when he refilled her coffee cup: he had watched for her needs and tended to them.

Four hours of lying in bed, and sleep would not come. She got up and performed her milk routine and crawled back into her sleeping bag and lay there, her mind alert.

Could Fee really have mistaken her pup for a coyote? Coyotes got habituated around the guest ranch, she knew, and became quite bold at times. They were drawn to look for the grease from grills, scraps the dudes might leave on the trails. Sometimes ranch guests, before they could be educated otherwise, would deliberately set out food for the wildlife, feeling they were doing a kindness. But bears got shot once they became habituated to humans, and wherever deer or other ungulates were fed by people, cougars preyed. Besides, human food was never nutritionally valuable to wildlife. Baby Huey's fur was similar to the color of a coyote's, but there were considerable differences in the shape of the ears and tail, though apparently at a distance not to Fee's old eyes.

Still no sleep. Last year when her grandmother had died and Cassie had flown home for the funeral service, the minister from her family's church, Reverend Hayden, had spoken about living with loss. He had offered three points: First, acknowledge the loss—whether of physical ability, mental ability, health, family, friend, lover, business, home—and grieve. Second, know that since you are still living, you have a purpose and it's your job to discover that purpose. Third, know that you have the power to fulfill this purpose, and begin to act on it.

Cassie had to wonder tonight whether she had moved at all into points two and three, before being thrust back into point one again: grieving. If the losses of her husband, grandmother and pet were to become meaningful, hadn't she better move on to points two and three? And if so, what was her purpose? She had neither discovered it nor acted on it.

Or had she? The words "living" and "purpose" chased themselves in her head, like her pup once did his tail. Perhaps purpose was found by following the trail toward liveliness. What for her instilled the most liveliness? Two things rose to mind: enjoying the natural world and painting it.

Robbin had advised that she paint with the intention that her art would play a central role in supporting her life. What if, along with that, she also enjoyed the outdoors with the intention that it would play a central role in supporting her life? What would that look like; how would that work?

The answer came swiftly: a small guiding business—hiking in the summer, snowshoeing in the winter.

She had no desire to sleep now; she was too invigorated. She got up, wrapped herself Indian style in a blanket, grabbed paper and pen and headed for a picnic table with her lamp to make lists. Becca would help her design and print a brochure at the ad agency where she worked. Erin had a head for business and would help set up a financial structure. Lacy worked as a concierge at the Four Seasons and would send her clients. Cassie could contract with other hotels and even guest ranches, starting with Cross Wave. She would begin small; her only financial outlay at first would be the brochure.

Points one, two and three: grieve, figure out your purpose and act on it. She could see it coming; she was going to be fine. She tiptoed back to her sleeping bag and slept the couple hours until dawn.

Though emotionally tamped down with missing Baby Huey, she blew through breakfast, energized by her business plans. After lunch she borrowed a vehicle, left camp and went in search of Fee. She needed to hear about what happened with her pup.

Cassie longed to be around a dog, any dog; she missed dog fur, panting, and tail flicking. When she spotted Cody and his dingoes, she couldn't resist stopping. Besides, maybe he'd know where to find his father and save her some trouble. She parked alongside the fence line, got out of the truck, and walked over to him.

Cassie sat right down on the ground and both Kelty and Cairn came over to her. She petted them and sighed. "Oh, gosh, I miss him."

Cody was tightening the top wire of the fencing with a tool designed especially for this. He stopped his work. "Fee's real sorry."

"I wouldn't know. He hasn't said."

"He is. He never wanted to hurt your pup."

"No, I guess not." She fell silent and lavished her attention on the dogs, whose heads were propped on her knees.

Cody watched her. She felt him wishing to cheer her somehow. A moment later he said, "Want to know a secret?"

"What?"

"I asked Diana to marry me and she said yes. So did her girls." He looked up to the sky with his big smile. "I'm going to be a husband and a father all at once." The flash of Cody's white teeth against his tanned face and dark mustache distracted from his cloudy eye, and as always he was dressed with pizzazz. Today a yellow silk scarf was knotted around his neck in such a way that it ballooned in front and made Cassie think of sage grouse during courtship display when the air sacs on the male grouse's upper chest puffed out in a flash of vivid gold.

Cassie smiled. "That's so wonderful."

"I gave her a ring. Got two little ones for the girls. It was damn fun. We haven't announced it to our families yet."

Kelty and Cairn rolled over onto their backs to give Cassie a chance to scratch their tummies. Once, she would have laughed out loud at such shameless pleas, but now she felt such a longing for one particular tummy.

"I got one worry, though." Cody stooped down to her level. "You know how we talked about caring about two people?"

"Sure, I remember."

"Now it's Robbin and my dad. They seem to be going at it. Robb's got questions out the yin yang and Dad gets pissed at every one of them."

"Questions?"

"About running things around here. But that's not my problem. My problem is—Dad doesn't know I know—but he's the reason we got all these reporters hanging around."

"Why would your dad want that?"

Cody was scraping his tool into the ground, gouging out lines and uprooting the grass. He tossed it aside and sat all the way down and stared at the horizon, his cowboy hat tipped back. "I'm not sure, but I'm supposing he'd much prefer Robb switch his attention back to movies instead of our ranching operation. We're used to making our own decisions." He took his hat all the way off, wiped his shirtsleeve over his forehead and ruffled up the hair plastered from the hatband, then put the hat back on. "My problem is, do I tell Robb or protect my dad and just stay out of it? My God, it's getting so I don't sleep all through the night. Wake up after two hours and argue with myself."

This news jarred Cassie. She asked Cody how he knew for sure, and he said that reporters were staying at the Snake River Lodge and Diana overheard them talking in the spa and caught Fee's name. She got that Fee wasn't directly involved and had himself refused to talk to the press.

Cody said, "Also, I've been approached by some of the younger ranchers to join in their 'games'—as they're calling them." He dropped his head and shook it in regret. He had learned that Fee had riled the other ranchers over Robbin's new interest in land conservation, suggesting that if their movie cowboy wasn't lured back to Hollywood soon, he'd have the local cattle ranches replaced by wind farms. So they had contributed to stirring up the interest of the press and given out information.

Cassie tried not to expose her shock at this news; Cody was upset enough. "What kind of games?"

"I think one of their *games* was the attempted cattle theft."

Cassie took a sharp inhale of breath. "But how would that lure Robbin back to Hollywood?"

"That one was to lure you away from him . . . and the ranch. I'm guessing Dad wanted it to look like something your conservation friends would pull. He knew you and your husband were supporters of the Land Trust, and he's been telling the other ranchers you were active in getting other valley ranches to pass some of their land on to the trust."

"That's not how the organization works. I'm only a volunteer, helping out with fence removal sometimes. What does he think, that I'm working undercover or something? I would never do that." She shook her head.

Cody said, "I know about the Land Trust; they're good people. I tried to tell Dad. He's got a lot of worries about the ranch and our future these days. When Robb checked himself into that hospital last year . . . it scared Dad. Well, all of us."

They both sat quietly for a moment.

Cody said, "I've got to decide whether to tell Robb what I know or protect Dad." He stared at the ground between his knees a moment. "Diana says maybe tell both. What do you think?"

She had to pull her emotions away from Fee's betrayal of Robbin; she had to let go of the urge to label him a bad guy and wish he'd get what he deserved—that was her pain talking, her longing for her pup, and her reaction to the unreasonable way that man had treated her all along. She took a big breath and tried to be the fair person Cody needed just now. She became aware of the rattle of grasshoppers in the tall grasses and the call of a red-tailed hawk circling above them.

Cassie said, "You don't have to choose one over the other. You can tell your dad what you've learned and give him the chance to clean that up with Robb."

"He might refuse."

"That's when you have a decision to make. But for now, I'd say the decision belongs to Fee."

Suddenly Cassie imagined how messy things could become. She stood up to leave, explaining that she had just enough time to ask Fee about her pup before needing to get back to work. Cody told her where to find him.

Ranching was jeopardized by many factors. In one respect it was a tradition that had outgrown its purpose. The manly skills of providing food, taming the wilderness, partnering with harsh weather, land and the forces of life and death had been glamorized for centuries. On the other hand, people still needed to have food provided, and they needed a way to make open land profitable in order for it to remain open.

The often-used argument of ranchers that if they had to sell out they'd be replaced by development was somewhat true. But for this to work for everyone involved—ranchers, the public, the wildlife—change was imperative. Fee didn't want to hear about it. Cody, being younger, starting his family, couldn't afford to wear blinders. Looking ahead, he had to see the big cattle truck, horn blaring, barreling down the road ready to hit him square in the pocketbook if he didn't comply with some land conservation.

Cody had directed her to the pasture behind the Barlows'

ranch house, so Cassie drove to the main house and parked in the drive. As she walked through the trees, she felt her pup's bounding energy beside her like a phantom limb.

"Fee, can I talk to you a minute?"

"What is it, missy?"

"It's my pup, naturally. I'd like to understand what happened."

He lifted his hat, black with a gray band of old sweat around it, the brim in front where he handled it grimy with dirt and grease; he wiped a hand down his face, and Cassie tried not to read impatience in the gesture.

"Come on over here in the shade." He climbed up and sat on the top of the buck-and-rail fence.

As Fee sat there seeming to take in the view, Cassie moved between hating him and trying not to cry, as if there were only those two choices. Was there a third choice, a fairer one? she asked herself. And the answer was yes, she could listen with an open mind.

"Sit?"

She shook her head no and rested her mind on her breath—in, out—calming herself.

"I'm feeling pretty riled at you, missy. I didn't like finding I'd shot a sweet little pup when I'm thinking it's a stinking coyote out to get my stock. I walk over there, and look down and find what I did and I feel like some kind of bad guy."

Cassie barked out a sob. Even so, she kept her face from crumpling and she kept her eyes on Fee. Some people never took responsibility for their actions, always found someone else to fault. Was Fee one of them? He didn't come to her; she had to go to him. She said nothing.

"So I'm sure sorry the little tyke got himself killed, if that's what you're asking here. But I don't take the blame for it. That lies with you. You should of taught him not to chase stock. I'd think with all your ecological interest, you might of learned him not to chase wildlife. Then he wouldn't have transferred that skill to my stock."

If she said anything in her defense it would just give him an opening to argue with her further; she didn't come for argument and she didn't come to place blame; she came to try to understand what had happened with her puppy and to try not to hate Fee for having shot him. She said one thing. "I did teach him that." And then she turned to leave.

"You train ranch dogs not to get in the stock. That's all I got to say."

Cassie turned back to him. "That's all you've got to say?"

Fee dipped his head, his hands grasped his knees, and then he looked up. "I also got to say that I am full sorry for your loss. I know it hurts."

That was better. Cassie nodded. Then she left.

So that was that, and Baby Huey was gone. She had thought it was safe to love this puppy. But she had forgotten one true fact of life: love beckons loss and it was her job to love anyway.

By nightfall she was feeling the awful stretch of hours; her eyes were scratchy and a continual hum resounded in her ears. She was daft with the need for sleep. Yet, at each departure of a guest from the campfire, anxiety mounted. Soon no one would be left to accompany her in the dark if she wasn't able to fall off. She was washing popcorn bowls and the last of the cups when Robbin came from his tent with his bowl of popcorn and requested the paper towels.

Cassie looked on the ledge beside the grill where the roll usually sat, then rapidly and with mounting panic darted her eyes around the cook area. She bent, rifled the cupboard and emerged wailing, "I can't find them. I don't know *where* they are."

Robbin stood immobile and silent at the response his simple request had set off. He recovered and asked, "No sleep?"

Cassie shook her head. The hot sand surface of her eyes yearned to close, but her mind burned with agitation from the talk with Cody, and then Fee. She worried about Fee's betrayal of Robbin, and how Robbin could participate in the management of the land without intruding on Fee and Cody's livelihood. They were all family, dependent upon one another. Like the Snake River channels that braided through the valley, separating and intertwining while feeding the earth and the wildlife, the ranch families had flowed in a braid of responsibility that had worked for years—Robbin supplied the finances, Boone ran the guest ranch, Fee and Cody operated the cattle company, and now like a beaver damming up and rerouting the stream, Cassie entered the scene, raising questions about conservation and concerns for the wildlife. Was this all a result of her recycling? Did Fee see the future laid out before him when he stood in the barn viewing the carton of reusable water bottles? No wonder kings once killed the messengers of bad news.

She rubbed her scratchy eyes.

Robbin said, "Get ready for bed. I'll bring you some tea with a shot of Mrs. Penny's Drambuie in it. We'll talk until you get sleepy."

She felt the warmth of his offer wash through her body the way the tea and Drambuie soon would. Her muscles relaxed. They'd talk; perhaps she'd get some answers. Then she could sleep. "I love you," she said gratefully. Then amended that. "I love . . . your wonderful idea."

Shortly after she crawled into her sleeping bag, Robbin approached her tent and softly called through, "Ready?"

Cassie said in a bored housewife's voice, "Yes, dear."

He came in with a steaming enamel mug and set it next to Cassie's lit lamp and made himself comfortable against a rolled blanket.

Cassie said, "I talked to Fee today."

"Really? How did that go?"

"Okay, I guess."

Robbin said, "I don't suppose he apologized."

"Eventually, though I had to prompt him for it. Still, it turned out okay."

"Good for you." He looked at her admiringly.

She sipped her tea and thanked him for it. It was cozy in her tent with the lamplight and whispers, the steamy tea and Robbin filling the space vacated so recently by her pup. But she felt agitated with unanswered questions, so she charged right in. "Robb, who's in charge where?"

"It's a mess, but there's a logic to the disorder. First of all, Cody said he told you about the accident with his eye."

"Yes."

Robbin shifted to sit upright. "When Cody lost the movie, Fee lost his windfall. He'd been—like his father and grandfather before him—Cross Wave ranch manager, but he wanted his own land, wanted it badly. Pale Feather Ranch, adjacent to Cross Wave, went on the market. Fee made an offer that was dependent on the movie deal for financing, and the offer was accepted. Then the accident happened. So I took Cody's place in the film, as you know, and that money then went for Cody's eye surgery. Boone hoped to follow through for the Barlows and put a down payment on Fee's land, but then we learned Cody would need a series of eye surgeries. It was going to be a long-term, expensive deal. But also about that time we learned there would be another movie."

Cassie sipped her tea.

"So it went like that. Sometimes Boone had to put up some of our land to get loans for the medical bills, when the surgeries went on year after year. But eventually new film projects came along to pay for them all."

Cassie offered Robbin a sip of her tea and he accepted, then made a face at the sweetness of the Drambuie. "So who owed who got murky, and no one wanted to be in the position of figuring out the answer anyway. The fathers called it even some time ago. Fee and Cody have a place to live the rest of their lives and the ranch to run like they've always had. My film work has earned enough to carry us through bad years to the next good ones. Nobody worries about groceries, and we all get to do what we love doing in this beautiful place, where we love doing it."

"Except you," she reminded him. "You no longer want to be tied to a movie a year. You don't love the work you've been doing . . . or the place you've been doing it."

"I know. That probably worries everybody. They're not used to me having any say around here. I was just the drunk that brought in the money."

"That's putting it harshly. But I'm sure everybody is wondering how much of a role you'll want to play now."

Robbin lay on his back beside Cassie with his knees bent, resting his head on the bedroll. He stared at the tent ceiling and said, "I don't want to take charge of either the cattle operation or the guest ranch. I only want to carry out my financing of the two with responsibility. And I haven't done that. I've just been doling out money and not caring how it was spent. It matters to me that the land is used well. I've always trusted Fee and Cody to do that, but now I wonder if they're resisting some realities here."

Cassie said, "Fee, I suppose, most of all is having trouble with this."

"Fee carries some real concerns, I know. He could handle me as the star full of myself for a couple summer months, as long as I returned to Hollywood at the end of it. That was a lot easier than putting up with me as the financial backer for the ranch, with questions and ideas and plans to stick around to see them through. He has no regard for my ranching opinions—with good reason. Who am I to have any? Aside from my money."

"You are someone who cares. But I see you'll have to go easy. And I see I better go easy myself. I haven't helped your situation here." She had had no idea, really, when she began her recycling and water bottle projects just what she was stirring up. But then how could she have known that these simple changes would unearth concerns that involved two families and their tangled histories? By these small acts of hers, large shifts in the plate tectonics of the ranching relationships were scraping against one another, the way the lithospheric plates of the earth's crust and mantle collided and scraped in Yellowstone, spewing scalding fumes and water. This was good and necessary for the planet; she hoped that could be true for the family members as well, because she didn't wish any one of them harm.

"It's nice to have you on my side," Robbin said. "You care, too."

She was getting sleepy, but there were remarks of Robbin's she wondered about. "You mentioned you have plans to stick around," she said.

"I want to build my own home on a piece of land here. But even that will stir up issues. I'll have to use some of Fee's grazing land no matter where the site is and that's how he earns his living, from the cattle income."

"What happened to Pale Feather?"

He turned on his side to face her. "Some investment group from back east bought it." Robbin looked at her for a moment, then smiled. "Mrs. Penny's Drambuie kicked in." He leaned over, kissed her on the forehead and pushed himself to his feet. At the tent flap he said, "Don't let the bedbugs bite."

"Don't talk about bugs!" She rolled over inside her sleeping bag and that was the last she knew until morning.

CHAPTER TWENTY

The only rainfall during the week since Baby Huey died drizzled for twenty minutes one morning, and the raindrops lay like spent bullets on top of the hard earth before spreading into a brief smear of dampness. Grasslands were scorched. To drive down a dirt road demanded windshield wipers. Everything in sight was sheeted in dust. With afternoon temperatures stuck in the high eighties and some days rising into the low nineties, the upstairs room where Cassie painted was stifling even with all the windows open and a fan aimed at her face. She carried her work downstairs and outside to sit beneath the Douglas fir. She was mixing colors on her palette, creating lush, voluptuous shades that detonated a physical response in her. A purple like the inside of a womb or a poppy, dark and mysterious. Pink like dawn on the glacier below Mount Moran, and a turquoise like a chunk of Wyoming sky—late winter, about two hours before sunset. She could eat these colors; she could paint her nude body in them, and they would perfect her spirit, heal abrasions and heartache.

Up on her knees now in a tension of expectation, Cassie prepared to swipe the three colors on paper to see what happened when they met each other.

"Cass?" Robbin stooped down near her. She hadn't heard him approach. "You busy?"

She said without looking up, "Hmm?" She dabbed her brush into the turquoise and made a single stroke on the heavy paper. She felt herself swing from a silence that allowed her to listen to her response to feeling almost hyper in her eagerness to lay down the next color.

"I was wondering . . . can you stop a minute, or should I come back?"

"It's okay," Cassie said. "What?" She rinsed her brush, dipped into the pink and laid a stroke beside the turquoise, swished the brush in water again and sat back on her heels to look.

"Well . . . never mind. Maybe later," Robbin said.

"Go ahead," she said and hunkered over the board she had taped her paper to, daring herself to make a stroke of the purple.

"Shit, you haven't even looked at me."

She looked. "Get a new haircut?"

Very evenly Robbin said, "Never the fuck mind, Cassie." And he stood up.

"Okay." She laid down her brush. "Here I am. What did you want?"

"I don't want anything from you. A simple damn thing— would you like to go out—and you have to make it into a goddamn struggle. Dinner and the symphony, and I have to bleed over you to get your attention. Shit." He walked off.

"I'd love to," she called after him.

He slowed some, then stopped and turned. "Okay," he said congenially. "We'll leave about five." He headed off again.

Since this week's group of guests—five couples who'd known each other for two decades—had requested the weekend evenings free to sample local restaurants and the cowboy nightlife, Cassie's only duty was to write out a list of wild and noisy bars. She had the afternoon to paint beneath the tree and get ready for her first date in years.

About three thirty, Cassie began preparations. A long, cool shower and shampoo. Painted toenails. Makeup. Now she stood before her narrow camper closet and pulled out the hanger with her black Laise Adair. Cut on the bias, it had sensuous folds that clung to her breasts and hips and skipped around her calves when she walked. Her mother had sent it last Christmas—"You mustn't always dress like a camp counselor, Cassie." The accompanying note had been spurred no doubt by her wearing a ski jacket to her grandmother's funeral earlier in the winter. Also, Cassie decided to wear Robbin's gift, the lapis lazuli pendant. CASSIE LOVE ROBBIN. While she was digging around in her storage area to pull it out, she removed Jake's watch and put it away there.

"My-my, my-my," Boone responded when Cassie entered the main house just before five o'clock. "Who?" he asked, when told her date was Robbin. "Our Robbin?"

"I think he's practicing on me," Cassie explained, and reminded Boone about Cody backing off on lining up Robbin's dates. She suddenly felt self-conscious: dating the boss' son didn't usually lead to the best circumstances for an employee. Mostly, though, she was warning herself that she shouldn't invest too much in this evening.

"Welp, you look just beautiful, Cassie-hon."

Unsure how tutorial her role might have to be tonight, Cassie feared Robbin would honk and holler from his truck. But promptly at five he arrived at the front door of the main house, wearing pressed khakis and a blazer. He draped her black fringed shawl with tiny blue flowers over her shoulders and handed her black evening bag to her just like a pro. All those old movies he and Boone watched probably helped.

Tonight's special guest at the Grand Teton Music Festival was Oxana Yablonskaya, a Russian pianist of renown. During the intermission, outside on the covered walkway that wrapped around the rustic wooden music hall, Robbin introduced Cassie to the former U.S. senator from Wyoming, Alan Simpson, and his wife, Ann. The senator was a longtime fishing buddy of Boone's. Referring to the rousing piano performance of Miss Yablonskaya, Senator Simpson said with hearty appreciation, "She just *pawed* the heck out of that thing, didn't she?"

Robbin and Cassie strolled the raised deck that surrounded Walk Festival Hall and next ran into Dale and Molly, old friends of Robbin's. They had first met in grade school and had kept up the friendship through the years. Most recently, Molly reported, they had used Robbin as a babysitter for their infant daughter. Cassie hoped her jaw didn't drop noticeably. She listened to the story about how at the end of January, shortly after Robbin's truck accident, which spurred his avowal to stop drinking, Robbin had babysat the newborn Jessie.

Dale said, "He walked our screaming daughter, who was suffering from severe colic, from midnight to eight in the morning the first month of her life, so we could get some rest."

This was the thing Cassie loved the most about human beings: the surprises they held.

She learned that Robbin had driven illegally into town, using side streets to minimize the chance of detection by the police, and given Dale and Molly sleep time.

"He saved our sanity," Molly said.

"He saved our marriage," Dale added with a laugh.

Robbin said, "I was the one that was saved. Jessie acted out all my own desires: she sucked on a bottle and wailed."

So, Cassie thought, the surly Robbin she drove into a snowbank that cold January morning was not drunk, but rather sleepy and driving the side streets with a suspended license. If her carelessness had involved the police, everyone would have been out in the cold.

Finally, it rained. As the four of them stood there, it began not with single drops but sudden opaque sheets. It blew and howled. It drummed on car roofs in the parking lot and hammered on the roof of the deck above Cassie and Robbin and bounced off the grass below them like hail. And as they watched, it became hail, slushy splatters, then ice balls a half inch in diameter that tattered leaves and snapped twigs from tree branches around them.

Before the concert, the sky had offered no hint of what was to come. It remained cuttingly blue, monotonously serene. Now, mean spears of rain sliced the air and hailstones ricocheted off the sidewalks that led to nearby shops, and Cassie regretted missing the anticipation of the coming storm, that delicious buildup of rowdy clouds and spirals of dust. The shiny deck became littered with matted cottonwood leaves and geranium petals from the pots swinging dangerously from the overhang above them. The smells were pungent, almost acidic, stinging and good. Like cattle, people all ran in one direction, faces away from the slanting slices of ice and water. Cassie and Robbin returned to their seats inside the hall.

After the concert they drove up the mountain behind Festival Hall to a reception the two of them had been invited to at the maestro's home. Maestro Harrold greeted them at the door. He seemed a pleasant man, tall, thin, with dark hair that grew as straight as ebony chopsticks around a chalky bald spot on the center of his head. Cassie wondered who cut his hair. The strands appeared to be styled only if each chopstick lay in its assigned slot around the bald spot, which it rarely did, as the conductor threw himself into his music and conversation, tossing his head until his hair looked like a game of pickup sticks.

Like Cassie had in the past, her friends had attended tonight's concert by volunteering to usher, and they were now pouring wine for the guests at the reception in trade for next week's free pass. Later, huddled with her friends, Cassie put forth the suspicion that Mrs. Harrold cut her husband's hair in revenge for the maestro's penchant for patting the butts of female guests. Cassie had spotted his impropriety in time to guard herself against it in seasons past and had long ago warned Erin, Becca and Lacy.

"Cass." Robbin leaned close to her from behind, laid his fingers on Cassie's shoulder to get her attention and spoke quietly, not wanting to interrupt her friends' talk. "Where's our purse?" The group, however, talker and listeners, all halted and watched as Cassie picked up her purse from the sofa and handed it to Robbin, who touched a point of hair lying in front of Cassie's ear and greeted each of her friends before moving away.

"He's in love with her," Becca announced to Erin and Lacy. "Robbin McKeag is in love with my friend." Becca looked at each of them. "How come *I* feel special?"

Cassie laughed and set them straight: Robbin didn't even *believe* in love. Her throat clogged momentarily at the words, then eased. Becca refused to accept that—his eyes, all that touching. "Sexuality," Cassie explained. "He believes in that."

Lacy said, "And you share a purse." She watched Robbin

retreat through the crowd and leave through the front double doors. "What does he keep in it?"

"His money, car keys. He's probably going out to lay a cellist in the cab of his pickup while I'm finishing my drink," Cassie said, to test the perspective, though she didn't believe it. She took a sip of her wine. Erin had always been clear-sighted about Robbin; Cassie invited her support. "Isn't that right, Erin?"

"You've become cynical, Cassie," Erin stated in her preemptive manner. "And prickly enough to mate with a porcupine and come out of it unscathed."

Cassie was just trying to take good care of herself, because according to Erin, in the past Robbin *marketed* affection. But before Cassie could react, Robbin was followed back into the front door by two slight Japanese violinists, whom Cassie recognized as guest musicians at Festival Hall. He came directly to Cassie with her purse chain hanging from his shoulder, pulled her aside and stood behind her with her arms outstretched. "Will it fit, dudes?" he asked the two small men.

Much nodding and smiling. Then the two men wiggled their fingers above their heads and mirth spilled in high, silly sounds. Robbin explained, while sticking his keys back into Cassie's purse, that they'd all been out to his pickup, where the Japanese men had spotted a pile of elk antlers tossed in the truck bed, found around the ranch after the elk shed them the past spring. Robbin had moved the truck to park beneath a streetlamp, so the men could photograph them, and now they wanted to make a trade with Robbin. "The antlers for some embroidered jacket thing. Think we got a deal."

He began to rush off behind the Japanese men, halted himself halfway across the room and returned to drape the purse chain over Cassie's shoulder. "Yum," he whispered in her ear.

"You are velly pletty." And he stood staring at her, arrested, Cassie thought, by some new response she felt in her eyes. Her friends had removed an emotional hurdle—the doubt Cassie had felt about her own sense of reality concerning Robbin's affection.

It occurred to her that her father had been wrong. Leopards *did* change their spots—that old adage being one of her father's favorite sayings. Robbin was *not* out laying a cellist, and she had known that all along.

After he left, Lacy said, "I'd like to move into that purse with you two—I'll pay a third of the rent and clean up all the lint."

Becca said, "You could *sell* the lint."

Erin was not engaging in the conversation any further. As Cassie knew, Erin made statements and waited for others to see the unwavering light of them. The nature of her friendship with Erin was a symbiotic understanding that Cassie's realm was the inner and Erin was mistress of the outer. Cassie was the artist, the seeker of elusive truths; Erin was the businesswoman, the spotter of stable realities. They rarely disagreed, unless one or the other felt her territory of expertise was being trod upon, which Cassie guessed they both felt at the moment.

But before the evening ended, Erin appeased her by saying, "It's like a power failure, Cassie. Complete darkness for so long you lose belief in light. But sometimes another person can tell that any minute the lights will come back on—no flicker, but a preceding hum—then suddenly the room fills with a glow, and heat pours through the vents." This was supposedly Cassie, humming to beat the band, but squeezing her eyes closed against the light.

Though Cassie knew what was happening. Since Robbin had learned that she loved him but wasn't settling for a sexual relationship, he had constructed, as carefully as his own career, as layered as the log cabins on the ranch, his relationship with her. He passed on the benefits of his experience in living a creative life, he supported her as an artist, he shared her interest in philosophy books and, together, they talked about improving the ranch land for the wildlife. Inside, she was singing to have her knowledge confirmed by her toughest friend.

News of the storm's effects on the valley began to swirl around the party conversation. Power was out in many areas, and rivers and creeks were swelling at alarming rates, as the rain pummeled down faster than the hardened ground could absorb it. The temperature had dropped forty degrees during the concert, and the winds had gusted up to sixty miles per hour. Robbin said they had better head home, before the bridge crossing Elk Tooth from the highway to the ranch washed out.

The evening was still early when they arrived at the ranch, and Cassie agreed to stop in Robbin's cabin. First he needed to check in with Boone to learn how the ranch had fared during the storm.

"Wait for me here. I won't be long."

By now the storm had passed, calm had settled, and the warm air was returning, lifted into place by the moisture rising from the ground. It felt as balmy as the tropics outside. Cassie watched Robbin jog across the yard and vanish into the darkness.

Twenty minutes later she emerged from the shower in Robbin's cabin, tying the belt of his bathrobe around herself. He hadn't returned yet. She wandered around the one-room cabin feeling that she'd left something undone. Or maybe just left something undecided. She tightened the robe ties again, and she touched items around the room—a lone sneaker on Robbin's desk holding down his manuscript of "The Countess and the

Cowboy," a stack of reference books on Cissy Patterson, then a long quartz crystal wand on the bookshelf. She stood by Robbin's bed. The vibrations here were denser. What did he want exactly? What did she want?

At the screen door she looked out to see if he was in sight. It was as black as onyx out there.

"I like seeing you in my bathrobe, Cass."

She jumped at his quiet greeting.

He approached the cabin porch and stood below the step, outside the rectangle of light cast onto the wide, uneven floorboards, her robed silhouette creating a shadow. Cassie set her hand on the door handle, she thought in order to open it for him.

Robbin continued in a quiet voice. "I missed you something awful these past few minutes—did you just lock that door?"

Cassie dropped her eyes to the source of the betraying click. Sure enough, her thumb had slid the latch into the lock. She felt foolish. Also reluctant to undo it. She lifted her eyes helplessly.

Robbin stood unmoving and spoke in a tone used to soothe the insane. "Undo the lock, Cassie, and come out."

This being the opposite of what her resistance was building toward, she obeyed the instructions gratefully.

Robbin sat down on the porch steps with his back to her, his arms stretched outward over his knees. He bent his head and pressed his mouth into the upper arm of his blazer sleeve.

Cassie wandered over to the porch post behind his shoulder and sat with her hip on the railing, letting one bare foot dangle off the floor. In the silence that followed she noticed someone walking down the dirt road, beyond the lodge next door, white shirt glowing in the dark—Fee—and she guessed he felt his forecast about her and Robbin was proven correct tonight. She wound the end of the bathrobe tie all the way up in a fat wheel, then let it unwind like a window shade between her legs.

"Not exactly wholehearted about this, are you?" He didn't look at her.

"I could ask for an autograph." When on the defensive, turn offensive.

He sighed. "So this is the joy of being with a woman who knows me well. This is having a *relationship*."

Silence. Then he stood up, went to the door and opened it. Without looking back at Cassie, he reached behind himself, grabbed her wrist and pulled her inside the cabin with him.

A point in his favor, Cassie thought. Jake would have stomped off as the injured party, leaving her to mend things with him on her own. Come to think of it, she herself was using Jake's tactics tonight, taking the offense once she had instigated the defense. Or was she doing the opposite? She had lost her place in the exchange, or Robbin had robbed her of it in throwing over his own easy out. Maybe Robbin wasn't adept at having a girlfriend, but neither was he versed in the ritual game playing.

He pulled out of his blazer, rolled up the sleeves on his dress shirt, and sat on the floor before the TV. He picked up the remote and flicked to the Idaho Falls channel for the late-night news. It was the likeliest station to give a report on the damage tonight's storm had created in the Jackson valley, even though Idaho Falls was a hundred miles over the pass and in another state. But this station, with its amateur newscasters and cameramen, was rarely worth watching for any reason, in Cassie's opinion. For one thing, the newscaster, a guy in his twenties, could never regulate his breathing with his talking, and Cassie would become short of breath watching the struggle.

With eyes on the TV, Robbin said, "Did I see you in my

bathrobe and say, 'Hey, baby, let's hit the sheets!'? No, I did not."

Cassie sat cross-legged on the floor beside Robbin, and she noticed a wasp sluggishly flying around the TV news desk. She said, "You want a *relationship*?"

"You're so goddamn ambivalent, it's a fucking insult."

The wasp made a killer dive, and the young newscaster deftly ducked his head as though to check his notes *very* closely.

"Monogamous?" Cassie asked, after mentally scrabbling for the word, as though it needed rediscovery after decades of disuse in Robbin's vicinity.

"We have to discuss the particulars? We have to negotiate?"

Now who was being ambivalent? she wondered. The newscaster was making wide, exaggerated gestures with his notes in an attempt to appear naturally enthused over his story, while directing his papers to collide with the wasp's flight pattern. "What do you really want for us, Robb?"

Robbin didn't answer immediately. His jaw was tensed and his eyes, murky and hooded, watched the TV screen. The wasp was becoming more intentioned, having awakened to its full power beneath the fake sun of the camera lights. The angry buzzing was as easily heard as the drone of the announcer's voice. But Robbin wasn't consciously following the situation any more than she was. They were both using the TV the way she accused her parents of doing—as a third focus to drain off the energy of one-to-one exchanges. With annoyance that she had pressed him to this, he answered her.

"A romance, okay? A *romance*, Cassidy." He punched off the TV and slumped back against his arms, watching the dark screen as raptly as when it was turned on.

"Okay," she said.

They exchanged glances as unemotionally as business cards.

"Hold it. Did you see that? That was a *wasp*." Robbin abruptly sat upright, punched the TV back on, then scooped Cassie up in his arms and sat her in the circle of his crossed legs.

She rested her back against his chest and they both watched the newscaster in his struggle.

"Oh, damn," Robbin cheered, "look at him."

The announcer was fast losing his composure, which was always tenuous enough to make Cassie squirm on the best of nights. A trickle of perspiration glistened in the studio lights on each side of his hairline. The wasp circled closer and closer around his head. The announcer, completely unaware of his words, reread an entire paragraph he had just completed, using all the practiced emphasis of his first reading. And his eyes sneakily followed the wasp zeroing in tighter. Abruptly the announcer leaped to his feet, the camera now on his belt buckle. Cassie heard the slap of papers through the air. The announcer sat back down and stared vacantly at the camera. In the background a hissed voice said, "Good night, good night." The announcer waved good-bye and the screen became dark.

Robbin switched off the TV and turned Cassie around to cradle her in his lap. He slipped his hand beneath the robe and along her leg and watched her laughter die down and her eyes get smudgy as his hand moved up to trace her hip bone. Once he had her full attention, he bent down and touched his tongue to her bottom lip. Then he said, "Hey, baby, let's hit the sheets."

He was funny, and she laughed on that account alone, but it also struck her as more than quick and clever twisted humor. He trusted her to get it in the way he meant—self-parody—and she thought it was somehow sexy as all get-out that Robbin could get inside their two heads like that and trigger a joint reaction so spasmodic and pleasurable.

Robbin was more succinct. "Oh, God, you're fun."

The next day Cassie and Robbin roamed the ranch to check on the changes wrought by the wind and water of the night before. Fragrances from sage and pine, weeds and wildflowers steeped in the sun and in the moisture rising from the earth. The pasture grasses were flattened, all bent northward, as the storm had come in from the Snake River Canyon and ripped its way toward Yellowstone. The river ran full and muddy. Pairs of trumpeter swans floated serenely with young families of Canada geese, mallards, goldeneye ducks and cinnamon teals. Where the river swamped the fringes of wetlands, Cassie spotted two sandhill cranes, bigger than fawns, stalking long-legged through the marshes. Mosquitoes buzzed fiercely around her bare ankles. She bent to gently move them on their way with a swish of her hand, then listened beneath the moving wings of insects, beneath the combing of air by the pine boughs, to the deep silence. The air felt twenty degrees cooler than yesterday.

Later that afternoon, Mrs. Penny rallied as many people as she could bully into greeting more of her recruits—this time two elderly men who were longtime, dear friends of hers. But during the night the bridge over Elk Tooth Creek had given out from the constant pummeling of high water, so the guests were arriving by taxi, and Boone planned to meet them on the far bank with the fishing dory to bring them across the swollen creek to the ranch. Mrs. Penny herself planned to wear hip waders and walk beside her guests as they sat in the dry dory to assure them of the safety and fun of the adventure. Mrs. Penny promoted the arrival of her old friends as though it was an event of major, though unnamed, significance to Cross Wave.

Cassie excused herself from the greeting party and cooked instead. She began a soup, made up her ten-piecrust recipe and baked a double batch of sour cream sugar cookies for the coming week.

CHAPTER TWENTY-ONE

As Cassie finished squeezing the oranges for juice, Robbin came in the kitchen door. A half hour earlier, she had slipped out of his bed from their second night in a row together. He circled his arms around her from behind and kissed her neck. Cassie heard Boone's steps coming down the staircase and eased out of Robbin's embrace and began to toss ham into the omelet. She directed Robbin's attention to the browning potatoes, so as to smear his dreamy look into a passable expression of early-morning hunger in time for Boone's eyes.

Boone entered the kitchen. "You know what I woke up realizing?"

"What?" A glance assured Cassie of Boone's preoccupation with his thoughts; he was tucking in his tan corduroy shirt and heading for the back door for his customary prebreakfast walk around the yard.

He cheerily divulged his realization. "Breakfast has been a very pleasant time for quite a while now. You two don't fight anymore." He pushed through the door to gather his clues on what kind of weather would arrive during the day.

Cassie froze in place with the juice pitcher poised over the breakfast table. Robbin grinned at her over his shoulder and lifted a spatula full of potatoes to turn. Stricken, Cassie whispered, "I don't want him to know."

"Don't be crazy. He'll be pleased as a punch drunk," Robbin said, using one of Cassie's mother's convoluted clichés, which Cassie had reported to Robbin from her last phone call home.

She had not moved a muscle and stood statue-still with the juice pitcher. How could she let Boone know she was sleeping with Robbin? The summer help shacking up with the boss' son. How could a nice woman like her be involved in a deal like that? That was what Boone would want to know.

Surveillance only half accomplished, Boone popped back through the door. "How come, you suppose?"

With a happy countenance Robbin said, "We found something better to do." He leaned his back against the stove and waited for the glad surprise he was confident of seeing on his father's face.

Sure enough, Boone delivered a little chuckle. "Welp." He looked to each of them and smiled broadly and benignly. "Doggone," he said, and chuckled again with the pleasure and surprise of it.

"He's happy for us, Cass." Robbin's expression invited her to join the two of them in their pleasure. He moved closer to her, but knew not to touch. Cassie held the ceramic juice pitcher with such pressure between her two hands that a lesser piece of crockery would have shattered.

"It's good, Cassie, and Boone sees that."

She was making a scene. It *was* good; Boone probably did see that. She let Robbin take the juice pitcher and accepted the chair he pulled out for her.

As if sensing surrender, Robbin came in for the cleanup. After directing Boone to sit down, Robbin brought over the food, setting it on the table in the pans it was cooked in. Then he put his hands on Cassie's shoulders and spoke from behind her chair. "She made me work for it, but finally she consented to be my girlfriend." Cassie knew he was trying to help her out. "Congratulate me, Boone; she's my first real one."

Chuckles from father and son, and Cassie thought, Oh, well, what's the big deal? And she smiled at her plate.

"If you two need a bigger place to stay . . . welp, let's work something out." Boone ate heartily, forgoing distribution of the newspaper sections this morning in honor of the big news here at home.

"That Randy-girl," Boone went on, "was another matter altogether. I'm all for a steady relationship."

Boone was trying to show his comfort with this, Cassie knew. He probably figured he needed to correct the notion she may have gotten about his position on such matters the last time Robbin presented a bedmate at breakfast.

"I'm steady. Robbin hasn't decided." Oh, heck, right out with it. What was she trying to pull off here—sibling rivalry? Robbin's been bad, but not her? Still, she added, "He's holding on to the option of seeing Randy again."

"Cassie . . ." Robbin said quietly. He brushed a forefinger across her thumb, lying idle beside her plate.

She raised her eyes and looked at him. "And that's fine with me," she said.

"Cass . . ."

"Because I understand he isn't ready to commit to one person."

Boone chuckled. He poured his coffee. "No, of course not— Robbin's too *young!*"

"Hasn't had enough *experience* yet," Cassie contributed, to make Boone laugh again. She was finding an old familiar rhythm coming to her rescue.

Robbin set his coffee mug down hard.

"Aw, heck," Boone drawled, halting his laughter and catching, finally, the drift of hot air.

A potato slice was enroute to Cassie's mouth when Robbin grabbed her fork. "I'm committing to you." He nailed her eyes. "But *after* you, I'm sticking to strangers. I don't need my past tossed in my face with breakfast another morning."

Did he even *hear* the incongruity in his words? She was in no mood to shrug it off as humor; she pushed back her chair and got up.

Robbin caught her around the waist. "I'm committing—did you get that?"

"For how long, Robbin? Till the next trip to L.A. or the next trip to the Cowboy Bar?" She pulled away. And because she could hide her face faster if she didn't turn toward the outside door, she headed for the upstairs room where she painted. Walked through the dining room, palmed the banister and swiveled around and up the staircase.

"Cass! Cass!" She heard Robbin's chair scrape back. "She doesn't understand," he said to Boone. "I love her."

"Tell her!" Boone cried. But he couldn't wait. "Cassie! Did you hear that?" he shouted. And Cassie heard Boone also leap to his feet, chair scraping back. "He loves you!"

Midway, she halted her race up the stairs and turned to see Robbin arrive at the foot.

"Cassie, I love you." He looked pained. "I *love* you."

Boone hurried up beside him. "He *loves* you!" he shouted up to her with a proud grin and an arm slung around Robbin's shoulders. "How *about* that!" He gave a congratulatory pat to Robbin's back.

Just look at that, Cassie thought, standing above them on the staircase. He can act, he can write, he can fall in love—what a boy.

Then she slipped through cynicism into utter happiness and sat down on the steps and cried.

Robbin's body was around her in a second. He sat sideways on the step, one leg awkwardly sprawled on the step above, and he drew her between his thighs and held her.

Through blurry lashes, beneath Robbin's enfolding arms pressing her head to his chest, Cassie saw Boone's feet retreat toward the kitchen a few steps, return, and retreat. Finally, he approached the banister beside them. "Could someone just tell me . . . does she love you?"

"She loves me," Robbin said.

The next morning as Cassie was leaving Robbin's cabin to head for the main house, she was met with the sight of a freshly severed elk head, antlers blood-smeared, mounted on the front of Robbin's pickup like a bloody hood ornament.

Robbin was following her, and they both stopped short.

"My God." Robbin turned to Cassie. "That's Earl." He looked stunned and confused. "What's going on?" All Cassie could do was shake her head and reach for his hand. She thought

Robbin was going to weep as he smoothed Earl's nose, already buzzing with deerflies. Cassie herself was nearly sick with the wanton destruction of this immense and beautiful creature.

Clearly this was a message of some kind, a warning, Cassie thought, or an act of revenge. And it was directed toward Robbin, the head sitting as it was on Robbin's hood, facing his cabin, designed to greet him in the morning when he awoke. The cattle rustling was still referred to as a prank, but not this. This was a crime. Cassie had enjoyed greeting Earl mornings and evenings as he confidently roamed the ranchlands, watering at the river's edge, matting grasses for his bed, browsing shrubs, lately bugling wildly in the night in preparation for gathering his harem for fall mating. This was murder, first degree.

Mrs. Penny, alerted by the rising commotion of Cross Wave residents waking to this gory sight, demanded that no one disturb the head until she roused her two friends, whom she paraded past the spectacle in their bathrobes. Why she went to such effort to protect her eastern friends from the terrors of the creek, then dragged them to this scene, Cassie had to wonder.

Fee arrived. "Dear God," he said. He shook his head, then let it drop, his eyes lowered. "The stupid bastards."

Silence reigned as everyone stood around, not knowing what to do or say next.

Fee said, "I'll send a hand to take care of this." Fee said again, "The stupid bastards." How come he seemed angry, instead of sad? She could never read that guy.

Robbin watched Fee leave. Boone appeared. "Something's going on, Boone." Robbin searched his father's face. "Things have been feeling wrong for a while now." Again he turned toward the direction Fee had walked. "I need to find Cody. Get him to take a look around with me." Boone nodded, and Robbin jogged off.

Boone said, "I guess we should call the authorities," though he made no move to do so.

Mrs. Penny said, "No, Boone. I think not. Give this a little time." She, too, cast her eyes toward the direction Fee had taken, then hustled her two friends back toward their cabins.

Cassie said to Boone, "Come on. I'll make some coffee."

While they walked back to the main house, Cassie tried to analyze why she felt somewhat responsible. Not outright responsible, she reasoned, more inadvertently connected. "I'll be right there," she said to Boone and veered off toward her camper to pick up a sweater. She stepped up into her doorway and almost fell inside, her foot seeming to rise too high for the threshold. She grabbed a fleece and pulled it over her head as she rushed back out the door, this time her foot plunging too hard to the ground. She turned to check her footing and saw with astonishment that her camper tires were flat.

She walked around the camper and examined each tire. "Slashed," she said out loud. She stood there a moment, feeling puzzled, victimized, mad. She forgot about the coffee and went directly to Mrs. Penny's cabin and knocked on her door.

"Why, dear, hello," Mrs. Penny said.

"What's going on? Earl is dead. My tires are slashed. And you know something about this. Who are these men you've brought here?" She said again, "What's going on, Mrs. Penny?"

"Come in. Sit, dear." Mrs. Penny gestured toward the end of the sofa and sat on the other end herself.

Cassie had no patience for sitting in this stuffy cabin. She chose to remain standing.

"Those men, dear, are bankers. I've brought them around to

promote the investment in some land here in the West that I'd like them to appreciate."

"You dragged them in their pajamas to view the bloody head of an elk in order to convince them? Mrs. Penny, will you please tell me what is going on?"

"Dear, rather than the answers, I just know the questions. You might say I see the possibilities, but like seeds, they may or may not sprout. When you get to my age, you've seen so much you don't need to wait until harvest time for results. I am an old dried pod, rattling with seeds. Now, take a seat."

Cassie took a seat, only because like everyone else on the ranch she'd become used to minding Mrs. Penny. "You're not going to tell me a thing, are you?"

"I have little information to pass on. Though I can tell you one thing: since you've come to Cross Wave with your loveliness and eager intelligence to preserve the land and its wildlife, you have charmed some people and frightened others."

"I don't try to frighten people, Mrs. Penny. I live my life; I give my best care to what comes my way."

"Dear, I know that. I admire you very much. I see that our Robbin admires you as well. However, right now . . . right now, the balance is touchy, and whether you intend it or not, you do provoke change and that frightens some."

"Are you blaming me for Earl? For the slashed tires?"

"Of course not. Nor the cattle rustling, nor the publicity leak."

"Nor the shooting of my dog, I hope."

"That was a dreadful mistake, dear. The situation can't handle another one. In that regard, I suggest you take very good care of your heart. Love and be watchful."

That's when Cassie realized the extent of Mrs. Penny's awareness of events on the ranch. She met the old lady's gaze; she felt she fully understood the message she was sending: Robbin is a wild card; you are fragile still. What she didn't understand was the lump she felt swelling in her throat. As if her body knew something she hadn't become conscious of yet.

Cassie rose and reached for the doorknob, and Mrs. Penny said, "If you would, please, keep the identity of my friends to yourself for now. It would be too hard on the others to know just yet."

Cassie nodded and left. She walked quickly across the compound to the main house; Boone was probably wondering about the whereabouts of his coffee and his cook.

He was in the office talking on the phone when Cassie entered the kitchen. He soon hung up. "That was Robbin calling from the Barlows' place. He's picked up Cody and the two of them are trailing the blood and the tire tracks. Cody is one hell of a tracker. We'll be getting some answers soon."

"My tires are slashed. All four of them."

Boone spun around and returned to the office to call the Barlow house and report that. Cassie hoped her footprints hadn't disturbed the ground too much. She began an extra-large pot of coffee, in case it would be needed.

A few hours after Cassie had given up on Robbin returning for breakfast, he and Cody drove up and came into the kitchen, looking exhausted. Cassie had made lemonade and was taking a quiche out of the oven. Boone walked out of the office when he heard voices, and the three of them pulled out chairs and sat around the kitchen table. Cassie reached for glasses and plates, set the pitcher of lemonade and the quiche on the table and excused herself. She was aching to know what they had discovered, but sensed that her knowledge of certain information, which Cody and Mrs. Penny had requested that she keep to herself, could put her in an awkward position, could make her appear to be a liar by omission. Besides, she needed to get to camp and begin lunch preparations. This morning Fee was taking Mrs. Penny and her two guests on a driving tour and a couple of the wranglers had several guests out fly-fishing. Both groups would be hungry when they returned.

Later that night when she and Robbin were alone in his cabin, she learned that Cody had tracked the poachers to the river. Apparently two men had approached the ranch from that access, killed Earl and removed his body to their boat, probably dumping his remains downstream. Furthermore, Robbin and Cody had driven to various put-in accesses along the river in hopes of discovering signs that would indicate where the boat had originated and to match boot prints Cody found on the ranch's riverbank.

"Cody knows the weight of the two men and has an image in mind of how they walk. Isn't that amazing?" Cassie agreed; it was amazing. "He's been good at this since we were kids. The guy just has this incredible sense of what's been disturbed. You wouldn't believe what he picks up just by standing still a moment. Reminds me of some research I've uncovered about Cal Carrington. They say he didn't track so much as intuitively sense where the animals were and often he'd intersect their path at a right angle."

"But now what? Cody has this information, but the world is big."

"Not so big. And he's got a lot of information. He spent the day driving around, checking the bars, the marinas. He'll just watch. The guy's got patience like I've never seen. He'll come up with something."

There were so many things they didn't know much about; to curb their frustration they moved their conversation in other directions. They talked about how stock tanks for watering the cattle would save the creek banks from the destruction of hooves breaking down the native grasses, which in turn allowed erosion that muddied the creek.

Then Cassie asked how his work was going on "The Countess and the Cowboy." They got comfortable in bed, and Robbin began to tell her the next installment of the story.

Soon Cissy was considered a westerner, rather than a greenhorn at the guest ranch, and she dressed the part in men's clothing and a five-gallon hat. She rode, camped and shot like a westerner. And did all this with Cal beside her. Most hunting guides were successful because they learned where the animals ate and slept, but Cal became one with the forest, the atmosphere and the spirit of the animal he hunted, and he rode directly to it.

Cal carried a stillness within himself that contrasted sharply with Cissy's restlessness. She invariably wanted whatever she didn't have and enjoyed conniving until she got it. By the time she came to Wyoming, that list had become quite short: she had everything there was to want. But once she saw Cal's Flat Creek Ranch, she had a new goal.

Cal held out. He had built his cabin there and a couple other buildings and he liked to go there to be alone. But eventually he conceded, sold her the land, and the following summer Cissy moved to Flat Creek Ranch, with Cal along as hunting guide. Her daughter, Felicia, was dragged to this remote setting, a full day's horseback ride from town, along with a cook, a Swedish maid and a chore boy. At first Felicia was happy there. Cal gave her a pony of her own and took her out riding, but as she grew up and the relationship with her mother—never a smooth one—worsened, Felicia was often miserable. Cissy had never acted lovingly toward Felicia and seemed to see her as a reminder of the husband who had beaten and humiliated her. "You look like your father," Cissy told Felicia, "just as many of the children do in his Polish village."

The ranch changed Cissy somewhat; she learned to love solitude as much as Cal did. Often she rode out into the mountains and spent long hours on her own. And Cissy and Cal loved to be alone in the wilderness together. During those years, Cissy stayed with Cal on the Flat Creek Ranch until the serious storms of winter arrived, and then she headed to her life of parties, high fashion, and the company of powerful people back east.

CHAPTER TWENTY-TWO

Cassie hadn't forgotten about the Beaver Creek Burn and the metaphor she had constructed to remind herself what consorting with Robbin could lead to. But she no longer worried that she would come out of her own picnic sooty and charred; she remembered other things about the aftermath of the fiery catastrophe. She remembered the healing growth of grasses and the sturdy shoots of new lodgepole pines. Each summer those pine seedlings seemed to double themselves, growing strong in fertile ground created by the lost trees now decaying. Yellow violets grew there and the breezes freely swept through the bared forest. And the hundreds of straight-poled trees that stood thickly without branches or pine needles had begun in those first few years to drop their charred bark in great sheets that the rain and snow had worked loose. Beneath the blackened bark, smooth creamy wood was exposed, as satiny as baby skin, freshly kneaded bread dough, Robbin's penis.

After that, those black and cream trunks began to loosen

their grip on the earth and winds blew them down to lie in cross-hatches atop the forest floor, providing shelter for the new pine seedlings and the small creatures that had returned. Now, many years after the fire, those trees once again closed the view to the mountains and grew in a dense and feathery forest.

Still, Cassie took the words of Mrs. Penny, "Love and be watchful," to heart, and in the days following the advent of their formal romance, while Robbin read one after another of Cassie's philosophy books, Cassie began to read about insanity. Craziness acquired a fascination for her. She didn't understand this; she didn't read these books in front of Robbin; she didn't entirely register her own insatiable interest. She just perused them at the library for hours. She hid in nooks at the Valley Bookstore and swallowed them whole. But she always left having purchased something else.

One day she found what she'd been unconsciously seeking. And she wrote down this quote from R. D. Laing and put it in her pocket: "Madness need not be all breakdown. It may also be breakthrough. It is potential liberation and renewal as well as enslavement and existential death."

She left the bookstore on a swell of relief. She surfed on it through tourist traffic around the town square and crossed to the park in the center of the square and found a bench.

If that quote was true, and it struck her intuitively that it was, then many other things were also true: she wasn't crazy for having fallen in love with a man who once considered himself crazy. And Robbin himself wasn't merely exhibiting another form of insanity with his interest in her philosophy books or his professed love for her. This might not be another side trip to the edge for him, but a progressive widening of consciousness. If so, there was hope for all that she could imagine.

She felt energy surge up and out and rode it playfully: eyes closed up to the sun, silly smile on her face. *Of course*, a small voice said, *there's no guarantee he'll choose this potential liberation and renewal*, and she beached abruptly on rough sand.

But there were no guarantees in life for anything, she reminded herself. She knew, too, that if growth was not part of a relationship, then passion dissipated or abruptly turned negative. Passion was energy, after all; the idea of it encompassed movement. Passion moved out of lives if it didn't move lives onward.

Late August, Cassie thought. If she wasn't careful to screen her perceptions, she could detect signs of the approaching autumn, and she wasn't ready for that. Something in the air suggested waking one morning not too distant from now and crunching a foot on frosted grass. The earliest snow was expected mid-September—unless the errant July blizzard counted. When asked about the weather by a newcomer, these days she would answer like an old-timer: "We have nine months of winter and three of poor skiing."

But, she reminded herself, summer officially continued for another month and her future need not be decided this morning—a litany she repeated often lately. The office phone interrupted her thoughts. Erin knew Cassie was busy cooking, but a rumor had just hit her real estate office that a change of ownership was being recorded on Pale Feather Ranch at the county office and she wondered what Cassie knew about that. Cassie didn't know a thing . . . exactly. But once she hung up from talking to Erin she began to wonder how that fit in with Mrs. Penny and her eastern friends. She wasn't sworn to secrecy on Erin's news, so she told Robbin moments later, when he came in the back door.

He said, "That's probably nothing. Pale Feather is owned by an investment group; it likely changes names once in a while for legal purposes."

As it turned out, Robbin shouldn't have dismissed Erin's phone call so lightly. By the time Erin phoned again that afternoon, she had traced the newest records on Pale Feather Ranch to the New York investment company Bachelor, Woods & Pew. She'd had a reporter friend at the *Jackson Hole News & Guide* call the firm to ask friendly questions regarding the firm's intentions for the property. The reporter gathered nothing but a reluctance to give out information. Which according to Erin's friend was unusual; most prospective newcomers to the valley were eager to be a part of the community and welcomed introduction via the local newspaper. Asked if the firm was representing another party with its bid, the firm's spokesperson had replied, "Of course. That's what we *do*."

And, of course, what else they did was keep the identity of that party confidential.

In bed that night Robbin said, "Today I learned two secrets."

Her head resting on an elbow, Cassie looked at his face in the glow of the ranch yard light shining through the window. He was smiling and looking expectant. Cassie hoped fervently that they were two of the secrets she'd been carrying. Of all of them, the secret Cody had told her about Fee's involvement with stirring up the ranchers to alert the press was the weightiest.

"First of all, Cody is engaged to Diana and her girls. Isn't that great?"

One down, she thought, and was pleased that this news made Robbin happy. "It's wonderful."

"We should have a party, a big one."

"What's your other secret?"

"You know how Mrs. Penny introduced her friends by their first names? I didn't even think about it, but that isn't her usual style. Guess who they are?" He didn't wait for her to reply. "Mr. Woods and Mr. Pew."

Cassie sat up. "Of Bachelor, Woods and Pew?"

"The same. Cody said Fee told him."

Cassie lay back down. "Now what the heck does that mean?" She was asking herself more than Robbin, but wouldn't mind an answer from either.

He said, "Maybe we should get engaged, too."

"We're not there yet," she replied matter-of-factly, covering up her surprise. Robbin was content not to pursue the subject.

Cassie had been through the stages of love before; she knew she and Robbin were just at the starting gate. But Robbin didn't. Like a kid infatuated with his fifth-grade teacher, he was making plans to run away from home, hop a freight train south with his lady love and wrestle a crocodile to make her a new pair of shoes. It could be that she should get used to being ahead of him emotionally. It could be that he wouldn't catch up in these matters for a while yet, and for Cassie to have an area in which she was more experienced was good. It balanced the relationship, because in the practical ways of life Robbin was way ahead of her.

He told her later that night in bed how he'd achieved his success in the film business. Perhaps in light of what she learned about this, she shouldn't have been surprised at his perspective on their relationship. He was goal-oriented by nature.

"I wasn't the best actor in the world; there were thousands better than me. But one by one, they took themselves out. They had all kinds of excuses, Cass; a million original, valid excuses for taking themselves out. I allowed myself none. So all that time

I hung in there, I moved up. Somebody gave up hope, somebody believed what the world told them about failure, and another space opened. I was in line for it every time."

It wasn't talent, he claimed; and ambition didn't explain his success either.

"Discipline?" Cassie asked.

"Discipline is for dieters. Artists use ritual and vision. They don't set limits—they set direction." And she could do the same with her painting.

The next evening Robbin asked Cassie to join him in a visit to Mrs. Penny's cabin. Her two friends, Mr. Woods and Mr. Pew, had left, and Robbin hoped to find out more about the reason they had come all the way out to Wyoming. Also, he had an idea he wanted to bounce off Mrs. Penny. They found her on the porch, just rising from her rocking chair with a book in her hand. This late in the summer the evenings became dark shortly after eight. Robbin and Cassie were invited to come inside with her and have a cup of tea.

Mrs. Penny headed for her stove and reached for the kettle; Robbin followed and told her that he had learned her friends were visiting here in regard to the purchase of Pale Feather Ranch and he was thinking that he'd like to save it from development, if that was in the works, by investing in it himself.

"Thought we might talk about a partnership, Mrs. P."

It would jeopardize the financial well-being of Cross Wave for him to do it alone, but together perhaps they could purchase it and protect it by handing it over to the Jackson Hole Land Trust. "Cassie says that land is valuable to the wildlife. For one thing, the antelope migration path cuts right through it."

Mrs. Penny turned her back to fill her kettle at the sink.

Since she didn't answer, Robbin elaborated. They'd keep their identities concealed. If John D. Rockefeller, Jr., hadn't concealed his identity behind the formation of the Snake River Land Company back in the 1920s, Robbin argued, Grand Teton National Park, in its present state, would not exist. Clearly, Bachelor, Woods & Pew and whoever they were working for would deliberately jack up the price if they knew he was involved—just like the landowners did to Rockefeller—because everybody believed Robbin was loaded with money and because, politically, a lot of people didn't agree—just like the ranchers back in the twenties and thirties—that land should be permanently taken out of the free enterprise system. Behind the guise of the Snake River Land Company, Rockefeller paid fair-market price per acre, and so would Robbin and Mrs. Penny.

"First we must acknowledge *why* you don't have the funds to accomplish this on your own." Mrs. Penny turned from the stove where she had set her pot of water to boil and rested her hands on the back of a kitchen chair. "There were years, Robbin, when Cross Wave needed to hold itself together without your support, because your money disappeared in considerable chunks as you gambled it away in Las Vegas. There were other years when nobody would work with you in films due to your drinking and drug indulgence. Lastly, you've recently emerged from a mental hospital." Mrs. Penny held up her hand to halt Robbin's interruption. "I know. You put *yourself* there as an act of healing. I congratulate you on taking that responsibility. However, the result is that you have once again jeopardized your career." Mrs. Penny spooned tea leaves from a flowered tin into a china teapot. "I believe I am correct in surmising that the recent attention stirred is primarily curiosity. And that your flood of offers does not include anything involving a long-term commitment from you." She clapped the lid on the tin. "The reason for that? You have no record of stability."

"Stability," Robbin repeated and began to move around the cabin in a restless pacing from woodstove to window to bookcase.

Mrs. Penny poured the steaming water into her china teapot and carried it to the coffee table on a tray with three cups and saucers. She sat down.

"I'm sorry to say this, Robbin. I cannot go into business with you."

Near the large front window glowing from the porch light beside it, where the arrow of words pierced his flight of aggression, Robbin dropped into stillness.

"Why?" He was ten years old, asking Mom how come no bike for a week.

"You're an honest man, Robbin. I know that."

"Then, why?"

"You like to play the edge. All of us who have watched you grow, become an adult, know that. And . . ." Here her eyes moved to Cassie, then quickly scanned past her, and she looked back at Robbin and finished. "And you know that."

"What do you mean?" It came out "whadoyamean," trailing up on the end, a plea—just give me my bike back, I won't do it again.

Cassie felt uneasy. She considered excusing herself, but then she'd miss something. Something that might explain herself to herself. Because Mrs. Penny almost said, "Cassie knows," and Cassie didn't know at all.

"You grew up in the wilderness, Robbin; wildness does not daunt you. The unknown is your challenge. Unmarked trails excite you; getting lost is a game. Without map or compass you can find your way to the center of every mystery." Mrs. Penny's voice softened, and for the first time Cassie heard her use an endearment when addressing Robbin. "But, honey, you arrive every darn time unprepared for what greets you."

Robbin dropped his gaze to the center of the floor between himself and Mrs. Penny and put his hands into his pockets.

"It's admirable, Robbin, that you have this courage to get to the center. Most don't. You figure out methodically how to get there. Yet, I think you stay just long enough to touch the signposts: here is the center—now get me the heck out."

Robbin glanced up with a slight smile of recognition, then lowered his eyes again.

"And you know why I think that is? You haven't earned the ability to handle the power there. The center is a place of responsibility and great control over one's life and often over others' lives. Money or fame alone is a false power. It is the image, the face of power, not the power itself. One who resides there can often afford to relegate the responsibilities of the position to paid employees, enjoy the power, yet never use it to benefit others. In your case, the aim was not to grow into that place of power, just to acquire its mystery. Then you scrambled like crazy to barge back through its misty walls."

Robbin shrugged and stepped behind the counter of Mrs. Penny's kitchen and poured his tea down the drain and filled his cup with water from the faucet. Cassie felt his discomfort, his wish to barge back through the misty walls of Mrs. Penny's diagnosis and get the heck out of this cabin, too. But mostly Cassie felt her own uneasiness. Mrs. Penny knew Robbin a whole lot better than she did, and she should not dismiss that.

Mrs. Penny said, "I'm going to risk pressing this point. I want you to get it." She allowed Robbin his barrier of kitchen counter, even rose herself and stepped behind her overstuffed chair to give further distance between her and her godson, but she continued her fierce gaze. "You penetrated fame; you drank and used drugs to experience unknown realms; you followed that path to the deep center of the shadow world—you followed it to the asylum. Now, you are here tonight with me and want to push into the realms of philanthropy, which you think I have the keys to. . . ." Mrs. Penny hesitated, then plunged on. "And there is Cassie. She, too, holds the keys to realms new and unknown to you. None of my business—if indeed any of this is—except as it pertains to my representing your interests with this land. There, now, your intentions and staying power are very much my business."

Cassie felt both a deep affection for this man and a profound concern over their love affair. Mrs. Penny seemed to be saying there was a pattern in his behavior: work hard for a thing, then trash it.

Mrs. Penny released a big breath and returned to her chair. She reached for her teacup and took a sip. She said, "We'll give this a little time, then discuss it again. I do commend you, Robbin, on your recent choices. I had always believed that you were heading in this direction. Though I cannot bet my funds on your following through just yet."

Robbin approached Mrs. Penny and knelt down on her level. He lifted one of her hands from her lap. "I'll think about what you've said. I don't know . . . I don't know if you're right."

CHAPTER TWENTY-THREE

Cassie held an armful of old catalogs in the living room of the main house. She pondered the two sofas, plus Boone's favorite overstuffed club chair, done in a dull brown corduroy so worn it was rubbed white in places, and figured how she might change the room arrangement while still maintaining visual access to the fireplace and the television. She heard the kitchen screen slam.

"Where's the Girlfriend?" Robbin asked Boone, who was sitting at the kitchen table, last Cassie had seen him, studying ledger sheets that she'd printed out for him. At every opportunity, it seemed to Cassie, she was introduced as and referred to as "the Girlfriend." Robbin took some odd delight in the title.

"She's rearranging the living room furniture," Boone answered.

"Again?"

"She said it's been a few weeks."

Beneath sounds of the dishwasher rattling open and a cup clinking on the stovetop, Cassie heard Robbin say he was still bumping his shins from the last time. She heard coffee pour and the enamel pot rattle back onto the burner.

"Elene says we should toss all that furniture out, or at least reupholster it. She says nobody's got TV lamps anymore."

"Hey, that's a *black panther* TV lamp. That's a cool piece of art deco, or something."

"Elene says if I expect her to live here, she's got to have some say over things."

"Live here? Like marry her?"

"Welp, Elene says—"

"What do *you* say?"

"She knows about that kind of thing better than me. She says we need to commit to our . . . uh . . . friendship. She says it's time."

"Are you ready for that?"

"It's time, Robbin; people don't commit, they get in a rut, become old, then they . . . I don't know . . . die, I guess."

"If you don't marry Elene, you'll die?"

"No, no. She says committing could be most anything. Deciding and agreeing on it is the crux of it."

"What are you going to do?"

"Reupholster the furniture, I guess."

There was a bit of a silence then.

"But," Boone stated emphatically, "I'm going to remain firm about my chair staying brown."

Cassie heard a hand thumping a shoulder or back, a chair pushed out, then Robbin's footsteps coming through the dining room.

"What's up?" Robbin asked at the archway between the living room and dining room.

"The usual." Cassie smiled at him.

Robbin looked down to the front of his pants. "Good God,"

he said in chagrin. "You're right." And came over with this romantic gambit to coddle her out of her usual disgust at such remarks. Instead of hugging her as he'd seemed intent on doing, he stopped short of her. "What do you think about this black panther lamp, Cass? You like it okay?"

"I'd like it if someone would accidentally drop it on the stone hearth."

"Yeah, well, *someone* better not." He stuck his hands in his pants pockets and turned to go, then changed his mind and came over to smooth things out with her. "Sorry, babe." He sat down on the hearth. Cassie sat cross-legged on the floor before him, and Robbin sifted her bangs through his fingers. "I love you, Cass."

"But?" she asked, sensing his trouble.

"I'm stirred up all the time. Makes me sleepy." He said, "Sometimes lately I want to draw the shades and sleep for weeks."

Cassie thought about how Robbin had accused Boone, during their argument earlier in the summer, of teaching him that sleeping—one way or another—was how to handle problems. She acknowledged that he had a lot of unresolved situations going on right now. "It works like that when you change direction in your life and rearrange your values. Both the rewards and the obstacles rear up at once." She knew that actually, both were there all along in people's lives; they just weren't acknowledged until a certain time of acceptance.

Her only advice to him was the traditional western retort when someone bemoaned that life was presenting a challenge. She leaned over, kissed him softly on the mouth and said, "Cowboy up, Robbin."

The press of longer, cooler nights and shorter days shifted the center of Cassie's thought to a need to look ahead. Summer was ending. They all played cowboy golf after dinner in the newly mown hayfields around the ranch, propping their balls on the stiff and dried four-inch stubble left by the swathing machines. Even Mrs. Penny enjoyed this sport and arrived at the hayfields suitably garbed in skirt and golf glove, a visor on her head, looking to Cassie like a society matron playing at Carmel's Pebble Beach, until Cassie noticed Mrs. Penny's handmade leather cowboy boots: pointy toes, cabbage roses embossed in deep red-brown leather to match those on her personal saddle. In a couple of days she'd be leaving for the season.

Yet all the while Cassie felt Robbin groping for balance in a forest of questions. Where did he belong in the hierarchy of decision making on the ranch, and could he take his place without destroying the sense of belonging of those he loved? How could he gain Mrs. Penny's trust? Who would he be without his series of starring film roles? Would Boone and Elene make major changes that affected home and work? Was there a link between Fee and the dirty pranks played on the ranch? What would Cody discover in his search for Earl's poachers?

Robbin's world was further nudged off center, Cassie believed, by Cody's engagement. It wobbled some on its new axis, but appeared to Cassie to be orbiting steadily, once again, the following Sunday afternoon, when Robbin invited Cody and Diana, along with the wranglers and their dates, to a cookout.

With the front lawn to themselves after the week's dudes had departed, food and drink were spread out on the front porch and a couple dozen people sat in bunches on the grass. Robbin perched on the porch railing with his plate balanced on one knee and shot off made-up-on-the-spot limericks as toasts. Cassie laughed with the others as she listened to Robbin from the yard, his mind fast as fireworks.

Now Robbin instigated plans for a big engagement party, a blowout celebration for his buddy. He'd rent a hall, hire a band, invite the whole valley. He stirred up excitement with the ease of an electric Mixmaster plugged into an endless source of energy and frothed the others like egg whites into exuberant peaks. Soon Cassie saw him with a napkin on his knee, recording all the names suggested for the guest list. She and Diana, like two yolks set aside for the batter to come, talked between themselves.

With the engagement party scheduled for September 22, the equinox, Robbin made decisions with caterers, reserved a ballroom, hired a band. Cassie presumed all of this was the reason he had seemed preoccupied during the past few days. Preoccupied and abrupt.

Perhaps it was her imagination, perhaps she was a bit sensitive, perhaps she should heed Robbin's frequent suggestion lately to "lighten up."

There could be other reasons for Robbin's mood as well. Change was looming in every direction. Soon Cody would be married, and perhaps Boone, too. Cassie might stay to cook throughout hunting season, but during the winter she would be working elsewhere and would need to live closer to town. Robbin's self-imposed sabbatical was scheduled to end and he had accepted some invitations for public appearances. Still, all the decisions were weeks away, and all this was likely a figment of her insecurities about the summer's waning.

One other ungenerous possibility: she had been having her period the past four days. But even as she knitted the thought together with Robbin's behavior, she felt she was selling him short and quickly unraveled the idea.

During lunch the next day Fee tapped on the kitchen door, then entered. He refused Cassie's offer of a sandwich, but accepted a cup of coffee. Uneasily he announced that he had some bad news. He took off his grubby black felt hat and pulled out a dining chair but didn't sit.

"I got a call a little bit ago from Bachelor, Woods and Pew. Mrs. Penny died."

Cassie exhaled audibly. Boone and Robbin both stood up from the table and seemed about to approach Fee to join together in commiseration. But Fee stood unmoving behind his chair, as if it were a barrier he needed, and so Boone and Robbin ended up patting each other and murmuring regrets over this news. There was sadness, though no one cried. Mrs. Penny was elderly, so her death wasn't entirely unexpected. Yet the woman was so robust in spirit and character that she belied any physical frailty. Dismay filtered through the room with the afternoon sunshine. No one could imagine a summer tourist season without her.

Fee sat down, rested his hat on the floor beside his chair and relayed what he'd learned about her death. She had left the ranch a week ago, earlier than planned, to join Betsy and Alexander Slater and one of the mistresses in Taiwan. Alex was spending a month's residency as guest conductor of the Taiwan Symphony. Heart attack in the night, Alex reported to her law office, found dead in her hotel room the next morning by a maid.

As if wanting to get this next announcement over with, Fee said, "I'm executor of Mrs. Penny's will."

The McKeags glanced at each another in surprise.

Fee apparently held further information he wasn't eager to pass on. He folded his hands carefully on the table. "One of my duties is to sprinkle Mrs. Penny's ashes on her land."

Boone said, "We'll go back east with you."

"Absolutely," Robbin said.

Fee said, "Mrs. Penny's ashes are being sent here."

"Here?" Cassie asked in unison with Boone and Robbin.

"Alma Katarina Pew Penny," Fee said.

Not hard to figure from there. As in Bachelor, Woods & Pew.

"Mrs. Penny owns Pale Feather Ranch," Fee said. "Or soon will, once the legal situation clears. Messy at the moment, they tell me, but thank God she dragged those two Bachelor, Woods and Pew partners out here last month, the day after the flood." Fee said the two men would serve as witnesses of her enthusiasm and intention, so they could close on the deal as participants in the negotiations. The sale would proceed and clear title passed through her will.

"Who are her heirs?" Robbin asked

"She doesn't have any children," Boone said.

"That we know of," added Robbin.

Fee said he couldn't fill in too many of the blanks yet, and Cassie wondered whether that meant he didn't know the answers or wasn't at liberty for some reason to disclose them. Meanwhile, Fee said, he was conservator of Pale Feather, and the land was safe from development. "Of course, I can tell you that she left you a little something," Fee said to Robbin.

"'A little something' is the way she always referred to my five-dollar birthday check." He laughed. "God, I'm going to miss that lady."

Fee seemed to be considering whether to say more or not. He gripped his coffee mug with both hands and stared at it. "And one more thing." He cleared his throat. "I've invested in Pale Feather myself."

Gently he explained that though Robbin was doing great now, just great, there had been times during the past few years when he'd felt he needed to do something on his own to hold them all together. "I'm full-hearted proud of you, son. I just didn't know there for a while what might become of us."

Robbin had pushed his chair away from the table earlier and now he bent forward and rested his elbows on his knees, and looked down at the floor. He said, "I'm sorry."

Cassie could barely hear him, he spoke so quietly.

"We shouldn't of leaned on you so. It'd wear out a crew of men, son, holding all this up so many years." Fee released his grip on the coffee mug and relaxed his arms on the table. A silence held in the kitchen.

Then Boone scooted his chair around, bent over and patted Robbin on the back. "Fee's right. We should have done more to help out after that slump in the cattle market, followed by a couple lean years in the dude business. It was a lot for you, Robb, knowing you had to keep going whether you wanted to or not."

"We thank you mightily for that, boy," Fee added. "I hoped it would relieve your burden to know that a parcel of Pale Feather is registered under my personal ownership in a side deal I made with Alma some weeks back. I asked her to cosign on that piece holding the old house. Plus, Alma insisted I accept the usual twenty percent executor's fee, which she added to my parcel. Said she put that in the will."

Both McKeags nodded.

"We'll keep it in alfalfa . . . some winter grazing. Work it along with the Cross Wave. Hoping the old Calloway house will suit Cody and his Diana, though those young ones will have a trot to the school bus, same like you boys did."

"Whew," Robbin said. "A lot of changes."

Cassie put some cookies on a plate and thought the air in the room seemed stiff and awkward. Talk reverted to plans for Mrs. Penny's ashes. It was agreed they'd wait until after Cody and Diana's engagement party tomorrow night, then arrange a memorial service.

Fee rose from his chair, as if to leave, then sat back down again. He cleared his throat. Another silence spread. Cassie's heart beat faster. Boone and Robbin sat fully alert.

"I've done you wrong, son." Fee looked straight into Robbin's eyes.

Robbin's whole body stilled. He watched Fee's face.

"Cody will give you the particulars, but he suggested I tell you first myself." He took a deep breath. "I riled the boys up and they got their sons involved and everybody got carried away. I told them missy, here, was checking the irrigation canals and finding seepage. Probably reporting us to somebody, and complaining to you. I told the boys we needed to make her look bad, get her off the place."

His eyes lifted to Cassie, leaning against the stove. "Missy, I owe you a set of new tires and an apology for blaming you for the cattle rustling. I'm sorry. You plain scared me, girl. I learned you and your husband promoted the Land Trust and did volunteer work for them around the valley, and I figured we needed to do something quick or another one of our ranches was going to fall under their rules. We like to have control over our own place. Those people get involved and there you are, accepting their money and moving your cattle places they tell you to. The old ways are good. They've gotten us far."

He paused, shook his head. "Still and all, I've lost us Earl and I stirred up the press about you being in residence, Robb.

My doing, all my doing." He took in a big breath. "Those questions you've been asking about how your money was spent these years. You got a right, and I know it. But it set me off."

Cassie felt relief over this news coming out, but the feeling was overwhelmed with a kind of misery for everyone.

Boone said, "I'm sure you aren't all to blame."

"I am, Boone. I'm all to blame."

"Oh, now," Boone added, hating to see his friend so despairing.

Fee scraped his chair back to make room to cross his legs, and the sound, abrasive and jarring, seemed to mimic the mood in the room. "My fears got the worst of me. Got all turned inside out. Everything changing on us. They just got the worst of me." He looked to Cassie. "Those water bottles and the recycling. I looked around at my hands, all following you like kittens do their mama's teat, and I figure it won't be long till me and my cows are moved right off the place."

Robbin said, "That would never happen. This is your home."

"My heart knows that, son; my head just kept on worrying." Fee gave a big sniff, turning his head sideways, as if to avoid a sneeze.

"I didn't mean to worry you so," Cassie said.

"I know that, too. You're a real decent girl."

After a pause, Fee said, "Alma saw the problem from both sides, and her determination was to keep us together as a family. So she got her backers and pulled from some of her other investments and moved events toward the acquisition of Pale Feather. Calloway is real pleased to move off the place. That old cowboy got so broken up from his rodeo days, his poor bones could hardly take another winter managing that ranch."

"It's all going to turn out, then," Boone said.

"The joke on me is that Alma has got rules and regulations about conservation on that parcel of mine that would put your Land Trust to shame, missy."

Everybody smiled, Cassie included. That was good news. But as much sympathy as she felt at the moment for Fee having to make his confession and express his regrets, there was still room to be irked at the man. If everything had turned out the way he had intended and she had been fired, Cassie wondered whether he would still have felt regretful. Maybe he would have; she didn't know him well enough to say.

Fee rose, exchanged sincere eye contact with each of them in turn, and said, "Cody, he'll tell you what he learned. I knew once he got his nose to the ground, I wasn't going to come out looking so good." He shook his head. "It got out of hand, it did. Some of the boys headed down to the bars in Pinedale and dragged up oil workers for their games and that's how poor Earl got himself on the hood of your truck that bad morning."

A silence spread as the memory of that discovery stirred.

"Mrs. P, she never did leave a scrap to waste. She used poor Earl to convince her partners that war was breaking out on Cross Wave and if they didn't help her acquire Pale Feather so we could all spread out, she was pulling every dollar of her money away. God love her."

Boone said, "She thought of all of us as her family and didn't want to see any trouble."

"And there won't be any more trouble," Fee promised. He bent to retrieve his hat. "I'm full sorry to each of you." He nodded to the three of them in turn, put his hat on, then walked out the kitchen door.

"Everything will turn out just fine," Boone said after the screen door closed.

Robbin didn't respond.

Cassie wondered what he was thinking, but when she asked him later, he said nothing much and wouldn't elaborate on that. Still, she hoped he felt exonerated for the uncertainty that had led Fee to purchase his own land. Because she saw now that Fee was right: it was a considerable burden on Robbin and had been since he was twelve. He couldn't have said no to the first film he'd made or to the last. She hoped now he would realize he had been released from a lifelong responsibility. To Cassie that seemed the point of Mrs. Penny's actions as they affected Robbin.

Later that afternoon Fee reported back from talking further with Mrs. Penny's lawyers, and while Cassie was putting the final touches on dinner, Boone repeated what Fee had said.

"Welp, it went kind of like this. Fee asks how long till that will gets read and settled. And the lawyers say there's one heir that is holding things up, won't say who. But there's money set aside for the care of this party. So Fee phones his lawyer in town to see what kind of holdup that could be, and he says it could be a kind of probation time for an heir, could be a stall to search for a missing person—like a child given up for adoption or something. Or some relative that cut himself off from family ties years ago."

Robbin said, "Wouldn't it be something if Mrs. Penny had an illegitimate kid she was keeping secret?"

Cassie repeated, "'For the *care* of the party.'"

"A *retarded*, illegitimate kid," Robbin said. "That could explain it. A retarded child whose lifetime care she wanted to ensure. I'll bet that's it." He took a spoon and tasted the sauce for Cassie's famous Cincinnati Chili Spaghetti Five-Way. She had a reputation among her friends for preparing this dish and tonight was the third time—by request—that she had fixed it for the

McKeags. It was a popular dish in Cincinnati; Cassie had grown up eating it, and whenever she returned home, it was the first thing on her list to do: head for Skyline Chili and order Five-Way. The sauce was made with a tomato base, the ground beef was grated, the spices a secret. Not everyone ate it Five-Way. But that was the best: spaghetti, sauce, kidney beans, grated cheddar cheese, diced onions on top.

The next day, the day of the party, the last Cassie saw of Robbin was during lunch. The minute he was finished eating he pushed through the kitchen's screen door and said to her, "See you at the party."

Cassie got up from the table. "Robb?" She caught him stepping off the porch. "What do you mean 'see me'? Aren't we driving in together?"

"We don't have to do everything together; we're not Siamese twins. I'll see you there."

Even before her dropped jaw clamped shut again, Cassie's mind—in some survival tactic known best to women dealing with men—began to accrue excuses for him: he was anxious about the preparations for the party; he wanted to get there early to greet the first guests; he needed to assure himself that his instructions had been carried out. Then she attacked herself: he didn't want to arrive with her on his arm wearing the same black getup she wore to all their dressy outings; her hair was still too short; she wasn't a party kind of woman.

Lately, Cassie had been parking her camper beside Robbin's porch, making it something of an extension to his cabin, a sort of mobile closet for her belongings. After Robbin left his cabin, Cassie showered there, then stepped into her camper to get her outfit together. She spotted a tiny gift-wrapped box on her camper bed. Her first reaction was relief: everything was okay between them. Her next reaction was gratitude: she was a lucky woman; this was a generous and thoughtful man she'd fallen in love with. She undid the black-and-gold-striped paper and opened a hinged velvet lid. A pair of earrings, oval-cut sapphires, faceted and a deep dark blue, dangled on slender stems of gold. As she placed them in her ears, she suggested to herself that she feel relieved now, that she relax and anticipate a good evening with good people.

She slipped on her black Laise Adair dress and over it she buttoned a black-and-blue-striped silk shirt, which she knotted at the waist. Rolled up the sleeves, tucked her hair behind her ears to show off the sapphires, and decided to drop in on Boone, who wasn't heading for the party for another couple hours. On his way he planned to pick up Elene at the airport when she came in from her late-evening flight. Maybe he'd tell Cassie that she looked good. Maybe she'd learn how effective the striped silk shirt was in disguising her uniform.

"Thought you'd left," Boone said from his favorite brown chair, a stack of catalogs on his lap, the television remote in his hand.

"Just Robbin."

He stopped his channel shopping on CNN. "He went without you?"

"Well, he had . . ." Cassie flicked her own remote, mentally surfing channels to a reply.

"Robb's been jumpy. Got things on his mind," Boone supplied. "Welp, you have fun now. Sleep in tomorrow. We can fix our own breakfasts." His eyes wandered toward the TV and his hand lifted to point the remote.

Suddenly Cassie wished she could kick off her high heels

and snuggle into the corner of that ratty sofa and watch TV with Boone. "You think I look okay?"

His glance flicked her way. "Oh, sure, fine."

Perhaps Boone had things on his mind, too, and who didn't around here?

"Well, bye, then." Cassie walked through the dining room archway.

"Keep that boy in line, Cassie-hon," Boone called after her.

During the drive to the Teton Village hotel where the party was being held, Cassie worked herself into a party mood. It took a pep talk: Hey, wasn't she cool? Wasn't she Robbin McKeag's girlfriend? Didn't he just give her a romantic gift? And didn't she look great in it? She was cool.

She sounded to herself like Lannie. And there he was, standing guard at the entrance to the parking lot leading to the party room entrance of the hotel. A roadblock was set up under the guise of welcoming and passing out roses to the guests, in order to screen out crashers and oglers.

"Wow. You look like a fucking star."

As usual Lannie emulated Robbin in his use of his hero's favored modifier, his stance, his dress, down to a leather jacket with the sleeves pushed up past his elbows in Robbin's own fashion.

A whiskey bottle dangled from two fingers of Lannie's right hand, and his left draped the neck of a flashy young girl with wildly curled blond hair that fell to her waist, whose two giddy friends sat on the hood of Lannie's truck. Another wrangler, Rill, stood in self-conscious attendance with the guest list. Two sheriff's deputies leaned against their Bronco, watching the parade.

Lannie offered Cassie a swig from his bottle. "Famous lips have schlepped here."

Whether he intended the joke or just couldn't speak straight,

Cassie didn't know. She put her gearshift in drive, gave him a sideways look and considered reminding him that he and his leader were on the wagon—just last week Lannie had been spouting to Rill, "Root beer, man, that's the way to go." But she was nobody's mother. She drove into the parking lot.

Just past the entrance, Fee flagged her down. He'd parked his SUV with its Cross Wave logo alongside the road and seemed to be waiting for her.

Cassie braked and pulled over. She armored herself, as she had learned to do from past encounters with this man. Despite his apologies to her, she sensed his choice would still be to have her gone from his territory. He approached the open window on the driver's side beside her.

"I been hard on you, missy."

"My name is Cassie."

"Cassie, I'm not your enemy. I know you're not mine. I'm sorry I've been acting like that, is what I mean."

Cassie was surprised. Then a bit suspicious. This was hardly the time or place for such talk. It seemed to be a prelude for something he wanted.

"I need you to know that, so you'll let me help you now."

"Help me?"

"You need to go on back home; park right over here, and I'll drive you. Boone's waiting; I called him. This party is no good, and we should of seen it coming."

"I don't know what you're talking about. I'm . . . my friends are here."

"You don't have a reason in the world to do what I ask you, but I full-hearted wish you would, missy . . . Cassie. Let me make some of it up to you."

Cassie tallied the reasons she had for not heeding this man:

publicly he had blamed her friends for rustling Cross Wave cattle; had her tires slashed; shot her pup. She lifted her foot off the brake and coasted past him, drove to the other side of the parking lot, pulled into a spot, slipped out of her truck and entered the hotel.

Erin, Becca and Lacy were right inside the door of the party hall. They surrounded her immediately. "It's my fault," Erin rushed in. "I was wrong; I should never have butted in and pushed it."

"Cassie, here's a drink," Becca said kindly. "Have a sip," she urged.

"I can't believe this," Lacy mourned, her neon blue contact lenses staring somewhere into the throng. She looked about to weep.

Cassie tried to see around her huddled friends. The place was hyped. Loud music, colored balloons, spotlights floating around the room.

"Okay," Becca said after she and Erin exchanged eye contact, "but go slowly."

"What?" Cassie asked.

Erin began. "You were right about Robbin. I was all wrong."

Cassie eased sideways to gather a fuller view of the party. With the security of her friends around her she was eager now to move past the entrance smack into the middle of it. She tried to spot Robbin.

She said, "No, *I* was wrong. Robbin and I . . ." So much she hadn't filled them in on during these last busy weeks of summer. Maybe she wasn't wholeheartedly in favor of Robbin's engagement suggestion, but her friends would be. She hadn't told them one thing about their late-night talks discussing philosophy, for instance. And though Robbin's gift was the least of the events that marked their relationship, it was a start and Cassie tilted her head toward Erin, who would be most in awe of real gems. "Look, sapphires."

"He's a shit, Cassie. You were right."

Becca reached a taming hand to Erin, while moving her right arm more protectively around Cassie.

"Erin. *You* were right. Don't worry about it. It's great. We're great."

"Hey, Cass!" It was Robbin. Cassie spun around, searching the wild masses. He wasn't far and he was to the right of her from the sound of his voice. "Cass!" There he was. Sitting on a high stool at the bar, people crowded around him. The crowd split when Robbin shouted, "Keys," and cupped his hands between his knees.

Secretly pleased to have her friends again witness her sharing things with him, Cassie waved and tossed her keys to Robbin.

It became quieter around her. In the space between her and Robbin, people stared, some whispered, but Cassie had expected that. She asked herself if she was ready. This looked to be it. Robbin would make a big deal out of introducing her. He'd do it while she was yards away like this. She'd have to walk down that path opened between them, and if she was lucky, Robbin would not put his tongue in her mouth when he kissed her in front of everybody.

While she watched, Robbin swiveled a quarter turn to a red-headed woman who, Cassie saw now, was hanging across the seatback of his barstool. A pretty woman, dishy, voluptuous, wearing leggings and a long glittery top that hung off one shoulder. The woman held a bottle for Robbin, feeding him like an infant in a parody of nursing him. With the woman between his knees now, where he had guided her with his hands low on her hips, Robbin took the whiskey bottle, and holding the bottle up high, dribbled liquor down her bare front and caught it in his mouth.

One of the five spotlights, which lined the narrow balcony above and floated their beams across the crowd, danced once over the scene, then flicked back to center on it. Another beam, trained most often at the entrance to greet and announce those coming in, moved now along the opened path leading to Robbin, gracing those faces that made up the audience of the small drama. Cassie felt it singe her cheeks, move onward, then snap back like the eyes of a cougar spotting a lame doe.

She watched Robbin dangle her keys in front of this woman; he shook them like a rattle and said, "Come on, mama, baby needs to be rocked."

By way of introduction—perhaps for the benefit of media clever enough to have slipped past the drunken guard, Lannie— the woman offered her name. She said, "Winnie."

Loud and high as a stud near a mare in heat, Robbin tossed back his shag of hair, bared his teeth and whinnied.

A certain part of the crowd closest to Robbin laughed uproariously. And Cassie heard one of these people shout, "Ya-ha! Robbie Mac is *back*!" Apparently these people didn't catch the tension that Cassie felt humming around her—or if they did, they fed on it. Yet even a few of those lining the pathway between Cassie and Robbin, in special sympathy with the seedy sight of watching a drunk jump off the wagon, cracked reluctant half smiles at Robbin's infectious sense of the silly.

A deep and spreading dislike of the slack-lidded goof so at one with the leering spotlight and the crude howls around him spilled over Cassie, stinging her eyes. But her eyes, like those of the rest of the enthralled pack, were in the firm grip of the master showman. Robbin's hair, dark blond and sun-streaked, flashed highlights, and his blue eyes exuded excitement and promised surprise. If bluebirds had sprung into flight out of those eyes, no one would have expected less. Half the females looking on in entranced disgust at what Winnie was allowing him to use her for also felt Robbin's tongue stroke their erect nipples, and Cassie knew this, too, though her eyes never left the show.

One arm draped around Winnie, Robbin, haloed in a white spotlight, sauntered toward the door, swigging his bottle with his eyes closed as he passed Cassie. Winnie, perhaps used to spotlights herself, moved with the music and smiled like the winning beauty contestant at those she passed.

Then they were gone, out the door, moving toward the parking lot.

The spotlight beams moved off, the crowd closed the gap and the surge of noise washed in waves toward another direction.

Cassie said—she thought to herself, but heard her voice speak out loud—"Not in my camper." She pushed past her friends.

Out of the crush of bodies Cody caught Cassie's arm as she began to press through the glass doors to the outside. He pulled her in against his chest, and Cassie rested there a moment to be polite. Cody said, "I'll handle it."

"This time it's not your job." She sent him back to the party.

Out in the parking lot, Cassie wended her way to the camper, easy to spot, as always, with its high profile. Tonight, the setting sun glazed its side window orange; the half circle with leaded flutes of glass meeting at center bottom glittered like a slice of candied citrus, a gilded Japanese fan, a fiery archway to the lower realms. Cassie put her hand on the doorknob leading into the back of the camper and paused. So quiet inside—the thought briefly flashed that she'd made a mistake: they weren't in there.

Then she heard Robbin drawl, "Don't take your shoes off, Winnie—we're getting company."

That being her cue, Cassie swung the door open. Winnie looked startled. Robbin sat on the edge of Cassie's bed with his face in a hand, arm propped on his thigh, the half-empty bottle dangling from his other hand between his legs. He glanced up as far as Cassie's knees. "Take me home, Cassidy." To Winnie he cocked his head toward the exit.

Cassie waited for Winnie to descend the step, watched her tug her glittery top up over her shoulder. Then, not receiving any clear directions from herself, Cassie followed Robbin's instructions to take him home. This was simple, demanded movement, had purpose and a goal, and she could manage it. Robbin held out the keys without looking at her and Cassie walked through to the cab and started the motor.

Ten minutes down the road the empty bottle dropped to the camper floor. She tipped the rearview mirror. Robbin had passed out on her bed.

She asked herself why she hadn't pushed him out the door behind that woman. Why, now, she didn't stop anywhere in this desolate rangeland and roll him off her bed and out onto the road. Run over him a couple times. But she was still shoring herself up, as though the worst hadn't happened yet. As though she needed to conserve expenditures of thought and energy. She was holding on—to the road and the steering wheel and the single effort of burrowing into a safe, lone place inside, where she had lived for some time before coming to this moment.

She drove at the speed limit, carefully, meticulously measuring the middle path between the center line and the shoulder gravel. Dusk settled into deep dark as she drove, and after a few vehicles passing in the opposite direction flashed their headlights at her, Cassie thought to turn hers on.

A t Cross Wave, she pulled the camper up to the front door and honked the horn one long howl, leaving the motor on, the headlights undimmed. Boone appeared at the front door immediately, as if he'd been waiting, hovering nearby. Even so, he stood with his hand on the screen door handle for a long minute. Finally, he walked out and stood beside Cassie's lowered window.

"Get him out of here."

Boone waited for more, an explanation, some clue; Cassie kept her eyes down the path of headlight beams. Finally, Boone walked back to the camper door. Cassie felt the weight of his body as he stepped tentatively in at the rear. His way illuminated only by the glow of headlights and the front porch light, Boone paused a moment inside the door. Then Cassie heard him take one step, and his foot sent the empty whiskey bottle bouncing against a cabinet door.

Cassie sat immobile, upright, face to the windshield, and she waited.

"Robb . . ." Boone spoke cautiously. Then the camper rocked as Boone bent to shake Robbin, prone on the bed. "Robb!" he said more urgently.

"I was almost a goner, Boone." Robbin's voice was flat, detached.

"What have you taken?" Boone's words were lilted with fear.

"Took myself back. Almost a goner."

"*What*," Boone repeated, spacing his words, "*do you have inside you?*"

"A river of Jack."

"Whiskey?"

"Whiskey River, Willie."

Boone groped for the empty bottle that had scooted before his foot; Cassie heard him grab it. "This all? Anything else? Tell me!"

"That's it."

The bed creaked with Boone's weight.

"Didn't have to do a lot. It was over in a minute. I had an audience; a performer can't ever undo what's done before an audience. I'm safe now."

Boone asked, "You going to be sick?"

"For a bit, then after that I'll be sorry, then I'm going to be fine." There was a pause. "Some guys go right on living their lives with this extra event of a woman in the background, but I lost myself inside her, Boone. Didn't know who the fuck I was."

"We better go in," Boone urged.

"One morning I wake up next to Cassie and before I open my eyes I think, What's wrong? I feel crampy and heavy down low. I know it's something odd, not like the flu. Then I see Cassie hugging her knees. She hurts, too. I say, 'What have we got, Cass?' Oh, fuck, Boone. You're not going to believe this. It was our period—I mean *her* period. *She* was having cramps. I knew I was a goner then."

Cassie sat with her eyes following the path of light into the bushes beside the drive, watching as more and more moths abandoned the porch light to investigate the twin beams from her truck. Then she laid her forehead on the steering wheel.

"All I wanted was to keep taking it a little bit further with her, you know? Then pretty soon, I love her. That's okay, I get used to the idea. A little blending. I liked it. But, Boone, having a period! That's way, way out there."

Boone said, "When you were born, I got labor pains. And remember how I kept scratching myself when you got the chicken pox?"

"I won't live like that."

"After a while you get the hang of it. All you need is the *notion* of what's going on with somebody; then you figure out what helps them and separate yourself to do that. Like feeling itchy—I gave you a bath in baking powder."

"Was supposed to be baking soda. We got that wrong." Another silence. "What about when Mom died?"

"I wanted to die, too."

"See?"

"It's worth it," Boone said.

"Having monthly periods and a death wish—it *ain't* worth it." Robbin said, "All I wanted was to be around her. But I felt too happy, like I was growing out of my psychic clothes. Inflated all the time. Like one of those balloon men somebody keeps pumping up. It gets lighter and lighter; it tips up on one foot, then pretty soon floats completely off the ground. It looks stupid with its smile all stretched. Still, it's tethered to that pump and it keeps stretching and stretching. Its eyes get bigger and bigger . . . then *boom*! It's little shreds of plastic." Robbin inhaled in jagged breaths.

He said, "I cannot be pumped that full. I'm not *designed* for full inflation."

A bit of a pause. Then Robbin said, "I had to make a leak."

Boone asked with nervous concern, "Is that what happened, then? Cassie's there, and you took a leak?" Boone probably remembered how that set Cassie off her first week on the ranch when Robbin used the toilet while she was showering.

"I leaked all the fuck over her."

"No! Robbin, say you didn't."

"*Ssss.* And it was finished, my skin sagging around me."

"Cassie . . . was she . . . *wet?*"

"No, I poured whiskey on some other woman."

"Oh, my."

Robbin said peacefully, "I'm probably going to throw up now."

Boone instructed Robbin's movements one limb at a time, until he had him upright and ready to walk.

Robbin said, "Wasn't she something, though? And she loved *me.* Still, I got out in the nick of time. I would have made history as the first male hospitalized for toxic shock syndrome."

Cassie heard Boone struggling with the weight of Robbin, heard the empty bottle strike the cupboards again, then the camper door close behind them.

"My failing . . ." Robbin's voice drifted across the yard. "I'm not a gentleman. I regret that. But what do you do when you fall into quicksand? You grab at anything, right? A nearby branch, a passing pair of boobs."

The screen door slammed.

Then, from indoors, "I think I'm going to black out. . . . I can hardly wait."

CHAPTER TWENTY-FOUR

November 3 was Cassie's birthday. On the second she decided to call her family, before her parents could phone the Cross Wave, find her gone and worry. The last they knew, she was planning to cook through the fall hunting season. When she had driven away from the ranch the night of the party she had headed straight for Erin's house and found her pacing the driveway, waiting and worrying. For the next five weeks Cassie had kept close to Erin's home and asked her friends not to disclose her whereabouts until she felt ready. She had been used to laughing, touching and talking every day with Robbin, and his sudden absence was wrenching. She longed for him and wondered if he thought of her at all.

She had sold the camper and now had a used Toyota and a savings account. She had purchased a computer and a cell phone. With the help of her friends, her guide business was in place and bookings for snowshoe hikes were coming in for the winter tourist season, which would begin next month. All she needed now was snow. A few stray flakes drifted past the window as she dialed her parents' number.

"We know all about it," her mother said when Cassie began the generic version of needing a change from ranch life. "He's such a *nice* boy."

All those phrases Cassie had readied about why she'd left the ranch fragmented and bounced like buckshot around her head. She attacked the one statement she was sure the rest of her mother's position rested upon: she said, "No, Mom, he's not."

"Good-looking, too, I must say."

"You've *seen* him?"

"Your father thinks you've picked well. Your brother, Dole, likes him; your sister-in-law says he's great with the kids; and we all had a wonderful time at the charity concert."

"Concert?"

"Cleveland's a nasty town, but Robb maneuvered your father's car through it beautifully."

"Mom—what?" Nobody drove her father's car. "Robbin was there? He drove Dad's BLT?" That was what her mother had always called it.

"That's a sandwich, Cassie. Robb stood center stage and whipped his arm out before him, finger directed to the audience and those people loved him like he could walk on eggs."

"Water," Cassie corrected. Walking on eggs was what she generally undertook when talking to her mother.

"That boy is in pain, while you've been gallivanting around the country wasting gasoline."

"He's used drugs, Mom."

"Oh, Cassie, don't be petty. He's told us all about himself."

"He was crazy once. He might be an alcoholic. And he's

definitely a womanizer." She waited for her mother to express alarm. When she didn't, Cassie added, "He was raised a Catholic." Her parents thought Catholics were silly. "Robbin calls the Catholic church that his father took him to Saint Placebos."

"Saint Placebos! That's good. Your father will like that. He thinks Robb has a wonderful sense of humor. Where are you, dear?"

"Mom . . ." She had a lot of questions: Why had Robbin been in Ohio? When had he gotten there? How did that totally improbable meeting come about? She said, "He and I . . ."

"I know all about it, and I think you're pouting. You always were a pouter."

"I was not. That was Dole."

"Tell your mother where you are."

"You'll tell Robbin."

"Your father says to stay put. He says running off is no crime and to just tell Robbin you're sorry."

"*Me!* Sorry?"

"He says Robbin loves you and wants to care for you. He says it's time you settled down."

Cassie repeated those words to herself—*Robbin loves you*—and felt herself loosen and expand inside as if she had been chilled for weeks and now was wrapped in warmth. *Robbin loves you.* She said, though, just to test the situation further: "Remind Dad he always told *me* that a leopard never changes its spots."

"Your father says, spots or not, no one deserves to be treated like a leper."

He said no such thing; those were words straight from her mother's scrambled idiolect. *"Leopard!"* Cassie rolled her eyes.

"Your father says to tell us where you are."

Just as in the game Simon says, Cassie was conditioned to

respond seriously to any orders prefaced with "Your father says." She felt the old training rise to defeat her once again.

"I haven't gone anywhere."

Her mother tipped the mouthpiece of the phone away, and Cassie heard her say, "She's been right there all this time." Then back on the phone to Cassie she said, "Well, you have a pile of letters from your young man just waiting for an address. I'll overnight them to you."

And she had more to say about Cassie's "young man." "Your father and I could tell that he was brought up very well. He has good table manners."

And so the conversation continued until Cassie eventually gathered the essential parts of the story: Robbin had phoned every night for two weeks. Then he came to visit, stayed in her room, met the family. Last weekend he was one of the presenters for a benefit concert in Cleveland, her entire family were his guests at the hotel, her folks thought he was the Prince of Light.

Robbin's absence from her life these past five weeks had flooded Cassie's mind and sent her feeling adrift in the world, like a motherless beaver kit in a strange pond. Now his presence seemed to infuse every sound and fragrance in the air. He was under these stars, this moon, on this planet Earth and he loved her.

She pictured him in her childhood home, dining with her parents, listening to their stories. He slept in her old bedroom, perhaps checked her bookshelves, read her old school annuals. Why was he doing this? What would his letters tell her?

The next day Cassie picked up the packet of letters from her mother and, rushing to meet Erin on time, kept the packet on her lap as she drove up West Gros Ventre Butte to one of Jackson

Hole's most elite resorts. Erin had invited her to meet for a drink at the Amangani, her treat, which suggested to Cassie that Erin had made a big sale that day and they would be celebrating her commission. Erin met her inside the front doors.

"I took a chance, Cassie. You've been so happy since you called home yesterday and learned about Robbin and the letters." Her eyes glanced at the package Cassie held clutched to her chest. Erin held up an overnight bag of Cassie's and slipped the strap onto Cassie's shoulder. "He's in the library." Erin nodded toward a room to the left. She added, "You still have a choice." Then she walked out of the hotel.

Cassie's heartbeat sounded to her like a woodpecker tapping fast and hard against a tree trunk, carving out its nest. He was there, just behind those doors. She turned toward the library and paused. If this didn't work out, she would be left with fresh-cut loneliness, as if her heart were an apple with another sliver removed, leaving the fruit with the job of browning and toughening its edges once again to seal off the escape of juices. Erin's words echoed: she still had a choice.

She opened the door.

"Cassie. Thank God."

All alienation fell away. She dropped her bag and the packet of letters on a nearby sofa. Then she was in his arms, home again. She buried her face in his neck and breathed in the fragrance of his skin. He held her tight, then pulled her face back to look at her. Tears streaked his cheeks. He shook his head, smiled, and held her close again. Together they stood with their arms wrapped about each other, silent except for the punctuation of their breathing.

After a bit Robbin said, "I've got a reservation for us here. We'll go to our room. We'll take it step by step."

He slung her bag over his shoulder; she picked up the packet of letters and they walked to an elevator that took them upstairs.

Once inside their room, he opened a small refrigerator by the bar and pulled out a bottle of white wine and another bottle of root beer. He poured her a glass of the wine and opened his root beer, then gestured for her to sit on one of the tufted leather chairs near the wide windows overlooking the valley.

"We'll fix this," he said.

With Robbin there with her, their separation over, the reunion in progress, unease found room to insert itself, followed by hurt, spiked with anger. She looked around this beautiful and spacious room and felt both assured and a little annoyed by his confidence.

He said to get them started, "This will be hard, but it's worth it."

"Last I heard, you feared death by toxic shock syndrome, and the work of loving someone, you told Boone, was decidedly not worth it."

He nodded. "I was scared. I had trouble with the boundaries—yours, mine—mostly mine." After a pause he said, "I've learned some things."

"How?"

"We love each other," he said. "We don't have any choice. We go ahead with this. Step by step, we'll get back on track—"

"We never had any *track*; we had a fiasco. Fiascos you forgive yourself for and move on."

"No . . . well, never mind. We aren't supposed to argue about petty side issues."

"Who says?"

"You've got questions," he replied. "Shoot. Every little one."

"What is this, an agenda of some sort?" She narrowed her eyes at him. "You didn't answer—who have you been talking to?"

For the first time Robbin looked defensive. Defensive, Cassie realized now, had been what she'd expected all along from him.

He tipped his root beer bottle to his mouth, then glanced out the double glass doors to the balcony. He eyed her seriously and warned, "Not one damn smirk."

She didn't promise a thing.

"I saw a marriage counselor."

"What?" She smirked. She pulled the facial expression right out of her snotty adolescence.

Robbin kept his gaze to himself after catching her drift and scraped a thumbnail against an edge of his bottle label.

"A marriage counselor," Cassie repeated scornfully.

"He said you'd have lots of questions. And possibly rage and cry."

"Then crawl into bed with you. And you paid him for that." She was beginning to feel the rage, all right.

"A hundred and eighty-five dollars a session, and we had ten sessions in the past five weeks. Bed he couldn't guarantee."

Robbin was gaining in strength. Cassie could feel it across the room. He didn't *need* any defense, she thought; he knew the program. She was the one who'd been ambushed by his sudden appearance. She was the one without a schedule, and how was she to be prepared for *his* moods and actions when he refused to give in to any of the ones she instigated?

"My job is not to give empty excuses for myself or tell you your feelings aren't valid or to get angry in retaliation." He stared at his root beer bottle.

Then her job, she intuited, was to make him angry, tempt

him to offer excuses and have feelings so exaggerated he *had* to argue against them. "Stonewall, is that it?" she asked him.

"No. Respond fairly and express my feelings honestly without blame to you or others. And especially listen." He waited a moment and then said, "Every little question—start."

She began with her basest and most haunting suspicion that Robbin had returned to the party and played out his scene with Winnie after it had served its initial purpose. "Did you see her again?"

"No."

"This is embarrassing. . . ." It was Cassie's turn to stare out the glass doors.

"This is all I know to do. Another one."

"Other women?"

"No. But I called Erin. She told me to go fuck my horse. Next I phoned Becca. She was using the DVDs of my movies as Frisbees for her neighbor's dog to catch. Lacy sobbed. Then one day I just barged in on Rin at her office and made her listen to me. She felt guilty mainly because she had encouraged you to drop your guard with me." He shrugged. "God, she's got a rough mouth."

Cassie smiled to herself. Erin could be searing; she hoped Erin had said every nasty thing she herself might not think of.

"Then last night when I learned from your folks that you were here in the valley, I phoned Erin to ask if she'd help me meet with you. Eventually I convinced her."

Robbin knew how to do everything. As childish and unpolished as his scene at the party had appeared, Cassie realized that somewhere beneath it all he had known how to use the technique of embarrassing her with her own affection for him. The memory of that night was painful.

Cassie said, "My most profound feeling the night of the party was shame over caring for you."

Robbin's expression cracked. He set his bottle of root beer down on the coffee table, bent over and held his head. The thumb and forefinger of one hand swiped tears from his cheeks. "I wanted to shame myself . . . not you."

But that wasn't true. As spontaneous as his escape from the relationship had seemed, he couldn't have covered all the bases better if he had choreographed the severance for months. But Cassie didn't argue with him. She gave in to hiccupping sobs herself and stared out the window.

Robbin dipped his head farther and wiped his face with the bottom of a red T-shirt he pulled out from beneath his navy sweater. He lifted his face and said, "You don't know how I've missed you. All I knew to do was to make myself ready for you . . . for whenever I found you again . . . to try to measure up to this thing we've got between us." He got up and went in search of tissues and returned from the bathroom with a fistful. He kept a couple for himself and handed the rest to Cassie. He blew his nose, then spoke in a reasonable voice, calm and knowledgeable. "All anybody wants is to find the one person they will love the rest of their lives. We've got that; now we do the work."

He sounded like the man Cassie had dreamed of loving. Still, she said, "You're so sure of yourself."

He sat on the edge of the chair with his elbows on his knees, hands dangling between them, leaning toward her. "I'm sure of two things: I love you. You love me. You're deeply horrified by the notion just now, but you do."

They stared at each other, she furiously, he patiently.

"I betrayed you and what we built together. I made a fool of myself and humiliated you. I did my best to ruin what we have together, and I regretted every bit of it the second I became half sober. Still," he said, leaning closer—and defending himself, Cassie was pleased to note—"I did not sleep with another woman, Cassidy, or do any number of worse injuries men and women forgive one another for. This can be fixed. Others have done it before us."

"Oh," Cassie said, "for two thousand bucks your therapist gave you an *easy out* on 'loss of trust.' I don't think so."

"Cassidy, knock it off. I'm not so goddamn fucking bad!

"Shit," he said to himself, and pinched his eyes between his fingers and thumb. He addressed her calmly again. "No. Loss of trust—it'll take years. I fucked it up for years."

That settled, Cassie took a shower and got dressed for dinner, rummaging through her bag to put on whatever Erin had packed for the night. When she came out of the bathroom, Robbin was talking on the phone.

"Champagne," he said. "I'll try that." His cheek muscle puckered as he caught Cassie's glance, and she knew it was Boone he was talking to. "Thanks," he said, "I'll tell her. Bye." He put the receiver down. "He sends his love. He hopes you'll come home soon. He misses you."

Across the table from each other in the restaurant, they waited for their orders to arrive. "We just sit here," Cassie said, "as if nothing's wrong."

"We sit here like our world has broken in two. But both halves are present. So we press on."

Robbin was somber, but it was only on her account, Cassie decided. What he would really like to do was celebrate. His mission of tracking her down had come to success. The rage was spent, the tears, the questions. Could kiss and make up be far behind? His regrets were something he'd lived with already for over a month now. His rehabilitation was grounded and authorized by a therapist, her best friend, Boone, even her own family. He was progressing along the prescribed route without undue relapses into the no-no's of anger and self-serving explanations. Why didn't she lighten up? That was probably what he was thinking.

Occasionally she felt Robbin's foot tapping energetically under the table. She knew him well enough to surmise he had a thousand things to tell her, funny stories about Boone, the ranch, the hunters staying there now. And she suspected he was eager to impart ideas he had about their future. He might verbalize his understanding that betrayed trust took years to restore, but she couldn't see him living with the tedium of that. He wanted to get on with it even now.

He said to her, leaning over the table and laying a hand close to hers, "Cass, I love you so." Something was settled for him.

Cassie unwrapped one of the chocolate mints left on the pillows when the bed had been turned down for them by a maid while they were dining.

Robbin was watching her.

She said, "What?"

"I'm not sure. You seem . . . cooled out."

Exhausted was more like it. But to keep the discussion going she said, "I want my own room." Which was ridiculous; she could just go home if she wasn't going to stay with him. She took a bite of the chocolate.

Robbin said, "No need. You can eat both of the mints." As if her motivation was the extra candy she would acquire with her own room. He waited to see if she'd laugh at his silly remark.

She did, surprising herself. Robbin's ability to make her laugh had always struck her as being as intimate as only a lover who knew her very well could be. She had missed that so much.

He apparently felt encouraged by her reaction. "I want to show you stuff. I've been working on our life together." He reached for a long tube and placed it on the table set before the two easy chairs and pulled out a rolled-up blueprint. "We have decisions to make. How many baths, did I figure the right closets. They're already digging the foundation." He began to move quickly, smoothing the plans out and anchoring them with a phone book on one end. He was darting around in search of something to hold down the other end.

Cassie watched Robbin fill the void she left at the retraction of her anger with heightened emotion of his own. He stepped away to reach for a tennis shoe, and the house plan zipped up into itself. The shoe wasn't clean enough, he decided, and like a frenetic window shade the plan snapped closed again when he bolted across the room for his bedside book. He grabbed Cassie on this trip and steered her over.

"I don't know what you've got here," Cassie said, preferring to play dumb to give herself time, "but I'd rather hear about your screenplay and what's going on at the ranch and . . ."

"You're not going anywhere."

"I'll stay tonight," she assured him.

"I mean, when you were in the shower, I took the coil from your distributor cap."

Cassie laughed.

"Funny? You don't know where it is, and if you find it, you can't put it back—you don't know how!"

"Oh, come on." Cassie grinned and took her shoes off to settle in.

"Come on, yourself. You're not going to cool out on *me*. That's my job. 'Stay cool. Stay calm. She'll be in a fury. She'll sob and say you don't love her. The cycle will repeat. Keep telling her you love her. Give her time. Talk softly!'" He was getting louder and louder, gesturing dramatically, taking steps toward her, then turning around to retrace them. "'She's hurt—she'll cry. She's angry—she'll shout. Remember it's *her* pain she's trying to tell you about. Don't bite at her barbs, don't attack, don't defend yourself. Stay cool, calm, centered!' Oh, God." He slumped down on the side of the bed with his head in his hands. He talked to his shoes. "She messes me up every damn *time*." He lifted his face. "I'm telling you, Cassidy, you throw me one more curve, I'm . . . I don't know." His voice faded out.

Cassie sat on the alert at the edge of a chair. They'd both lost their places, she thought. And that was because they both had assumed unreal roles to play. Yet, to get real here was somehow unseemly. To get real, she'd have to throw some food around and Robbin would probably have to try to solve it all in bed.

Robbin stood up and unbuckled his belt. He pulled his sweater off over his head and flung off his boots and socks.

Here it comes, she thought.

"I'm going to take a shower." He removed his pants.

Cassie watched his naked body with interest. She admired his lack of self-consciousness. She could never be nude in front of anyone who was mad at her. She needed the gauzy shield of lust to undress behind. "Is that what your therapist said?" she taunted. "Take a shower if she rattles you?"

"Go to hell," he shot back and slammed the bathroom door behind himself.

She got the brown envelope from her mother and opened it. It held more than a dozen letters from Robbin, plus a CD.

Scanning the letters, she could see they were a faithful reflection of his progress with the marriage counselor.

"I believe the keys for a good relationship are embedded in being fully awake. Being right *there*, eyes open. Honesty is important. Upholding agreements. But surpassing all the fair-play laws of a good citizen is a fundamental alertness to one's self and the engagement with another's self."

Oh, my, Cassie thought. She found other entries that were very touching to her, romantic, with a deep longing expressed eloquently. The shower continued to drum in the next room. Cassie sorted the letters into sequence and began to scan them for news of home events.

October 4th: Boone and Elene are engaged. I gave them a lifetime membership to the Valley Opera to celebrate. Boone says I'm jealous and spiteful; Elene thinks I'm a dear.

October 9th: Lannie couldn't handle my topple from the wagon. I had to send him to the dry cleaners. A rehab in Salt Lake. The aftershocks of my behavior still ripple, cracking the good people around me. Cody and Diana eloped. I'm pretty sure Cody didn't want to chance me as best man. I robbed them of their wedding and Diana's daughters of their chance to be flower girls.

October 12th: I have finished the screenplay. CD enclosed. Bottom line—Cal and Cissy never married. We can't let that happen to us, Cass. They loved each other, but never committed for life. Cissy continued with her newspaper and social life in the East during the winters and Cal involved himself with his ranch on the other side of the Tetons, staying out west. Cissy died first, alone. Cal had Felicia, Cissy's daughter, at his side.

October 16th: Fee left for California today to comfort his ex-wife. Laraine's church is crumbling around her. Mother

Flame is reported to have ovarian cancer. To heal herself she's had gems surgically implanted in her womb. Sometime back, Mrs. Penny had stipulated that she would cosign for a parcel of Pale Feather for Fee if he set aside some acres for Laraine and her church to use as a retreat. Fee is going to tell Laraine about the land. He says there're no further disclosures about the rest of Mrs. P's instructions. Fee expressed further regrets to Boone and me about needing to keep quiet about this and his executorship. That sweet lady always considered me an imbecile. "Incapable of guiding my own protoplasm toward evolution," is how she once put it. God, I miss her.

October 18th: Fee reports back that suspicion rises over Mother Flame's cancer diagnosis. She and her implanted gems have fled. Some say translated to Pluto to prepare a new world order, some say to Argentina to party.

About Pale Feather Ranch, I did learn that provisions are made in Mrs. Penny's will that lifetime care and future land maintenance and taxes are to be prepaid out of the estate, all legally in place before the property is passed on to the beneficiaries. My lawyers surmise the holdup is that one of the heirs is severely retarded, just as I had guessed. So great, Laraine's flames and a retardo as neighbors.

Here, Cassie began to laugh. She couldn't wait to read the letter where Robbin discovers *he* is the retardo. Retardo himself. Recalling Mrs. Penny's questions about how long Robbin would stick with his new life plan, Cassie figured a timeline was put into place before she handed further power over to him. Yet, apparently, she had also made provisions for him whichever path he chose. Cassie rifled through the letters, strewing pages across the bed, searching for that entry.

But another paragraph snagged her eye first: We are family,

you and I. You know it, Cassie. We are involved in a lifetime's growth together, and although you'll often be ahead of me, Cass, you'll be there in part because I'm pushing you from behind. This isn't to relieve myself of the blame for being a jerk. I may always be a jerk, but I can promise you two things: I will give you children one way or another, and I will love you for the rest of my days. So, if life is a series of errors faced and challenges overcome, I can be counted on to provide our life together with a full spectrum of obstacles for us to surmount!

Staring wet-eyed at the bathroom door with this letter of Robbin's held to her chest, Cassie abruptly noticed she no longer heard the shower. Robbin opened the door and walked toward the closet while drying himself with a towel.

He drew on a clean pair of Levi's. "I have a proposition for you," he said, starting at the bottom of his 501's and buttoning upward. He left the top button undone and reached into the back pocket of his other pants, lying on the end of the bed, for his comb. Cassie continued watching him. He walked to the mirror and began to comb his wet hair.

Also, she alerted herself to this new approach. This was Robbin the legendary businessman, the dealmaker, the brain behind the fame. Robbin had apparently calmed down, centered in and was now calmly centered on a *proposition* for her.

"These are house plans." Robbin gestured toward the table. "The land is a parcel near the river at the end of the ranch road." He moved to the table set beside the bed. "This," he said, opening a drawer and pulling out a folder, "is the paperwork making it yours." He tossed it onto her lap. "This," he said, and again pulled out another folder and tossed this one also onto her lap, "is a medical record proving I am physically capable of giving you children. What I want in exchange is marriage."

The folders lay on Cassie's lap; she didn't touch them. She watched them, though. She registered the cold, businesslike aspects of this proposal and didn't know who to blame—Robbin or herself—for pressing it to this black-and-white exchange.

"I don't have anything else to work with. You're not going to listen to my promises for the future, and I haven't got a past record to deal from. So I'm bargaining with what I *do* have, and with what you want. Sperm."

Involuntarily, Cassie reacted with the short beginnings of a laugh. She cleared her throat to cover up and kept her eyes on Robbin's bare feet, sometimes glancing beneath her lowered lids to the folders on her lap. A weepiness set in with the realization she had somehow become the kind of woman a man would propose to with land and medical records. She had never meant for this to happen.

As further argument, Robbin said, "I have a hundred and thirty-eight million."

Pained, Cassie looked up and pleaded, "Don't tell me about your *money*."

"Sperm. That's my sperm count."

He acknowledged the lunacy of this talk before she had to do it alone. Even as her eyes misted with congested emotion and before she knew for sure which opposing reaction would spurt out, Robbin's cheek muscle tucked into itself and he dipped his head and shielded his own grin behind a thumbnail he scraped above his upper lip.

Together, they broke into extravagant howls of laughter.

Robbin bent and scooped Cassie off the bed with one arm behind her back and the other beneath her knees. The folders slid to the floor.

He sat with her on his lap and told her she wasn't going

to *believe* the story of what had happened to him at the Salt Lake City Medical Center, where he'd had to go for his sperm count.

"I figured with my bad standing, I'd better have *documents*."

So off he went to Salt Lake City, Utah, a five-hour drive, and when he arrived at the hospital, he was sent to a room in the basement. They offered him magazines. "With pictures, you know?" His first error was replying to a nice motherly sort whose short-sleeved Mormon temple underwear was clearly outlined beneath her white nurse uniform, "No thanks, I think I can pull it off without the porno." And she got the unintended pun.

"I followed their directions and filled this jar with sperm. Then they sent me up the elevator to the ninth floor with my jar. I was nervous, you know? I didn't realize until I was in the elevator and then joined on the fourth floor by two nurses that my fake mustache was hanging off my lip. Worse, I hadn't zipped my pants! I didn't know until the nurses looked at my jar, looked at my unzipped pants, exchanged eye contact and immediately pushed the STOP button and rushed each other off.

"They thought I had filled that jar in the elevator! They weren't sure I was done!"

Cassie's laughter came from such an overcharged clenching inside she didn't even make a sound at first, but just clung to Robbin with her head thrown back, unable to inhale until the laughter volcanoed out.

"Oh, God, Cass, the whole ordeal was goddamn awful. But afterward, I said to myself, 'Cassie is going to love this story. If I ever find her again, she's going to love this.'"

Once she was back in control of her vocal cords, Cassie said, "That is the most wonderful thing anybody has ever, ever done for me."

"I've been trying to tell you, Cass—I'm goddamn romantic!"

He lowered his head to test the possibility of a kiss.

First he asked, "How many sperm did Jake have?" Thinking better of his question, he added contritely, "Never mind."

And then he kissed her.

Tina Welling lives and writes in Jackson Hole, Wyoming, with her husband, John, and four-legged family members Zoë and Miko. You can reach her at www.tinawelling.com.

COWBOYS NEVER CRY

TINA WELLING

This Conversation Guide is intended to enrich the
individual reading experience, as well as encourage
us to explore these topics together—because books,
and life, are meant for sharing.

A CONVERSATION
WITH TINA WELLING

Q. What inspired you to write Cowboys Never Cry?

A. While talking with you (my editor, Ellen Edwards), we both realized that people who don't live in the West often hold somewhat unreal images of the cowboy culture. And even those of us who do live in the West glamorize the lifestyle. We may not have ridden a horse for years, but we sure have a snazzy pair of cowboy boots in our closet.

The lifestyle comes from an industry that is more than a hundred years old. Yet nothing other than the fashion designs—Levi's, snap-front shirts, cowboy boots, Stetsons, silver and turquoise jewelry—is the same today. There are serious conflicts between the traditions of land use in the past, when running cattle in wilderness areas was the norm, and the needs of land conservation in the present. We have finally learned the interconnectedness of life-forms on our planet, so we know that however we treat the water, air or land in one place affects every other place. I wanted to explore the conflict between past ranching traditions and present realities and write about how we could keep the good parts while healing the practices that wound the land and its wildlife. Flowing beneath all that were the energies of my two characters—Robbin and Cassie—that began to embody in my dream world the opposition of the older value system of ranching and the newer realities of the shrinking wilderness. I saw these two people as strongly attracted to each other, yet carrying opposing views on this matter of the cowboy mystique. One rode the wave of that universal lure all the way to the peak of glamour; the other moved quietly in the opposite direction, toward finding solace in the wilderness. Along the way I knew that writing about the two of them would teach me things I wanted to know about fame and grief, because those two experiences epitomize the high and low of our culture's value system—people often long for one and fear the other.

Q. In the novel you explore different kinds of cowboys. You also live in Jackson Hole, Wyoming, both the novel's setting and where lots of real and "pretend" cowboys live. Explain what led you to write about cowboys and what personal experience you drew on.

A. Sorry, no juicy story of a personal romance with a cowboy—unless you count my husband, who looks darn good in a pair of Levi's. Though there is certainly a romance on my part for the whole cowboy culture. When I first moved from Cincinnati, Ohio, to Cheyenne, Wyoming, I was enthralled with the drama of the lifestyle. I was a big rodeo fan, my first friend

was a born-and-bred cowgirl, and in no time at all my ward-
robe included cowboy boots and a classy Stetson. A few years
after that I moved to Jackson Hole, home of Grand Teton
National Park, and I began to hike and ski. I fell in love with
the outdoors.

Following that I became alerted to what it means to take
care of the land, how all our actions affect the wildlife, and
how very precious our wilderness is to each of us. From there
I realized that those ranchers who cling to certain traditions
often jeopardize the wild places and wildlife that belong to
us all. In Jackson Hole today the ranchers comply with the
land conservation practices that honor the migration paths
and protect the wetlands, the streambeds and the predators.
Yet in areas of Wyoming and other western states traditional
views still reign. I knew a rancher who was proud of having shot and buried the last bear in the county on his ranch.
He was carrying on the tradition of his grandfather, who had
homesteaded the ranch and had worked hard to protect his
livestock from predators, which were abundant then.

*Q. I was certainly surprised to learn that long-standing ranching
practices are often destructive to the environment. As in the novel,
are the ranchers you encountered during your research learning
new ways that might help sustain their way of life?*

A. Sometimes I was shocked that my perceptions were so far
off the mark. One thing that comes to mind: it is astounding
how much damage cows can create on stream banks. They tend
to gather around water, so destroy the plant life by trampling

the banks, which causes erosion, which muddies the water, which in turn kills further plant and animal life. But, yes, things are definitely improving.

Still, there are plenty of holdouts around the West at this point. Ranching is a hardscrabble life, so anything that might cut into profit is resisted. As always, it is a matter of education. For example, ranchers all over Wyoming are still randomly shooting coyotes and teaching their children to do so as well. Recently a young boy told me he does it to help ranchers.

Oddly, many ranchers who want to reduce the coyote population are also strongly against the coyote's natural predator—the wolf. In the 1940s ranchers were mainly responsible for killing off the wolves in Wyoming, killing the very last one ever spotted for the next fifty years. In the 1990s the wolves were reintroduced in Yellowstone National Park, and since then the number of coyotes has been reduced in the greater ecosystem. I used to hear them every night before falling asleep; now I rarely do. Yet I now have the pleasure of listening to wolves howl around the valley. Balance is everything in the natural world.

Q. Although the novel opens three years after Cassie's husband died, she's still finding her way toward a new life. Explain how you see her healing process.

A. I see Cassie as embracing her grief rather than numbing or distracting herself from it. She held the pain lovingly and stayed present with it, and this allowed her to be supported by the liveliness around her, most especially by the natural world, which can be very healing. For many of us a period of grief is almost a time-out, a stretch of life in which we do little other than survive, but I wanted to examine the possibility of coming through that period having gained useful life skills and a deepened sensitivity to oneself and others.

Q. Robbin is a man searching for new ways to create a meaningful life. Through him, do you hope to convey some general ideas about where meaning lies?

A. Yes, I do. Our culture has it backward: it is not the outer appearance but rather the inner experience that offers our quality of aliveness. Many of our media messages suggest that if we look good, that's all that matters. But these images of success do not take into consideration our inner well-being. Many people suffer from a lack of self-esteem or a sense of not measuring up while trying to form themselves into acceptable versions of the culture's idea of success and happiness.

When I speak to writing students, I notice they put very little emphasis on the value of creative writing for the deep personal pleasure it brings to the writer. Rather, the emphasis is put on the outer event of publishing. I see success as a sense of satisfaction, a calm happiness in experiencing the moment.

Exchange with others is often a component of our satisfaction; so is being acknowledged and recognized for one's authentic self. This can happen on a very small scale and still offer all the real benefits that world fame offers. Some people can manage world fame without it also stealing their life force, but it's a skill to be learned and not many people look at it like that. Most people just go racing after it, expecting that it will fulfill all their inner needs of self-acceptance. In the novel Robbin gets to the peak of the fame and wealth that many people dream about acquiring and discovers it's just flashing lights and applause that does little for his inner experience of fulfillment.

Q. Tell us more about Cissy Patterson and Cal Carrington—how their story first came to your attention and why you felt drawn to include it in the novel.

A. I adore the story of Cissy and Cal for its drama and romance and conflicts.

When I first moved to Jackson Hole twenty-some years ago, Felicia, Cissy's daughter fathered by Count Gizycki, occasionally visited the valley and published stories about her girlhood here with her mother and Cal Carrington on the Bar BC Ranch and Flat Creek Ranch. To me it seemed Cissy and Cal epitomized the contrast in the cultures of the East and the West in the 1920s. Cissy lived for society and the accumulation of status; Cal lived for a sense of oneness with the land and wildlife. She couldn't be alone and quiet; he loved solitude and stillness. The two of them were full of opposite qualities and yet the legend is that they fell in love. Felicia says no, they were only friends. But the two of them were in the prime of life, both very physical in their own way, and the places within themselves where they did meet were powerful and magnetic. Aside from their summers together in Jackson Hole, Cissy often invited Cal to her home in Dupont Circle to meet her society friends and on several occasions the two of them traveled together around Europe. They took turns introducing each other to their respective lifestyles and in the process they widened their lives and became lifelong companions.

Q. Your descriptions of Jackson Hole make it sound like a place of stunning natural beauty, out-of-sight prices, and an odd combination of cowboys and actors! What first drew you to the area and what keeps you there?

A. I was first drawn by the beauty. Unlike most mountains that have foothills in front of them, the Grand Teton Mountains rise dramatically from flat meadows. The immediate sensation is one of sheer, towering spires against the sky. One day my husband, John, and I were hiking while on a visit to the valley. I said, "People should live in the place they think is the most beautiful." He said, "Okay." And we moved here. It was that abrupt. I felt kind of embarrassed at first telling anyone; we had children and responsibilities. But here in Jackson Hole that story isn't one bit unusual. Many people arrived here the same way we did—they fell in love, moved in.

What keeps me here is the community. It is the most awake gathering of people I have ever encountered. The people care about what happens regarding everything from town regulations to Bear Number 349. Because we host so many visitors, we have a lot of culture for a small town. And the valley is home to many creative people—artists, writers, entrepreneurs. In some ways it's not an easy place to live. We can have very harsh weather, it is extremely expensive, and I have to drive a hundred miles to the nearest place to buy underwear!

Q. You wrote this novel in about a year—much faster than your previous two novels. How did you manage it?

A. I managed it with the love and support of my family. I began the novel while visiting my sister Gayle and my brother-in-law Bob Caston in Florida. When I arrived, they had set up a desk for me on their deck beneath a palm tree and overlooking the river. I watched herons wade while I wrote. Suddenly I'd hear wild splashing in the water and look up in time to see a tarpon strike. I reveled in the glorious pandemonium of these huge fish feeding. It was an exciting contrast to the serene dipping of palm fronds and soft breezes. I ended the novel by coming back down to Florida at the end of the year and leasing a condo for a month to spend more time with Gayle, Bob, my brother Tom and my sister-in-law Debbie Welling. In between, my husband was on call for supplying just the right word when I'd holler for help and cooking just the right meals to keep me going in tight times.

Q. A loving relationship between a man and a woman lies at the center of each of your three novels. Is that by accident or design?

A. That's by design. The intimate relationship between a man and a woman intrigues me. It is certainly the center of my own life. I have been married to the same man for decades. I find long-term loving partnerships—whether of the same sex or opposite sex—to be full of mystery, misery and elation. Love between two lifetime partners has so many layers to it. It holds heartache, disappointment, joy, comfort, companionship, surprise, romance, history and hope. Many important life skills are demanded in such a relationship. It's a real trick to stick with it, to keep alive the core of love and respect under constantly changing circumstances and challenges. I wouldn't be surprised if my next book carries deep love and commitment as one of its themes as well.

QUESTIONS
FOR DISCUSSION

1. *Cowboys Never Cry* is, at its heart, a love story. What do and don't you like about Cassie and Robbin and their developing relationship?

2. Discuss the other couples in the novel—how do those relationships add to the main romance?

3. Are cowboys your weakness? What attracts you to them? Do you distinguish between real and pretend cowboys?

4. Discuss Cassie's way of life. What about it appeals or doesn't appeal to you? What changes would you have to make in your own life to live like that? Or do you, like the guy in the bar, need the security of insurance?

5. Do you find Robbin's crisis of meaning, and his effort to create a new life for himself, believable? Have you, or some-

one you know, ever suffered a similar crisis? What did you do about it?

6. The author suggests that women have come so easily to Robbin, he doesn't even know how to ask one out on a regular date. In what ways is Robbin secure and sophisticated when it comes to women and in what ways is he backward? Have you ever felt inexperienced for your age when it came to romance—maybe as a "late bloomer" in your youth or as someone starting to date again after a long marriage? Did you call upon a friend for help, as Robbin calls on Cody?

7. How do you feel about Cassie's efforts to make Robbin, Boone, Cody and Fee more conscious of the environmental impact their decisions have on the ranch? Do you think it's important to preserve ranching as a way of life?

8. Were you surprised to learn that cattle ranching comprises only one percent of Wyoming's income, or that legislators in the western states are often ranchers because the two jobs neatly dovetail? Discuss the implications.

9. Several of the older characters in the book develop unique romantic relationships—Cissy Patterson and Cal Carrington, Boone and Elene, Fee and Laraine. What do you think of the accommodations they make in order to have a relationship? What makes their situations different from Cassie and Robbin's?

10. Cassie finds solace and renewal in the natural world. Do you?